PRAISE FOR THE NOVEL

"This charming, exquisite, and poet... light of Venice and the heavenly music of the coro as it portrays two orphaned sisters full of ambition, heart, and steadfast love."

—*Booklist*

"Fans of Tracy Chevalier's *Girl With a Pearl Earring* will welcome another novel about how a masterpiece is created. Corona shines when showing musicians at work, especially through secondary characters both real (opera star Anna Giro) and imagined (violin teacher Silvia the Rat)."

—*Publishers Weekly*

"Corona's *The Four Seasons* is historical fiction as it is meant to be written—a gripping exploration of the twisting byways of both eighteenth-century Venice and the human heart . . . a stirring story of love, ambition, and music that will keep you reading long after the last note of the concerto has ended."

—Lauren Willig, author of *The Betrayal of the Blood Lily*

"I've never been to Venice, played a violin, or for that matter carried a tune, but after reading *The Four Seasons* I feel that I've experienced all three, and through them come to a better understanding of the many forms love takes. Brava, Laurel Corona."

—Sally Gunning, author of *Bound*

Penelope's Daughter

A NOVEL

LAUREL CORONA

BERKLEY BOOKS, NEW YORK

THE BERKLEY PUBLISHING GROUP
Published by the Penguin Group
Penguin Group (USA) Inc.
375 Hudson Street, New York, New York 10014, USA
Penguin Group (Canada), 90 Eglinton Avenue East, Suite 700, Toronto, Ontario M4P 2Y3, Canada
(a division of Pearson Penguin Canada Inc.)
Penguin Books Ltd., 80 Strand, London WC2R 0RL, England
Penguin Group Ireland, 25 St. Stephen's Green, Dublin 2, Ireland (a division of Penguin Books Ltd.)
Penguin Group (Australia), 250 Camberwell Road, Camberwell, Victoria 3124, Australia
(a division of Pearson Australia Group Pty. Ltd.)
Penguin Books India Pvt. Ltd., 11 Community Centre, Panchsheel Park, New Delhi—110 017, India
Penguin Group (NZ), 67 Apollo Drive, Rosedale, North Shore 0632, New Zealand
(a division of Pearson New Zealand Ltd.)
Penguin Books (South Africa) (Pty.) Ltd., 24 Sturdee Avenue, Rosebank, Johannesburg 2196,
South Africa

Penguin Books Ltd., Registered Offices: 80 Strand, London WC2R 0RL, England

This book is an original publication of The Berkley Publishing Group.

This is a work of fiction. Names, characters, places, and incidents either are the product of the author's imagination or are used fictitiously, and any resemblance to actual persons, living or dead, business establishments, events, or locales is entirely coincidental. The publisher does not have any control over and does not assume responsibility for author or third-party websites or their content.

PRINTING HISTORY
Berkley trade paperback edition / October 2010

Library of Congress Cataloging-in-Publication Data

Corona, Laurel, (date)
Penelope's daughter / Laurel Corona. — Berkley trade pbk. ed.
p. cm.
ISBN 978-0-425-23662-8
1. Penelope (Greek mythology)—Fiction. 2. Odysseus (Greek mythology)—Fiction. 3. Mothers and daughters—Fiction. 4. Adventure and adventurers—Fiction. I. Homer. Odyssey. II. Title.
PS3603.O7687P46 2010
813'.6—dc22
            2010013002

PRINTED IN THE UNITED STATES OF AMERICA

10 9 8 7 6 5 4 3 2 1

For all the children left behind
when fathers and mothers go off to war

Penelope's Daughter

SOMETIME IN THE
FIRST MILLENNIUM B.C.E. . . .

. . . Greek warlords have combined their armies and sailed for Troy, to sack the city and bring home Helen, wife of Menelaus and the Queen of Sparta. On the small and remote island of Ithaca, a young queen, Penelope, is left behind with a one-year-old son when her husband Odysseus, King of the Cephallenians, joins them.

Still in her teens, and far from her own family, Penelope discovers she is pregnant again. Within a few months of Odysseus' departure, she is struggling to be a mother to her son Telemachus and daughter Xanthe, and to maintain Odysseus' household and kingdom.

Ten years pass, and the siege of Troy drags on. Penelope grows in beauty, stature, and confidence. Without a father to inspire him, Telemachus is failing to show the budding manhood and leadership that will keep the kingdom secure if Odysseus does not return. Xanthe is nearing the end of a carefree childhood and has taken her place beside her mother at the loom, to learn the skills by which the value of a woman is measured.

The kingdom and family are in good order and prosperous, awaiting the end of the war and Odysseus' swift return. Then the news arrives. The siege of Troy is over. The Greeks have won. The heroes are on their way home, after ten years of war.

All but Odysseus arrive.

By the time two years have passed, dire stories and ugly rumors abound. Men from neighboring islands descend on Ithaca, seeking to persuade Penelope that her husband is dead and she should marry again. Nearing puberty, Telemachus and Xanthe are powerless victims of the suitors' struggle to win Penelope's hand. Fearing that the most cunning and unscrupulous of the suitors would not stop at the murder of her son and abduction and rape of her daughter to force his way onto the throne as her new husband, Penelope realizes that the key to everyone's survival will be her skill at outwitting the suitors long enough for Odysseus to return and set everything right.

In the twentieth year of his absence, she acknowledges defeat. Xanthe is safe only because she is barricaded in her chambers, where she passes the time by weaving the story of her life on her loom. Telemachus has once again narrowly escaped being murdered, and Penelope is so shattered she does little but cry and sleep.

And then, on the remote north coast of the island, Odysseus washes up on shore. . . .

BOOK I

Ithaca

CHAPTER 1

A Splash of Yellow

The loom weights tremble, sending a quiver through the warp, as if to mark the departing spirit of another human soul. I hear somewhere below me the roar of a man confronting the tear in the flesh that will kill him. Was the voice my father's? I would not recognize it if it were.

I close the door of my quarters to block out the sobbing of the women, and I reach out to touch the cloth I have been working on in the months since I returned to Ithaca.

"It's worse than pointless, Xanthe," I can hear my mother saying. "Not beautiful, not harmonious, not even useful."

It's not worthy of my time. That's what she means. I need sheer veils in bright colors to accent my beauty, linen supple enough to define my breasts and cling to my hips. Men need warm cloaks for winter and tunics sturdy enough to resist their misadventures. For guests, the best of what is packed away—linens and blankets for their beds, and luxurious robes for their shoulders. Fabric is the treasure that wives and daughters bring to a royal house. Even more than our wombs, our weaving is the measure of us.

5

I have made enough worthy things for a nineteen-year-old, turning out neat stacks of cloth that do not challenge or confront, but on the private loom in my own quarters I weave for myself, without concern for those it might frighten or confuse.

And since my return to Ithaca, I've spent every day in this room, with nothing else to do. Weave and remember. Weave and remember. At some point, I'm not sure exactly when or how, the two came together and I decided to use my loom to tell my story.

Harmonious? Sometimes.

Beautiful? Often.

Useful? The usefulness of a young princess to the ambitions of ruthless men is why I am locked upstairs, a victim of the disharmony and chaos that took over this house when my father, Odysseus, King of Cephallenia and Lord of Ithaca, did not come back from Troy.

My mother, Penelope, is a victim too, though a much more celebrated one. For the people of Ithaca her suffering is magnificent. But just as my weaving hides many secret thoughts, she too has her own. Hers are stored away like jewels, taken out privately only from time to time, marveled over, and put safely away again.

The best of these is that the men who invaded our palace only thought they were in control. Even from the beginning they never understood how outmatched they were. Perhaps the reason she is sleeping in her own corner of the palace right now is that she believes her victory is at hand.

I wish I had her confidence. The gods speak to her more often and more clearly than they speak to me, and they pluck heroes from this life as easily as villains. Now all that matters is the mood they are in, whom it will please them to leave standing, and what that will mean for those of us who will be the victor's reward.

* * *

I started at the top of the loom with a splash of yellow, for the bright sunlight of my childhood and the radiance of Halia, the first person I ever loved. The daughter of a fisherman, she was my wet nurse until I was weaned, and afterwards my companion and attendant.

Halia was seventeen or eighteen and I was probably not quite four years old when a memory first lodged permanently in my mind. Every few days in nice weather, she would bring me down to the beach to watch the boats unload their catch. On that day the fishermen were struggling with their nets to get the fish to spill on the pebbled shore. A few dozen flashed silver as they tried to make their escape into the tiny waves that washed around them. Halia put me down so she could help out by throwing them onto the pile.

An extraordinary creature must have gotten trapped and then fallen from the net—a huge and luminous bubble, trailing threads behind it. As it swept back and forth in the turquoise water lapping the beach, I saw what looked like puffy, pink clouds inside it. Halia and I had watched a number of sunsets together, making up stories about what flavor each color of cloud would have if we could only reach out and pop a piece of it in our mouths.

And now, one of those clouds seemed to be within my grasp. Unnoticed, I went in the water up to my knees to see it better. A wave caused my hem to lift, and the soft appendages of the creature splayed outward. Though I did not see it touch me, my leg exploded with pain.

I must have been shrieking, and Halia's contorted face meant she must have been screaming too, but in my memory, the scene is completely silent. I remember her running across the beach carrying me in her arms. When she laid me down, the faces of the fishermen made a circle above me. The water they poured on my leg felt like burning oil, and the slightest touch sent ripples of fire through my whole body.

I don't know how long it took for the pain and panic to recede enough for me to be aware of anything else, but eventually I heard sounds again. Halia was sobbing, but her father reassured her that I was breathing normally and would be all right.

I struggled to sit up, and Halia helped me to my feet. When she picked me up, she grasped me tightly around the leg. I cried out in anger that she was hurting me, but I could see by the wounded expression on her face that she hadn't meant to. I buried myself in her chest, needing to forgive her because everything else in the world seemed unforgivable.

When we arrived home, my mother was at her floor loom in the megaron, the great hall of the palace. She must have seen the expression on Halia's face, because she dropped what she was doing and hurried toward us.

"My queen," Halia said, putting me down and lifting the hem of my dress. "I'm so sorry."

My mother knelt beside me and touched my leg. I cried out on the assumption it would hurt, but the pain by then had died down. Her soft fingers traced the halo of pink prickles around the red welt where I was stung.

"A jellyfish," she said, and I heard for the first time the name of the creature that had hurt me.

My mother stood up. "Eurycleia!" she called out.

The woman who had been my father's and my brother's nurse came in through a side door and walked with a hitching limp across the megaron. The three people I cared most about in the world surrounded me, and it seemed that such a reward was well worth the injury.

Eurycleia clucked in sympathy as she examined my swollen leg. My mother's personal servant, Eurynome, had also come into the room and was looking over her shoulder.

"I can get some vinegar," Eurynome said. "It's supposed to help."

"I think it's too late for that," Eurycleia said, turning to me. "Is it starting to itch?"

I nodded. My mother's fingers seemed to have unleashed a swarm of ants under my skin, and I reached down to scratch my leg.

She bent down again and pulled my hand away. "No, darling," she said, putting her arms around me. "Don't do that."

She looked up at the two women. "Can you make a poultice for the itching?"

The two women scurried off, Eurynome in the lead and Eurycleia a few halting steps behind. My mother stood up again and turned to Halia.

"What happened?" she asked. Though her voice was barely above a whisper, I heard the accusation in it.

Halia was crying as she explained, and when she finished my mother stared at her with cold, unnerving eyes.

I adored Halia, and the idea that she might be punished caused me to dissolve into tears. "Please," I said. "Don't hurt her!"

My mother was not a cruel person, but servants had to be kept in line, and ordering the occasional beating was an effective tool with the others. Still, she seemed surprised at my alarm.

Her face softened. "Xanthe obviously trusts you," she said to Halia, "so I will too."

Halia let out a hoarse cry of relief.

"It was an accident," my mother went on, "but you were careless and let it happen."

"I won't take my eyes off her again," Halia rushed to say. "I swear by the gods."

My mother's face was solemn. "Be careful what you swear to. Especially if you ask the gods to listen."

I didn't understand what she meant. All I remember is my relief when my mother sent Halia back home unharmed.

When Halia's footsteps died away outside the megaron, I recorded my first, and in fact my only early memory of being alone with Maia, the name Achaean children call their mothers. She was always too busy to have time for me, but like any young child I assumed my experience was typical. She was eighteen when her husband went away to Troy—nineteen when I was born—and her situation was more difficult than I can fully comprehend even now.

Halia was the center of my world anyway. Others like my brother, Telemachus; my grandparents; and my mother circled around outside. Of the more than seventy servants in the palace compound, only a few were important enough to know by name—the baker, Ponteia, who made bread in funny shapes just for me; the kitchen helper, Tecta, who put extra honey in my cider; the maid, Clytia, who tucked flowers in my hair.

But every child knows who bore her, and that afternoon in the megaron is as vivid and important to me as if it had happened yesterday.

"I'm so sorry that mean thing hurt you," my mother said, tears in her eyes. "And I'm sorry I wasn't there to protect you."

How odd, I remember thinking. *Mothers aren't supposed to cry.*

Of course I assumed at the time the tears were for me. I think now they may have been more for the mother she was never able to be.

CHAPTER 2

Unfurling

From sequins made of iridescent bits of shell I set a jellyfish swimming in the yellow stripe at the top of my loom. At first the barbs were neatly cut bits of pink thread, nicely contained within the yellow, but as I wove further, the tidiness of it felt wrong.

What was I trying to convince myself of by keeping everything within its allotted space? That events are finite, that stories have endings, that meaning can be constrained to one time or place, one set of circumstances? Now my weaving is as tall as I am, and the threads hanging from the top are long enough to unfurl until they spread out on the floor. Memories have barbs with which to sting us again and again.

Halia remained part of my life until I was five. I was underfoot at home, so I continued to spend much of my time with her in the fishing village where her family lived. My mother had decided that training in the skills expected of princesses could wait until a more convenient time, by which I think she meant when my father came home and she did not have so many other obligations to attend to.

In those days, little reason existed to fear for my safety. Everyone thought the war would be over soon and that my father would return home. In the meantime, farmers, herders, fishermen, and craftsmen had jobs to do. At home, their wives continued to prepare food, wash clothes, clean house, and look after children. Since my father was the king, no one wanted to risk punishment for harming his daughter in even the smallest of ways. Everyone watched out for me wherever I went. I had the cup with no chips, the chair with no splinters, the fish with all the bones taken out.

I know now that most bad things that happen are not caused by those who live in fishing villages. For the first few years of my life, not many other kinds of people existed on Ithaca. Noblemen in their prime were off fighting in Troy, and their fathers and sons were either too old or too young to cause much trouble. But boys who had been too small to go to war became young men as the conflict dragged on, and little by little the need to keep me safe began to constrict my world.

For the time being, however, I was free to roam. Once I grew to trust the water again, Halia taught me to float on my back and then to swim a few strokes out over my head and then back again. Fish darted around her legs as she stood beside me in the shallow water, her hand cupped under my waist. I felt my hair streaming out like the spiked crown of Apollo, and my dress felt weightless around my legs. Only when I turned my head to try to see the palace imposing itself on the skyline above the bay, and felt my weight pull me under the surface of the water, did I feel as if I had any substance at all. When I finally stood up, and my hair turned to ropes and my clothing stuck to my skin, it felt wrong—as if the real me were meant to float forever without experiencing the insult of a world that was rough, or hard, or heavy.

Back at her house, Halia's mother let me help slap and pound the bread dough, and best of all, she let me press into each unbaked loaf the wooden stamp that marked it as belonging to that particular family. When we went to the village oven, she made me stand aside as she transferred the loaves from her paddle to the oven with a deft flick of her wrist. I was close enough to feel the blast of heat, and if I craned my neck, I could see the red glow of the burning olive pits used as fuel, but because I liked Halia's mother too much to deliberately make her nervous, I kept what she considered a safe distance without needing to be told.

She would not allow me near the cauldron at home, and though she let me rub off the skin from garlic and mash cold, cooked lentils to a paste, she would never let me near anything that might cut or burn me, and she refused to allow me to clean up after my rather messy efforts to help.

"That kind of work is beneath the dignity of the king's daughter," I remember her saying as she grabbed a wet sea sponge from my hand or dashed to pick up onion skins from the floor. At such times I was aware of being treated differently from anyone else, but most of the time I was just Halia's little shadow, and nothing more.

The times I liked best were spent with Halia's two younger brothers. They were not yet big or strong enough to go out with the boats, and they spent their days collecting whatever was edible from the tide pools. With their bare hands, the boys caught fish that had not been able to escape at low tide, and in the deepest pools they used spears to catch some of comparable size to those brought in by the men. They left Halia and me alone to collect whatever we could find in the shallower pools, at a safe distance from the waves that surged onto the rocks.

I spent mornings turning beautiful flower-shaped anemones into tight little wads by poking my finger into their sticky centers. I ran after crabs and shore birds to make them scurry away. I tried for a long time to catch one of the small fish left behind until the next tide, and when I finally got one, I felt so sorry for it flopping around on the rocks that I threw it back in the water.

I loved to sit on the sand at the water line and let the waves come up around me in little crackling hisses. As the water surrounded me, I splashed my hands and sucked the salt water from my fingers over and over again, until Halia ordered me to stop before I gave myself a stomachache. We sat on the beach in the afternoon eating the meal Halia's mother packed for us, and to this day some foods do not taste right to me because they are not salted and gritty with sand.

Shortly before I turned five, life with Halia came to an abrupt halt. One day I sat eating a fig while I waited for her, as usual, on the steps of the palace. Eurynome came out to get me.

"Halia won't be coming today," she said. I was disappointed but not terribly concerned, since this happened from time to time.

Eurynome glanced over her shoulder to make sure I had followed her back inside.

"Actually, she got married," she said, "and she's not coming back at all."

I watched Eurynome continue across the megaron and disappear upstairs. Even today I remember how my jaw went so slack that I forgot to swallow the last bite of fig and had to catch an unexpected trickle of saliva in my hand. The whole world felt wrong, and I stood in the huge, empty hall crying so hard and long with betrayal and grief that the whole house was disrupted. Finally, to put an end to the noise, my mother ordered Eurynome to take me one last time to the village to say good-bye.

We went first to Halia's house, but it gave off such an aura of gloom it frightened me, and I didn't want to go inside. When her mother came out, she tried to smile and act happy to see me, but I could see by her red eyes and puffy face that she had been crying. She blew her nose and rubbed her apron over her face to tidy her appearance as she took us in the direction of Halia's new home. It was in a group of squalid huts up the path from the village. I had never had a good feeling about those huts, especially after I saw a huge rat run out the door of one and into another, and I don't think Halia liked going near them either, since she usually guided us as far away from them as possible. The fronts were not tidy, as Halia's family's house always was, and the walls and roofs on some of them seemed about to cave in.

And now Halia—so fresh, sweet, and young—had gone to live in one of them. Her new husband, Terpias, was quite a bit older than she was. I knew what he looked like already, but the easiest way to recognize Terpias was by smell. He never seemed to care about washing the remnants of fish guts and scales from his clothes and hands, and what I remember most about him was the odor of rotting fish that preceded and followed him.

I knew a little about him from Halia, how his wife and baby had drowned a few years before, when Poseidon, angered by something or perhaps just wanting to remind the village of his power, had come across the bay, driving his team of stallions. The outline of their bodies could be seen in the massive rise of water, and their manes were the white crest riding atop. The god and his horses thundered onto shore, trampling huts, people, and boats, before making an indifferent turn and heading back out to sea.

Perhaps that was what made Terpias so distant and cheerless. He was just a fisherman without any reason to have come to the gods' attention. One day, Poseidon came to the village and ruined what little Terpias had. Why did it happen to him? At the time I was too young to think there might be reasons to offer, or blame to cast, for terrible things that occur. I accepted them as part of a world too big for me to understand. Even today, I'm not sure there's any better conclusion to draw.

What I didn't know until we walked into the cheerless hut where Halia now lived was that a nice old lady who often came down to the beach to see me was Terpias' mother. Her broad smile revealed so few remaining teeth that I know she could not have made for herself the delicious sweets of pounded dried fruit and chopped nuts she always gave me, since it wouldn't have been possible for her to chew them.

The one bright thought I had all afternoon was that at least Halia had someone who might be nice to her. The hut itself had only one bed for all of them, and that was no more than a pile of dirty cloth on a bare frame. The air smelled sour, like the odor left behind by a dead fire, hinting of rotten seaweed buzzing with flies. The gloomy hut made such a horrible impression that for one shameful moment I was glad I would not be seeing Halia again.

Halia was vacant and listless, completely unlike her former self. After a while in which little if anything was said, she asked me to come outside with her.

"I'll miss you, Xanthe," she said. Her eyes were large and sad.

"Why did you marry him?" I asked.

"Why not? I have to get married, don't I? And besides, he—" She looked away. "He put a baby in me."

I had spent enough time around dogs and livestock to have some sense of how this occurred, but I could not imagine Halia and the fish man engaged in anything of the sort. "Why did you let him do that?" I asked.

"I didn't." Her voice sounded so different I turned to look at her, but her hair was hiding her face. "When he did it anyway, my father made him marry me."

After that neither of us could think of anything to say. We went back inside the hut, and when Terpias' mother offered me a piece of freshly baked bread drizzled with honey, I refused because I was sure I could not swallow it.

I kept my eyes on the dirt floor, tracing a meaningless pattern with my toe, since I could not bear the sight of Halia in that awful place. When I finally spoke, it was only to say that I wanted to go home.

Walking up the hill toward the palace, I told Eurynome what Halia had said about Terpias making her pregnant.

"Well, it's not like it's the first time," Eurynome said, as if that were the only thing that mattered.

"What do you mean?" I demanded. "Halia doesn't have a baby."

Eurynome grumbled and told me to forget what she had said. Apparently she didn't have enough experience with children to know that the one thing that will pique their curiosity more than anything else is to be told to ignore something.

I stopped in my tracks and put my hands on the fronts of my thighs. "I'm not moving until you tell me what you meant."

"You are a willful child who should be beaten," she scolded.

I stood my ground. A slave had no right to hit me. At five I already knew that.

"Stand here all night then," she said. "Until the Sea People get you." It was a bluff, and we both knew it. She would carry me back to the house, pounding on her back and screaming in her ear if she had to, but she would not leave me there.

I glared at her until she gave in. "Halia had another baby," Eurynome said. "It's how she had milk for you." She said this in a voice so matter-of-fact it was obvious she thought anyone would understand, but I didn't.

Eurynome went on. "At the time you were born, we heard about a young girl in the fishing village who had just had a baby."

"How could Halia have a baby?"

It was Eurynome's turn to glare at me. "How would I know? A little something behind the boats, maybe?" She was deliberately talking in a way I wouldn't understand just to make me feel stupid, and I hated her for it.

But I persisted. "Well, where's her baby then?"

"It was born sick. Your grandfather visited the house and offered the family the chance to have Halia nurse you instead. It was a good offer. You see that they live in the nicest house in the village."

I don't know if it was just meanness on Eurynome's part that made her go on, or the fact that the rest of the story would surely get my feet moving.

"They left her baby out to die," she said, "because you needed a nurse."

I took off running to escape from what she was saying, but her words chased me all the way home.

That night I was woken by a nightmare, certain I was drowning. Eurynome came to my chamber, though she was not the one I wanted. She dispatched a servant girl to go bring me some warm goat's milk with honey to help me sleep, and an extra blanket to cover the cold spot where I had wet the bed.

Eurynome ordered the girl to sleep in a corner of my room for the remainder of the night. The girl threw down skins and blankets and settled in, but I still could not sleep. I thought of a runt puppy I had seen, alone in the dirt after its mother shoved it away from her teat. I thought of fallen nestlings waiting motionless on the ground for whatever would happen next.

I could not get warm, nor could I make my body settle into the contours of the bed. Eventually I got up and crawled in beside the servant girl on the floor. When I woke the next morning, I was back in my bed and the girl was gone.

CHAPTER 3

Soft White on Green

I hear my brother's voice and know he is still fighting. He has called out to someone, and I have heard a voice call him son in reply.

Telemachus. I blow a gentle breath over a tuft of white in the next part of my weaving and watch the delicate threads flutter. He is woven in green, with little tufted knots of white, like the olive grove in bloom where we used to play when I was six and he was eight years old.

How strange it is that such a clear line can be drawn between when my life did not involve my brother, and the first time he became important to it. Green for naïveté, soft white for weakness, because colors are not perceived only by the eyes. If he is alive at the end of the day, I will probably see him differently. For now what I remember are the places we explored, as the person inside each of us began to emerge to shape our lives.

When I was very young, I had little contact with my brother. I sometimes saw him playing with boys who were part of our household, but I always felt a little sorry for Telemachus because he had no one like Halia for company.

A man named Mentor took a special interest in him, and I saw the two of them together from time to time. Mentor seemed ancient to me, but I suppose he was not much older than forty. His hands were gnarled in a way that added to his wizened appearance, and his skin was the color and texture of leather. My father put him in charge of his *oikos*—his house, land, slaves, and servants—when he left for Troy.

I still don't know exactly what being in charge was supposed to mean. Eurycleia muttered under her breath whenever Mentor came to the palace, and I could see why he annoyed her. She needed no supervision, and it was hard to imagine what skills Mentor possessed that could be much help running a household. Though Eurycleia walked with a limp, she could chase rats out of the storeroom with the ferocity of a whirlwind. When she ordered servants to prepare a feast, they worked so quickly they sometimes had to slow down so the meat had time to roast. The banquet hall was clean almost before the guests had picked the last strings of meat from their teeth.

Mentor underestimated the old nurse. I can picture her now, allowing Mentor to overhear her musing about the timid and soft little boy Odysseus had left behind as a baby, and how in the absence of his father he was unlikely to become much of a man, especially if he spent his days in a household full of women. What chance did Telemachus have to be brave and learn to lead, when the only thing to practice on was the flock of geese in the courtyard?

I see now how helpless Mentor was when Eurycleia set her trap. Of course he would want to make sure the king's most precious asset was budding into manhood when Odysseus came home. I can picture Eurycleia's lips pressed together in a thin line to keep from laughing when Mentor insisted to my mother that it wasn't right for Telemachus to be coddled so long by women and demanded from that point forward to take charge of the boy himself. Quite a victory it was, for someone who only wanted a meddler out of her kitchen.

Even after his decision to take on the princely education of my brother, Mentor was never in Telemachus' daily life the way Halia was in mine. Mentor was an elder in the town, left behind when the others went to war, because his twisted hands would be of little use in battle. His friendship with my father elevated him among the people of the island, who looked to him for advice and to settle disputes. I saw him often as Halia and I walked down the main street of our town, usually with a group of men around him arguing about something, or sharing a meal at a table outside a tavern.

He had his own *oikos* to tend to as well, so I suppose he paid as much attention to our family as he could, which in truth wasn't much. To me he paid no attention at all, at least when I was very young. Mentor had time only for people who mattered in my family, which meant Odysseus' wife and son. The rest of us were about as important to him as the frescoes on the wall.

Mentor's idea of making a man of Telemachus consisted of sending him away from the palace to learn about the skills involved with running an estate—where the food on the table came from, how the wool came to the women to spin, how to keep wild boars from ruining a garden, how to prune the vines to ensure that wine would be plentiful each year. Telemachus was too young to till a field or slaughter an ox, but he could watch people at work and lend a hand whenever a child his age could.

In Ithaca almost every man, regardless of his status, knows

how to plow, plant, and harvest. They know how to fish and how to herd animals, how to stun a bull and cut its throat, and how to wrap the fat around a thighbone and burn it as a sacrifice to the gods. In Ithaca, only a ruler with calluses on his hands and sweat trickling through the dirt on his skin could command respect. Living among men he would eventually rule, Telemachus would learn the skills he needed to earn the admiration of other noblemen and the affection of his servants and slaves, as Odysseus had done before him. At least that was Mentor's plan.

In the period of time just before Halia's marriage, Telemachus lived with Eumaeus, the king's swineherd. Halia and I walked down from the palace many times to visit the pig farm, and though we always talked about how nice it would be to see my brother, I have to admit I was always more excited about seeing the pigs.

The piglets' eyes squinted and their snouts turned up with what looked like smiles as they trotted over to greet me. One of them in particular was mine. When others in its litter had grown enough to be taken to the palace for slaughter, Eumaeus left it behind. I had saved this particular pig from death once, he said, and as far as he was concerned I had saved it forever.

The story of how the pig came to be mine is so gruesome I can recall it in perfect detail today. Halia and I heard the clamor from the new litter long before we reached the pens. Pink splotches of vomit splattered the stone wall in the corner where Telemachus was cowering. Eumaeus and his helper were splattered with blood. They flipped a male piglet onto its back, and the helper fought to hold the struggling, squealing animal in place while Eumaeus slit its scrotum with a knife. Eumaeus' crooked fingers reached into the wound and pulled out the testicles, slicing them off at the base and tossing the bloody package to the ravens gathered at the fence.

Seeing the small pebbles of bloody flesh landing on the dirt and being fought over brought up my stomach as well. I stood crying next to my brother, hating the swineherd more than I could imagine hating anyone.

Eumaeus forbade me to go near the wounded piglets, which had bunched together in one corner of the pen, for fear they might be frightened and try to defend themselves by biting me. Nevertheless, I made Halia bring me back the next day and the next, so I could see how they were. By the third day, most of the piglets were recovering, but the wounds of two others were red and swollen. They lay, sides heaving, as Eumaeus approached.

"No use in keeping them," he said, and I watched in horror as he pulled back the head of one and slit its throat.

"No!" I screamed. Somehow I managed to cross the pen and throw myself on top of the other piglet before Eumaeus got to him.

"You can't have him!" I screamed. "He's mine!"

Eumaeus leaned down to take the pig from me. "He's sick," he said. "He's going to die."

"No, he's not!"

Halia took Eumaeus' side. "He's suffering," she said. "Do you want that?"

Eumaeus was still trying to take the piglet from me, and I tightened my grip around one of its legs. "I'll make him well. I will. You'll see!"

Eumaeus stood up. "You shriek like the Furies," he said. He wiped his knife and put it in the scabbard dangling from his belt before walking off to tend to his other chores.

Even when I realized I had won, I couldn't stop sobbing. The piglet wiggled free, and I got to my feet. My chiton had ripped away from the pins holding it at the shoulders, and I was naked from the waist up.

Halia came over to get me dressed again. She was shaking her head too, but her eyes gleamed with approval. "A Fury indeed," she said, fastening my chiton back into place.

I was still mad at Eumaeus and I didn't want to leave, because I imagined him hovering just out of sight, waiting for me to be gone so he could finish off my new little friend.

"You can't hurt my pig," I told him. "You have to promise."

I suppose the long, quizzical look he gave me was to decide whether the demand of a five-year-old princess was something an old and honored slave had to give in to. Then his eyes crinkled at the corners. "I promise," he said.

Though now I know that Eumaeus' word is enough, at the time I was still too young to know I could trust him with something so important.

"Ask the gods to witness!" I demanded.

Eumaeus was laughing by now. His eyes swept the sky. "I swear by all the gods, I will not harm that piglet!"

Since no one would be foolish enough to break such an oath, I was finally convinced it was safe to go home. But one important matter remained.

"It needs a name," I said.

Eumaeus shook his head, amazed. "Pigs don't have names!"

"Why not?" I asked. "You talk to them like people."

"Very well then," he said, I think a bit abashed to have his soft heart noticed. "Go ahead and name him. But don't expect me to call him by it. He's just a pig to me."

I thought for a moment. "His name is Circe."

Halia and Eumaeus burst out laughing at the idea that a male piglet should have not only a girl's name, but that of a beautiful goddess. Though Telemachus and Halia came up with a dozen different boys' names, I would not budge, because to me, naming the piglet after someone with the power to turn men into swine and then back into men again seemed like a good idea. Perhaps the name itself would cast a spell, I thought, and someday I would walk down into the valley and find in Circe's place a human girl just my age to play with.

Needless to say that didn't happen, and Circe soon grew too big to be any sort of playmate at all. My visits to Eumaeus stopped when Halia got married, and whether Circe ended up on the banquet table, I couldn't say, but I do know I caught Eumaeus on several occasions calling the pig by name.

In time I forgave Eumaeus for the death I witnessed. He was more careful when I visited not to upset me, in part because he was fond of me, but also because he was a busy man. He had better things to do than tend to one sick little piglet when a hundred or more animals needed his attention. He must have spent a great deal of time bringing Circe back to health, and he probably didn't want to run the risk I would force him to do the same for some other animal I pitied.

If Ithaca were made up of men like Eumaeus, my story would be different. If the world were made up of people like him, so would his. Like mine, his life was swept off course while he was still a child, by people without any of his sweetness and sense of honor. Born the youngest of several princes in some kingdom I never heard of, he was kidnapped as a child and sold into slavery. Eventually my grandfather brought him to Ithaca, where he has tended the pigs ever since.

When I was younger I didn't understand why, being of royal blood, he didn't insist on his freedom. I understand his answer better now, having spent years among slaves, posing as one of them. What would he do but stay right where he was? Better to be a worker on the *oikos* of a great man, he once told me, than to be in his own country with no crown, no land, no possessions. His life could have been different, but it wasn't, and he was satisfied.

Eumaeus told Telemachus and me story after story of my father's bravery and cunning, as if he were describing the adventures of his own kin. His pride in Odysseus surpasses anything I ever heard Laertes express for his own son, although my grandfather is not one to brag, or in fact say much of anything.

My mother rarely speaks of Odysseus at all. I know she married him at sixteen after he won her hand in a contest set up by her father, King Icarius. Odysseus was twenty-six, or thereabouts. They had barely laid eyes on each other and had time for no more than a few words of conversation before they were married. He took her immediately back to Ithaca, and a year later my brother was born. Shortly after Telemachus learned to walk, my father left for Troy. Eurycleia told me later he was gone before Penelope knew she was pregnant with me. To this day, I do not know for certain if the man fighting downstairs knows he has a daughter.

Two years together and twenty apart. Perhaps my mother speaks so little about her husband because she doesn't have much to say.

I can imagine what my mother must have thought of Ithaca when she first laid eyes on it. I have seen enough of the world now—the lush fields of Lacedaemon, and the rich seaside kingdom of Pylos—to suspect she may not have been too pleased with a rather barren island, and a palace (though the grandest in the kingdom) with only a packed dirt floor.

Before their marriage, Odysseus was one of several powerful lords on our cluster of islands. With his own hands he built his palace before going off in search of a wife. As part of my mother's dowry, Icarius created a new Kingdom of Cephallenia from the lands of Ithaca and the surrounding islands, decreeing that whoever married his daughter would be its king. That was how my father came to be not just the largest landholder on Ithaca, but its ruler as well.

And then he left. I suppose it didn't matter at that point whether she liked living on Ithaca. It was her fate.

It took a while for my mother to accept the turn her life had taken, to accept that two children were part of it. Perhaps she was overwhelmed by my father's absence, but I think it more likely she was intimidated by motherhood, afraid Telemachus and I were like fruit that would spoil with handling. She had Eurycleia and Eurynome to advise her about some things, but not a single female friend of her own social rank to talk to. Her mother and an older married sister were too far away to be of any help. Whatever the reason for her disinclination to take over my care, I had to wait a long time to attract more than fleeting moments of her attention.

Though I recall wanting more from my mother when I was young, I can't say I was unhappy when she sent me away to live with my grandparents after Halia left my life. Their house was laid out like the palace, but much cozier— small enough that I never had to take more than a few steps to find who I was looking for, but large enough to get temporarily lost when it suited me.

Their lands were not far from the house of my birth. In fact, from my grandfather Laertes' groves and fields, I could look out across the end of the bay and see the outline of the palace walls on the hill above it. My gaze did not go there often. From time to time I felt pangs of longing for my mother, but I was still too young to comprehend that she was going about her day somewhere inside the walls I saw in the distance.

In any case, life on the farm was much more exciting than the best moments I spent in the palace. Outside my window was an apple orchard so close that in spring the breeze wafted hundreds of petals into my room. On the other side of the house was my grandfather's vegetable garden. He let me gather beans and pull garlic, and I loved the sharp smell of pollen clinging to leaves and the soft dirt I brushed from roots.

Anticleia, my grandmother, gave me my first lessons in weaving and embroidery, but at six, I struggled to work a needle and thread, and I made a mess every time I touched a spindle. Anticleia grumbled that it wasn't worth the trouble to keep me working for more than half a morning, so after helping my grandfather pick vegetables for dinner, I had nothing more to do.

Their farm included an olive grove tended by a man named Dolius, a slave on the *oikos*. By coincidence, within the same moon cycle, Telemachus came to stay with Dolius to learn about olive production. For the first time in my life, I would have my brother as a frequent companion.

Work stopped for a while in the middle of the day, so one day I set out to look for him. I found him by the sounds of children laughing and shouting. He was on a ridge overlooking a small dry streambed, standing next to a boy and girl. They were throwing stones and trying to make them land on the opposite bank.

"Hey!" I called out, and they all turned around to look.

"Who are you?" the girl demanded. She was thin as a stick. Her hair was sun-streaked, and her blue-green eyes stood out from a face as brown as the skin of almonds.

"I'm his sister," I said, pointing to Telemachus.

"Hey, come here, Xanthe," Telemachus said. He was so wrapped up in throwing stones that he didn't greet me or ask what I was doing there. "Watch me kill a Trojan!"

He made a loud *phhtt*, like the sound of a spear whizzing to its target, as he let go of a stone. It fell far short of the bank, and the boy next to him growled with disapproval.

"It's easy," the boy said, cocking back his elbow and shoulder. He launched the stone forward with a smooth motion of his whole arm, and it rose in a high arc, falling on the other side far beyond the rim.

The boys had stripped off all their clothes in the heat of the afternoon. The girl was wearing a shift that came barely to her knees and when she bent over, I saw she had nothing on underneath.

I looked away, as if I hadn't noticed. "What's your name?" I asked her.

"Melantho," she said. "That's my twin brother, Melanthius. We're eight." The boy's coloring was the same as hers, but he was half a head taller than Melantho, who herself was a little taller than my brother. Though Melanthius was the same age as Telemachus, the muscles of his back and arms were already beginning to take on the contours of a grown man's.

Melantho pulled up her hem toward her waist and dropped the stones in the fold made by the cloth. "What are you looking at?" she asked me. "My slit?" She giggled and turned to take her load of rocks over to where the boys were standing.

I was fascinated by this girl. Men sometimes stripped to work or exercise, and seeing Telemachus and Melanthius naked had not been worthy of note. Women bared their breasts sometimes, but below the waist? Even by my age, no one had to tell me to keep myself covered. Whenever I went out to play I had to bunch up a cloth between my legs and tuck the ends in at the sides of my waist, then pull my chiton over it just to make sure no one saw what they weren't supposed to. Melantho either didn't know or didn't care about that, and I found myself drawn to her, wanting to know why she was so at ease flouting the rules.

Melantho aimed one of her own rocks across the streambed. It hit the other side below the top and fell into the water, but it was still a longer throw than any of my brother's.

"Try it," Melantho said, tossing me a small stone.

When I let the rock go, I didn't open my hand at the right time, and the rock plummeted down the bank straight into the water. Everyone groaned, Telemachus loudest of all.

"Watch me!" he said, "I'll show you."

He bit his lower lip in concentration as he drew back. The throw was a little better than the last one, but when he crowed "Almost!" we all knew it wasn't so.

Except when the weather kept me indoors, I went to the same place every day to be with the three of them. Near the spot where they liked to throw rocks, an oak tree clung to the top of the bank. From a high branch the twins had dangled a rope knotted in a loop at the end. A lower branch protruded just enough to serve as a place to stand and secure their feet inside the loop. From there they jumped, clutching the rope with their hands and thighs.

The rope stopped short of the streambed by about one body length. When it was taut at the bottom of their fall, they would jerk up, but if they had jumped at the proper angle they would swing back and forth in big swooping arcs before letting go and flying to the streambed. A bad launch would bring them crashing into the sharp branches and ferocious thorns of the bushes growing on the side of the bank. This happened often enough for their arms and legs to be perpetually bruised and scratched.

Melanthius was fearless. Whenever he came crashing into the

bank or was knocked to the ground by a slip of his foot or hand, he would shake his head and scramble up the path to the top, stopping only to suck away blood that had risen in his scratches before jumping again.

I was too afraid to try at all, but no one pressured me because I was two years younger, quite a bit smaller, and a girl. Of course, that last point didn't stop Melantho. She loved the swing, especially when a little apple tree that had somehow managed to root itself a few feet up from the streambed was in bloom. She would reach out and try to grab sprigs of blossoms, bringing them back to tangle in her hair and mine. I loved every bit of attention I got from that wild girl. Being around her was like glimpsing a goddess at play. I was completely in awe of her.

Before the olive harvest consumed all their time, Dolius and his sons prepared for winter by chopping enormous quantities of wood and doing whatever else would help get the family through the winter. Little of this work was considered suitable for a young prince, and as a result, my brother began sleeping at our grandparents' farm and walking over each morning to see if he was needed. More often than not, Dolius sent him right back.

Laertes and Anticleia found ways to keep us both busy, but one day when we were being particularly rambunctious, they shooed us out of the house by midmorning and told us not to come back until mealtime. Our feet led us through the orchard to the swing. It was nice to be there alone, with no one yelling or hurtling through the air.

With a few quick motions, Telemachus had climbed up onto one of its branches, dangling his feet and scowling.

"I hate Melanthius," he said. "He's such a bully."

I didn't think I needed to reply because what he said was obviously true.

"Well, he is!" Telemachus insisted.

"I didn't say he wasn't!"

"You don't even see half of it." My brother tossed a small piece of bark in my direction and started prying at another one. "He's better than me at everything."

"You're getting better," I said. "Look at how fast you got up that tree."

Telemachus grinned. "I wish he could have seen that!"

I was sure Melanthius wouldn't have been impressed, but I didn't say so.

"It's not fair," Telemachus said, tossing another piece of bark at me. "He's bigger and stronger, but he says as long as we're the same age, he isn't picking on me."

Often as not, Telemachus gave Melanthius the first shove. I offered that point, because to me it looked like a game they both wanted to play, and I couldn't understand why Telemachus kept at it when the outcome was so certain.

"I wouldn't mind if he just chased me," Telemachus said, "but he throws himself at me and knocks me down. Pins me and pulls back my arm till it really hurts."

"Well, that's the game, isn't it? Say you don't want to play."

"I *do* want to," he said, exhaling in frustration at my failure to understand. "I just want to win. At least sometimes."

The conversation was starting to worry me a little. Telemachus wasn't just any little boy scrapping in an olive orchard. Hadn't our father won our mother's hand by being the best athlete at Icarius' competition? Hadn't every story Eumaeus told us about Odysseus been about how strong and brave he was against man or beast, or even the gods? For now, Telemachus didn't have to be special, but not forever.

"There must be something you can beat Melanthius at," I said.

He got down from his branch and went out to stand at the jump spot. "Give me the rope," he said.

My heart pounded. Though the twins had taunted him for it, he had never been confident enough to take a chance with the swing. Over time his failure to do what was expected of a boy his age had become embarrassing, because I thought it made me look bad as well.

I can't say I hoped for much when I handed him the rope. He had stood on that spot many times before, taken a few deep breaths, and then backed away. There he was again, contemplating the ground, the tree, the air. Then, to my amazement, he jumped.

Telemachus had not remembered to push off at an angle, and he plummeted straight down. When the rope reached its full length and bounced him up, one of his feet flew out. The rope slipped through his hands, and he tumbled to the ground.

"You did it!" I yelled, scrambling down the path so quickly I lost my footing and tumbled to the bottom. Though my ankle hurt, I barely felt it as I jumped up and danced in circles around him.

He was still sitting on the ground. "Did what?" He looked down at his hands. Red rope burns cut across both palms, and though they were not bleeding, the broken flesh had begun to glisten.

I stopped dancing. How could he see this so differently? He had jumped, and that was all that mattered. *Don't be a baby*, I pleaded silently. *In the name of all the gods, don't cry.*

I could see him struggling to hold back tears, but he composed himself. We got up and walked home without saying a word.

CHAPTER 4

A Fade of Purple

The next stripe of cloth is so finely woven it shimmers, in a color so delicate I run my finger just a hairbreadth above it to avoid touching it.

To weave my mother into the story on my loom, I started with a purple dye that comes from a sea snail so tiny that tens of thousands are needed to color one robe. So rare and valuable is this dye that only those of royal blood ever wear the hue.

What other color could I choose for a woman who was not just my mother but also the queen? To stretch the small quantity of dye I was able to bring back from Sparta, I made too dilute a solution, and the thread came out so pale it was still almost white. I boiled the dye again and it darkened a little, but it was still far from the royal color I intended.

For the first of many times, the story my loom would tell was more important—and truer—than the one I first intended. The thread wasn't purple because she wasn't really royal yet. She was too young and inexperienced to make much of a queen, or a mother.

After I wove a little of the pale thread, I tore it out and started again. I

had made another mistake. I had created a distinct line between Telema-
chus and my mother, as if they were separate people with separate destinies,
but that was never the way it was. I gradually worked my mother's color in
and faded his out, because their fates have always been intertwined. Only
my father, if he survives, has the power to make what happens to one not
unravel the other along with it.

My brother and I spent a while longer at Laertes and Anticleia's farm, but shortly after the olive harvest in the late fall we were both called back to the palace. I can't say it was entirely unexpected. Even before the harvest I overheard my grandparents talking about how things needed to change.

More accurately, I heard my grandmother talking. Though I couldn't see my grandfather, I could picture him bending over a row of vegetables, giving his beans and garlic far more attention than they required, to block out her intrusion into his place of solitude.

When Anticleia started in on something, regardless of how hard my grandfather tried to ignore her, the subject would not change until she got her way or grew tired of arguing. In those cases she would storm off, muttering how he was never interested in any of the right things, and how it was a shame that men had so much power when their skulls were so thick.

I know so much about their arguments because I took every possible opportunity to overhear them from one or another of my favorite hiding spots. I used to think spying on the world of adults was more entertaining than anything else, and it is painful to recollect now that I ever chose not to go outside and enjoy the world when I had the chance.

I was still young enough to think I was the center of any

conversation that had my name in it, and this one in the garden seemed to.

"She shows no interest at all," Anticleia insisted.

"I don't think that's true," Laertes said. "You're too hard on her."

"How long has it been now? A year? What am I supposed to think?"

My heart moved in a sickening way inside my chest. What had I done wrong? I didn't need help with a needle and thread by now, and I had learned enough about weaving to think my grandmother wasn't just being nice when she thanked me for helping at her loom. I was rarely scolded for lack of effort, although I admit my speed was quickest when I was heading out the door to find Telemachus and the twins.

"It's her responsibility to raise her daughter, wouldn't you say?" Anticleia went on. "I didn't put the responsibility for Ctimene off onto your mother."

Ctimene? The conversation wasn't about me after all. But who was this Ctimene I'd never heard of? I leaned forward to hear more.

"I wasn't away at war when Ctimene was a baby either," my grandfather said. "Penelope has enough on her mind. You should help her without complaining so much."

I heard him grunt as he stood up. "I'm going to check the orchard," he said, signaling that the conversation was over.

I knew I wasn't supposed to be there, but I was determined to understand a conversation I had gone to so much trouble to overhear.

"Who's Ctimene?" I asked, catching up with Anticleia in the courtyard.

"You were snooping again." She was still upset with my grandfather, and I wished I had waited for her to be in a better mood, or followed after him instead.

But it was too late now. "I walked up and I heard the last thing you said, that's all."

By now we were in the kitchen and Anticleia looked around the empty room. "Where are the servants? They should be making dinner."

I knew she was trying to change the subject, but I wouldn't let her. "Who's Ctimene?" I repeated.

"She's my daughter, little has-to-know-everything." Anticleia's knife banged on the table as she attacked an onion. "And don't just stand there. If you're going to ask questions, at least make yourself useful while you're doing it."

I picked up a handful of chickpeas and rolled them in a cloth to clean them. "I didn't know you had a daughter."

"You don't know a lot of things."

I was on dangerous ground. Anticleia's temper could flash in an instant, and I had felt the sting of her palm on my cheek more than once. Still, I had to ask one more question. "Does that mean my father has a sister?"

"What else could it mean?" she snapped.

"Well, what happened to her?"

"We married her to a prince and sent her off. Is that enough?"

I could not absorb what she was saying. How could a daughter disappear like that? How could I spend the first seven years of my life not knowing she existed?

I fell silent. Not until I felt the towel flatten did I realize I had been rubbing the chickpeas so inattentively that they had broken into pieces under my hand.

* * *

Even at that age, I sensed that Ctimene's story contained some message about what might happen to me when I grew up, but I quickly pushed thoughts of her aside. Perhaps if my father were real to me I might have been able to hold on to images of his sister, but he wasn't, and as a result, neither was she. But the main thing that turned my attention elsewhere was the olive harvest, which got under way shortly thereafter.

Getting the olives down from the trees was one of the big events of the year. It had to be done quickly, between the time they were ripe enough and the first winter storms turned the harvest into bruised and dirty windfalls. Almost everyone got involved in one way or another, and for days we worked our way through the orchard. The women set up nets under the trees, and men tapped the branches deftly to dislodge the olives without harming the tree. Melanthius and other boys climbed into the trees to hand-pick fruit that refused to fall. When the olives were in the nets, they were hauled off, and the process began again with the next group of trees.

Only days before, the orchard had been filled with the sounds of birds and the clicks and buzzes of insects. Now the clamor was almost enough to shake the bark from trees. Poles banged against wood, and olives thudded softly against each other as they brushed past the leaves and fell into the nets. From time to time a branch cracked and fell, followed by curses and loud arguments about who was at fault. Some of the older men brought instruments and set up nearby to play music, while workers sang along. The dogs got caught up in the excitement, chasing after each other, barking and wagging their tails until they fell to the ground, covered with slobber and panting from exhaustion.

I found Melantho with a group of young women carrying pails suspended from both ends of a pole balanced across their shoulders. From the time I first met her, I always checked to see if she was wearing underwear, and this time she was. She was scowling about having to do women's work when she would rather be scrambling up and down trees, and her mother was threatening not to let her go to the celebration at the end of the harvest unless she settled down and behaved like a girl.

Melantho glanced over at me with a glum look. I picked up a pail to follow after her, but though it was only half full, it was too heavy for me.

"You're too small for that," Dolius' wife said, taking me over to where Melantho and the others were dumping their pails on large cloths so heavily stained that the remaining white fabric looked like bird droppings on the brown. She gave me a little basket and left me with a couple of other young girls who were looking for damaged fruit in a mound of *kolymvades*, my favorite type of olive, which was preserved swimming in oil.

All around me, girls a little older than I was crouched over the vast quantities of olives destined for the presses. They filled shallow baskets and brought them over to another part of the clearing where women bent over mortars and pestles. The olives were dumped in and pounded to a coarse mash, after which—pits and all—the mixture was scooped into large sacks woven from bristly animal hair. These sacks were loaded into boxes secured to the backs of donkeys and sent off to the presses.

Children no older than three or four crouched between the sorters, examining the edges of the piles with the seriousness and deliberation of a jeweler choosing among his stones. From time to time they fished out a stick or a piece of rock and set it to the side. When the sorters grew bored or just wanted to stretch their limbs, they made a game of sneaking close enough to the mortars to coat their fingers with the oil that oozed through a hole near the base and collected in a stone bowl. Some of the women made playful slaps on the children's hands when they reached for the oil, but others scowled so fiercely that no child came near them. Everything about the harvest was serious work, and rarely was anyone foolish enough to misjudge an adult's tolerance badly enough to earn a beating.

I was so busy trying to be helpful that for a while I didn't notice Telemachus working alongside Melantho, looking even more miserable than she did. Only a few boys had been relegated to what was clearly women's work, and I knew that he must have been told to leave the tree climbing and pole swinging to others.

Mentor had been right that manual labor would make Telemachus stronger. He had baskets dangling from both ends of a pole resting on the back of his neck, and I could see the shape of his arm muscles as he balanced the load. The job was hard, and he was doing it well, but I knew without having to be told there was no honor in it.

I looked away, embarrassed for him, and saw that Laertes had arrived and was talking with Mentor at the edge of the work party. The two men were casting glances in the direction of Telemachus as they spoke. Laertes beckoned my brother to put down his pails and come over. When he got there, Mentor put his arm around his shoulder and bent down to say something to him. Then the two men walked away and took Telemachus with them.

It was the end of my brother's apprenticeship. Telemachus stayed behind in my grandparents' house until the harvest was over. I continued to pick through olives when the mood struck me, but mostly I did whatever I wanted, as long as I stayed out of the way of people with real jobs to do.

I walked alongside the donkeys as they took olives to the pressing huts. These were built around large exposed rocks into which had been carved a flat platform, lined with grooves that fed into a single spout, under which buckets lined with beeswax were placed. The sacks were placed on it, and a wooden press was brought down with great force onto them. To work the press, men lifted boulders secured with leather straps and hooked them on the end of a long lever. The extra weight brought the press down with a force far beyond what they could have exerted themselves, and the green-gold oil poured out into the basins as swiftly as rivulets after a rain.

The men were wet with perspiration, and their muscles bulged. Everyone knew the oil would keep far better all year if pressed within a day of harvest, and I didn't have to be told that this was a place where I would not be welcome underfoot. Elsewhere around the groves, women laid out the olives we called *drypeteis*, which shriveled into delicious, chewy bites as they dried in the sun, while others brined tangy, cracked *thlastes* olives. Everyone was nice to me as long as I didn't ask too many questions or expect anyone to pay attention to me. I spent most of my time with the donkeys, because at least they nodded their heads when I talked to them.

After the last trees were stripped of their crop, the oil pressing was completed, and the olives for eating had been stored away, it was time to celebrate. The day of the harvest festival had been cloudy, with gusts of wind and a few drops of rain, but by sunset the sky was clear and the air felt warmer than it had all day.

No perfume, no unguent or incense, has the power to transform the air around it quite as much as a rain that has lasted only long enough to wet the dust. The birds rejoiced, and I sang along with them, swinging Anticleia's hand, as my grandparents, Telemachus, and I headed for the olive grove. As the sounds and smells of the festival overtook everything else, I dropped her hand and ran ahead. The first person I saw was Melanthius, who was part of a group of boys throwing windfall olives as they chased each other through the grove. I stepped out of the way to avoid being knocked down, but I don't think he noticed me.

In the clearing, someone had already laid down a cloth for us to sit on, along with a full wineskin, cups, and a large piece of bread in a basket. All around us, other families sat on their own cloths. Mothers nursed infants and chatted among themselves while toddlers stooped on chubby legs to examine everything on the ground nearby. Girls of about my age watched the little ones to keep them from wandering off or making themselves sick by putting dirt-caked raw olives in their mouths.

Some of the men had brought instruments from home—different types and sizes of flutes mostly, but also some drums. I sat and listened for a while, watching a group of children jump and wave their arms in front of the musicians, in anticipation of the dancing soon to come. Some of the older ones held their arms out like eagle wings and swirled in loops around the little ones. When they pounced they turned their fingers into claws, and tickled the children until they screamed.

Another boy, whom I remembered seeing throwing olives at Melanthius, stood in the middle of the children and pretended to be the god Argus, who had a hundred eyes all around his head. Children stood at the edge of his vision making faces and posing in funny ways. Without moving his head, he described them, as they clutched their stomachs and fell to the ground in laughter.

Why had Telemachus and I never thought of any of these games? Why had I gone around making up wild stories in my head while he acted out other ones that didn't involve me at all? And why did I not get up and join the fun? I am not sure today why I thought I couldn't. I sat in the space someone else had laid out for me on the ground, feeling more isolated than I ever had in the fishing village and believing my life could never grow big enough to include much of anything at all.

The sky had turned deep blue by then, and the first stars came out. As I lay on my back, looking up at the moonlight trickling through the branches, my mood softened. The grove was lit from above by the heavens and below by the warm glow of the fire, and I felt as if I were floating somewhere in between, no longer lonely but complete all by myself. I shut my eyes, and my ears took over, bringing me into a realm of music, happy voices, and the cries of children at play. The clearing hummed with magic. The pigs and goats roasting on spits over piles of firewood gave off an aroma so sweet and smoky I could not imagine how anything, even wine itself, could be more intoxicating.

I was startled out of my reverie by excited shouts from the crowd. My grandfather was standing near the fire, honoring the gods by offering them a thighbone wrapped in fat and pouring a libation. Whole goat carcasses had been removed from the fire and shredded, and large roasted chunks of ox and beef were chopped into pieces on a few tables. People took what they could with their hands, or with anything else they might have thought to bring from home. Someone handed me a bowl full of the best pieces, and I ate until my stomach rebelled at the idea of another bite.

Then, after everyone was clutching their stomachs and groaning with pleasure at the rare treat of as much meat as they could manage to stuff in their bodies, two men lugged a huge clay krater into the middle of the gathering. Laertes gave yet another invocation thanking the gods for a successful harvest and the gift of life-sustaining oil. Everyone stood in line, and men ladled new oil into our cups for us to drink. No thicker than skimmed milk, it smelled like trampled grass and did not taste like olives at all, but had a hint of spice and the tanginess of fresh cheese. Perhaps it was because I contributed to the harvest and had a sense of belonging among the people with whom I was sharing the feast, but I can't think of anything I have tasted since that surpasses it.

The day after the festival, Telemachus went back to live in the palace. Though no one ever said anything to me, I suspect now that Mentor took one look at Telemachus carrying pails with the women and judged his project an embarrassing failure. I don't see it that way at all. I remember my brother sweating and straining, but not giving up, as he carried loads people much older and bigger than him also had trouble with. But most of all I remember the leap from the tree, and how much I wished Mentor could have seen the moment that held out the best hope for the kind of man Telemachus might become.

Soon after, I too was summoned home. My mother, I was told, had decided it was time to take over my education. My grandmother cried at my departure, though I am sure she had insisted on it, and Laertes walked me back along the shore of the bay and up the hill to the palace by himself.

I had returned home briefly perhaps a dozen times, accompanying slaves bringing produce from my grandparents' estate, but I had seen my mother only twice in the year and a half I had been away. The other times I was there she was sleeping, or off somewhere else, and because my visits had been unplanned, I was told I shouldn't expect otherwise.

When Laertes and I walked through the pillars of the megaron, she stood up as if she had been waiting for us and hurried over to me. Her hair was the color of honey, just as I remembered. It was pulled up off her neck and secured with a comb, from which a few curls were worked loose to soften the borders of her face. Her eyes are hard to hold clearly in my mind even today, a combination of every color I have ever seen—blue-tinged or brown in different lights, and a tawny greenish yellow when the sun shines on them. Her skin was almost as white as her gown, which hugged the contours of her ample breasts and slender waist, and gathered at her hips before falling away in soft, graceful pleats to the floor.

I had no one to compare her to at the time, but I see now that those who deemed her a great beauty could not be accused of empty flattery. I felt proud and important that such a woman was coming toward me, arms outstretched, smiling and saying my name. I felt as if my life were starting at that moment, that no time had passed at all, that my mother had always been in my life, and I was now truly at home.

To my mother's credit, she took her commitment to my upbringing seriously from that time forward. When I finally mastered a spindle, my mother declared that the thread I made was her favorite. I worked days on end to produce what seemed at my age to be enough thread to reach from Ithaca to Troy and back, but it always was used up in no time at all.

The palace was full of looms, and while working together at ours every day we became inseparable. My mother had several looms of different sizes in her quarters and a large one in the megaron, near the circular hearth in the center of the room. We stood at it much of each day working on cloth that would be folded and pinned into garments for my brother and the two of us. In another part of the palace, servants and slaves made cloth for the rest of the household. Once a year, soft wool was combed from the sheep and goats before it became too coarse, and then it was brought in mountainous quantities to workshops where women carded it, turned it into thread with their spindles, and wove it into fabric.

Every woman and girl wore a chiton secured over both shoulders by sturdy pins and tied in place with a belt. Women's chitons covered their legs to just above their ankles, but girls wore theirs shorter, at the knees. The only distinction between royal clothing and everyone else's was in the cloth itself and the decorations on it. Our garments were more finely woven, mostly in linen, which could be oiled to a beautiful sheen. Occasionally we also wore a peplos, a square of cloth with a colorful border that draped over the upper part of our bodies.

Men and boys of all ranks wore tunics made from larger pieces of fabric with a slit in the middle to poke their heads through, tied around their waist with a belt or in some cases a simple piece of rope. Underneath, another cloth was pulled between their legs and tucked in at the ends to secure it around their waists.

Densely woven cloth of sheep's wool and goat's hair kept everyone warm in the winter. These served as cloaks draped over both shoulders, or as himations flung over one shoulder and secured under the other arm.

My mother and I wove more than we could use ourselves, storing the best of it away for better times. With few visitors and so little cause to celebrate, we had no need for fancy things. But when my first summer back at the palace turned to fall, my mother surprised me by stopping work and going to a chest to get out several pieces of our best cloth.

She sat me down. "You'll soon be a woman," she told me. "It's time I shared something important with you."

I did women's work, but I knew I was not of their world. At nine years old, I still wore my blond hair styled like a girl's, clipped close to my head at the sides and neck, with a single short lock dangling over my forehead and one long, thick strand down my back. With my hair and my short chiton, suggesting that a little wisp like me was close to being a woman was odd, but I wasn't thinking about that. All that stuck in my mind was that my mother had something important she wanted to share.

Though I spent almost all my time by my mother's side, our conversations were mostly about whatever we were doing, and I actually knew very little about her. On a few occasions I had gotten her to talk about her life when she was my age. Her face would light up briefly as she described the megaron in her childhood palace blazing with torchlight, the banquet table cluttered with gold and silver serving dishes piled with meats and fruit, and the kraters of wine mixed with water, from which servants would ladle goblet after goblet for the guests.

Inevitably she would stop in the middle of the story and make a dismissive comment about how it was a long time ago and had nothing to do with now. Afterward, she would remain silent for a long time.

"I wish you could have been there to see it, Xanthe," she said once, describing the feasts and games in honor of a visit to her father by the King of Crete, but almost as soon as the words were out of her mouth her face fell, and she rushed from the room. Later I found her asleep on the couch in her quarters, her hair still wet with tears. After that, I resolved never to ask her about her childhood again.

Though the sun would scarcely change position in the sky between the times gods were invoked for one reason or another, and

I could recite huge numbers of stories about them by heart, I had gotten almost no training in how to honor them. My mother, I soon found out, had a great deal more to teach me than how to weave.

Hera was who she wanted to share with me. I thought I knew everything about her already. She was the wife of Zeus, and the mother of the great smith god Hephaestus and the war god Ares. Halia's mother told me her children were born not with the help of a man but by eating some kind of leaf. Eurycleia scoffed at that, saying that they were born when Hera slapped her hand on the ground and willed them to exist. I remember that after she told me this, I spent most of a morning slapping my hand on the ground and ordering things to happen, but I soon grew bored and decided if I really wanted something, I was probably going to have to figure out how to get it myself.

I knew from stories I'd heard that Hera was terribly jealous of her husband. He was always looking at other women, even though she was the most beautiful goddess of them all. She could be very mean, and I told myself I should be as careful as possible to make sure she was never mad at me. Even someone as powerful as Zeus could not control her at all. For at least a month I examined my bed thoroughly before getting in, after I learned Hera put poisonous snakes in Heracles' cradle. I was so upset by her revenge against a poor girl named Io, who had been unfortunate enough to catch Zeus' eye, that I pleaded with my mother never to leave the palace again. She was so pretty I was afraid she too would be turned into a cow if Hera ever saw Zeus looking at her.

I had grown up quite a bit since those early days, and it was time for me to move beyond listening to stories of the gods and start developing my own relationships with them. Hera had to be first, for she was the one who saw not just the nine-year-old girl I was, but the woman I would become. It was she who would watch over my whole life, and I needed to learn how to be worthy of her attention.

We spent the next few days getting ready for my first visit to Hera's shrine. It lay down a path I had been forbidden to take for fear of incurring the wrath of the gods. They could pick me up and dash me against the rocks, or send huge birds to eat me alive, or weigh me down with a boulder and throw me into the ocean to drown if I displeased them. Much as I hated not having the answers to everything I was curious about, I had done no more than stand at the top of the path and wish I could go down it. And now that was going to happen.

My mother and I went to a pomegranate orchard, where we examined one fruit after another, rejecting any whose skin had started to turn dry and brown, and stopping only when we each found a perfectly shaped orb with no hint of a flaw. These we blessed before we picked them, and then we carried them home in our cupped hands, as if the slightest jostling might shatter them.

We took them to my mother's chambers and laid them on a cloth my other grandmother, whom I had never met, had helped my mother embroider when she was about my age. It was a square piece of fine linen bordered all around in a pattern of intertwined pomegranate blossoms, with a design of a beautiful ripe fruit in the middle. A piece of the skin was missing, revealing a wedge of glistening seeds made from little red beads my mother had sewn to the cloth.

I spent most of the next few days working on my own cloth for Hera and listening to my mother talk about her patron. "You could spend your whole life trying to take in everything she offers us," my mother said. "She is there wherever a woman marries and when she gives birth, and even though Hera's a mother, she's still a virgin."

I screwed up my face, wanting to show my sophistication in such matters. "That's impossible," I said. "Isn't it?"

My mother smiled. "For us, but not for the gods. It's not so strange, really. Every year the pomegranate puts out newflowers that only later bear fruit. Just like that, every year Hera goes to the spring at Kanathos, and renews her virginity in its waters."

She looked at my cloth. "Keep your stitches a little smaller. You want this to be the best thing you've ever done. You'll only work on it these few days each year, but by the time you've had your first blood, you'll be ready to take it to the shrine and show it to her. Once you know she's pleased, you can start using it the way I've used mine."

I bent over my work, but since I couldn't make tiny enough stitches without losing track of what my mother was saying, eventually I laid my work on my lap and just listened.

"Hera isn't just one goddess, you know," she told me. "She's really three at the same time—Hera Pais to young ones like you, Teleia to wives, and Khera to widows."

Her expression clouded. "I guess at this point I don't know whether she's Teleia or Khera to me."

I rarely considered the possibility that my father might be dead, and I realized, to my shock, that my mother must think about it all the time.

"I miss him," I said.

Her laughter was brief. "How can you miss someone you've never met?"

"I just do. Don't you want him to come home?"

It was a silly question, I thought, as soon as I asked it. That was why her answer came as such a surprise.

"It would certainly make a lot of things easier," she said. Nothing more than that.

"Don't you miss him?" I asked.

She cleared her throat. "Of course I do."

I thought our conversation was over when she said nothing more, so I picked up my embroidery again.

"Hera tried her best to help me," my mother finally said, her voice so distant it seemed to emanate from the other side of the room. "To help all the women whose husbands are at Troy. Have you heard about how Paris was forced to choose whether Hera, Aphrodite, or Athena was the most beautiful?"

Halia had told me the story. "He chose Aphrodite." In the past, I had treated it as a story of no particular note, but now I snorted with indignation. "Everybody knows Hera should have won."

My mother gave me an approving smile. "Hera offered to make Paris the king of all men if he chose her, but do you remember what Aphrodite offered?"

"Love?" I had forgotten a few of the details, but because Aphrodite was the goddess of love, it was a safe guess.

My mother sniffed. "I'm not sure I would call it love. She promised him he could possess Helen of Sparta, so he took her off to Troy—and your father and the rest of the Achaeans went to get her back."

I knew all this, but I had never heard it from her. "Ten years ago they went," she said, pumping her hands into the tops of her thighs for emphasis. "Ten years! Helen was already married, and Hera tried to distract Paris with an offer of more power than he could have imagined, but he chose Helen anyway. And now, who knows what will happen to all of us?"

She got up and went to the window. She slid her fingers

through her hair from her temples to the back of her head, and held them there a moment before turning back to me.

"It's important to pray, Xanthe. The gods don't always come when we call. That's just the way they are. But whenever I feel Hera isn't listening, I believe in my heart it's because she's away helping your father survive to see his home again."

She came over to me and touched my shoulder. "But you are old enough to invoke her now. That's what I must teach you to do."

Her hand stayed on my shoulder, and I reached up to clasp it with my own. She laid her other hand on top of mine and left it there for a moment. Then she bent down to kiss the top of my head before pulling away and going back to her work.

On the day my mother had chosen for my first visit to the shrine, we ate a quiet meal in her quarters before setting out at midday. I knew we were not supposed to treat this like an ordinary outing but spend the entire time thinking about Hera. If we spoke, it should be only about her. Our path took us down to the bay and across the beach, then up through one corner of Laertes' farm to the low and rocky hills behind. Because the walk was long, I began to sing a song my mother had taught me the day before.

"Sing we now of Hera, the goddess of women," I began. "Ruling from heaven on your golden throne."

My mother joined in. "Let us sing now of the goddess greatest in beauty. Let us raise our voices to the queen of gods."

I took her hand. "There is no one we love more than you, Divine Hera, no one we honor more." We finished in unison and sang the whole song again, beaming at each other.

When our voices died away, my mother cocked her ear, listening. I heard it too. Across one of Laertes' fields, ragged and yellow from the recent harvest, a crow perched alone at the top of a dead tree, calling out as if it were trying to talk to us. In a nearby thicket I heard cuckoos singing.

The crow and the cuckoo. Hera's birds!

The glow in my heart was more than mere happiness. The sun prickled my skin as if it were leaning over to tell me its secrets. Everything around me shimmered, as if I had stepped into another realm where gods embodied themselves in birds and other creatures, and nothing was ordinary at all. The crow cawed again, and a shiver went down my body from my scalp to my toes.

We walked through the rich afternoon light of autumn, until we reached what could not really be described as a hill, but more a protrusion of spiky rocks between which a little dirt was scattered. At its base was a small hut of wood and stone, covered by a lattice of woven branches taken, I suppose, from the ragged olive trees that stood on either side.

Anyone happening upon it would see nothing more than a shabby and abandoned hut, but they would be blind to what it really was. The gods want to be honored in the houses mortals make for them, even if all we can offer is something meager and plain. Not just the hut but its surroundings were radiating, as if Hera had already arrived and was waiting for us.

My mother took a pouch from our basket and took out a handful of barley, which she poured in a line across the entrance to the shrine. "Come, greatest of goddesses," she said, "most highly renowned and revered Queen Hera. We prepare this shrine for you and pray that you find our devotion worthy."

I recognized the invocation we had practiced. "And bless us with your kindness, as we rejoice in your majesty," I said with her.

My mother gestured to me to go in. When I stepped through

the door, I heard a rush of wings. A pair of birds flew out, so close that the feet of one of them grazed my head, pulling out a few hairs. Clutching my scalp, I rushed outside screaming.

I wanted to tell my mother this new world was too overwhelming, and I wasn't ready for it. I wanted to go home, to try again next year when maybe I would know a little more and be less fearful. But her expression was less concerned for me than puzzled, as if she were trying to interpret the hidden message in what had just occurred.

She gently detached my grip and nodded to me that it was time to try again. I resisted for a moment, but something inside me must have wanted to go in, because I felt my feet move without my head telling them to.

The interior was illuminated only by light filtering through the branches. They had been pulled aside in one spot to allow a column of light to shine down on a flat stone altar at the far side of the room. On it, a large object was covered by a dusty cloth.

My mother came in behind me and went to the altar. "Royal Hera," she said, addressing the covered form in a voice somewhere between speech and song. "Majestic in demeanor, formed from divine air, enthroned in the bosom of the blue sky, we mortals are your constant concern and care."

She lifted the cloth. The clay figure of Hera was perhaps a third my height. She had one arm crossing her chest, supporting her bare breasts, and she held her other arm up, bent at the elbow. A face and hair were painted on her round head, and her lower body, which was shaped like the bottom half of a chiton, had marks like folds of cloth scratched into it.

My mother sprinkled more barley on the altar, and afterward she blew the air around the statue to dislodge any dust that might have crept under the cloth. Then she took a small piece of fabric from the basket she had brought with her, and after asking Hera's permission to dress her, she placed it around her body, fastening it at the shoulder with a jeweled pin.

"You nourish life with your breath and know what every being needs and desires," my mother went on, taking the gold bangles from her earlobes and hooking them over the tops of Hera's clay ears.

All this time Hera had not taken her eyes off me. They were not cruel eyes, nor were they kind. All I remember is that they were huge, taking up nearly half her face. I stood without moving, wondering if I should avert my eyes out of respect, but finding myself helpless to unlock my gaze.

My mother unwrapped a bejeweled golden orb shaped like a pomegranate with a small spike on the bottom. This she inserted through a hole in Hera's raised hand and finished by placing a gold crown on the goddess's head. "Come, beloved Hera," she murmured, "famed eternal queen, bless us now and forever with your serenity."

She put up her hands to cover her face, and if it weren't for the fact that she was not moving at all, I would have thought she was crying. I pressed myself next to her, like a nestling tucked in beside a mother bird, and waited, not wanting to breathe.

My mother came back from wherever her thoughts had led her and bent over the basket. She took out my pomegranate and handed it to me without saying a word, before disappearing through the doorway. I knew that was my signal to approach the goddess and make my offering to her in private.

I stood a few arm lengths from the statue, afraid to go any nearer. I took one step, then another, until I could reach out and lay the fruit on the altar. I backed away as suddenly as if I had touched a hot coal, and returned to where I had been standing.

What should I say? I tried to remember some of the words my mother had used, but they all formed a hopeless jumble in my head.

And then it came to me, not as a thought enters the mind, but more as an understanding takes over the entire self. Hera had granted my greatest wish. She had given me my mother.

"Thank you," I whispered, and since there was nothing more I could think of to say, I backed out of the hut.

My mother was seated on a rock outside. When I came out, she took the second pomegranate, and after offering it to Hera, she wedged a small knife into it and broke it in two, revealing the tiny crimson jewels inside.

She left half of it on the rock for the goddess and broke the other into two pieces for us. The juice ran over her fingers and down to her wrists. Raising her hand to her mouth, she cleaned it with movements of her lips that were less like licks than kisses. She handed a piece to me, and I felt the seeds burst in my mouth, sweet at first, then bitter at the core.

"We'll come again in the spring," she said, almost too soft to hear. "We'll decorate our hair with pomegranate blossoms, and weave branches through the roof so Hera can be in a beautiful orchard."

She looked at me with a wistfulness I had never seen before. "You're a good girl, Xanthe," she said. Then, because we weren't really supposed to talk, she turned and started down the trail before I could open my mouth, though I can't imagine what I would have found to say.

Because we would spend the night with my grandparents, we went back by another route that climbed briefly up before descending to the farm. When we reached the top, the cliffs fell away to the rocky shore below, leaving us with an unobstructed view of cloudless sky and sea. The sun was flattening on the horizon, turning the water around it into a pool of molten bronze so bright it tinted the sky around it green.

High above us, a crow made a perfect circle directly over our heads. Gulls and other seabirds wheeled and soared, their cries disappearing into the vast air. Everything was new, as if the world had been born that day and not just I but every living thing was experiencing it for the first time.

Something came over me that I can't explain today, as if an invisible hand were touching the small of my back, pushing me forward, while another gave wings to my feet until I was so light I thought I might be floating. Suddenly I was running down the path, waving my arms over my head, and twirling in place, greeting the huge sky and the beautiful earth and telling it I was glad I was here.

I turned to look up the path toward my mother. Her golden hair shone with the last rays of sun, and her skin seemed almost impossibly white against the growing shadows. The oiled cloth of her chiton wasn't reflecting the light as much as absorbing it, warming it, and sending it back out into the world.

I wasn't sure the radiant figure was my mother at all. I thought she must have stepped out of sight behind a rock or a tree, and I was looking at a goddess.

As the light faded, the vision did as well. My mother began walking toward me.

"What are you looking at?" she asked.

"You're very beautiful."

"You are too," she said. "I saw you dancing with Hera Pais and I said to myself what a marvelous woman you are going to be."

I had been dancing with Hera Pais? "Did you see her?" I asked.

She smiled. "I can't explain it. You don't see her presence as much as know it." She looked at the darkening sky and took my hand to hurry me along toward home.

That night as I lay in my bed at the farm, I fell into a kind of slumber I had never experienced before, as if I were dreaming while I was still awake, or perhaps was no longer here at all but in another world. Today I no longer remember the details of the visions that came to me that night, or the next few nights when I was back home, except that I emerged knowing in my heart that Hera was as real as I was, that she was my protector, that she would find me if I was lost and know me wherever I went.

Eurynome went alone to the shrine four days later, to cover the statue against the weather, and to bring back for safekeeping Hera's crown, golden pomegranate, clothes, and jewelry. I begged my mother to store them in my quarters, and she did. I feel their presence now. They lie safe inside a chest in the corner, wrapped in my embroidered cloth, awaiting the day I am once again free to take them to her.

CHAPTER 5

Air and Absence

The texture here is not at all like the smooth purple linen above it. I used olive juice to dye coarse wool to a color I hoped would be as rich as the bark of cypress trees but instead turned out a dull and rather morose shade of brown. I wove so loosely in this part that sunlight passes through, picking up glints of the spun gold I streaked in to break the monotony of the hue.

I had the gold thread already, left over from one of the first projects I did on my own loom, which my mother gave me as a present when I turned nine. It was a cloak I wove as a gift for my father when he returned home. I wanted my mother's approval so badly, and what I most remember is how proud she was of me. The cloak itself is of so little importance now that I had forgotten about it until, rummaging around in a basket, I found the gold thread I used to trim it.

Each piece of the story on my loom began as a concrete memory, but often I become aware of something deeper when I step back and let what I have woven speak to me. This stripe of air and light is not about the cloak at all, not about my first loom, not about my mother's relationship with me. It's about my father himself.

I was wrong about him not being part of my life. He was everywhere and nowhere at the same time, the backdrop for everything that happened to all of us, a fabric made of air and absence.

After the olive harvest that year, I was weaving in the grand megaron with my mother when I looked out and saw Melantho in the courtyard. I was almost ten, so she must have been close to twelve. She had grown several inches, and though she was still too thin to have anything resembling hips, I noticed that under her chiton her breasts had grown to the size of apples.

Though Melantho's wildness had always intimidated me, she was the only girl close to my age I had spent much time with. When she told me Eurynome had brought her to the palace to train as a maid in the queen's quarters, I was thrilled, thinking I would finally have someone to talk to. I should have realized that the olive grove was a far different world than the palace, and that someone whose role in life was to serve me could never really be my friend.

In some respects, after Melantho's arrival I felt more alone than ever. The first time I saw her giggling at a secret another maid had whispered in her ear, I went to my room and cried, because I was sure no one would ever do that with me.

For a while I thought I might die of loneliness. Much as I had hoped my time at Hera's shrine with my mother would bring me closer to her, it didn't. She began complaining of headaches and spending much of her time alone in a darkened room. Though from time to time she would bustle around with enormous energy, within a day, or sometimes less, she would be gone again, back into her own world.

Telemachus was out of my life again as well. Mentor's new plan involved private tutors who came to the palace to teach what seems to be the real calling of a king—to go off to war with a shield and sword, and to play at mock battle with his peers at home. On those rare occasions when we entertained visitors, Telemachus sat with the men rather than eating with my mother and me in our private quarters. He took his other meals with his tutors and slept in the same wing of the palace where they were housed. I caught glimpses of him from time to time, but that was all.

Slowly I accepted that Eurycleia was the nearest thing to a friend I was going to have. Her upstairs counterpart, Eurynome, was devoted to my mother, but she did not like children very much. In many ways I was already more like a small adult, mostly from lack of opportunities to behave like a child. As a result, Eurynome seemed to approve of me most of the time, but her heart could go no further.

Eurycleia, on the other hand, hugged me every day, brought treats from the larders to help me grow, and clucked with sympathy if I so much as pricked my finger. And she loved my father even more than she loved me. When I asked her what Odysseus was like, she didn't talk about how strong he was, or how he could get the better of everyone. I think she admired him for all that but loved him for other reasons. She talked about how handsome he was, and how when he was young he was able to do things that were difficult for much older boys.

I noticed that when Eurycleia talked this way, her thoughts seemed to wander, and she would grow quiet. At first I thought she was remembering old times, but the look on her face was more concerned than a person needs to be for anything that has already run its course. Looking back now, I suspect she was thinking about Telemachus, and how unlike his father he seemed. She must have been worried that Telemachus would turn out to be a disappointment as a man. I think everyone was, although we never spoke of it.

Eurycleia was as close to Telemachus as anyone could possibly be. When he was a baby, she could not feed him from her own body, as she had with Odysseus. My mother once told me how Eurycleia sat each day with the wet nurse and held Telemachus in her arms afterward, as if she had just offered him her own shrunken breast, and how she had from that time forward referred to herself as his nurse.

One of Eurycleia's recollections disturbed me greatly, because of how different my father seemed from the man portrayed by Eumaeus. A few years before he married my mother, my father had been unsuccessful at winning the hand of Helen of Sparta. He had already set eyes on Penelope, and to gain Helen's father's support for his suit of my mother, he made all those who vied for Helen swear an oath to defend the winner if anyone in the future dishonored the marriage. When Helen went off to Troy with her lover, her husband, Menelaus, called on Odysseus and all the others to remember their oath and sail to Troy with him to destroy the city and bring her back.

My father did not want to go. Penelope had been in Ithaca only two years. At seventeen she had given birth to Telemachus, and she was at that point only eighteen and unready to take charge of my father's *oikos* and kingdom. He had to make a terrible choice between his honor and his family's need, but so strong was his feeling he should stay at home that he did not respond to Menelaus' summons. When a small group of men came to Ithaca to force him to honor his promise, he went around shouting things that made no sense and talking to voices no one else could hear, hoping the men would believe he had lost his mind and would have to be left behind.

In the end, when the men refused to depart without him, he hitched his plow to an ox and donkey, and instead of seed he began sowing salt on one of his fields. Neither Eurycleia nor my mother was in on the ruse. Penelope picked up her baby and the two women ran to the field, crying out in despair. One of the visitors grabbed Telemachus from my mother's arms and laid him in the path of the plow. I try to imagine my father's desperation when he saw this, but he did what any sane man would do. He turned the plow away to save his son's life.

The next day he left for Troy.

Since my return from Sparta, I have seen the ruin other men have made in the great Odysseus' house. I wonder if he sensed that this might happen. I wonder if he realized that his wife was too young and his kingdom too new to be safe without him. I try to imagine what he was thinking as he pulled the ox out of the path before it reached his son. Perhaps he saw it as the noblest fight he had ever undertaken, the most crucial battle he ever lost.

When I wasn't weaving with my mother, I followed Eurycleia around the palace. She was the only one except the queen who had a key to the storage rooms beneath the house, where our supplies of food were kept. Every morning Eurycleia and the other kitchen servants brought up olive oil, wine, dried fruit, and other things we needed for the day and stored them in a small pantry off the kitchen. The stairs to the storage rooms were dark and very steep, and I never liked going down them, but one day she told me she had forgotten something and needed my help getting it, since no one else was around.

She had never allowed me to hold the torch before, I suppose for fear I would somehow manage to set myself on fire, but that day she had no choice but to hand it to me while she rummaged in a crate for what she had come for.

I swept the light around the storeroom, noticing for the first time several double doors along the far wall.

"What's inside there?" I asked.

"Those?" She stood up and put a round of cheese in her basket. "Your parents' things, mostly."

"What kind of things?" The house was already full of possessions, and I couldn't imagine what could possibly be missing.

"None of your business," she said. "And give me the torch back if you're not going to shine it on the stairs."

I sighed loud enough for her to hear, but she ignored me. I assumed when we got back into the kitchen that she would change the subject, but to my surprise she answered my question.

"Gifts, mostly. Things people gave your father. Silver, gold . . . brooches, bowls. . . ." She shrugged her shoulders as if she could go on forever but assumed she'd said enough. "And of course his weapons," she added as an afterthought.

I was confused. One wall of the megaron was decorated with great bronze shields, flanking a row of spears and axes hung on a rack. "Whose weapons are those in the megaron, then?"

"Your father's," Eurycleia said. "He has dozens more like them. He put his favorites downstairs for safekeeping when he left. His best bow—things like that."

"Why don't we take them out and show them to people?" I asked.

"And bring pirates to our harbor, and make thieves of the men of Ithaca?" Her eyebrows shot up as if she were surprised I needed to ask.

"Ahh." I nodded, trying to look a little wiser than I felt. Pirates and thieves stole children too. Perhaps a band of them were hovering around the walls of the palace as we spoke, waiting to sneak inside to grab a shield in one hand and a foolish girl who wanted to flaunt her family's wealth in the other.

"And besides, Ithaca is a poor island," Eurycleia went on. "People know how important Odysseus is. I don't think he ever felt he needed to prove it by showing off." She patted my shoulder. "Now run along, my flower."

Eurycleia was the only one who ever called me that, and then only when what she meant was that even though she loved me, our conversation was over. I went upstairs with my head filled with images of dark rooms piled to the ceiling with treasure, but the room I really most wanted to know about was the one the old nurse hadn't described. My mother's storeroom. How many more secrets did she have? And more important, how was I going to steal Eurycleia's keys and brave the dark stairs to find out what those secrets were?

I thought of nothing else for several days before deciding that the price I would pay for being caught was just too high, and that I was better off waiting for a chance to wear the old nurse down and get her to open the door herself. As things turned out, I could never have imagined how drastically my life would have to change before she would do just that for me.

Little by little my world closed in around me as I grew older. By the time I was ten, I spent almost every day indoors. The most notable exception was laundry day. Every piece of cloth had value to the *oikos*, because it took so much time and effort to produce, and that meant that a princess could properly be involved in attending to it. I knew how much work was involved in getting wool off an animal and into a cloth to be wrapped around someone's body, but what I really cared about was that laundry day involved me.

Once the men had helped load the carts, the day was for the women and girls of the palace. Eurycleia and I rode in a donkey cart because of her bad hip, while the others walked alongside the donkey carts, singing songs and teasing each other. Melantho and one of her friends led the animals down a trail in the direction of the rising sun. We meandered up through rocky terraces that looked as if they had been formed by Titans hurling huge boulders from the mountaintops. Here and there the parched terrain gave way to a spring-fed meadow or a grove of trees where we could stop to rest and drink.

From the donkey cart, I looked around at the hills, green from the spring rains. Here and there in the distance, poppies had completely overrun the land, turning it into a solid mass of red, broken up only by the ragged gray rocks that more than anything else defined the landscape of Ithaca. Perhaps it was my imagination, but the sky seemed bluer than usual, set off as it was against the red and green and the patches of yellow and purple flowers dotting other slopes.

A hawk was circling overhead. It dropped lower and then plummeted, its talons extended and its wings arched back. Something—a lizard perhaps—was wriggling in its grip as it rose, and I watched it fly in the direction of the sun until the glare grew too bright and I had to look away.

"What does it mean?" I asked Eurycleia.

Today I am wary of omens. One person predicts something and another the opposite, and then a third thing happens. At the time, however, I had total confidence that Eurycleia and my mother knew with the wisdom of the gods themselves what it meant when grain grew or refused to grow in a particular spot, eggs did or did not hatch, or a cloud did or did not give rain.

Eurycleia's brow was furrowed. Seeing my worried look, she gave me a reassuring smile. "It's nothing, I imagine. Only that we'll have a good day of washing."

Whenever I think of the flowers blooming in such profusion that day, I see more than how beautiful they were in the fields. I see them in garlands on the heads of the servant girls, and one garland in particular, crowning a scene that is permanently embedded in my mind.

Shortly before we reached the stream, we skirted the edge of a field that had not yet been plowed. The air was full of the songs of birds and the buzz of insects on the wing. A light breeze sent puffs of air across the grass, shaking it like a veil of green silk. Melantho and the other young servants picked wildflowers to weave into wreaths for their hair and chains around their necks.

At the stream, we stomped on each piece of fabric in the shallow water and rubbed it against the rocks with such vigor that if cloth were alive we would surely have killed it all. When all the dirt had been dislodged and washed away, each piece was laid out on rocks above the stream to dry. We moved as quickly as possible, because the rest of the afternoon was for leisure. One of the carts had carried a meal for us and enough wine to make a celebration. After we had eaten, the only task that remained was to wash what we had been wearing. Except for Eurycleia, who went off on her own, everyone stripped naked and ran into the water waving our clothes above us.

I was allowed to enjoy the gaiety with them, although I knew that my status as a princess would put a stop to it in a few years. For now I relished it, especially in those moments when a few of them treated me as if I were one of them, splashing me with water and reaching out to tweak the tiny, hard nipples on my flat chest.

Even Melantho, who now made a point of not noticing me, took off a piece of the garland that had started to disintegrate around her shoulders and draped it over my head. The intimacy pained me, a reminder of how much I missed the time in the olive grove, but another part of me was thrilled at this small bit of attention from her. Nothing else can explain why, when later I saw Melantho disappear into the woods on the other side of the stream, I decided to follow her.

I could see the general direction she had taken by the broken twigs and indentation of her bare feet in the grass. Soon I pulled up short because instead of her voice, I heard that of a young man. It was the last thing I expected, because I had been told the punishment was harsh for any man or boy who came near the stream on laundry day. As I drew closer, I heard whimpering that sounded so much like a litter of puppies that for a moment that was what I expected to find.

Out of sight, I moved closer, careful not to break sticks underfoot and give myself away. When I came near enough a small clearing in the woods, I could see her. She was bent over a felled tree, holding her body with her arms to keep her chest away from the bark. She had gone naked into the woods, and her breasts swung free, brushing against the garland that still hung from her neck. A man—really a boy just a few years older than her—was behind her, grunting as he thrust himself into her over and over again.

Her face was hidden at the beginning, but as his thrusts grew harder, she began to moan, and her head turned toward me. I stepped back, but I needn't have, because her eyes were shut. I thought for a moment he might be hurting her—in fact, I didn't think it was possible he wasn't—but I could see by her open mouth and the way her eyelids were relaxed almost to the point of fluttering that she was enjoying it.

Suddenly the boy pulled himself back and stood up straight, holding his phallus out straight in front of him and rubbing it. A white liquid spurted from it and landed on Melantho's back. She laughed, rotating her shoulders and thrusting her buttocks toward him. I stepped further back, knowing they might see me now if they looked around.

I knew I needed to make my escape, and one small step at a time I moved away until I was close enough to the stream to break into a run. I jumped back into the water and submerged myself in it, uttering a prayer to Hera to come to me and cleanse my mind of what I had seen.

I spoke so little the rest of the day, and I lagged so much behind the group as we went home, that Eurycleia worried that something in the meal had made me sick. I told her the wine had not been cut with enough water and had given me a headache. As we walked, I could not take my eyes off Melantho, who skipped along with her friends next to the donkeys, as if nothing at all had happened.

The servants took the most direct route home, but Eurycleia and I took a short detour along a ridge in front of the palace that gave us a more open view of the bay than we had from our quarters. The route took us first by a pasture so barren it looked as if a Titan had reached down with his fingernail and gouged out a narrow piece of the landscape. The field my father had sown with salt in his desperate attempt to avoid going to war still produced at most a few bedraggled weeds chewed to nubs by goats. The spot where he had turned away the plow formed a scar that jutted out like a thumb pointed toward us.

We rarely took this route because it caused Eurycleia such pain, and I was relieved when we were past it. Not long after, when we reached the ridge, we got out of the cart. Eurycleia shielded her eyes, watching for Achaean boats at the distant end of the bay. I was more interested in looking at the shoreline, seeing off in the distance to the left the tiny boats in the cove where Halia's village lay, and then, directly below us, the movements of ships and people in the harbor.

I was the first to notice a new ship at anchor. When I pointed to it, Eurycleia grabbed my hand so hard I cried out.

"That ship!" she cried out. "It's just like the one your father left in."

I forgot all about the barren field. I forgot all about Melantho.

We jumped back into the cart. Eurycleia lashed the poor donkey to make it move faster toward home, stopping only when I burst into tears at its pitiful brays. We were intercepted just before the palace gate by Mentor. He had climbed the hill so fast he was gasping for breath.

"The war is over," he said. "The Achaeans are on their way home."

CHAPTER 6

The Color of Hope

Hope is what I wanted to weave, the belief that everything was opening up, that we were all being lifted free of the heaviness enveloping our lives. I began with thread dyed blue-green, from a mineral collected in the sea caves on our island. I wove a pattern of cresting waves because in the early days all we did was watch the sea and ready ourselves for my father's arrival.

The row of waves is about as thick as two of my fingers. It's tidy, the way we all wanted Odysseus to find his oikos when he returned. The row below is in the same colors and patterns as the designs on the columns and walls of the megaron, freshly repainted in anticipation of my father's return.

Life sparkled. My mother made coverlets and pillows, brightening the palace with ochers, reds, and greens. Glints of light splashed the walls as Eurycleia and the maids wore their arms out rubbing silver, gold, and bronze. Outside the palace, torches stayed lit all night, ready at any moment for the king's arrival.

We watched, and we busied ourselves. Two thin stripes—one for sea and one for land. Any day now. Any day.

* * *

When the ship appeared in the harbor, two feasts were held. The first, for the ship's crew, took place on the beach. After the proper sacrifices and libations, the crew and all the people in the village gorged themselves on roasted meat and drank wine until they could do no more than stagger to bed.

As evening fell and preparations for the second feast were finished, Mentor accompanied the sea captain and the other guests into the megaron. I'd learned by then that the captain was part of King Nestor's returning army, separated from the others by a fierce storm. His boat had been blown north of its destination, and he planned to leave the next day to continue home.

I'd also heard that he had news of my father. I was livid that Telemachus got to sit at the table and hear the captain's stories, but I would have to wait because only men attended such feasts. Didn't I have an equal right to know? My mother would speak to the captain privately later that night, but even she knew only that Odysseus was apparently still alive.

I knew only a few of the other guests' names at that point, although I can list them all now, for the very men who toasted Odysseus' prompt return that night later tried to destroy everything that was his. Antinous, Eurymachus—they and the others ate our food and drank our wine until they could swallow no more. It was only the first of hundreds of times they would do the same.

The next day Telemachus and I were left on our own. Everyone in the palace was far too busy to have time for us, since the captain's tale made it seem as if it were only a matter of days until Odysseus would walk through the door. Though I could have stayed in my room to avoid bothering anyone, I wasn't about to do that. I always waited for Eurycleia or my mother to be distracted enough to agree to whatever I wanted because they didn't have time to think of a reason to say no.

And besides, I could not wait to hear what Telemachus had learned. We set off in the morning with no real plan for the day, taking one of our father's hunting dogs, Argos, with us. For the most part we just followed along after him, since Argos seemed clearer than we were about what was worth investigating.

In truth, by this point I didn't like my brother's company that much, but I couldn't wander the island alone. Telemachus was not mean by nature, and he rarely teased me, so being around him wasn't difficult in that sense. But he always seemed so ineffectual at whatever he did, and if I were his big brother, I don't think I would have been as decent to him as he was to me. Certainly not that day, when I was still pouting about how he got to hear the stories firsthand and I was at his mercy to hear them at all.

Telemachus could not stop talking. He waved his arms and jumped around as he told me how our father was the most daring, crafty, and brave of all the heroes of Troy. I was so wrapped up in all of it, and so happy to be Odysseus' daughter, that I reached the top of a steep mountain road without noticing I was panting for breath.

As my brother talked, Argos ran around him, barking to play. Telemachus, caught up in the stories he was telling, chased after him with a stick, calling him a dirty coward for leaving the battlefield.

When he came back in my direction, I could see he wasn't pleased I was smiling. "What are you laughing at?" he demanded. "I'm a good fighter."

I was still glowing from the stories he had told about my father, and I wasn't really watching him at all. My good mood faded as I realized for the first time that spending his days in mock battle with his tutors had made my brother believe his own fantasies. Watching Telemachus spar with the tufted seeds that floated in the air that afternoon, with Argos jumping wildly in front of him, I had to admit he looked quite confident. The rest of what he would need to be his father's son was coming along more slowly.

I was still wondering whether I was the only one who realized that Argos was not really a Trojan warrior when we came to a crossing in the dirt path. My heart fell when I saw a herd of goats coming our way. I recognized the goatherd immediately. Melanthius had left his home around the same time Melantho had come to the palace, and I saw him from time to time moving my father's herd around the island. He had gotten a reputation for mean-spiritedness as he got older, and seeing him was always unpleasant.

I turned around, hoping to warn Telemachus he was coming, but I saw him about twenty steps back, still fighting imaginary opponents with his stick. Melanthius saw him too, and I watched his lips curl with contempt.

By now Telemachus had noticed the goats, and his hands fell to his sides as he stood watching Melanthius.

"Isn't he the little warrior." Melanthius sneered as passed me. "Think he wants a real fight?" Melanthius screwed up his face to make himself look ridiculous and pranced around imitating my brother before starting again down the road.

The way Telemachus had been acting, I thought he might decide a little stick fighting could settle the old score between them. I knew a goatherd wouldn't dare get into a real brawl with a prince, but my brother would lose even a mock battle, and I couldn't let him suffer that disgrace.

"Look at me," I said to Melanthius. I saw how he hated doing it, but he turned around and raised his eyes to mine.

"My brother is a prince," I said. "He will not stoop to fight with the likes of you. If you say one word to him . . ." I didn't know how to finish the sentence without appearing foolish, but Melanthius just glowered at me for a moment before taking his walking stick and prodding a goat that had stopped near him. Then he spat, not exactly at me but because of me, leaving a thick glob of green slime in the dirt, before continuing past Telemachus as if he were not even there.

The following morning we went out for the day again. Dark clouds had been forming all that afternoon, and though it looked like rain, we were in no hurry to go home. We had taken the path to the stream where the women did laundry, and since no one was working there that day, Telemachus could come along with me. When we got there, we hopped onto a large, flat stone in the middle of the stream. It was still warm from the midday sun, and as the water murmured and gurgled around us our eyes grew heavy and, following Argos' example, we both fell asleep.

The thunder woke me, and I saw a few drops of rain on the rocks around us, but the sky immediately above was not yet completely dark with clouds. I scanned the sky and saw the opaque black mass that hid the top of the mountain above us. Heavy rain must already have been falling upstream. I had been told that water could come rushing across these rocks faster than seemed imaginable, faster than anywhere else on the island. "Like an ocean wave big enough to knock you down," Eurycleia had said, "and it just keeps coming."

I jumped off the stone and onto the bank, calling out to

Telemachus to do the same. He got to his feet as slowly as possible and stood on the rock, taking time to adjust his tunic under his belt, just to make the point that he didn't have to do what I said.

"Hurry!" I said. "Get over here!"

"What's the matter with you?' he called out. "It's barely raining."

Just as a flash of light and a thunderclap filled the air around us, I heard a rumble upstream and the sound of a branch snapping.

"Jump now!" I screamed to Telemachus just as the first of the water came into view. He saw it and leapt just before the water swept over the rocks. Argos, who had been waiting beside him, lost his footing and was pawing at the water as he was carried downstream.

"We have to do something!" I screamed. "He'll die!"

"We'll drown if we jump in!" Telemachus yelled over the sound of what was now torrential rain.

I remembered that farther down the stream a newly fallen tree made a bridge between the two banks. On laundry day, several of the girls hoisted themselves up on to it and dared each other to walk across. The trunk was not much bigger around than their waists, and because the tree wasn't dead yet, it still had most of its lower branches and foliage sticking out in all directions, which made footing difficult. In the end, no one had taken more than a few steps.

I ran, blinded by the rain, until I saw the tree. As I had hoped, the trunk was still above the water, but barely. Argos was pinned against it, his head caught under one of the now-submerged branches. By that point I was already crawling over the roots of the tree. I didn't look to see if Telemachus was behind me as I straddled the trunk and started wiggling my way out. Telemachus had already gotten up on the roots, and I called to him to crawl out behind me, and to hurry because Argos couldn't last much longer.

When he was right behind me, I shouted to him over the roar of the water. "Hang on to my ankles!" I screamed. "If you let go, I'll die."

I lay down on the trunk, extending my legs. When I could feel Telemachus' grip on my ankles, I inched out until I reached Argos. Hanging on to the tree with one arm, I tore with the other at the small branches and twigs holding Argos down.

I was crying with rage at the tree, the stream, the rain pouring down over my head into my eyes, and I think it was that rage that gave me the strength to break off or pull aside just enough of the foliage to grab Argos—I don't remember exactly how—and lift his nose out of the water. He was nearly unconscious, but when he felt the air he revived enough to muscle himself free and get his front paws over the tree trunk. Snorting and gulping for air, he hoisted himself out of the water right on top of my back, scrambling over me so forcefully I had to hang on to avoid going into the torrent myself.

I crawled back onto the bank laughing and crying in hoarse gulps of air. I had challenged the whole world, and I believed, at least for that moment, that it would never be able to deny me what I wanted.

Telemachus was kneeling next to a gagging and heaving Argos, petting him and calling him a brave dog. When Argos saw me, he pulled away from Telemachus, and soon I was knocked to the ground having my nostrils and eyes licked by a whimpering, but most grateful dog.

Finally I managed to get up. "You did a good job," I said to

Telemachus as we started along the bank toward the path for home. It was true. I felt the strain on my ankles as he held me, and I knew I could not have done it without him.

Though he must have heard me, he did not say anything in return.

My legs were trembling with cold and exhaustion, my hair was matted on my shoulders, and my chiton was covered with mud and torn open in the front. Scratches on my stomach bled pink into the soggy cloth. Telemachus was filthy too, and neither of us knew what to expect when we arrived at the palace.

We sneaked through the courtyard unnoticed, but when we reached the door to the kitchen, Eurycleia and Eurynome came rushing toward us, their faces pale with worry.

"We saved Argos from drowning!" Telemachus crowed. "We crawled onto a tree to grab him and pull him back."

"You brave child!" Eurycleia said to him. "Your father would be so proud."

My jaw dropped, but Telemachus just looked at me with a smug grin and said nothing.

After Eurycleia bustled Telemachus off to arrange for his bath, I stood alone with Eurynome in the kitchen. I hadn't moved since Telemachus stole my moment from me, until Eurynome, to my surprise, asked me what really happened. Wet, dirty, and half clothed, I flung myself into her arms as the truth came out of me between bursts of tears.

"He wouldn't jump off the rock when the water was coming. He's so stupid! And I was the one who figured out what to do, and I crawled out to get Argos and all he did was hold my ankles!"

Eurynome knew nothing about what had happened, of course, and all I suppose she understood was my hurt. She held me in her arms until I had sobbed my way through the whole story.

"So," she said, when I had finished. "What are you going to tell your mother?"

I pulled away in surprise. Why would I not tell her the truth? And then I thought of her face, of everyone's face whenever they looked at Telemachus. My brother needed the acclaim even if he hadn't earned it. And though I would have liked it for myself, I sensed it would be far better for all of us if I gave it to him.

"Nothing," I said.

Eurynome smiled. "But I know," she said. "And so do you."

From that moment in the kitchen, the distance closed between Eurynome and me. I love Eurycleia with all my heart, but she loves more easily, and she loves others as much as she does me. Eurynome's affection was something I earned. And though it might be unseemly to sound so arrogant, she had to earn mine as well.

She bathed me herself that night, to make sure no rumors spread among the maids, and she burned the chiton I had been wearing so my mother would not be angry I had ruined it. By the time she saw me later that night, my hair was washed, my chiton was immaculate, and she did not remember I had been gone.

CHAPTER 7

Darkening

*I kept weaving with sea-blue thread, because we kept hoping. I worked sil-
ver filaments into the blue, remembering how, when everything was pol-
ished, painted, and scrubbed, the sun made ribbons of light from the dust
dancing in the air of the porch, as if the great sun god Apollo himself were
preparing a welcome.*

*When I finished the last of the blue thread I had already dyed, I dark-
ened the next batch, and the next even more, so that by the end the blue was
gone entirely. The silver is tarnished now, and the two colors have merged
into a hue as gray and miserable as our lives became.*

Over the next two years, ships appeared regularly in our harbor,
mostly merchants and travelers, the clearest sign that life had returned to normal.

For everyone, of course, but us. Menelaus, the ruler of Sparta,
was the only other straggler, but we had heard news he was in

Egypt. Of the Achaean leaders at Troy who had not been dispatched to the eternal realm of Hades, my father was the only one besides Menelaus who had not come home.

I was eleven now, and Telemachus was thirteen. He was much taller than I, and his voice broke when he got excited. In the sunlight I could see dark hair forming on his upper lip, but ever since he took credit for saving Argos, anything about him that hinted of manhood was a joke to me.

I wanted as little to do with him as possible. Fortunately, that was easy, because by then my brother had almost no interaction with the women of the house. Mentor often took him into town, where he learned whatever it is men do when they have nothing important to occupy them. From what I've seen, they chat, roll dice, watch women as they pass, play pointless games where they move pebbles back and forth or throw things at lines in the dirt, eat, drink, argue, and go home. To me, it seemed about as promising as the training he got in the olive orchard.

For the first two years after the end of the war, it seemed reasonable for Odysseus not to be home yet. Sea travel was unpredictable, and the list of things that could delay a voyage was long. Travelers occasionally said they had seen Odysseus in some distant port, readying a ship or collecting treasure for the return voyage. In the beginning my mother believed them all, showering each one with gifts to thank him for his news, but when she realized she had become a target for lies she stopped giving audiences to strangers at all.

By the time the war had been over for two years, all explanations for his absence were unpleasant. Some of those who anchored in our harbor said they heard he had been killed, and others said he was in prison. The worst story, the one that sent my mother to her bed for days and threw the household into chaos, was that he had settled down in a new land, taken another wife, and started a second family.

The megaron was silent. The torches outside the palace burned out and were not replenished, a layer of dust covered the new paint, and the silver was allowed to go dull.

By this point, my mother always went heavily veiled, not from modesty but from indifference. At thirty, she was still beautiful regardless of how little attention she paid to herself, but now she preferred to hide her hair rather than groom it, and she no longer bothered with the skin oils and creams she had used so regularly when she expected Odysseus home.

The household had taken on my mother's indifference, so when the number of men coming to the palace to see her began to grow, I thought anything new had to be good. The day my mother first swept into the megaron to greet a visitor with her hair in place and her skin glowing under a nearly transparent veil, I wanted to cry with happiness. She was going to care again, and that was the first step in fixing everything.

I always spent the morning downstairs in the megaron weaving with my mother, and that did not change when we started having more company. Business matters did not involve eleven-year-old girls, and I was as good as invisible at her side. Occasionally Mentor would ask for a private moment, and they would either go off for a walk, if the weather was nice, or ask me to leave if it wasn't. For the most part, I heard and saw everything that happened between my mother and the men who visited her, and I did not think for a moment that anything other than concern and kindness motivated them. After all, my father had now been gone twelve years. Anyone could see the toll it was taking.

My mother appreciated their attention too, especially when one of the men, a local nobleman named Eurymachus, took a special interest in my brother. He began inviting Telemachus along when he went hunting, and I could see from my window how Eurymachus would put his arm across his shoulder as they started up the path toward the mountains. On the rare occasions when I saw my brother, almost every one of his sentences began with Eurymachus' name.

Other men competed for his time as well, and I could see that Telemachus was enjoying feeling so important. Even the way he walked changed. He held his shoulders back and his chest high. His stride lengthened. For the first time he had men around him of his own social standing who were not as old or as physically limited as Mentor, and by the time another year had passed, he no longer looked or acted like the soft and timid boy he had been.

With his increased confidence came arrogance he must also have learned from the men of the island. I remember the first time his new attitude rattled our lives. When my mother requested that Telemachus have dinner with the two of us in her quarters, he didn't want to come. He wanted to take Argos and go off hunting with Antinous, another of our regular visitors. My mother's command to join her for the midday meal had spoiled his plans, and he came in scowling. He flung himself into a chair with a loud and exasperated sigh, and I heard him mutter something under his breath about how he would someday be giving her the orders rather than the other way around.

My mother asked him to repeat what he said. He refused, but she had heard him well enough.

"Is this what the men fill your head with?" she demanded.

I was sure she would set him straight and tell him that as long as she was in this house she would be giving the orders. But she didn't.

"You're right," she said.

I felt my heart climbing up my chest. It grabbed my throat and made it difficult to breathe. Telemachus giving the orders? The same Telemachus who stood on the rock with the water rising around him, refusing to jump because it was his little sister demanding it? The Telemachus following behind me while I thought of the plan and took the risk that saved Argos? The Telemachus who waved sticks in the air while his little sister faced down a bully for him?

Though it had always been obvious how men and women's lives were different, in that moment I understood what my mother's words foretold for me. Shocked as I was at the thought he could ever give orders to her, I was enraged that he would be able to do the same with me—the person who, more than anyone else, knew how undeserving he was.

The only thing that saved my mood that day was what my mother said next.

"You are at the moment a boy, not a man," she said. "One who has behaved most rudely to his mother and disrespectfully to the queen, and must be punished for it."

I can't separate out how much of my glee was in seeing her stand up to that puffed-up little coward, and how much was plain and simple gloating that I was the good, obedient child, and he was in trouble. All I remember is the glow I felt as I saw him tracing the grain in the planks of the wood table, eyes averted, as he received his scolding.

The next time the men came to the megaron to ask permission to take Telemachus out, my mother chastised them for turning the head of a child, and she refused to let him leave the palace with any of them for a month. I expected we had seen the last of those men for a while, so I was surprised when Antinous and Eurymachus continued to show up as usual.

This caught my mother by surprise as well, and I think it occurred to her for the first time that the men really came to the palace because of her. The next day and the next, she did not come downstairs, and I stayed in her chambers with her.

"Why do you think those men are always here?" she asked me, as we worked side by side at the hand looms on our laps.

I was by then almost twelve, and I suppose I might have seemed older, because my reaction to the growing somberness of the palace was to become as quiet and dutiful as possible. Still, I was taken aback to be asked my opinion, because she rarely consulted me about anything more important than a choice of thread.

I wanted to rise to the occasion, to see things as they needed to be seen, but the truth was that I had no idea what the men wanted. I suspected they just didn't have anything better to do, but that didn't sound like the kind of counsel a girl wise beyond her years would give.

"Because they like you?" I asked, picking up a length of blue thread for the belt I was making.

"That's what I'm afraid of," she said.

I screwed up my face. "What's wrong with them liking you? Don't you want company?"

"It's not that." She was quiet for a long time. "Do you ever think your father might be dead?" she finally asked.

The question was so unexpected, my mind went blank. "No," I said.

My mother smiled. "It's good to be hopeful." She hadn't understood that what I really meant was that I rarely gave my father any thought at all.

"It's going to be difficult to continue much longer this way," she went on. "I want you to know that."

"What way?"

"Me here, without a husband."

Before I could ask her to explain, my mother put her hands to her face and began to weep, softly at first and then uncontrollably. I didn't know what do, so I put down my hand loom and went to stand beside her.

I felt her weight sag toward me, and I pushed hard against her to keep her from falling. "I feel so sleepy," she said. "I need to lie down."

I had to use all my strength to help her to the couch on the other side of the room. It's a strange skill my mother has, this ability to fall asleep so quickly it's almost a faint. It comes over her often when she cries, which she did more and more as time passed.

I learned a great deal about narcotics at the court of Helen and Menelaus in the kingdom of Lacedaemon, watching powders and potions sweep over people in much the same way. But my mother was not drugged, nor did she wake in the same dazed state I so often observed there.

I think sometimes it must be the pity of the gods that releases her, at least momentarily, from her life. Even now, with the tumult of the battle downstairs, she sleeps in her quiet room, while the rest of us suffer and wait. When my mother returns to this world, she will look radiant, having forgotten why she was crying, while all those around her will still wear our burdens of woe.

When my mother cried about not being able to continue without a husband, I assumed it was because she missed Odysseus. I suppose she did, but over the next few months, I saw that her tears were less about him than about the difficulties his continued absence created.

Since I'd never known a father, I couldn't see what use a husband was either. The household ran smoothly, the crops were good, the herds were healthy. Everyone accepted my mother's authority except, increasingly, my brother, and he limited his objections to furtive scowls and grumbles. If circumstances had been different, we could have flourished under the rule of someone with her intelligence and compassion. Instead her power dwindled, as men with little of either of these qualities forced her out of the megaron where she had once been the center of attention.

The growing crisis in the palace centered as much on Telemachus as on my mother. Whether Odysseus came home or not, Telemachus would inherit the *oikos*, except the portion of the land and property necessary for my dowry. But the kingship was another matter. Because Icarius had created the kingdom as part of my mother's dowry, and dowries belonged to the bride for life, the most obvious way to the throne would be the way Odysseus had gotten it—by marrying her. With the sole other contender someone as weak as my brother, such a strategy might work to make a king of her second husband.

And it's not bad at all to be the king. In Sparta, Menelaus demanded rents and taxes from everyone who lived there. Gifts poured in from everyone seeking the smallest favor or protection. If he liked to hunt in a certain patch of forest or graze his horses in a particular meadow, he decreed it to be a royal holding, off limits to anyone else. And though my father hadn't been present long enough to shape Cephallenia to his liking, who wouldn't yearn for the chance to do it in his place?

Telemachus was alone in the world of men. If his right to the throne was challenged, he would be naked among wolves. The throne would go to the strongest, the wiliest, the most ruthless, and we all knew that would not be him.

The solution was simple, or so it seemed. All my mother had to do was spurn any proposal until Telemachus came of age. Odysseus could then be declared dead, and his son would have it all. And that might not turn out to be necessary because my father might still be alive and headed home. My mother had no reason to take the drastic step of remarrying. We were fine the way we were.

If I had been right about that, there would have been no need for her tears. We were not fine—not then, or ever again.

The first inkling I had that the growing number of men who visited the palace might have the power to turn our lives upside down came one afternoon when Telemachus had been forced to stay inside by a rare winter storm cold enough to have deposited ankle-deep snow in the courtyard. With no letup in sight, Telemachus was sitting in the megaron, glowering as if even the chairs and footstools had done him some kind of offense.

"There's nothing to do!" He shook his head in disgust. "How can you stand being here?"

He got up and went to the porch that served as the entry to the megaron. He looked out over the snow and shook his head again. "How long is it going to be before it's gone?" he asked the air in front of him.

For my mother and me, life indoors was normal, and the only difference was having my brother for company that day.

Telemachus flung himself into a chair by the fire. My mother and I exchanged glances at each of his complaints as we worked at the great loom. I remember it was so cold that day, and so drafty from the fire on the hearth, that we had to pile animal skins under our feet and wear himations we usually needed only out of doors to keep the chill from seeping into our bodies.

I took the shuttle from my mother, locked the thread around the edge on my side, and passed it back to her. Over and over we made the same movement, scarcely noticing the tiny touches of our fingers as we handed the shuttle back and forth, and unconscious of time except as measured by the growth of the cloth.

"Come feel this," my mother said to Telemachus. "Look how nice and warm it's going to be."

I loved how the blue and red border enhanced the gray of the wool in the cloak we were weaving for him, and I stopped to run my fingers over it.

Telemachus was staring at the fire, stroking his cheeks. Though he knew we were taking extra care with his new garment, he didn't glance up or acknowledge what my mother had said.

Then a moment later, as if he had just realized she was there, he stood up and went over to her.

"I'll soon have a beard," he said, picking up her hand and stroking it over the dark fuzz that was now substantial enough to color his cheeks. "A full one, like the men."

He didn't seem to be boasting, just making idle chatter to while away the time, so I couldn't understand why my mother was growing agitated. Eventually she stopped weaving and turned to face him.

"You talk as if once you look like a man, the *oikos* will be yours," she said. "Do you think all it will take is a beard?"

Her tone was so uncharacteristically sharp that both of us looked up, startled.

"Your father would have to be dead for that to happen." She turned back to her weaving to avoid having to look at either of us. "Is that what you think?"

I saw Telemachus' eyes dart in the reflected light of the fire. "People say he is," he replied, picking up a stick to poke at the embers. "And that it's only a matter of time until you see it too."

"And who are these people?" Her voice was so calm it unnerved me.

"Everyone!"

Her back was still to him as she continued to weave. "And what do you think?"

"I don't know!" Telemachus whined in a way that always set my teeth on edge.

"No you don't, do you?" My mother wheeled around to face him. "And they don't either. But you'd better hope they're wrong."

"Why? Just because you don't want to get married again?" Telemachus jumped up. "Just because you don't want to leave the palace to me?"

My mother was now standing directly in front of him, and I noticed for the first time that he was taller than she was. "Those men are not your friends." Her voice was rough and low, like the growl of a wary animal.

"They are too!"

"You don't know what people are capable of."

"Well, I don't have a father to help with that, do I?" he said, in a tone so spiteful it made me gasp.

"You have a father, even if he's not here." She spoke so slowly that every sound of each word was emphasized. "I don't want you to associate with those men any more. They fill your head with foolishness."

Telemachus turned and left the room without saying a word. My mother watched him for a moment before rushing out of the megaron up to her quarters. All of a sudden the room was silent, except for the rustle of embers settling in the fire.

What had just happened?

I went upstairs also, just to be doing something. I looked out the one window with a view down onto the courtyard to see where Telemachus had gone. He was kicking at the snow as if he were in a battle with it as he trudged over to his quarters.

For a while I stood, watching his tracks fill up, but eventually the cold of the open window was too much for me. I went back to my room and poked at the glowing coals on my own small hearth, while outside the silent and indifferent snow obliterated everything familiar.

My mother's confrontations with my brother took more and more courage as his beard grew thicker and his voice deepened. She was doomed to lose and fated to pay whatever price he might exact for having crossed him on his way to manhood. But her efforts would keep us safe a while longer from the men Telemachus called his friends.

Antinous and the others had good reason to act friendly toward him, at least for now. No threat existed that my brother would claim the throne any time soon. He was still too young, despite how impressed he was with the fuzz on his cheeks. On the contrary, they knew he might be useful in influencing his mother's choice of a new husband.

More than a hundred men invaded our house over the next few years, wearing my mother down to the point where she intended to accept one of their proposals just to put an end to their destructiveness. I was not in Ithaca to see the worst of it. When I left, the insults to my father's *oikos* had barely started. The suitors took their turns coming through the megaron offering their greetings, posturing about their wealth and connections, and leaving when my mother showed signs that she was tired of their bragging.

"Bring me news of Odysseus," my mother grumbled upstairs at her loom. "The rest I don't care to hear."

Part of my mother liked the attention. I could see that. I realize now how terribly bored she must have been. And worse. Now that the drives of my own body are strong in me, I also understand that to have no release for ten years would be to know the hatred of the gods. Perhaps my mother might have enjoyed the occasional pleasures of her imagination as the men passed through the megaron. But I would rather sleep alone the rest of my life than let any of them touch me, and my mother's refusals say the same. We all know how the gods, when they most wish to plague us, offer disaster in attractive packages.

Three years after the end of the war, my mother began her transformation into the cunning adversary of the suitors she is today. Her first step was to send Mentor on a secret visit to her father. Her dowry made Odysseus the King of Cephallenia, and it would be sensible to conclude that he ruled only because he was married to her. Oddly enough, Icarius had intended the opposite. Though the kingdom was her dowry, whomever she married had all the power, and she was the queen only because she was married to him.

Mentor's task was to ask Icarius to declare that Penelope was queen in her own right. It seemed a simple enough request. If he agreed and my mother remarried, she could eventually hand the throne to her firstborn son and fade away as Laertes and Anticleia had. Her new husband would be king, of course, but only while she was alive, and any children they might have together would be behind Telemachus in line for the throne. Such an outcome was unlikely to interest the suitors, and they would soon be gone when they learned of it.

Icarius refused. What man would control his daughter then? And what if this gave me ideas about being queen myself some day? It was preferable to declare Odysseus dead, he told Mentor, so Penelope could marry again and get on with the queenly business of producing more grandsons, no matter by whom, to strengthen her family's line.

It pains me to think how abandoned she must have felt. She had been thwarted at her first move, and I wouldn't have blamed her for seeing her situation as hopeless. But she didn't, or perhaps she had decided to fight even if she did. She was quieter than usual for the next few days, but I saw something different in her face. From that point on, I never saw fear. I saw determination. I saw quiet defiance. I saw the power of a woman whose only army was her own wits and wiles.

My mother kept most of her thoughts to herself, and at the time I did not understand why she was so hostile in private toward our many visitors, and so suspicious of their true feelings toward Telemachus. I didn't see anything to be concerned about. They were always willing to spar or wrestle, and though they were not willing to lose to him, they let him think the day he might beat them was not far off. I suspect they let him take the easy shots when they went hunting, so he would always come home with game, even if some of them did not.

Though they were rough men and not inclined to tenderness, their behavior toward my brother seemed kind and caring to me. What I didn't realize then seems so obvious to me now. The time would come when currying Telemachus' favor was of no further use and his adulthood began to pose a real threat to their ambitions. When that happened, they would not let such an insignificant matter as his murder get in their way.

All I noticed at the time was that a number of men paid a great deal of attention to my brother. I didn't see the warning signs that they were also watching me. I was twelve by this point, still flat chested, and completely mystified by what drove men and women to come together. When Antinous came to call and asked if he could speak to my mother alone, I assumed it had nothing to do with me.

The day was cold, and she did not want to leave the hearth, so I went upstairs to the loom in her megaron, where a fire had already been set. Not too long after, she came upstairs.

She was gulping for air to hold back sobs until she was alone. She might not have seen me but even if she had, she could not restrain herself any longer. She staggered to the far wall and held her palm against it to support herself as she wailed with the abandon of a wild beast.

Odysseus was dead. Telemachus was dead. What else could it be?

My mother's eyes darted around the room. "I'm going to be sick," she said.

I jumped up to find a basin, but it was too late. I saw her bend over and heard horrible gagging sounds in the corner.

"Eurynome!" I screamed, but it was Melantho who answered the call. My mother had been so charmed by her sea-green eyes and exotic brown skin that she hadn't much cared that as a servant Melantho was decidedly inferior to many of the other young slaves. Since Melantho was at least adequate, Eurynome had to accept my mother's decision as to who came into her chambers.

By now, I had relegated Melantho to a space in my mind where

I kept things I didn't think I needed to try to understand. To Melantho, I was even less important than that.

"Is the queen sick?" The question was asked not to me but directly to my mother.

The answer was obvious by the smell. Melantho went over and put her arm around my mother's back. I didn't hear what she said, but my mother nodded, and Melantho guided her out of the room. I ran after them because no one, not even Eurynome or Eurycleia, was permitted to enter my parents' bedchamber—no one, that is, except me and an old servant named Actoris, whom my father had made solely responsible for keeping it clean. I saw by the look on Melantho's face that she had been hoping this would be her moment to glimpse inside, and I stared her down until she transferred my mother's weight to me and turned her back to leave. I opened the lock only when she was out of sight.

When my father built the palace, he left a full-grown olive tree standing inside one corner of the courtyard. He created a bedchamber by enclosing the tree inside walls and running its trunk up through the floor of the upper story. Then he sawed off the top and smoothed down the stumps of branches until he had created a comfortable bedstead. He embedded ivory decorations into the wood and wrapped it round with gold and silver trim. I don't suppose there could be another like it anywhere in the world.

I rarely went in the room, and I had never been in my parents' bed before, but my panic was so deep that I could not stand or sit. I lay down next to my mother with my stomach pressed to her back and held her without moving a muscle.

Not too much later she stirred. When she felt my arms, she turned around and pulled me to her. I heard her hot breath next to my face and felt her lungs heave.

"Maia," I said. "You're scaring me!"

She pulled back, but she was still so close it took a moment for her eyes to focus. "My precious, precious Xanthe," she said, and began to sob again so hard she could not speak.

"Is my father dead?" I asked. She shook her head and lifted her body until she was seated in the bed.

"It wasn't about them," she said, as she pulled me into her arms. "Antinous wants to marry you," she said.

I gasped, and an animal cry from somewhere deep inside me broke through my throat. I hadn't grown much taller since I was eight or nine, and the size of most men intimidated me. Antinous was larger than most. He was not fat, but very muscular and tall, with a chest that made his gait more like a strut. His beard could not disguise his large jaw, and his brown teeth looked as if they could gnaw through the joints of an ox.

I had not even had my first blood. I was still amazed at the tendrils of hair that had begun to sprout under my arms and in the place Melantho had called her slit.

Actoris heard the commotion and came to see what was wrong. She helped us both from the bed and back into my mother's megaron. When she had left us alone, my mother took a fan from the wall, and though the day had been quite cold, she began to wave the air around us as if to dispel malevolent forces while she told me what had occurred.

Antinous had suggested an immediate betrothal and a wedding after my first blood, when he would take me to his estate as his wife. "I asked him why he was coming now, when you were still so young," she said. "He told me talk was afoot about what would happen to you. He said he could protect you better than either Telemachus or I could."

"Protect me from what?" I said, though I was fairly sure I knew.

She shook her head and pulled her lips in until all that remained was a line across her face. "Xanthe," she said. "You are not to leave this house without my knowledge. Not with Telemachus, not with Mentor, not with anyone. When you do go out, you will have guards, and you must never, never, leave their sight."

I was so frightened at that moment I didn't care if I died of old age having never moved from her olive-tree bed. I had heard enough stories of rape and abduction by both gods and men to fill in what my mother did not want to say, and I had no intention of disobeying her.

I did not come again with my mother to the megaron, at least when any visitor was present. Since she still spent her mornings there, I no longer had the time I treasured at her side. It was the first of many things I was robbed of by the suitors. They took me from my mother almost as completely as if they had carried me off to their lairs.

The pomegranate trees bloomed again, and my mother and Eurynome went without me to Hera's shrine for the spring ritual, walking alongside two donkey carts piled high with branches of pomegranate blossoms. I watched from my window, feeling a burning hole behind me in the direction of the chest where Hera's clothes and adornments had been until that morning, before being taken away for a ceremony I loved and was now denied.

The weather warmed, and the hills around the palace turned red with poppies. I stood at my window watching a swallow bring mud for its nest under the eaves. I heard the peeps of the nestlings when they hatched, and I watched as they grew so large their heads stuck out all day. There were three of them lined up in a row, and I named them after the Furies, for the loud cries they made when their mother returned with food. And then one day, I watched them fly away.

I looked out from another upstairs window as the suitors and Telemachus came and went between the palace and the town, ignoring things I ached to feel—the grass between my toes, the sun on my cheeks, the butterflies looking for a finger to alight upon.

I remember it all so well because once again I am trapped in the same room. The men downstairs now are not jolly with wine and stuffed full of food and self-importance, as they once were. Now they are terrified, anguished, agonized, just as I had hoped for seven years before, when I fantasized how the gods would make them pay for stealing my life from me.

My prison became so tainted with hopelessness that at times I stood at my window wishing I had the bit of extra courage I needed to jump. I took no pleasure in anything, and my laughter grew bitter as my spirit shriveled. I lashed out at everyone, not caring whom I hurt.

My beloved Eurycleia and Eurynome were among my victims. I don't remember what I said that made Eurycleia rush out of my mother's chambers in tears one day, but it was bad enough for my mother to slap my face.

"Slap it again," I said, not even reaching up to touch my cheek. "What else are you going to do? Throw me in prison?"

My mother's face grew scarlet before settling down again to its normal hue, but I could see by the glitter in her eyes that she had forced herself to appear calmer than she actually felt.

"No," she said. "You're being punished quite enough, but it is not Eurycleia's doing, and you have hurt her without cause."

She sniffed. "Perhaps I have misunderstood what kind of girl you are."

No one needed to tell me I had done wrong, and I already felt terrible about how I was behaving toward the only people who cared about me. The brashness with which I had challenged my mother to slap me again vanished into a cascade of tears, as I fell into her arms.

"I'm *not* that kind of girl," I sobbed. "I'm just so unhappy I want to die. Telemachus is outside, and I'm stuck in here, when I haven't done anything wrong. It's so unfair!"

By now Eurycleia had come back into the room, and I tore myself away from my mother and fell over her neck, wetting it with slime from my nose and another bath of tears.

"Sometimes I forget that I don't hate everybody," I said. "I forget who I'm talking to, and things spill out."

My mother came up behind me and put her arms around both of us, fashioning a cocoon as they held me tight, rocking me.

"I'm sorry," I said to both of them.

"I know," my mother whispered into my neck. "And I know just what kind of girl you are. I think you're very brave." She pulled away to look at me. The tenderness in her eyes made my own well up again, but she raised her hand as if to say it was time for me to get control of myself.

I sniffled but stood up straighter, feeling Eurycleia's arm still around me as my mother began to speak.

"The only way we have a chance to win," she said, "is to not let them break us. Don't give in to hate, Xanthe. It doesn't hurt anyone but yourself, and it doesn't change anything."

"But what am I supposed to do?" I asked. "Be glad they're there?"

"Of course not. We all have every reason to despise them. But we also have to endure them, at least for now. But I'm concentrating on something else, and that helps me get through every day, awful as most of them are."

"What?" I asked.

My mother picked up her spindle and flicked it. "How to defeat them," she said, staring at the growing length of translucent thread as the weight at the bottom made its way toward the floor. "That's what I'm wondering, because that's what I intend to do."

For most of a moon cycle, my mother brooded. She consulted Mentor almost daily, and though she did not share much with me, I gathered that Mentor felt the situation with Antinous was growing more dire.

Antinous' plan, Mentor surmised, was to put his baby in me—before marriage or after, it didn't really matter. It was easy to imagine how many ways a fatal accident might befall poor young Telemachus after I had given Antinous a son. With Telemachus dead, the person with the strongest claim to the kingdom would be me, once Penelope had also been pushed aside.

The next king, in this plan, would be the suitor who had been smart enough to figure out that the person they should be courting was not Penelope but her daughter. Antinous would have to get to me before some other suitor figured this out also, someone else who might think nothing of a little rape or abduction if it helped him secure a throne.

And if I was harmed, who would swing his sword in revenge? Telemachus? Laertes? Icarius? The only one who might was Odysseus, and it was a fairly good bet that he would never know.

My mother let Antinous think she was favorable toward his proposal, but she told him she did not have the right to consent to my marriage. Only my guardian could negotiate a marriage contract, and that was Odysseus. In short, I could not get married until my father came home. If he did not, Telemachus would be my guardian when he reached manhood and claimed the *oikos* and kingdom. He would see to my betrothal and marriage then.

My mother had her first great success with this move, putting off not only Antinous but any other suitor who might come up with the idea of marrying me. Once Telemachus became king, I would lose my value as a means to the throne, and the men would move on to other targets.

My mother seemed to have found a way to protect us all, but she was still so distraught that she could neither eat nor sleep. Finally, for peace of mind she decided to consult an oracle. She sent Mentor off to Lacedaemon to the oracle of Pasiphoë, where supplicants ask questions before going to sleep in the temple, and the answers come to them in their dreams. Mentor came back with two dream fragments for my mother—a shepherd looking for a lost sheep while lions stalked the flock, and a hand reaching down to pick a wildflower while a crow circled overhead.

That was all. He had no more idea what they meant than we did. I remember the puzzled looks with which my mother, Eurycleia, and Eurynome went about the palace over the next few days. Did the first prophecy mean that Odysseus was trying to find his way home because he knew his family was in danger? Or did it mean Penelope herself was holding out false hope and should be watching her two children more closely? Personally, I didn't think the prophecy told us anything we didn't already know, and I could hardly understand their excitement.

The second image drove everyone to distraction, and my mother eventually decided to consult Halitherses, the local prophet. When she did, Eurycleia's scorn was hot as coals.

"Better to rule out whatever he says, he's wrong so often," she muttered when my mother was out of hearing. "Doesn't anyone but me remember he said the Trojan War would be short? And Odysseus would be quickly home?" She snorted. "What about that?"

Still, my mother had nowhere else to go. Halitherses interpreted the second omen so quickly and with such confidence that the matter was settled on the spot. The message could only have come from Hera, because she had used her own symbol, the crow. This time, however, the bird was not the goddess herself but Telemachus. He had flown the nest, but my mother need have no fear for him, as he had the protection of the gods.

The second omen turned my world upside down.

I was the flower. "Your daughter is in great danger," Halitherses told my mother. "You must waste no time. Once the hand is in motion, no one can save her."

CHAPTER 8

Secret Blood

No way exists to make thread continue the tale except to soak it in blood. I sent word to Eumaeus that I needed blood from one of his slaughtered pigs for a private sacrifice. In my room I poured the crimson liquid into a bowl and daubed a handful of fleece in it over and over again until the wool was saturated.

I knew from the beginning it wouldn't work. How can it be that what comes pouring out as red as pomegranate seeds can dry to the color of caked mud? A few days later, the matted clump looked more like the undignified piles left behind by animals than the terrible forces I wanted to represent. Brown powder fell to the floor as I smoothed the roving to make it ready for spinning. I found some ground cinnabar among the dyes in my mother's room, and I soaked the thread again until it was bright red. I know the secret the dye covered up, and that is enough.

To be saved, I first needed to be dead. At least Antinous and the other suitors had to believe I was. My mother made offerings to

Hermes, the god of trickery and stealth, to ask for his help, and within a month she was holding a feast of thanksgiving for the inspiration he had planted in her mind.

My mother rarely went downstairs before a banquet, but on the night she privately declared war, she went down to greet the guests and bid them to eat and drink heartily. Since Antinous' proposal, I had not been downstairs at all when any man other than Mentor was present. The night of the feast, my mother forbade me to go down with her, but I made such a fuss she agreed I could go if I covered my face and stayed out of sight.

All the suitors were present when we entered. As usual, the men were paying attention only to each other, so no one noticed when Mentor dedicated the feast to Hermes instead of one of the usual gods. When the fat-encased thighbone he laid in the fire began to pop and sizzle, the men came to attention, and their voices rose in affirmation of his dedication.

A furrow had been carved years before from the center to the edge of the circular hearth in the megaron. This created a channel for wine to pass through before falling into a golden bowl atop a silver tray resting on the dirt floor. As Mentor poured the libation, the men cheered again.

When the sacrifice and libation were finished, my mother turned to leave, but not before saying she hoped the god her guests honored would hear the prayers made to him that night. I could see the smirk under her veil as she swept across the megaron and out the door.

In her chambers we held our own ceremony. We sprinkled barley as we invoked Hermes, Hera, and the other gods, and then, with the meat brought up by the servants, we made a special offering on the small hearth in her megaron. Then my mother took her goblet of wine, and we went to her window, which looked out over the palace walls toward the crags in the distance.

The moon was new, like the end of a fingernail pared off to keep thread from snagging. The smell of windfalls from a fig tree sweetened the night, making the air as substantial as the palace itself or the hills in the distance. Millions of stars set the heavens aglow, as if they were lit from behind by the breath of the gods. Perhaps on nights like these the heavens themselves drew closer, and I offered my own prayer that the immortals who inhabited them were listening.

My mother held her goblet at arm's length through the window. "I offer this to you, Hermes, sharpener of wits, protector of secrets, and crafter of ruses." She poured some of the contents of the goblet onto the ground below.

Just then a roar broke out from the feasters downstairs. My mother smiled out into the night. "The men downstairs join me in this offering to you. They have said it to you, great god, with their own voices."

She held out the cup to me and asked, "Do you want to do the next libation? Just pour a little when I tell you."

I held my arm out the window in the crisp night air. "And to Hera and all who protect women," my mother went on, "I ask you to watch over this house and keep my daughter from harm."

She put her arm around me. "Pour," she said. I let a thin stream drop earthward.

She examined the remains in the goblet. "There's enough for one more."

She shut her eyes. "Athena, great goddess and favored one of Zeus, you who protect Odysseus and his house, I call on you to guard what is his against those who wish to destroy it, and beseech you to bring him safely home."

Just as the last drops of wine fell from the cup, the silhouette of an owl passed in front of the gray haze of stars.

I felt my mother's shoulders tremble. "She's here," my mother said. "Athena heard us."

A shooting star crossed the sky, and then another and another—six total we counted, right after another. The first three came from Hermes, Hera, and Athena. The three others, we decided, were messages from hidden protectors we didn't know we had.

Finally the chill drove us back to the hearth, where we ate our dinner. Flicking bits of fat into the fire, we laughed at every sizzle and wisp of smoke that rose up. Athena hovered over the house in the form of her symbol, the owl. Hermes and the other gods had winked at us from the heavens. And, for that night at least, we believed the men downstairs didn't have a chance.

The plan was to fake my death and spirit me away to a safe place where I could live with a false identity until either my father returned or Telemachus took the throne. I loved being the center of attention for the next few months while the details were worked out. My mother and grandmother, and of course Eurycleia and Eurynome, were in on the plot, and they wept over me from time to time, which I have to admit was the best part of all. At my age I didn't really understand that the goal we all worked toward was a terrible one, a sudden amputation from my home and from everyone I knew.

I was not told where I would be going. No one knew, except my mother and Mentor, who was gone for more than a full moon cycle making the arrangements. When he returned, we settled in to wait for the pieces to fall into place. We needed a ship headed for a certain port, and Mentor spent his days at the harbor casting around for information. Then, after the time it takes for the moon to grow to half size, Mentor came to the palace with news that he had arranged passage for us, and we had less than two days to carry out the plan.

The following morning, Eurycleia and I went on a purported errand to deliver supplies to Eumaeus at the pig farm. He was waiting for us, sitting beside his hut next to several bowls of blood from an animal he had just slaughtered. He was working on a litter by lashing several tree branches together and wrapping a blanket around them. Folded and stacked next to him was every piece of cloth in his hut.

We tried to eat the food we had brought and to talk about anything other than what lay ahead, but the diversions didn't work for long. We knew there was nothing to do but offer prayers to the gods and begin our work. I lay down on the dirt, and Eumaeus poured one entire bowl of blood over my stomach. I felt the liquid seep through my chiton and trickle down my sides, and I had to resist the urge to vomit.

"Get up," Eurycleia ordered, and I rose from the ground, looking down at the gory mess Eumaeus had created. After they wrapped a large piece of cloth around me they both nodded their heads, satisfied that the blood seeping through the cloth had the authentic look of a mortal wound to the gut.

Eumaeus smeared and splattered some blood from the second bowl on the front of Eurycleia's chiton, and without a word to me, she set off running up the road to the palace, screaming about how a wild boar had charged out of a thicket and gored me.

I lay down on the litter, and Eumaeus continued his handiwork. Since it didn't take long at a full run to reach the palace, we knew that soon Eurycleia would be back with a party of men to carry me home.

The sweet, almost odorless smell of newly spilled blood had already begun to turn thick and cloying in the midsummer morning. I lay swathed on the litter, unable to move my arms to wave away the flies buzzing around the congealing blood, and feeling so close to panic that I began to moan.

Eumaeus leapt up and went into his hut. "We forgot this," he said, holding a wineskin in one hand and a cup in the other. "It will help you relax." The mix of honey and wine could not completely mask the bitterness, but whatever drug it was took effect almost immediately, and by the time Eurycleia came back, I had dozed off without a care in the world.

To look as if I had spat up blood, Eumaeus put into my mouth a fig-sized bubble of pig's blood inside a gut casing. Just before we set off back down the path to the palace, he made me turn my head to one side and bite it. Blood spurted down my cheek and onto the cloth underneath my head with such dramatic effect it caused Eurycleia to burst into tears.

Eumaeus bent down to give me my instructions one last time. I was quietly dying. Beyond help. I shouldn't try too hard to play dead, for an inadvertent sign of life might expose the plot. I was to avoid calling attention to myself—no screaming or writhing in pain, no pathetic last gasps or groans. In fact, if the drug let me sleep through the whole thing, so much the better.

No instructions were needed. I vaguely recall people swirling over me, but in my narcotic haze I may have confused this with my memory of the jellyfish so many years before. The first thing I remember with any degree of clarity is lying in the bath in my mother's chambers while Eurycleia sponged the blood from my body.

Eurynome was fashioning a corpse with the headless carcass of a goat that had been hauled through the upstairs window and secreted away the night before. She had broken a bowl into two pieces and placed one on each side of a bag of dirt, and she was busy wrapping it in cloth to create something the size, shape, and weight of my head.

"Here you are," she said, pointing to the shrouded form. "What do you think?" Before I could respond, I fell asleep again.

My mother propped me up and put a cup to my lips. "You need to get rid of the drug as quickly as you can, so you can help." she said. "They think we're up here performing the rites, and it's the only chance we have to get you ready."

She and Eurycleia assisted me from the tub and rubbed me dry with such vigor I yelped. My mother smiled. "You must be waking up," she said. "But dead people don't make noise. The rest of us have to keep talking, but you can't even sneeze."

Especially sneeze. Though everyone knows a sneeze is an omen that whatever a person is wishing for at the moment will come to pass, mine is barely a sneeze at all. It's more like a loud squeak, distinctive enough to give me away to anyone who might be listening outside.

By now Anticleia had been summoned from the farm, and I heard her mounting the stairs wailing at the top of her lungs. When she got inside my mother's quarters she dropped what she was carrying and rushed to hug me, but my mother had to remind her to shriek as if she were seeing my body.

After a few impressive screams, Anticleia got to work. She had brought a full change of clothes suitable for a boy, from shoes to cap, and a dark, oily concoction she was pouring into a bowl.

Eurynome pushed a chair next to the tub and Anticleia motioned to me to sit down. I stifled my tears as she cut my hair to a ragged chin length all around. Only in the last year had I been allowed to grow out my hair in anticipation of my first blood, and now, here I was looking like a child again—and not even a girl. My mother picked the strands of hair off the floor, holding them to her chest as if they were a bouquet of flowers.

Anticleia told me to tip my head as far back as I could. She massaged the oily mixture into my shorn locks, then rinsed it out and tousled my hair to start it drying. When I put on the tunic and the cap, however, it was obvious they had forgotten one important detail. My skin had the pallor of someone who was always indoors, and few boys, even house slaves, lived that way. Anticleia diluted the rest of her mixture and stained all my exposed skin a light and rather strange shade of brown.

"Mentor will have to make up some place where people look like this," she said. After all that had happened that day, a lie that small sounded as easy as breathing.

Eurynome handed me a shiny metal disk so I could look at my reflection. I had woken up that morning as myself. Later I had been a corpse, and now I was a boy with greenish-brown hair and a rather strange shade of skin. My lessons in the fakery that is the price of survival had begun.

While I was supposedly being sent off into the afterlife, the rest of the palace was as busy as we were. In order to occupy most of the women, my mother commanded that a feast in my honor take place that very night. The men were sent out to dig my grave for a quick and unceremonious burial. No one questioned the haste. After all, my only importance was as a bride, and since I wasn't going to be one, my life was of no further note.

To ensure that the palace was completely empty, my mother ordered everyone to attend my funeral. As the sun sank to the horizon, I crept down to the cellar unobserved. I had been given the keys to my mother's storeroom, where a lamp was lit, food was laid out, and a bed was set up on the floor. I was to wait there until everyone had gone to sleep, and then Mentor would come to take me to the ship.

I bolted the door of the storeroom behind me. The silence, especially after such a day, was thick as oil. Immediately I realized how hungry I was, and I wolfed down the food that had been left for me, stopping only to swallow huge gulps of water mixed with a little bit of wine. Afterward, I felt a wave of exhaustion so great it carried me to the pallet on the floor. I don't remember lying down, I fell asleep so quickly.

With no outside light and no sounds around me, I was unaware of how long I slept. When I awoke, the oil lamp was still burning and my eyes were acclimated enough to pick out more than just the shapes of the various chests and boxes in the room. To my surprise, the first one I went to look at more closely had no lock.

Even though I was alone, I set my teeth and held my breath as the lid opened with a scolding barrage of squeaks and groans. The air inside smelled of cedar and the dusty tang of boiled wool. A golden bowl and a jeweled mirror lay just underneath an embroidered cloth. One layer below was a diadem studded with gems and a silver platter with an incised design of women at play. They were wearing skirts that looked like flowers with overlapping layers of petals. Their upper arms were tightly covered but their breasts were bare and held high by a wide belt around their stomachs. Their hair was pulled up in front and flowed down their backs in long curls. Goddesses, I was sure, as I had never seen any women who looked like that.

I kept lifting layer after layer of cloth to peek at what was between them, but the weight became too much for me before I was near the bottom. My curiosity was overwhelming, and I went to each chest in turn to see what else I could find. Most of them were locked, but I found one more that was not.

Inside was a skirt just like the ones incised on the platter. Though the light was not bright enough to pick out the exact colors, I could tell that each layer of the skirt was different, many of them stamped with designs in contrasting hues. The next items were a belt and a sleeved top like the one on the platter.

This was my mother's clothing? I barely had time to form the thought when I heard movement outside in the storeroom. I got everything back into the chest and shut the lid just as Mentor opened the door.

"Come quickly," he said. "It's almost morning."

I was already on the path leading to the harbor before I realized I had never said good-bye—not to the house, not to my room, not to my mother, not to my grandparents, not to Eurycleia or Eurynome. My brother thought I was dead, and later I would wonder if he had grieved for me, but at the moment I wasn't thinking about him at all.

I turned and looked back toward the palace, but all I could see were the outer walls. Something came over me, and I broke away from Mentor and began running back. He hissed in the same way he might call back an errant dog. "Do you want to come home and see it again someday," he asked, "or do you want to ruin things forever right now?"

I stopped and turned around to face him. Over his shoulder I could see only one ship in the harbor, and I knew it must be ours. The sky was beginning to lighten, and a few wispy clouds were pink with the reflected light of dawn.

It was too late to change anything. When I reached Mentor he grabbed my elbow to keep me from bolting again, but I didn't intend to. I had been strong, I had been brave—everyone had said so. And now I felt as broken as the clay head on the pathetic corpse in my grave. He could take the pieces with him wherever we were going.

I spent the next five days on an open boat, with a crew of eight men. It was black on the outside, having been waterproofed with pitch, and it had one large square sail. The bow was covered over with wood planks, and it was there that the trade goods were squeezed in and lashed down for transport.

Mentor and I sat in the back with the captain and crew, who busied themselves fishing, trimming the sail, mending lines, and holding the rudder oars in position to keep us on course. The midsection of the boat curved down to allow long oars to be placed over the sides if the winds were not favorable. These were secured to a set of benches running the breadth of the ship, and though the men might crawl in to take a nap from time to time, that part of the boat was usually empty.

When the wind picked up, the ship groaned and creaked so loudly that in the beginning I thought the whole thing might explode into splinters. Once I got used to it, I barely noticed the noise, except to rejoice that a strong wind meant we were moving quickly toward our destination.

The ship was going to Pylos, the home of old King Nestor, who had fought with my father at Troy. Mentor said he would tell me then where he was actually taking me, but he did not want to run the risk that anyone on the boat would learn the secret. The plan had been to make the journey in several stages, so Antinous and the others would not easily find the trail leading to me. A five-day sea journey was nothing, Mentor told me, for an angry man whose ambitions had been thwarted.

I had no further part in the rest of the scheme, except to take direction without questioning and keep my mouth shut. Mentor would do all the talking for me.

I was the child of one of Penelope's slaves, born on Odysseus' *oikos* after my mother's abduction from some remote place on the Egyptian coast. This explained both my odd appearance and why I understood Mentor's language. My disguise could not make me look masculine of face or body, however, so to make a credible story, Mentor told the captain I was being sent as a gift to someone in Nestor's family who had a taste for young boys. Lest any of the crew get ideas, Mentor made it clear that the captain and his crew would all suffer grievously if I were to arrive with any signs of recent use.

After a while, the leers stopped, and I was more or less ignored. I spent the first day watching and listening to the slapping of the sail against the rigging, and the sounds of water rushing along the sides of the boat. Dolphins leapt from the water and raced with us. Fish boiled in schools on the surface while seabirds plummeted to eat their fill. The sea was so glorious it made me forget everything for a while, before a stray thought would bring my losses crashing in on me. Then I would crawl between the oar benches in the middle of the ship and cry until I could compose myself and go back to being a mute slave boy again.

When night fell, the boat was pulled ashore. We cooked the day's catch of fish on a driftwood fire, and the men drank wine until they staggered off to burrow themselves into the sand and go to sleep. Mentor slept next to me, tying one of my wrists to his with a rope, just in case drink might have made a sailor reckless enough to try to drag me off.

I had never had the experience of sleeping next to a man, though I hardly thought of Mentor that way. Much as I wanted to take comfort in him, his nearness was so oppressive I could not fall asleep. I lay looking up at the stars smeared across the vault of the sky, as embers collapsed, adding their smoky scent to the heady mix of night-blooming flowers and salt air.

All my senses were awake, vibrating like the strings of a lyre. A tingling spread out from my belly to the tips of my fingers and toes, and to every hair on my scalp, the way it had the day my mother first took me to honor Hera. The day I thought I could fly. But there I was, tethered to the man who was charged with saving me.

And then, suddenly I was outside myself, hovering above, looking down on my sad, stained body as if it had nothing to do with me. I whispered Hera's name, for I knew it was she whose presence I felt, knew that in the end she would protect me from whatever the next day, and all the days after, would bring.

The following morning I felt euphoric after Hera's visit. By the time the day was over, I felt nothing but horror. My stomach was hurting by midday, and I slept for a while curled up between the oar benches, before a painful cramp between my hip bones woke me up. I don't know what caused me to slip my hand down inside the loincloth, but when I touched myself between my legs, I felt something slick and wet. I yanked out my hand, and stared at the scarlet coating on my fingers.

My first blood as a woman was coming on the seas, surrounded by men who thought I was a boy.

Why had Hera bestowed womanhood on me then? I told myself she could not betray someone who honored her as I did, but secretly I was furious with her for letting it happen. I had only Mentor to talk to, and I would not do that, not about something like this. I would have to figure out what to do all by myself.

I was afraid if I stood up, blood might come pouring out, so I lay the rest of the afternoon on the bottom of the ship trying to think of a plan. By afternoon a spot the size of my thumb had appeared outside the thick folds of cloth wrapped between my legs.

Fortunately for me the wind dropped early. The captain ordered the ship into a cove because there was no point in either drifting or exhausting the crew with rowing when there was no hurry to get to Pylos. The anchor stones the sailors threw out sent schools of brightly colored fish darting away in the azure water, and before curiosity brought them back, their world was disturbed again by the splashes of men jumping overboard and swimming to shore. I jumped in too, taking my time getting to the beach in the hope that my cloth would be rinsed clean.

I knew it would be only a temporary solution. The blood would keep coming, and a wet cloth would hold less than a dry one. When everyone was preoccupied with settling in for the night, I went back into the water, glad for the fact that Halia had taught me how to swim at least well enough for what I needed to do. I splashed around until the crew forgot all about me, and then when no one was looking, I drifted back in the direction of the boat, hoisted myself on board, and opened a chest stored in the bow. It was full of gifts I was bringing to my hosts. My mother had me choose something I had woven myself for the woman whose guest I would be, saying that only the best and the most expensive would do. The one I had chosen, a piece of fine white linen with a complicated gold border, was lying near the top of the chest.

I had no choice. I took a knife one of the crew had left on the boat and tore the cloth in pieces, ripping off the border altogether and putting it back in the chest in case it might be of some other use. I tucked one piece of the new cloth under my belt and slipped back overboard, coming ashore before anyone missed me. I pretended I needed to relieve myself in the woods, and I found a clearing where I could leave one cloth to dry while wearing the other. Later I went back into the woods to retrieve the dry cloth. The wet one was already pink all the way through, and since I had no way to rinse it, I buried it under a pile of leaves.

I did the same thing where we landed the boat the next day, and prayed we would get to Pylos before I used up the whole cloth. Hera was with me, because we did.

We sailed into the harbor just as the sun was setting. Several bonfires lit up the beach, and I could smell the aroma of roasting meat before the rowboat that came to meet our ship brought us ashore. At least a hundred men were gathered around the fires, and at the edge of the beach I could see crowds of village women. Excited children ran up, urging us to hurry because the sacrifice that opened the annual feast of Poseidon was about to take place.

Mentor and I were swept along with the crowd moving toward the central fire. There I saw the most ancient human being I had ever laid eyes on. King Nestor was an old man before the war with Troy. He brought his fleet there in person anyway, though he had not been in battle himself. Now, thirteen years later, he had to be helped to the altar by his sons Peisistratus and Thrasymedes.

Nestor nodded to Peisistratus to place a fat-wrapped ox thighbone in the fire. I watched as the flames rose up and licked it. On Ithaca, we had feasts like this in our own harbor, but I hadn't attended since I was forced indoors by the suitors. And now here I was, sharing the pleasure again—suspected by no one, coveted by no one—standing so near the fire my eyes were watering from the smoke and I could hear the fat pop and crackle.

The crowd hushed so they could hear Nestor's voice, and I was surprised at how loud it was, despite his stooped shoulders and wizened frame. "Hail, Poseidon," he said, "god of the wine-dark sea, tamer of horses and savior of ships. Shaker of the earth, by you the land moves as well!"

His sons helped him forward and steadied him as Nestor poured the libation. "Hail, Poseidon," he cried out. "Carrier of the earth, commander of the sea! O blessed one, show us your kind heart. Help those who voyage in ships, and those who live on the edge of your mighty waters!"

The voices of the men around me rose in a cheer so loud and sudden it made me jump. They began to move away, since the ceremony appeared to be over and the feasting could begin. Nestor called them back.

"I wish to make a second sacrifice," he said as Thrasymedes handed him another, smaller bone wrapped in fat. This one he placed himself on the fire. "Mighty Poseidon, it is by your blessing that my men and I are home over your seas from Troy, and by your anger that one among our heroes is not. I speak of Odysseus, the bravest of them all."

I opened my mouth and took a step forward, but Mentor held my arm.

Nestor continued. "We beseech you, great Poseidon, if the great wanderer has not already gone to join the valiant dead in the halls of Hades, that you bring him safely home."

A loud assent broke from the crowd as Nestor turned from the fire and was led away by his sons.

I beckoned to Mentor to lower his ear. "Does Nestor know who I am?" I whispered.

"He doesn't know we're here. I need to reach Peisistratus to tell him we've arrived. He's the only one involved."

"Why did he mention my father?" Mentor glared at me and I realized my error. "Odysseus, I mean."

"Odysseus," he emphasized each syllable in a tone more scolding than kind, "is admired everywhere, and his absence is breaking more hearts than yours."

Sometimes I wished I had no father at all, but that moment I wanted to cry out with pride and tell the crowd who I was. I imagined Nestor's sad face breaking out in a wrinkled smile, and his handsome sons accompanying the daughter of the great hero to the bright palace I could see illuminated on the hilltop overlooking the harbor.

But I stood on a moonlit beach, dark skinned and dark haired, as close to invisible as a person could be. At that moment I began to understand that although my journey to my new home might come to an end soon, I would not resume being Odysseus' daughter even then. My skin would eventually be fair and my hair long, but until my father came home, there would be no Xanthe, just a young girl living a lie.

I should have been ravenous, but I could barely eat. Eventually, servants of Peisistratus took us up to the palace, and I fell asleep, free from Mentor's rope, on a corner of the pallet they had laid for us on the porch.

The following morning I got up at dawn and watched the crew row out of the bay at Pylos. Hundreds of marsh birds filled the air above a green lagoon at the edge of the bay, their faint cries carrying on wisps of air toward me. Curious gulls circled the boat that had brought me there, as it slipped around the barrier island just off shore and was gone.

I turned in a full circle to look at the coastline and the hills of the interior, thinking how strange it was that a place could be made of the same rocks, water, and sky that we had at home but contain not a single familiar sight. Back in Ithaca I was sure Hera would always be able to find me, but now I was not so certain. The world seemed too large for a single goddess to be able to watch it all.

As I turned to look inland, I saw an expanse of land stretching farther than any I had ever seen. Almost everywhere in Ithaca, the outlook was blocked by crags and hills, and the only distant views were across the bay or out to sea. I watched in wonder as the mountains pulled their shadows in as the sun rose behind them.

Mentor came up behind me. "We have to hurry," he said. "It's best to leave before the entire house gets a good look at you."

We walked toward another walled enclosure I could see ahead of us. As we went through the gate, I stopped in my tracks and cried out in fear. Two animals larger than anything I could have imagined were tossing their heads and letting out loud and unearthly sounds. They were led by a rope around the neck by two men who came barely up to their chests but who did not seem frightened by them at all.

"What are they?" I called after Mentor, too afraid to follow him into the courtyard.

He turned around. "Horses." He beckoned me forward with an impatient flick of his hand. "Come on. They're nothing to be afraid of."

I still wouldn't move. "What are they for?"

Mentor charged back toward me as if he were prepared to drag me if he had to. "They're taking us where we are going. You see that chariot? They're bringing the horses to hitch them to it."

The thing he called a chariot was painted gold and decorated with stark red and black designs and figures of men doing battle. It was a cart of some sort, but a strange-looking one, with an opening at the back, and huge compared to the ones at home. I could not imagine why anything more than a single donkey and wagon was needed to carry my belongings as we walked to our destination. Not until a man hopped aboard through the gap in the rear did I understand that the chariot would be transporting us as well.

I followed Mentor's orders to get on and sit atop the chest of my belongings, set to one side behind the driver. When I was settled, Mentor got on and stood next to him. The driver made a loud cracking sound with his whip, and the chariot lurched forward out of the courtyard.

I had never imagined anything could go as fast, or as painfully, as we moved across the low plains of Nestor's kingdom in the direction of the mountains I had noticed that morning. Try as I might, I could not keep my body from being bashed against the sides of the chariot or thrown forward so quickly I could not stay seated. Finally I gave up, and Mentor let me stand and brace myself against him. The horses' sleek brown haunches rippled with the effort of pulling our weight as they loped along, snorting from time to time in the dry and prickly air.

Over time, I felt safe enough for my thoughts to wander to something Mentor had told me back in Ithaca. "You promised you'd tell me where we're going when we got to Pylos," I yelled over the drum of horses' hooves and the clack of wheels.

"What? I can't hear you."

Dust blasted my face and my mouth was gritty, but I shouted out my question again. I was not going to leave him alone until I got my answer.

I was expecting to hear the name of my grandfather Icarius or possibly my mother's rarely mentioned sister, Ipthime, but the name sounded nothing like that.

"Who?" I cried out.

"Helen," he shouted. "Your mother's cousin."

I sat down on the chest, absorbing what he had said. Helen of Sparta. The cause of the war. I had spent the last few years cringing at the mere mention of the name that had stolen my father from me, heaped such burdens on my mother, and wrecked my life.

"Why?" I whispered to myself. "Why her?"

And why me? What I had I done to deserve such a fate? Betrayed by everything and everyone, I sat down on the chest, shrinking into myself and moaning with every jerk and bounce as the dirt rose up in huge swirls, swallowing the road behind me.

BOOK II

Sparta

CHAPTER 9

Beckoning

*What I wove of my thirteen years before I arrived in Sparta takes up the
distance from my fingertips to the pit of my arm. The five years I spent with
Helen fills the loom to below my knees.*

*My transition to life in Sparta is woven in linen the color of fresh cream,
so sheer it glows when sunlight passes through it. It is bordered on both sides
by the same gold pattern I copied from the cloth I had ruined with my blood.
The fabric has a magic to it, demanding that I come closer, whispering to me
like a spirit at an open door, beckoning me into another, boldly luminous
world.*

When we pulled into the stables of the palace at Phera that evening, I felt as if every bone in my body had crumbled to shards
that were now stabbing me from the inside. But as I hobbled away
from the chariot, I took solace in the thought that at least I had
arrived where I was going. The mountains I had seen in the

distance that morning towered over us, rising almost straight up from the plain, and of course it would be impossible for anyone to go further.

"We'll sleep on the porch tonight," Mentor said, "and get an early start tomorrow."

"Tomorrow?" All I wanted tomorrow was a long nap in a soft bed and a change of clothing. "This isn't where I'm staying?"

"We have to cross the Taygetos," Mentor replied, waving his arm in the direction of the mountains behind us.

"No," I said, pointing to the highest peak, now a dark purplish-green against the white sky of twilight. "No one can go up that high."

"We go through there," he said, pointing to a gap between two mountains. "The pass will take us to Sparta."

I went to sleep thinking a pass was some kind of magical road lying unseen at the base of mountains, like the channel that separated Ithaca from the neighboring island of Same. I had seen the channel only once, peering down at a tiny boat making its way along the narrow strip of water between the massive cliffs, one of which rose up to where I stood, and the other towering on the far side.

The following morning we started out at daybreak, and by the time we had been on the road a little while, I knew far more about passes than I cared to. I was so terrified that I wet the top of the chest on which I cowered. When we stopped at a spring to water the horses, I braved a look at the cliffs and peaks surrounding me and was sure the Taygetos Mountains were alive. I saw their glowering eyes and grimacing mouths. I saw their powerful shoulders and arms ready to reach out and knock me from my perch into a gorge so deep I could not see the bottom. *What are you doing here?* they asked. *Get out, before we eat you.* I lost my balance and fell to my knees, vomiting onto the dark, mossy rocks by the spring, until my stomach screamed for mercy.

The horses strained until midmorning to carry our weight up a road far steeper than any in Ithaca. Once we had climbed high into the mountains, the journey got a little better. From time to time we raced down to streambeds and back up again along ledges so narrow I closed my eyes and cried. But on other stretches we crossed stone bridges over cascading streams, and soggy meadows thick with wildflowers and butterflies, where carefully laid stones made a road high enough to remain firm and dry. While we were moving, the chariot and horses made too much noise to hear anything else, but whenever we stopped, glorious sounds of thickets full of birds, eagles and hawks screaming in the sky, and the buzz and click of insects offered a defiant reply to the menacing and silent peaks.

We arrived at our destination not too long after nightfall the second day. Mentor had made good on his promise to my mother, and no one but the charioteer and a few stable hands had laid eyes on me since we left Pylos. I was miserable but safe, and he was obviously relieved.

We were spending the night at the home of a vineyard keeper and his wife. Though the dwelling was modest, their generosity was not. The woman laid the table with a basket of bread much softer and tastier than any on Ithaca, a large round of cheese, and bowls of fragrant lentil soup. Then, while I was satisfying my stomach, she prepared a bath for me. Taking me out of sight of the men behind a screen in one corner of the room, she helped me undress and get into a wooden tub once used for stomping grapes, and now waterproofed with a heavy coating of pitch.

"What have they done to your skin?" she asked.

I was too tired to answer. I leaned back in the warm water while the woman ran a scraper made from an animal bone over my arms and legs, collecting up rows of dirt and dead skin. I watched, amazed that without hurting me she could get rid of so much of the horrible stain I had been looking at for days. Then she took a sponge and rubbed my whole body with such vigor that water sloshed onto the floor. She took a piece of gritty rock and rubbed it in circles on my cheeks and forehead, using a fingernail to work into the creases of my nose. When she was done, she helped me get up out of water as black and slimy as olive brine, and handed me a mirror. I was chafed and glistening, but much of the way back to my normal color.

As she dried me, I thought of the day not long before when my mother and Eurycleia had done the same thing. When I sat on a stool and leaned back against the tub so the woman could deal with my hair, I almost cried with the memory of Anticleia and the loving way she had massaged my shorn locks. Still, I couldn't wait to get rid of the hideous tint, and I sat as still as I could while powerful fingers kneaded olive oil into my scalp until I thought I would have no hair left at all.

She was disappointed with the results. Putting a cap over my head, she said that when the women from the palace came the following morning, they could figure out what else to do. She brought me a clean piece of cloth to wrap around myself, securing it with my own pin and belt. When I came out from behind the screen, Mentor—uncharacteristically jolly by then with our host's wine—let out a cheer at my bright pink body.

Mentor and I had barely spoken during our journey. With all we had gone through together, I felt less like a traveling companion than cargo he was delivering. I'd never seen more than a flicker of emotion from him, either at home or on our journey, and I don't recall him showing interest in what we experienced along the way. I trusted him, but he was still a stranger to me, having never revealed anything about himself or his thoughts.

While our hosts were busy disposing of the bathwater and doing the last chores of the day in the yard, Mentor and I were briefly alone in the house. I knew he was leaving in the morning, so I had just one chance to ask him what had been on my mind.

I sat down on a stool next to him, broke off a piece of bread, and handed it to him. We chewed silently for a moment.

"So," I said, hoping the wine had loosened his tongue. "You haven't told me why you brought me here."

I saw his face tighten. "It was your mother's wish."

"I know that," I said, trying to hide my annoyance, "but I don't know why she wished it."

"Neither do I." Mentor's voice turned sullen. "I tried to talk her out of it, but Halitherses—"

"I don't want to hear about an omen." I was bothered for a moment at how sharp I sounded, but I didn't apologize. "I want to know why you didn't want me to come here."

"Who says I didn't?"

"You did."

His lip curled as he spat out his next words. "Do you have to ask? It was that woman!"

Relieved that he felt the same way I did about Helen, I blurted out what was really on my mind. "Why couldn't I go to live with my grandfather? That's where I thought I was going."

"And what I advised, but your mother wanted Icarius to believe you were dead. She thought there would be no other way to keep him from meddling."

The grandfather with the beautiful palace, where my mother dressed in the clothes in the chest and danced all night in Hera's temple—I would never go there, never be a princess in his kingdom, never be even a passing thought in his mind.

Mentor was still talking. "She was sure he wouldn't care what kind of a man he chose for you, once the suitors got wind of where you were. He didn't seem to care what happened to Telemachus, and his life is more important than yours."

I had long ago trained myself not to bristle, at least noticeably, at such insults, and in this case I wanted to hear what he had to say far more than I wanted to point out that my life mattered too, at least to me. "But only my father can choose my husband."

"Not if Icarius declared him dead. Then he would be guardian to all of you again until Telemachus came of age." Mentor snorted with contempt. "He'd already selected your mother's new husband."

"Who?" I dreaded all the possibilities.

"Eurymachus. Antinous would settle for you, I'm sure, and continue his scheming. They had both already visited him, separately of course. Not empty handed either, from what I hear."

The room fell silent. I saw now that despite his apparent indifference to me, Mentor was on my side, even if I wasn't the one he cared about first and foremost. And though I couldn't understand everything my mother was thinking and doing, she was fighting for me with every power she possessed. I felt a surge of love for her and vowed to make a success of my time in Sparta, if for no other reason than to make her proud of me.

"But why Helen?" I asked. "Why did my mother want me to come here?"

Mentor's sigh was resigned. "They're cousins, only a couple of years apart, and childhood friends. Your mother said that despite everything, she still feels closer to Helen than anyone else, and she knows she's strong enough to protect you, no matter what happens."

He shrugged his shoulders. "And besides, she doesn't hold against Helen what is really Aphrodite's fault."

I couldn't believe what I was hearing. "But Helen ran away from her husband with another man!"

Mentor put his finger to his lips, to remind me that it was best not to be overheard, even among the most trusted of servants.

"I've never seen my father because of what she did." My voice grew hoarse with tears, and I felt myself starting to shake. "How can you say it's not her fault?"

"I didn't say that. Your mother did." He looked me straight in the eyes, as if he were comprehending for the first time that I was a real person.

"There are many ways to see Helen," he said. "Your mother has hers and I have mine. I imagine it won't be long until you have your own."

The following morning the charioteer came back from the stables and fetched Mentor before I was awake. He was gone before I could say good-bye. What finally woke me were soft voices in the cottage. I opened my eyes and saw what looked like spirits standing in the doorway. The morning light streamed in, causing their oiled linen gowns to glow and sending glints of light onto the walls from the golden ribbons woven through their hair.

When the sleep left my eyes, I saw they were two young, but clearly mortal women. One of them was taller than the other, with dark hair and very pale skin. The hair of the second one was the color of apple cider, and the white lotion covering her face could not completely disguise a ruddy and freckled complexion underneath.

"Who are you?" I asked.

"Eirene's awake," the dark-haired one said in a voice as soft as a cloud, as they started toward my bed. I looked over my shoulder to see who they were talking about.

"That's you," the fair one said. "The queen has renamed you."

"We're going to oil your skin now." As the dark-haired woman unclasped the brooch holding my chiton, she saw the confusion on my face.

"I'm sorry," she said. "We've been rude. My name is Phylo." Gesturing to the other woman, she added, "and this is Alcippe. We're the queen's personal attendants, two of the three at least. Adreste is back at the palace. We've all been talking of nothing but you for days."

With only a glance at my naked body, Alcippe took the cloth from Phylo. "The queen thought for a long time about what to call you, since it wasn't safe to use your real name," she said, in a voice as tiny and breathless as a child's. "And when she thought of the name Eirene, she said 'That's it,' and never considered another!"

After all that had recently happened, I hadn't imagined that things could get any stranger, but they just had. Eirene. A name that meant *peace* seemed more a cruel joke than anything else, but it had been deemed perfect by someone who had never met me. I was standing completely naked, except for a boy's cap over my oily hair, in front of two stunning women who spoke with music in their voices and were treating me as if I were a goddess newly arrived to a festival in my honor.

Phylo removed my cap. Her face fell. "Oh dear," she said. "What happened to your hair?"

I wanted to blurt out that it was not my fault, that my hair used to be long and well cared for, rather like the color of Alcippe's, but when I opened my mouth to speak, the explanation seemed like too much effort. It didn't matter, because they had already turned away to consult with the vineyard keeper's wife about how to repair me adequately to finish my journey.

When the woman left to fetch supplies from the palace, Phylo trimmed the ragged ends of my hair to make it an even length while it grew out. Alcippe combed a mixture of coarse barley meal and flour through it over and over again to remove the excess oil and most of the tint, and soon the dirt floor was covered with little mounds of almost the same dull brown color.

While they were waiting for the woman to return, Phylo and Alcippe oiled and scented my skin with hands that bore no resemblance to any I had felt before. The night before, the vineyard keeper's wife treated my body as if it were bread dough she was preparing for the oven. From time to time in the past, Eurynome or Eurycleia caressed me with their callused and bony hands, but most often the task of oiling my skin or drying me after a bath was turned over to young slave girls who lacked the experience, or more likely the desire, to make anything about it truly enjoyable.

Alcippe's and Phylo's hands were devoted to the pleasure of touch. They rubbed their palms together to warm the oil for contact with my skin, making circles with their palms to press the heat down into my flesh. The oil smelled of a flower I could not quite identify, or perhaps it was a whole meadow of scents. When I sighed with pleasure, they purred and laughed in voices that sounded like melodies picked out on a lyre.

Alcippe moved her fingers with such delicacy it felt more like being tickled, not as a playmate would, but with slow and deliberate motions that sent tingles up and down my body. Phylo bore down so hard with each separate fingertip that I thought about telling her to stop hurting me, except for some reason I didn't want to. Every part of me that retained memories of the journey the day before was caressed until the aches vanished, and by the time they had finished I was as limp as the clean cloth they wrapped around my body.

By that time the vineyard keeper's wife had come back from the palace. She put a covered basket on the table before going out into the yard again. Phylo went to the door to make sure she was out of earshot and then came back to me.

"Best that no one hear," she said. "We have a lot to talk about."

Alcippe filled a basin of water from a small cistern near the door and poured in a vial of bright yellow liquid that Spartan women made from wildflowers and used to lighten their hair.

She put the basin on the table, and I dangled my head over it, taking in the sour, pungent scent of a field of grass. Phylo rubbed her hands over my back, not as she had when she was massaging me, but more like the reassuring way I remember Eurycleia touching me. The tenderness was almost more than I could bear, and I fought with everything I had not to break down and cry.

"Before you leave for the palace, the queen wants you to understand who you are going to be while you are here," Phylo said.

"Eirene," I mumbled into the bowl.

"Good. That's right," Alcippe chirped with the excited tone I remembered Halia using whenever I mastered something new. Phylo, I had already decided, was all business, but Alcippe seemed more like a child getting ready for a game of make-believe.

"We are the only ones who know who you really are, other than the king and queen, and Adreste of course," Phylo said. "The story is that you are a slave, sent from Egypt as a gift from Alcandre, the wife of Polybus. They were the host of the king and queen when they visited Egypt on their way home from Troy."

I didn't hear all she said very well, so stunned was I at the news I would live as a slave. I tried to lift my head out of the basin, but Phylo's hands pressed just hard enough between my shoulders to keep me down.

I wouldn't do it. I would run away. I would go back to Ithaca and hide somewhere until . . .

Until what? My father came home? Antinous found out where I was and raped me to ensure I was fit for nothing but to be his wife? Telemachus married me off as a favor to someone who had flattered him? I had no choice but to go along with what they said.

My hot breath rippled the yellow water in the basin as I listened.

"Your father ruled a Greek colony somewhere," Alcippe said in her high and breathy voice. "He was killed, and you and your mother were taken into captivity when the Sea People came to your town. Polybus bought you both, and you grew up in Egypt." She paused to examine my hair. "I think that's enough time."

Phylo murmured agreement but kept a hand between my shoulders. "Don't lift your head. It will run all over your face," she said. I heard Alcippe filling another pitcher with water while Phylo continued the story.

"Your mother was the chief handmaiden to Polybus and Alcandre's daughter. Your mother went with the princess to her new home when she got married. You were left behind, but since Alcandre remembered how much Helen fancied you, she decided to send you here as a gift to her."

"It's a very good story, I think," Alcippe said, pouring the fresh water over the back of my head and working it through. When Phylo let me sit up, they hovered so close to me I could hear their breath as they patted the drips from my neck and rubbed the cloth over my hair to remove the excess water.

"Better," Phylo said, rubbing a strand of my hair through her fingers. After she brushed out the snarls, she put a narrow strip of blue and silver cloth over the top of my head and tucked it behind my ears, pulling it tight and tying it at the back of my neck.

When she came around to look at me, Phylo saw the troubled expression on my face. "You're upset," she said.

"Of course I'm upset! I'm going to be a slave!" My voice filled the hut. "Wouldn't you be?"

Phylo fluffed out my hair behind the scarf. "That's what we are," she said in a tone devoid of any recrimination.

Ashamed, I whispered an apology, but Alcippe broke in before Phylo could reply. "I'd rather be a slave to Helen than a princess in some rough Greek colony," she announced. Her eyes grew wide and she put her hand to her mouth. "I'm sorry," she said. "I didn't mean the real you."

I thought of Eumaeus, happier on Odysseus' rocky island than he could have been in his own kingdom. I thought of Eurycleia and Eurynome, respected in our household almost as much as my mother. All three would probably agree there was some truth to what Alcippe said. Still, it was hard to be told I was no longer free, even if it was just a lie to protect me.

"Just wait," Phylo said. "You'll see how it will work out. Let's go outside to dry your hair."

When I walked through the door, my grim mood vanished. Lacedaemon stretched out before me, brilliant in the summer sun. Behind me, the Taygetos Mountains were like huge gray ax blades sunk in a long row by giants. The slope I was standing on was covered with neat rows of vines that gave way, over a series of other hills and ravines dotted with flowers of every imaginable color, to a marshy strip of bright green meadowlands. Two rivers wound through the middle of the valley, but in many places I could not see the water for the thick, dark green ribbon of trees on their banks.

Neat orchards bordered pastures where horses and cattle grazed. In one direction I saw men cutting swaths of hay, while in another, vast fields of wheat and barley shimmered in the heat. A cloud of dust swirled behind the wheels of a chariot roaring toward the hilltop palace in Sparta, whose white walls gleamed against another mountain range beyond.

Ithaca had pastures and orchards too, but nothing to compare to Lacedaemon's. Every plot of land on my father's *oikos* had to be coaxed to yield to the plow. Every flock had to be driven from one sparse grazing ground to another. Here, life exploded from the rich soil, willingly providing everything we desired.

Alcippe brought out two chairs and sat down beside me. Phylo went off to send the vineyard keeper down to the stables with the message that we were ready to leave. Since I was naked from the waist up, when I heard him coming toward the house I grabbed the loose top of my chiton and held it in front of me.

"Why did you do that?" Alcippe asked.

"The man," I said, assuming she would understand.

Her brow wrinkled in confusion. "You have a beautiful body."

My nipples had grown puffy and pink as rosebuds, but underneath them my chest was still almost flat. "Not yet," I said.

"Already," Alcippe replied, reaching over to brush away a tiny bug that had landed on my hand.

The vineyard keeper started down the road without a look in my direction. Phylo brought a chair and sat next to me.

"It's hot," she said, unpinning her chiton and exposing her breasts to the sun.

"We have to cover up soon or our skin will color," Alcippe said, baring herself as well. "But doesn't it feel wonderful?"

It did. Confident we were alone, I let my chiton drop again, and the three of us sat with our eyes closed. My eyelids glowed pink as the breeze brushed away the sun's heat from my face. A flock of songbirds settled into a tree near the house and just as suddenly flew off again, blending their chatter with the distant voices of people at work in the vineyard.

Far too soon I heard Phylo say it was time to go inside. Their chitons were still unpinned and draped over their belts, and their faces were within inches of mine as they dusted my skin with white powder and painted a design on my cheeks. They didn't see me watching them as they concentrated on their work, and the experience of having their eyes and bare breasts so close to mine was so intense I can't remember exactly what they said they were doing.

When they were finished I looked in the mirror Phylo handed me. My hair was the green of an unripe pear and the red sunbursts they had painted on my cheeks were so strange I didn't know what to think.

"You look like a princess," Alcippe said.

"I *am* a princess," I blurted out, but already that word was starting to feel out of place. Though I can't say I truly liked the way I looked, to be treated this way at home in Ithaca would have been splendid beyond imagining. But reality was otherwise. I was not free. I was not home. I was not Odysseus' and Penelope's daughter, except to a few, and they would be pretending I was someone else.

We sat in the shadows inside the hut, waiting for the retinue from the palace to arrive. Soon we heard the sound of men's voices, and when Alcippe and Phylo repinned their chitons and went to greet them, I did the same.

Outside, four men stood dressed in tunics so white they made me blink. They were carrying a chair painted in bright colors, attached on both sides to the middle of two long poles and covered with a blue and red canopy shot through with gold thread.

"What's that?" I asked.

"It's a sedan chair the queen brought back from Egypt," Alcippe replied. "There important people go around in them, so their feet don't have to touch the ground."

It took a while for me to realize the important person that day was me. "This is for a slave?" I asked, bewildered.

Phylo pulled me aside so the men could not hear, and Alcippe followed.

"Helen decided she couldn't let Penelope's daughter come to the palace any other way," she said. "People will forget soon enough."

"And most people won't know or care who you are anyway," Alcippe said, with the innocent thoughtlessness that would in time become one of the most endearing things about her. "Helen does what she wants," she added. "She's the queen, you know."

Too dazed to be anything but compliant, I went over and sat down in the chair, and the four men picked me up. When we reached the main road I stared at the distant palace walls, looking away at the details of the countryside only long enough to make the palace jump forward when I returned my eyes to it.

The ride gave me time to examine my clothing more closely than I could in the low light of the hut. The linen of my chiton was in a weave so tight and fine it clung to my body and gathered in tiny tucks rather than folds under the gold and silver sash at my waist. The veil draped over my hair was trimmed with gold and silver sequins, and when I shook the hem, tiny stars traveled across the skin of the men carrying me.

Just the day before I had been jostled nearly to death in the back of a chariot, and now here I was, bouncing along another road, in a world so utterly transformed it seemed I was crossing a portal into another world.

Eirene's world. I was already starting to think that was who I was, almost believed I really had been kidnapped and grown up in Egypt. Ithaca, the journey, Xanthe—they were all fog and dreams compared to this world of color and touch and sound, where every one of my senses seemed to prickle, like a limb that had fallen asleep but was now called back to life.

CHAPTER 10

Ripples and Shafts of Light

My entrance into Helen's world can be told as the story of a day, a single stripe on my loom. After that, I made one false start after another, condemning my work as shallow and lifeless as I destroyed days of effort. Eventually I resigned myself to my shortcomings, realizing that even now I am not sure I fully understand all that happened to me in Sparta.

I settled on a plan to weave one great swath of fabric, bigger than the total of what already existed, into which I would put everything I had to say about my five years with Helen. When I began, all I hoped for was that when I reached the center, I would have figured out how to do the impossible— represent the queen herself.

Once I knew what I wanted to do, I still couldn't weave for days. From the very first thread I had to show the power Helen had over everything, the way her existence saturated the air, and how even when she wasn't there, her presence filled rooms.

Without weaving, I had no escape from the fact that my life since I returned to Ithaca was controlled by inebriated and boastful men whose

armpits stank and who belched and farted as if that were their contribution
to the world. And then one morning as I stood at my window, the scent of
apple blossoms and meadow flowers wafted through the air.

"Helen," I whispered, sure that her spirit had somehow been carried to
me, and that the answer I sought had come with it.

I drew the design with my finger in the ashes on the hearth. Ripples.
Ripples and shafts of light.

I began the journey to the palace believing I could transform
myself into Eirene by the time I arrived. As we neared the white-
washed outbuildings of the compound, fear sent trickles of sweat
down my back, and my heart was pounding so fast I thought I
couldn't breathe.

The air in the courtyard lay heavy as a blanket on a feverish
sleeper, but just as I moved to get up from my chair, a puff of cool
air passed over. I would have thought nothing of it, except that
in the same moment a thought came to my mind, as quickly and
surely as a bird alighting on a branch.

Eirene. Daughter of Zeus. Goddess of peace.

Was she telling me that if I did not resist what I could not
change, I might find peace here in Sparta? A strange calm washed
over me, as if she were telling me yes, that indeed I had understood
her. When Phylo took my hand to help me up, I floated to my feet.
I might not have been ready to wrap my new identity around me
as if it were nothing more than a fresh chiton, but I knew I was
strong enough to try.

Alcippe went ahead and Phylo followed behind me as I
mounted a double flight of stone stairs leading to the upper floor
of the palace. When we reached the top they turned to walk to

one end of the building, but I lagged behind to look out over the courtyard.

Dozens of servants went about their business, coming in and out of the workshops and supply rooms on the ground floor. A man loaded bags onto a donkey braying with disapproval. Two women chattered as they carried empty sacks into one of the storerooms. In a corner, two young men pitched stones into a grid they had drawn in the dirt.

The buildings enclosing the courtyard were two stories high on my side and three on the other, painted in blinding white and shades of rust and pink. The ground floor was protected from sun and rain by a covered walkway whose roof was supported by columns painted in bright patterns. Near the far end I could see a staircase three or four times as wide as the one I had walked up, connecting the courtyard to the upper floors. Next to it was the entrance to the megaron, whose ceiling reached all three stories to the roof, and whose doors were many times the size of any I had ever seen.

The palace complex was bigger than whole villages I had passed through on my journey, rivaled in size only by Nestor's at Pylos. My ride from the outer walls to the central courtyard had taken me through a twisting warren of corridors and alleyways hemmed in by two- and three-story buildings on both sides, all with the same open walkways and painted red columns. How many people lived here? Had anyone ever counted all the rooms?

Phylo came back and took my arm to coax me along. "The king's quarters are there," she said, gesturing across the courtyard toward the two upper stories, before turning to nod in the direction of the wall just behind me. "And the queen lives here."

The queen. Right behind that wall, Helen might be waiting for me. I felt the blood rush away from my head, and I rested my hand on the railing in case my knees gave way.

Phylo took my arm and guided me down one hallway toward a smaller one, where she opened a door and gestured me inside.

"This is where we live," she said. "It's right around the corner from the queen's quarters. We'll go there after I've shown you your bedroom."

The megaron for the handmaidens was as large as my mother's in Ithaca. Looms and baskets of handwork were scattered here and there, along with an assortment of chairs, stools, and small tables.

The room was cool and flooded with light from a row of small open windows between the tops of all four walls and the roof. Blue waves with leaping fish were painted along the bottom of the stuccoed walls, and a fresco of women at play and work ran around the middle of the walls on all four sides.

Several curtained doorways opened onto the megaron. Phylo took me in the direction of one.

"This is yours," she said.

The room was taken up mostly by the bed, but big enough to walk around without bumping into anything. The bed, on which blankets and bed cloths had been neatly laid, was a platform built up from the floor.

Folded on top was a red coverlet, with a sheen I knew could only come from skilled hands with limitless quantities of beautiful thread to work with. Embroidered animals paraded around the edges, and a gold tassel ornamented each corner.

"The queen made that," Phylo said. "It's her welcome gift to you. I helped her pick it out."

I sat mute on the bed, stroking the folded coverlet on my lap as if it were a pet.

"Do you weave?" Phylo asked, breaking the silence.

"Yes," I murmured, "but not like this."

She smiled. "You'll learn. Helen is the best weaver in all Lacedaemon. People say a goddess guides her fingers."

I touched the tiny stitches of the embroidery. "She did this too?"

"Every bit." Phylo gave me a sly smile. "Unless it was the goddess." She motioned to the space next to me on the bed. "May I?"

I nodded, and she sat down next to me. "It would be nice if you made something for her in return, while you're here," she said. "To repay her kindness."

I sat in silent misery, remembering the beautiful gift I had destroyed to hide the secret of my first blood. Just then, Alcippe appeared in the doorway, standing next to an old woman whose back was curled into so severe a hump that she had to crane her neck to be able to look forward. She came toward me with a broad smile, revealing several missing teeth.

"Ahh," she said. "Xanthe—Odysseus and Penelope's daughter."

Alcippe and Phylo laid a finger to their lips in perfect unison. "Not any more, Adreste," Alcippe said. Her tone was that of a child grown suddenly solemn. "We're not to call her that, ever."

"I'm Eirene. A slave princess from Egypt," I said, trying to be helpful.

She came closer and looked me in the eyes. "You are Penelope's daughter," she said. "No doubt of that."

"How do you know?" I asked.

"Everything about you. You look just like her when she was young."

"You knew her when she was young?" I blurted out before seeing Phylo scowl. I was so proud to hear I resembled her, although I knew it wasn't true. My mother and I shared only the golden-brown color of our hair, and even that similarity was gone until mine looked normal again. Her eyes were soft and enchanting, and mine were dark and murky as olives. I've always thought my eyes belonged on someone else's face, so great is the contrast between their color and the fairness of my skin. Phylo's eyes in Alcippe's face. To me, it didn't make a very appealing whole.

I wanted to know what else Adreste knew about my mother, but she had given in to Phylo's stern look and would say nothing more.

Since Phylo and Alcippe were both in their early twenties, I had assumed Adreste would be very much like them. I don't know why I found her age and frailty so reassuring. Maybe it was because not everyone here spoke with a musical voice and walked as if their feet were barely touching the ground. And besides, a woman who could look into my face and see my mother might become my new Eurynome, my new Eurycleia.

But Adreste's presence offered another kind of reassurance. Another queen might have replaced her with a younger and more capable servant, but Adreste remained protected by Helen, living out the remainder of her life in dignity. Even before I met her, the queen of Sparta had already begun to make an impression on me.

And now the moment had come. Alcippe took Adreste's arm, Phylo took mine, and we walked toward the queen's quarters.

At Adreste's slow pace, I had time to review everything I had been told about Helen. Considering her fame, I knew surprisingly little. Menelaus had come from Mycenae to rule as Sparta's king when he married her, and after a few years she ran off with her lover, Paris. I knew the aftermath in much greater detail. The war with Troy had cost me a childhood with my father, and his absence was the reason I was now in Sparta.

I had far more questions than facts. Why had Helen run away, and what made her worth all that effort to fetch her back? Why hadn't Menelaus killed her when he first laid eyes on her again? How was it possible that they now ruled together, as if nothing had happened? And why did my mother believe that none of it was Helen's fault? Rules were rules, and she had broken every one. Why had she not paid the price?

The time had passed for questions. An open door beckoned me, and without a chance to take a deep breath, I was inside her chambers.

Helen was on a platform on the far side of her megaron, seated on an enormous gilded chair decorated with red and blue designs and studded across the top of the back with amber disks and other brightly colored stones. It appeared as if she had recently come in, because the fire was just then being stoked by a servant, while two young girls in white chitons and bare feet folded her veil and put it in a chest. They scurried away as the four of us made our way toward the queen.

Helen held out her hand but did not get up to greet me. "Eirene," she said.

I felt Phylo's hand in my back pressing me forward, and I moved to the edge of the platform. Though she was seated, its height put Helen at eye level. She gazed into my face, and though I normally would have reacted by looking away, something about her commanded my attention.

Many call her the most beautiful woman in the world, but how can I explain that with her it wasn't anything strictly physical, but the way she took you in when she looked at you, how you wanted nothing more than to stay in that moment forever. How when she looked away, you felt a pang of withdrawal until her eyes lit on you again. I saw many times in my years in Sparta how she could do something as simple as shift her weight in her chair and attention would be on her, not because she asked for it but simply because she was the most compelling force in the room. No games or contests, no music, no topic of conversation could compete with the simple fact of her presence.

I suppose that's why, in describing one whose beauty is supposed to surpass all others, I wouldn't begin with what she looked like. I had imagined someone of a size to match her story, but I could tell even when she was seated that she was small. Her full height and weight were scarcely more than mine at thirteen, and I towered over her before a year had passed. Her hair was black and lustrous, held off her face by a golden diadem and gathered in loose curls at the back of her head. In front of the diadem, short strands of hair were pomaded into tight, flat coils high on her forehead. Her skin was covered with a lotion that made it very pale. Red disks and lines like rays of the sun, similar to the ones Alcippe and Phylo had painted on me, decorated her chin and cheeks. Heavy gold ornaments hung from her neck and around each earlobe, and a blue and gold shawl was draped over her shoulders.

And her face? For the first moon cycle I lived in Sparta, the image I had of her as I lay awake at night was so incomplete I was always surprised when I next saw her by what I had failed to notice. She had a small black mole touching the bottom of her mouth, which she hid by extending red paint beyond the borders of her lips. The bridge of her nose was so straight and perfectly angled it could have been the work of a master builder. Perhaps it was a trifle too large—she thought so—yet Helen's flaws had the power to redefine the beautiful.

But her eyes are what made Helen most memorable. They were the shape of almonds, almost feline, and fringed with lashes as black as her hair. I am sure they would have been beautiful in any color, but Helen's had not a hint of the typical blue, brown, or green. They were the color of the sky before a thunderstorm, pure dark gray, inviting you in, but hiding more than they revealed—smoldering heat under a veneer of ash, the brilliance of a sun obscured behind clouds.

That was the woman who took my hand. "Eirene," she said again, squeezing it tight.

A table made of planks of oak had been set near the hearth, and after Phylo and Alcippe made sure we had everything we needed, they left us alone.

Before sitting down, Helen ushered me to the hearth. There, held upright in a bronze tripod holder, was an object unlike anything I had ever seen. I knew it was a rhyton, used for pouring libations, but this one was nothing like the simple stone jugs used at home. Carved to a point at the bottom, and about the size of my forearm, it was made from hollowed-out rock crystal the color of honey. The shatter lines in the translucent rock reminded me of the coarsely woven tunics worn in the winter by farmhands in Ithaca, but they gave the rhyton a glow richer than gold. Around the neck, coils of gold wire encircled a collar of dark amber, to which was attached a graceful, ear-shaped handle made of bronze beads alternating with round stones in different colors. To that point in my life, except for the things I had briefly seen stored in my mother's chests, nothing but the trims on fabrics were meant to be beautiful for their own sake. It was not so in Sparta. In Helen's world, beauty was a requirement for life, as much as food and water.

"Come," Helen said. "First, the libation in thanks for a safe journey."

I followed her to the hearth. She tipped the rhyton forward, and wine flowed from the lip into the groove on the hearth. It made its way to the edge, where it cascaded into a gold basin sitting atop a silver plate.

"Goddesses of Olympus," she said. "Your beauty is beyond compare, and we use your gifts faithfully in your service." She turned to me. "Was there anyone who helped you on your journey?"

"A man named Mentor brought me."

She smiled as best she could under the thick coating of white on her face. "I was referring to the gods."

I felt so stupid. "Hera," I said. "Hera was with me. She's always with me."

"Your mother has trained you well."

I was too absorbed in thought for the compliment to register. "And Eirene," I added.

Helen turned back toward the hearth. "Accept our thanks, Hera, Queen of Olympus, and Eirene, goddess of peace, for protecting your daughter who stands before you."

We went back to the table and sat on cushions of gold and white silk atop chairs of smooth wood, darker than any I had ever seen, and inlaid with colorful stones and shells. On a platter in the center of the table, pieces of sausage and bits of lamb sat alongside a mix of cooked lentils and onions. On another platter, a small whole cheese was surrounded by figs and other fruit. Though I suppose I should have been overwhelmed by being alone for the first time with Helen of Sparta, suddenly I was starving. Perhaps Phylo and Alcippe had eaten before they arrived at the cottage, but I had not had anything that day.

I'm afraid I made a disgrace of my first meal with the queen, but she gave no sign of disapproval. Pushing the platter of meat in front of me, she said, "It's all for you. I don't eat it."

Not eat meat? I had never heard of such a thing. I suppose the quizzical look on my face prompted her to continue. "I've had enough of blood," she said. "I've seen too much death for one lifetime."

"It's delicious," I said, picking up another piece with my fingers and swallowing it almost without chewing.

"I'm sure it is." She cut the cheese into wedges and handed a piece to me before putting another in her mouth and chewing it as if each bite gave her something to think about. She picked up a fig and bit into it with such delicacy that my own ravenous mouth stilled, as if it were impolite even to draw breath in her presence.

When she had finished, she was ready to talk. "I'm trying to decide which of your parents you most resemble," she said.

I forgot all about Adreste's certainty, forgot about how nervous the painted, impassive woman at the table was making me feel. "You know my father?" I asked.

"Of course."

I remembered too late that Odysseus had been one of the suitors who failed to win her hand, but she didn't seem to be thinking of that.

"I saw him in battle. Several times."

The subject was too serious to combine with food, and though I was still hungry I pushed the platter away. "What did he look like?" I had formed a vision in my mind, but I hadn't ever heard him described, and suddenly I wanted to know.

"Do you mean was he healthy? Did he fight well?"

I nodded my head. "That too."

When she answered, her voice sounded far away. "I used to stand on the ramparts of Troy and watch the battles. Your father looked like a god. His skin was golden and his strength . . ." She thought for a moment. "I have never seen such courage as he showed."

I grew up surrounded by stories about how brave and strong my father was, and if I wasn't going to hear something I didn't already know, I was happier if he wasn't the subject. I breathed a private sigh of relief when she said in a low voice, "It's a long time ago now," and fell silent.

After a few moments, she leaned back in her chair. "Tell me about your journey!" she said in a cheerful voice.

The sudden turn of the conversation caught me unaware. "My hair was chopped off and stained with olives," I blurted out. "Alcippe and Phylo tried to fix it."

"I wondered why it was green. You didn't get that from your parents." She got up and came over behind my chair to examine it, and for the first of countless times I was close enough to Helen to take in her scent, to hear her soft breathing, to glimpse why few men could have resisted her.

She came around the chair to look at me. "You're as pretty as your mother," she said, brushing away a tear before it could fall. "But crying will spoil my makeup, and this is a time for happy thoughts, isn't it?" A smile played at the corners of her mouth. "I suppose your mother's told you how mischievous we were."

"She told me about a temple at her father's palace, how you used to dance all night," I said.

"Dance, and more." She was close enough for me to see her expression soften under the paint. "And the way we danced . . ."

She shook her head as if to get rid of the memory. "I don't dance like that anymore," she said, sitting down again. "It isn't dignified for a queen, especially one my age. I don't suppose your mother has much wildness left in her either, after all that's happened."

Wildness? My mother? "I don't think so," I said. "At least I've never seen it." Our walk back from Hera's shrine came into my mind. "I danced like that once. My mother said she saw Hera Pais with me."

"Hera Pais?"

"I felt as if I could fly away." I looked away, suddenly shy at having told someone I barely knew anything that intimate.

"Dancing with Hera Pais . . ." Helen's voice was so dreamlike I looked up to make sure she wasn't floating away. "The girls dance with goddesses in Sparta too," she went on. "I imagine Hera will recognize you when she sees you. Even with green hair."

She patted my knee to let me know she was teasing, but then her look turned serious and quizzical. "Have you had your first blood?"

I shut my eyes, as the memory swept over me. Betrayed by my own body in a ship full of men. Lying amid the oars and benches, clutching my aching stomach as I imagined the warm crimson smearing my thighs. The furtive trips to the woods to bury the evidence. The ruined gift for Helen.

I wanted to cry, but I was momentarily distracted by the recollection of the beautiful coverlet Helen had left in my room. "Phylo showed me your gift, and I am ashamed I haven't thanked you for it."

Ingratitude to a host was the mark of a savage, my mother always said, and though she was referring to Antinous and the others in the house, I knew she would be most unhappy with me for having waited so long to mention Helen's generosity.

"I hope I can weave like that someday," I added. "I love to weave. My mother and I stayed at the loom all day sometimes."

"Then you will weave with me while you're here." She said it as if it were an order, but I knew it was meant as an invitation. "But I asked you about your blood," she reminded me. "You didn't want to answer?"

"No, I suppose not," I said, surprised that memories so vivid had not managed to spill out of my head into hers without the need for words.

"Didn't Hera pay you a visit the night before? Didn't your mother honor you? Wasn't there a celebration?"

I didn't want to cry. I refused to cry. And then I was crying.

I told her the whole story, and by the time I finished, Helen had given up dabbing her eyes and was weeping openly.

"I'll tell my husband I can't come down to greet his guests tonight," she said. "I'd much rather stay here." She clapped her hands and within a moment, Phylo came in with Adreste hobbling behind her.

"Oh, my!" Phylo said when she saw the queen's face. "Shall we try to repair it?"

"No," Helen said. "Wash it off. I'll be staying in."

After Phylo wiped the last remnants of a cleansing cream from the queen's face, she softened and rearranged Helen's hair with her fingers. "There you are, Jewel of the People," she said, stepping back. It was the first time I heard how others formally addressed the queen.

When Helen opened her eyes, I saw her natural face for the first time. Even as dazzled as I was by her regal attire on my first night in Sparta, the recognition that a real person lay under the paint made a far greater impression on me. Perhaps some people preferred Helen unreal and untouchable, but for me the experiences carved in the tiny lines near her eyes and mouth, the sorrows that so often clouded her eyes, were something to honor rather than hide.

Before I had a good chance to look at her, Phylo came over to me with the jar of cream. Only in that moment did I remember that I was painted as well and must have looked as streaked and blotchy as she did.

When my face was clean, I turned it toward Helen. She put her hand to her mouth as her eyes filled with tears, and I realized my paint had been as much of a disguise as hers. She took in a breath, as if she were about to say something, and then she dissolved into sobs. Phylo rushed to her side.

"Help me to bed," she murmured.

I was numb with confusion about the sudden change of mood in the room. My eyes watched but my mind barely registered how Phylo struggled to keep Helen's feet under her as they disappeared into her bedchamber. At the door, Helen glanced back over her shoulder at me. Her lips were parted and her eyes were narrowed into slits of pain as she disappeared from view, without a word of farewell for the night.

I only remembered Adreste was still there when I felt her hand on my elbow. "Come along," she said. "I'll get you to bed."

We walked back to our quarters in silence. My head was whirling. What had made someone as intimidating and self-possessed as the Queen of Sparta dissolve like that before my eyes? Had I done something wrong? Was I going to find myself unwelcome after that horrible journey? And if so, what would happen then?

Before my voice found me again, with Adreste's help I was out of my chiton and ready to get into my new bed. "What's the matter with the queen?" I asked her.

Adreste clucked. "Lie down, and I'll put the covers over you."

"No," I said, still seated on the bed. "I need to know. Am I in trouble?"

Adreste shook out the red coverlet Helen had given me. "Sometimes the queen gets overwhelmed with all—" Adreste looked away as if the air on the other side of the room had presented a sudden distraction. "With all that's happened." She laid the coverlet on the bed and smoothed it with her gnarled fingers. "I've known her since she was born, and I can read her face better than anyone can. You reminded her of how many people—even those she didn't know—were hurt by . . ."

I didn't have to ask what she meant, but Adreste finished her thought anyway. "By Troy," she said, as if somehow we could avoid annihilation only by giving our pain the name of a place far enough away to be safe from its shadow.

Even today I am not sure whether I was awake to hear the commotion in the hall outside the handmaidens' quarters, or whether it somehow worked its way into my dreams that first night in Sparta.

"Where is the little bitch?" I thought I heard a voice say. "I want to see her." The response was an indistinct murmur. "Little usurper!" the voice said as her voice trailed down the hall and disappeared.

In the middle of the night, a jerk of my limbs woke me from fitful and threatening dreams. The moon had risen, and I watched it pass across an open window. Beams of moonlight streamed down onto the coverlet Helen had made for me, and I pulled it up against the chill of the night air.

I had already shut my eyes when something caused me to open them again. Without a sound, an owl had perched at the windows, its black silhouette ringed by the full moon behind it. Before I could take a few breaths, the bird flew away.

I was still awake when dawn sent pink fingers of light into my room. In the window, the owl's phantom presence remained.

CHAPTER 11

The Other Side of Silver

Blue for the background. Not really blue at all, but a shade of purple, made from the same tiny snails that gave their lives by the millions to tint the cloaks and hems of royalty. It's the most expensive of all dyes, and I hear my mother chiding me for the waste, but what do I care? Better to spend it on my own story, I thought, than weave it into a garment for one of the undeserving louts downstairs.

I began what would become great swaths of silver woven through the blue, narrowing toward the center but so wide where I started that only a little blue shows at all. It was a nice way to start, but not completely honest. My weaving had a public face, but so far it had no private one. I took a charred ember from the fire and, going to the hidden side of my weaving, I darkened what I had woven about Sparta until it was caked with black. Sometimes from the front of the loom I stare where I know the black is hiding, imagining little holes burning through the cloth. We think we can control the story we present to the world, but the truth always lies in the background, awaiting its chance to illuminate and scar.

* * *

My arrival coincided with the annual festival of Orthia, the biggest event of the year for women. Families from all over Lacedaemon, and as far away as Pylos, Tiryns, and Mycenae, converged on the palace at Sparta for the occasion. From there, I was told, the mothers and daughters would go to a place on the banks of the Eurotas River, where, if Alcippe and Phylo's level of excitement was any indication, wondrous events would occur over the course of one sacred night.

Everyone in the palace was caught up in the excitement. In what I took to be an annual ritual, shortly after the guests arrived, Menelaus pronounced that the air contained more femaleness than was good for a man, and he and his friends left to go hunting in the forests of Lacedaemon. Without men Sparta was a different world, and every year the women conspired to drive them out as soon as possible so the main events of the festival could get underway.

The first night the men were gone, Helen took charge of the grand megaron, inviting all the women in the palace, from scullery maid on up, to be her guests at a table where the rest of the year they were not permitted to sit. She ordered the herdsmen to slaughter as many animals as they would if it were one of Menelaus' feasts, and because the women were well aware of just how much wine, cheese, and other stores were normally brought to the table in an evening, by the time the torches were lit and the feasting began, the table was heaped so high some of the smaller guests had to kneel on the benches to see across.

The men left behind to maintain the palace kept everyone's goblets full. They brought in platter after platter of beef, mutton, and goat, which the women grabbed with their hands, making a great show of the gluttony they had heard about, if not witnessed, when the men sat around the table.

Helen's handmaidens always ate before banquets, so we could spend the feast looking dignified behind the queen. I used the time to examine the grand megaron itself. Every inch of the gigantic wooden beams reaching across the length and breadth of the ceiling was painted with designs in reds and blues and whites. Wherever the beams crossed, a gilded pillar reached up from the floor to support them. I could have looked forever and kept noticing different things about the patterns, which at first looked identical and then only in time revealed their subtle and intricate differences.

And that was just the ceiling. Running around all four walls of the megaron, huge frescoes told stories of men and their adventures. On the far side of the room, hunting dogs had a wolf at bay, while the hunters came up on horseback behind them. On another wall, the sails of a fleet of ships were filled by the breath of a god, while another boat fought off an attack by a sea monster. Battle scenes were complete with victorious homecomings, including beautiful dancing girls. Every time I came into the hall, I saw some new detail, and though I can't say I wouldn't rather have been upstairs relaxing in my chair than standing behind the queen, the fantasies on the wall made evenings on my feet easier.

This evening, however, was entertaining enough all by itself. After a while the wine had gone to everyone's head, and the women called for the bard to entertain them.

"Forget the heroes," one of the women called out. "Sing to us about love."

"Sing to us about sex!" another chimed in.

"Even better!" the first woman replied.

The bard raised his shoulders and eyebrows, as if to say he

didn't know what they were talking about, but the women grew more raucous the longer he resisted.

One of them started a song without him. "Come in the forest with me, darling, please," she sang, as the others joined in.

"And heap the basket full of bread and cheese . . .

"And bring my favorite sausage 'tween your knees . . ."

The bard made a great show of indignation, as if he would rather do anything than hear the end of the song. He drew his plectrum across the lyre and picked out a beautiful melody once through before he began the words.

"I begin with the Muses and Apollo and Zeus," he sang. "For because of them there are singers and players upon the lyre. Happy is one beloved of the Muses, since across his lips song passes sweetly."

The women shouting for bawdy songs grew quiet as the spell of the bard took over.

"Sing of Orthia," Helen said when he had finished.

"Yes, Jewel of the People." He played a few notes and began.

"I sing of Orthia, great winged goddess, who makes mountains tremble and the woods echo as she flies. Awesome protector of women, she leads the dance of the Graces, who sing of the gods' children living supreme among the mortals."

He looked at Helen and played a grand flourish. "Hail, queen, grant the favor of honoring my song and give me leave to sing another."

And another and another. Between his songs, women danced and performed stories, most of which involved sex, the ridiculous behavior of men, or both. Some they made up on the spot and others were obviously old favorites, judging by the tears of laughter streaming down faces and the hoots of anticipation for the next development in the tale. When the time drew late and no one had the energy for another story, people started yawning and shifting in their seats, hoping the queen would notice it was time for the last formal libation, so they could drift off to bed.

The court at Sparta had a different rhyton to honor the specific god of each festival, and at Helen's signal, Phylo carried Orthia's rhyton to the hearth. It was made of creamy alabaster in the shape of a woman with upraised hands. Her head was encircled by a jeweled band from which gold balls in the shape of poppy capsules protruded upward, like the spikes of a crown. The base, where the wine was stored, was in the shape of a plain, cylindrical skirt, flat on the bottom so the rhyton could stand upright.

Orthia's breasts were bare. Each nipple was made from tiny pieces of pink shell arranged around a brilliant bead of bright red stone. To my astonishment, Phylo wiggled both nipples free with her fingertips, while Helen incanted a blessing. Then, taking the rhyton, Helen tipped it forward. Tawny wine came pouring out of each breast onto the hearth, and as it did, the room grew silent. For a moment I felt as if I were outside time, brought back only by the telltale sniffles of women struggling to hold in their emotions.

Helen broke the silence. Handing the rhyton back to Phylo, she excused herself in her most regal voice, inviting the others to stay as long as they wished. To great applause for her hospitality, she left the megaron with us by her side.

The air had turned chilly, and I was instantly aware I had left my wrap in the megaron. I retrieved it, and when I was back outside in the courtyard again, I saw the queen, Alcippe, and Phylo turning the corner at the end of the walkway on the second floor.

I was alone. I smiled at the happy voices inside the megaron as I made a slow circle in place, taking in the rings of torchlight, the painted pillars along the walkways, the glow of light in upstairs rooms, the black outlines of trees beyond the walls. My skin, which was flushed and hot from the stuffy air inside, felt soothed by thousands of invisible, cool fingers as I tilted my head upward to take in the stars. I was already starting to shiver, but I wanted to be nowhere else at that moment.

A loud crash at the opposite end of the second story from where we lived shattered the calm. I looked up and saw a young servant who had been at the banquet earlier. She was sobbing as she ran down the stairs and across the courtyard.

"What happened?" I said, grabbing her arm. She shook her head without replying and broke free, disappearing into the maze of the servants' quarters.

I went up the stairs, and after looking around to be sure I wasn't observed, I turned in the direction from which the noise came. I tiptoed down every corridor, but I heard nothing. Eventually I gave up and went to my room.

"Does someone else live here? Someone at the other end of the building?"

I directed the question the following morning toward Adreste, who sat with me sorting a pile of sequins and beads that had gotten mixed up when she dropped a tray. Phylo and Alcippe sat in their usual places, putting the finishing touches on the garments the queen would wear later at the main ceremony of the festival.

Phylo looked up immediately, and I saw the distress written on her face. "No one you're likely to meet any time soon," she said.

"Who is it?" I asked again. "I heard a loud noise last night, and a girl ran out crying."

Alcippe and Phylo exchanged looks. "I told you," Phylo repeated, trying to sound casual. "No one you need to know about."

"It isn't important, really," Alcippe said, as they went back to their work.

I stared at the tops of their heads for a moment. They might have decided the subject was closed, but I hadn't.

I turned to Adreste. "The night I arrived, I thought I heard you talking to a woman outside in the corridor."

Phylo answered for her. "We were talking among ourselves." Her eyes bored into Adreste, as if to warn her not to speak.

"No, I'm quite sure it wasn't any of you," I said. "She was saying things that weren't very nice, and the voice wasn't any of yours."

"It's unpleasant," Alcippe said. "We don't like to think about it."

Adreste stared at each of them in turn. "It's not a secret. The queen's made that clear." She shrugged and picked up another bead. "As if it's a secret that could be kept."

"She's also told us that she doesn't want it discussed." Phylo gave Alcippe orders all the time, but I had never heard her use such a tone with Adreste, who was old enough to be her grandmother.

"Discuss what?" I demanded, ignoring Phylo and speaking to Adreste instead. "Who is she?"

Adreste looked up at Phylo. "Who's going to tell her? You or I?"

Phylo put down her work. "No one will say anything until I have discussed the matter with the queen." She got up and, glaring at Adreste, she left the megaron.

Soon she returned. "The queen would like to see you," she told me. Alcippe and Adreste started to get up, but Phylo gestured them to stay where they were. "Alone."

Phylo stopped at the door to the queen's quarters. She told the girl stationed there to leave, and before sitting down in her chair, she gestured to me to go in.

"You asked," she said. "Now go find out."

The ornate chair that served as a throne in Helen's private megaron was empty. I couldn't pick her out immediately in the low light, and only when I heard her disembodied voice float across the room was I able to see she was weaving.

"Help me with this," she said, gesturing to the far side of the loom, where the first few inches of a blue robe were hanging. "It's a bit wide to do without a second pair of hands."

I came over and after pulling the shuttle the rest of the way to my end, I helped her press the new weft thread into the cloth above it. We lifted first one rod and then another, changing the sheds through which the shuttle passed to make the fabric. Pass, beat. Pass, beat. Pass, beat. We wove without speaking for a long time before Helen stepped back, rubbing her hands together as if she were cleaning them.

"Do you know that Heracles discovered this dye when his dog came back covered with blue saliva from snails he had eaten?" Not waiting for an answer, she motioned me to sit down at the table. "Are you hungry? I can call for something to eat."

I shook my head. The ordinariness of our weaving and her formal, flat tone was unnerving, since I didn't know her well enough to be able to sense her mood. I was just about to blurt out that I was sorry if I had caused any problem, when Helen spoke.

"Phylo tells me you were inquiring about my daughter."

"You have a daughter?" My voice came out as an incredulous squeak. "Why haven't I met her?" I cringe today thinking of how little tact I had.

Helen's cheeks, clean of makeup, grew flushed. "Because she hates me, I'm sorry to say."

If anyone was perfect, it was Helen. I shook my head. "What could there possibly be to hate about you?"

I might have cause to resent a mother who ignored me when

I was young, and good reason to be angry with a father who had never come home from war, but I had never for a moment entertained such a black thought as hatred toward either of them.

Though Helen's fleeting smile had more pain than pleasure in it, I could see she appreciated my undisguised adoration. "I suppose I should let Hermione tell you herself. I'm sure she will, in time. But I'd like the chance to be heard first."

She poured us each a goblet of water and took a sip before speaking.

"I've been a terrible mother, and a worse wife, if that's possible. But I will not be disrespected, and since she insists on telling me exactly what she thinks of me, regardless of who hears, I've had to confine her to her quarters until she gives me her word she will behave."

Helen let out a long, resigned sigh. "She said she'd rather be locked up forever than be forced to spend her days with me." Her eyes tightened with private pain, and since I had no idea what to say, I watched her in silence.

Eventually she spoke again. "She wants to return to Mycenae to live with my sister. Clytemnestra took her in and raised her while I was—" She paused, and I saw her swallow deeply. "While I was away in Troy."

Helen touched a finger under her eye as if to wipe away a tear, but so far none had fallen. "Hermione was only nine when I left, and my husband went off after me," she said. "The war lasted ten years, and even then we didn't come right home."

She looked straight at me. "That, I think, was my unforgivable crime, even more than his. After all, mothers are supposed to yearn for their children, aren't they?"

"I think so," I said, wondering if my mother was at that moment yearning for me.

The inadequacy of my answer made me feel a little stupid, and I was glad she hadn't seemed to hear it. "My daughter was twenty-three before I saw her again," she said. "Why should she care about me?"

Because I do, I thought to myself. I didn't want Helen to hurt. I wanted her to be above troubles, to be no more complex than a painted image on a pot. I had not yet understood that a person's story cannot be told as just a series of experiences, strung one after another like beads. If anything, life is a growing wad of complications and contradictions, knotted together like the tangles in our hair while we sleep. "How did that happen?" we ask ourselves in the morning, and we don't know the answer.

If Helen had asked me in that moment whether I wanted to walk down the hall to meet Hermione, I would have said yes, even though I had pictured the person at the other end of the hall as one of the Harpies, wild haired, with piercing, destroying eyes and mouth, snuffling around the palace like a she-wolf looking for prey. But now that I realized it was Helen's daughter, I knew the truth had to be quite different.

Ten years older than I, Hermione was halfway between my mother's age and my own. Being Helen's daughter, she had to be beautiful. I wanted to meet her, just to fix her image in my mind, but I instantly felt guilty, as if I were betraying Helen by not being satisfied just to know her.

But Helen didn't ask. Instead she got up and went back to her loom. "Weaving helps me think," she murmured.

I went with her and took my place at the other side. We changed the shed and passed the shuttle back and forth in silence, adding to the cloth one thread at a time until we had finished a section about the width of two of my fingers.

The next sound to come from her was laughter entirely devoid of joy. Rather than floating across the room, it seemed to fall to the floor under its own weight.

"Perhaps you haven't heard what kind of a person my sister is, this woman Hermione loves to throw in my face," Helen said. "She was married to Agamemnon—"

I nodded. "The leader of the Greek army. He was killed when he came home."

"Murdered. By Clytemnestra and Aegisthus. My sister and her lover are ruling Mycenae right now."

I gestured to a tiny bump in the fabric I knew would displease her. She took out several rows until she reached it and teased the thread smooth, but it was clear her mind was somewhere else.

"My husband is Agamemnon's brother," she went on. "He's waiting for his nephew Orestes to return, so they can kill Clytemnestra and Aegisthus together. It wouldn't be proper to do it alone and deny a son his revenge."

Her eyes narrowed. "They'll soon be dead, and even if it is at my husband's hands, I will not weep one tear for my sister, because of the way she turned my only child against me."

By now she was beating the weft threads together so forcefully that the clay warp weights were banging against each other. "You need to stop," I said. "The weights will tangle." She gave no indication she heard me, but her hands fell to her sides as she stared at the loom.

"I should calm myself," she said. "I haven't told you the least of it yet, and already I'm so upset I'm trembling."

Though I wanted to know more, my heart was so heavy I was glad she was finished. Then, as suddenly as it had come on, her mood shifted.

"Would you go to the door and ask Phylo to bring us some food and a little more water?" she asked in a voice as serene as if nothing had ever disturbed her. "I've kept you here far too long on an empty stomach. And besides, we need to start thinking about getting ready for tonight."

When I went out to speak to Phylo, I walked with her to the railing just to be able to breathe freely for a moment before going back inside Helen's chambers. I saw pairs of women and daughters heading in silence toward the shrine, where each one would honor Orthia privately and prepare with appropriate solemnity to encounter the goddess at her sacred ceremony. At sunset, Helen would make an appearance in the crowded palace shrine as head priestess of the festival, and from that point forward, just as at home, all frivolous and unnecessary conversation would cease, even among the slaves and servants, until after the main ceremony the following night.

Suddenly I heard a wave of noise come up from the people in the courtyard. At first I wondered why they were cheering for me, and then I realized Helen was behind me. She came to the railing and accepted the acclaim without waving or nodding her head, in fact without moving at all. The women's salute to Helen was nothing like the loud, hoarse calls of men, but high and melodious, as if their voices were taking flight and soaring away over our heads.

Helen touched the small of my back with her hand. "Look at all the excitement," she said. "I imagine you haven't seen much of this on Ithaca."

"No," I said. If times had been better, my mother might have brought such a life with her, but they weren't, and she hadn't.

"Was it like this when you and my mother went to festivals?" I asked her.

Helen smiled. "Grander," she said. "It's always better when you're young, and things are new."

She pressed her delicate fingers against the side of my waist to get me to turn around. "Help me get ready to go down to the shrine." The crowd was still cheering as we disappeared from view.

Before I went downstairs for my own private moment in the shrine, I closed the curtain in my bedchamber, so I would not have to talk to anyone for a while. I fought against the tiredness that overcame me as soon as I lay down, because I didn't want to go to sleep until I had pondered everything I had learned that morning.

A woman of such power and beauty, one in whose name thousands had gone to war, had a child who despised her and a sister who fanned, or perhaps created, that hatred. Underneath the serene and confident exterior was the saddest and possibly the angriest person I knew.

But the person at the other end of the hall interested me more. She was not some insane old crone, and though she was quite unpleasant, perhaps all she needed was a friend.

After all, we both had been sent away to live with a relative when things fell to pieces at home. Surely that was something we had in common. But I could already picture the scorn with which Helen's daughter might view me. Though I could be angry at my situation, I had no cause to be upset with my mother. She hadn't chosen to be separated from me, and Hermione would probably think I was nothing but a whining child for comparing my exile to hers.

She had been with her father for nine years before he sailed to Troy. Didn't that make my story sadder, since I never had my father at all? Probably not, I realized. Menelaus knew her, knew she was waiting, and still he did not hurry home.

I could at least comfort myself with the thought that Odysseus might not know I existed, although admittedly he hadn't come home to the wife and son he did know about. Still, my father's slight to me was imaginary. The injury to Hermione was not, and her pain was real and justified.

I should stay at my end of the hall, I told myself. Crazy as it sounds, I was mad at her for having a story that was worse than mine, though I should have been comforted by the comparisons. I hated the confusion Hermione had caused me, hated the way her existence threatened to complicate what looked like a pleasant life in Sparta. And I couldn't wait to meet her.

The sacred ceremony of initiation into womanhood took place the following night. My mind was so distracted—not just by Hermione, but by the work required to serve the high priestess of a festival—that I hadn't done much to prepare myself. Besides, although Helen explained to me that women were complicated enough to have more than one goddess watching over them, I still felt disloyal to Hera that my initiation would come at someone else's shrine.

No time remained to get a belated start on the preliminaries. The afternoon sky had already lost its blue, and Adreste was lighting the lamps. She was too infirm to travel to the sacred grove and would stay behind, ready to tend the queen the following day when we all returned exhausted from the festival.

Two servant girls came in with baskets laden with food for our supper. Alcippe and Phylo hustled the girls along, and when the four of us were alone, we wasted no time in sitting down to eat.

"We have to hurry," Phylo said. "The banquet will start when the sun goes down. The queen's eaten already, but she still needs to dress, and so do you."

The platters in front of us were heaped with chunks of meat, mounds of dried pear and apple slices, and a square of honeycomb oozing its amber liquid onto the round loaf of bread next to it. I poked at the meat, having by now adopted at least superficially some of the queen's distaste for it, but Adreste placed another piece on my plate and half a sausage as well, demanding that I eat it all.

"You'll be dancing all night," she said, "and you'll forget to eat. They all do."

I complied, but my stomach was tight with excitement and I had trouble with every bite. Phylo and Alcippe got up just as I sucked the last of the honey from a small piece of comb, and I joined them as they went from our quarters toward the queen's megaron.

Inside, Helen had just come from her bath and her skin was radiant with oil. She sat on a low-backed chair while Phylo and Adreste attended to her makeup. When they finished, Helen stood up, resplendent with black-lined eyes, scarlet lips, and the same red sunbursts on her whitened face I had seen the day I first laid eyes on her.

"Before I dress," she said, "I want to attend to Eirene."

To this point I had made myself busy being helpful in small ways—holding a pot of color or dipping my fingertips into a waxy pomade and touching it to the queen's hair to hold it in place. Now all eyes turned to me as she bid me drop my garment to the floor.

I stood naked in the middle of the megaron. The warmth from the fire in the hearth warmed the front of my body while my back shivered in the cold draft. Helen picked up the crystal rhyton. "Hear us, goddesses," she called out. "The girl of last year is no longer. Standing before you is a woman marked by her first blood."

She came over to me, and Phylo followed behind her, carrying a bowl. Helen took some unguent on her finger and touched it to my lips, spreading it from one side to the other and looking me deep in the eyes. Then she leaned forward and kissed me.

This was no brush of lips, but enough to make my teeth click against hers and to feel the wetness of her mouth as she broke away. My lips were afire. I felt Phylo and Alcippe on either side of me, rubbing my nipples with the same unguent and moving out in larger and larger circles until my whole chest was glowing. The unguent penetrated my skin and crept deep into my flesh as they moved to my buttocks and the crack between them. Their hands caressed my stomach and slipped further down onto my new triangle of thick, dark hair.

As their fingers pressed the inside of my thighs to pull my legs apart, I fought against them, thinking something wrong was happening, something I should want to prevent.

Helen held up her hand. "Let me," she said.

Alcippe and Phylo stepped back. Leaning toward me, she whispered in my ear not to resist, as she took unguent on her fingers and slid them between my legs.

"Part them," she said. Because she was the queen I obeyed, although my heart was pounding with fear.

She took her fingers and spread the ointment over the lips at the entrance to my body. With the tip of her finger she pulled back along the whole length, pausing to cup her finger under a nub in the front I didn't know I had. I felt a pleasant shudder come over me and shut my eyes for a moment, but Helen had already removed her hand. When I opened my eyes again she was smiling at me, so close to my face I could smell the honey on her breath.

"May you be blessed to follow the path of happiness and find little misery along the way," she whispered. Helen put under my nose the fingers with which she had touched me, but the unguent was so strong I could smell nothing of the odor that would later become so familiar.

"This scent is you," Helen said. "You are more than your sex, of course, but from now on, your body will have new importance. May it be a friend more than a betrayer."

Though it was hard to see her well underneath her makeup, I could see that her eyes glistened with tenderness.

"You may make wiser choices than I have," she went on, "and I hope you do. But it is better to act, even badly and in ways you regret, than to be afraid of life."

She stepped back and told Phylo and Alcippe to bring us our clothes. Mine was a new chiton of linen so sheer only the folds of cloth kept my nipples from being visible underneath it. Helen's robes were gold and purple, matching the ribbons Alcippe wove into her hair. Her neck, ears, and arms were heavy with gold jewelry. Phylo arranged the queen's garments after she sat down, and she finished by placing a diadem over Helen's coiled hair and slipping dainty shoes onto her fragile-looking feet.

The two of them helped me into my chiton and then excused themselves to go back to our quarters, leaving Helen and me alone.

"You're very quiet," she said. It was true. I had been standing like a statue, feeling the warmth of the unguent fading and trying to recall exactly how it had felt.

Helen interrupted my thoughts. "You were surprised when I touched you between your legs. I saw you tremble."

"What was that?" I couldn't think of any other way to ask.

Helen laughed. "The Gatekeeper, Aphrodite's Bower, the Kiss of Eros—women have many names for it. I heard someone call it the Tip of Zeus's Tongue, but that's probably a name you won't understand quite yet."

I was still overwhelmed and a little embarrassed to have been touched in that way, but I wanted to know more, wanted to touch the spot myself, wanted to know why it mattered to her to show it to me. I opened my mouth to say something—I'm not sure what— but before I could speak we were interrupted.

A woman stood at the threshold of the megaron. She was dressed in a chiton similar to mine but fastened in the middle with a cord of gold long enough to wrap around her body numerous times between her waist and the bottom of her breasts.

"I'm going tonight and you can't stop me," she said.

I knew immediately who it was, but I was so taken aback my jaw dropped. If I had never seen Hermione and I were asked to describe Helen's opposite, the description would be a perfect match.

She was tall and robust, a bit on the thin side, but otherwise rather masculine in appearance. Her hair was dark brown, and her face was long and large in the jaw. The kindest thing I can think to say about her physical appearance is that if she were a horse she would be the most attractive one in the stable. As Lacedaemon's sole princess, and Helen's only child, she was, to put it mildly, a disappointment.

Hermione came into the megaron. "Is this the little bitch you've brought in as my replacement?" she asked, tossing her head in my direction as she faced her mother.

The paint on Helen's face disguised most of her expression, but I could see her mouth contort.

"I warn you," she said, grabbing Hermione's upper arm and pulling her to within an inch or two of her face. "If you're planning to embarrass me, the shame will be yours. And Orthia will make you pay for spoiling her festival. I won't need to."

Hermione sniffed loudly and wrenched her arm away. She strode toward the door without a glance in my direction. Alcippe and Phylo were just at that moment coming into the room, and they jumped aside to avoid being pushed into the door frame as she passed.

For a moment I was so stunned by the interchange that I didn't notice how the two handmaidens were dressed. Then, as if a fog were lifting, I realized they were wearing clothing much like what I saw in my mother's chest back in Ithaca. Their skirts came to just above the ankle and were made of five or six overlapping layers in dark indigo, red, and saffron, from which dangled gold disks so thin they fluttered as they walked. An embroidered headband caught their hair off their forehead in the front, allowing huge gold loops to dangle free from their earlobes, while ribbons attached to the band cascaded over their shoulders.

Each wore an embroidered jacket tucked into a broad belt that reached up to cup their bare breasts, on which the nipples had been accented with dark pink ointment.

Much as Alcippe and Phylo enjoyed dressing up, that particular day was the only time I recall that they did not twirl in front of the queen or accept a brief reversal of roles and allow the queen to arrange their hair and rub her best oil into their arms and chests. Everyone seemed frozen in their tracks by Hermione's brief appearance.

"Well then," the queen said finally. "It's her right to go after all, to honor the goddess."

"I hate to see this happening to you, Jewel of the People," Phylo said in a voice so sad and low it was almost a whisper. Alcippe nodded, fighting back tears.

"Since it can't be helped, we make the best of it," Helen said in a tone that made it clear the subject was closed. "Put on your sandals, Eirene. We need to be off."

The first stop was the banquet hall, where the queen made an appearance to sit with her guests after everyone had finished eating. I had never before been in the grand megaron when it wasn't so loud I wanted to put my hands over my ears, but tonight the guests were a different group—not the servants who had made merry a few nights before, but the noblewomen who had remained behind in their rooms. Their faces were solemn, and the room was hushed with anticipation.

Alcippe, Phylo, and I stood as usual behind Helen and the empty seat that had been reserved for Hermione. Helen had recovered completely from the scene in her quarters, and with her usual grace, she poured a libation from the breasts of Orthia, after which the entire table finished whatever wine remained in their goblets.

Silent as an animal stalking its prey, and just as unexpected, Hermione came up and took her seat next to her mother. Her face was impassive to the point of total blankness, as if she had looked into a candle for too long and could see nothing except light swimming in front of her eyes.

Helen stood up. "My daughter, Hermione," she said in a tone of forced affection. An almost imperceptible change of expression flitted over Hermione's face as she stood up to be acknowledged. She sat down again with a heaviness devoid of grace, not bothering to glance at the assembled guests.

Helen stepped away from the table and went over to the hearth. Alcippe and I followed her, while Phylo carried a bowl of something that gave off a sweet and spicy fragrance I could not place. Phylo gave it to the queen and, turning to the crowd, announced in a loud voice, "The Jewel of the People! The Priestess of Orthia!"

The room held its breath. Helen turned to face the guests. "Night is upon us, the torches are lit, and we must prepare to leave for the sacred grove."

And then, without any preliminaries, Helen began to sing, not in a beautiful voice, but in a strange and captivating mix of cries of animals and songs of birds, a blend of amazement and awe, tinged with grief, and pain, and fear. She sang the praises of all the goddesses who protect women, asking them to accept as their newest devotees those who had recently had their first blood. When she had finished, Helen threw the mixture in Phylo's bowl into the fire, and the entire hearth erupted for a moment in a ball of blue and orange flame.

The only sound was a collective intake of breath, then silence again, dispelled after a moment by the sounds of benches scratching over the floor and the rustling of clothing as women got up from the banquet table and went out into the night.

Most of the guests at the banquet would go to the grove, but only the twenty initiates would be staying until morning, in the company of Helen and a few others. The rest would return to the palace with sentries waiting outside the grove for them.

In the courtyard, several dozen servants held torches as they stood at attention waiting to escort us to the sacred grove. Helen's sedan chair was ready, along with another one for Hermione. When the two were seated, they were lifted up and the procession began.

When we were outside the walls of the palace compound, Helen sang out another incantation to the goddesses, waving smoldering bunches of twigs covered with incense. Phylo and

Alcippe walked along opposite sides of Helen's chair shaking ivory rattles shaped like the capsules of opium poppies. Women in the procession sang hymns to the goddesses, verse after verse from memory.

Since there was nothing for me to do, I moved to the edge of the procession to look for Hermione's chair. Though her attitude toward everything was as sour and hard as unripe fruit, she had been born and raised in this fantastic place and had lived at least most of her childhood by Helen's side. Just that was enough to want to be near her.

I was curious, to be sure, but mostly just stubborn, both of which are attributes I have been told I possess in greater measure than is good for me. Even if Hermione rejected me, I would force her to do it to my face, so I would have at least the small victory of being acknowledged.

I drifted over to her chair. She was looking straight ahead, appearing not to notice me, though I'm sure she did. Although I was supposed to use my voice only for sacred things, I'm embarrassed to admit I had not yet made the transition to the proper state of mind.

"I'm not a usurper," I said. "I heard you call me that outside my door. And I'm not a bitch either." Hermione still didn't acknowledge me.

"I didn't ask to come here," I said. "I was sent."

Hermione's lip curled as she looked down at me. "Oh yes, tell me the story about the little Egyptian girl my mother fancied."

Her tone said she knew my identity as Eirene was a lie, but that was not the same as knowing the truth. Not sure what I was allowed to reveal, I shook my head and fell in walking silently beside her.

"Put me down," I heard her say.

The men lowered her chair to the ground. "Get in," she demanded.

The chair was large for one person, but not really meant for two, so I had to squeeze in beside her. The men picked up the chair and continued walking.

"I know who you are," she said in a voice too low to be overheard. "You're the daughter of Odysseus and Penelope. Your name is Xanthe."

"How did you know that?"

She sniffed. "I know everything that happens in the palace. If my mother passed gas, I would know if I wanted to."

"If you know so much, why did you say your mother sent for me?"

I could tell I had caught her by surprise, that it hadn't occurred to her that her assumption about me might be wrong. I wanted to tell her she didn't know as much as she thought she did, and that if anyone was a bitch it was her, but I didn't.

Hermione's expression closed again. "Because she did."

"You're wrong. My mother sent me away to keep me safe while my father was gone. He hasn't come back from Troy yet. He's the last one. Helen said she'd take me in."

She didn't respond, and for a while we rode in silence.

"Look," I said finally. "I'd just be happier if you stopped calling me names, that's all. And if you at least glanced at me when I was in a room. If you don't want to be any nicer than that, go ahead—it won't bother me—but you don't have any reason to be so rude."

She turned and in the torchlight I could see that her expression was interested, even quizzical.

I don't know where the boldness that swept over me came from, but I went on. "After all, you know the truth. I'm not a slave.

I'm a princess, just like you. I may be in disguise while I'm here, but I'm your equal, and you should treat me that way."

Foolish, foolish, foolish, I realize now as I look back on it. I should have seen that Hermione had the means to ruin my sanctuary in Sparta, to reduce my mother's efforts to ashes by exposing my story as a lie. I should have left well enough alone, but now it was too late. Hermione turned to me, responding in a tone so mixed with honey and bile that to this day I am still not sure what she was thinking.

"Well then," she said. "I see I've misjudged. Perhaps we should try to be friends."

We had come to the edge of the sacred grove, and the men carrying the chair could go no farther. Because we were near the back of the procession, Helen's chair had already been lowered to the ground and she had been helped to her feet. Helen was looking toward the entrance to the grove, but Alcippe and Phylo saw me in Hermione's chair and exchanged worried glances. I looked at Hermione, who was staring at them with an enigmatic smile.

Just then Helen turned toward us, but her painted face was so deep in shadow I could see nothing written on it. She beckoned me to join her in leading the procession, and without another word to Hermione, I followed the priestess queen into the grove.

CHAPTER 12

A Pulse of Black

The silver shafts narrow as they converge in the center, where Helen will take her place. To the blue background I added thick gold thread, contrasting it with white filament so fine I could send it aloft with my breath. After the night in the grove, I could never again see the mortal and the immortal as entirely separate, or look at Helen without seeing both a woman and a goddess. Helen was the force from which everything grand and wonderful about Sparta emanated. But in Sparta, another pulse also surged through the palace. Alongside the ripples of gold and white, black lurks, growing thicker and heavier as I near the center.

The torches made a snake of light as we walked down the path through the sacred grove. Soon we came to a clearing where earlier the servants had lit fires inside rings of stone. Empty standards for our torches had been placed in a circle, and soon we stood in a great pool of light in the middle of a vast, hovering darkness.

Helen sang more incantations while female musicians from the palace evoked from bone flutes melody after melody so strange they made my skin prickle. Some shook rattles and sistrums while others tapped out insistent patterns of sound on small, flat drums that rested against their shoulders. Dancers played hand cymbals and their anklets clattered as they twirled around the clearing, leaping into the air. Women sang soft nasal harmonies that shifted without warning into loud, repeated trills and cries. Alcippe found a sistrum for me, and I grasped the wooden handle, shaking the loose beads against the metal crossbars as I tried to follow along.

After some time, Phylo stepped into the middle of our circle. She beckoned the girls who were going to be initiated to join her. We all came forward, each holding a small votive figure, which we would give as an offering to the goddess. For the other girls, these statues in clay, stone, or wood were gifts from their mother, but mine was from the queen herself, carved from a piece of ivory small enough to cradle in my hand. It was in the shape of a girl with budding breasts, wearing nothing but a belt carved around her waist and a ribbon to hold back her hair. She was standing with her back arched like a strung bow, with one hand touching her forehead in devotion.

Phylo took us away from the golden light of the clearing, through trees so dense their black arms reached in to brush against us as we went down the narrow path. Soon we were in another, much smaller open space, lit by a single fire. On the far edge of the clearing was a hut that looked like a larger and sturdier version of my mother's shrine for Hera.

Phylo lined us up between the fire and the hut. I didn't so much as dart my eyes in the direction of the other girls, because the fear I thought I might see in their eyes would destroy my little remaining confidence.

"You will each go in alone to greet the goddess," Phylo said. "When you approach her, you will arch your back, close your right hand, touch your knuckles to your forehead, and say, 'Hail Orthia, I come to leave my girlhood at your feet. Grant that I may be worthy of you as a woman.' And then you will present your offering."

"Repeat it now." Phylo arched her back and pressed her hand to her forehead, and we all copied her, murmuring the invocation in dull, slow unison.

"You must remember the words," Phylo said. "It shows you are no longer a foolish and scatterbrained child."

Hail Orthia, I come to leave my girlhood at your feet. Grant that I may be worthy of you as a woman. I rehearsed the words over and over to myself as I stood with the other girls.

Phylo put her arm around one girl and brought her to the entrance. "Go," she said, giving her a gentle nudge between the shoulders.

After the girl disappeared inside, the silence was so total, I thought perhaps Orthia was going to gobble us up one by one. And then I heard a voice not really singing or talking, but somewhere in between. I couldn't say whether the voice was pleasant or unpleasant, only that it was so strange it made the hair stand up on my arms.

Soon afterward, the girl came out. Her hands were clasped over her mouth, and only her huge eyes were visible. She staggered the first few steps before righting herself and coming over to stand with us.

"What happened?" someone asked her.

Phylo shook her head and scowled at both of them. "No one speaks," she said.

When the second girl went through the door and the silence began again, the girl next to me whimpered. I didn't blame her.

After all, I was pressing my legs together and wishing I had thought to go into the woods to relieve myself while I still had time. Not long after, the girl rushed out in tears, and the whimperer was led in, shaking visibly. She came out as pale as her chiton and looking for a place to vomit.

And then it was my turn. I stepped through the door and was immediately assaulted by the acrid, unpleasant smell of whatever was burning in pots placed two or three to a wall around the room. Almost immediately, the fumes went to my head, making my head feel as if it were swirling up and away from the rest of my body. Through the thick haze of smoke I could see an altar illuminated by two oil lamps, one on each side of a statue about half the size of an adult woman.

I moved forward until I was face-to-face with the most terrifying image I had ever seen. A huge-eyed female carved in stone glared at me. Her nose dominated her face like a raven's beak, and her lips were parted, revealing a glimpse of sharp teeth. Her waist was cinched so tightly she was almost cut in two, and her crossed arms lifted her breasts as if her womanhood were a taunt.

"Say it," a hoarse voice whispered from behind me.

To this day I still wonder how I managed to remember the right way to stand, and to spill out the words without a mistake.

Once I had greeted the goddess, I came close enough to lay my little ivory statue at her feet. I stood staring for another moment, until I felt a presence at my back. I turned and saw a disembodied white face only a step behind me. I gasped in fear, but a moment later I saw it was a veiled woman dressed entirely in black, with only her face showing.

I recognized the disks on her cheeks and knew it was Helen. Who else could it be? She gave no indication that she knew who

I was, however, and in the dim light her eyes seemed glazed and unfocused.

"From the dark of the womb, women bring forth all life," she chanted. And then, without warning her voice went shooting up from a low growl, climbing higher and higher until it gave out in a crackling hiss of air.

She sang a few wild phrases to Orthia with words that made no sense, before she stopped for a moment and intoned the rest in a husky but more recognizable voice. "Here in Orthia's shrine, you leave behind the ignorance of childhood, returning to the womb to be reborn a woman."

She took me to a corner where a dozen or more figurines were grouped around a krater full of wine. Helen filled a goblet and ordered me to drink it all.

The wine was uncut with water, but the intense flavor could not entirely mask the bitterness of whatever had been dissolved in it. I gagged at having to take it in so quickly, but I finished every drop.

Afterward, Helen led me back to the statue of Orthia, standing me next to a small bowl. She lifted my hand palm up and stroked it. Before I could realize what she was doing, she had taken a small knife and made a shallow cut on one of my fingers. She pressed the cut to force drops of blood to fall into the bowl, squeezing so hard it hurt more than the wound itself.

"Revered Orthia," Helen said, "this virgin's first blood has already been shed, and we offer this token of it in your honor. May you be satisfied with this sacrifice, and not suffer any god or man to demand more."

She turned to me, still without a glimmer of recognition. "You may go."

I walked out of the shrine into the cold night air. The other girls cocked their heads to one side and leaned forward with curiosity. I could see by their expressions that they were looking for signs of horror on my face, but though my head was pounding from the fumes, I felt utterly calm inside.

I lifted my head skyward. The treetops were brushing the face of the full moon. The stars swirled and danced against the blueblack of night. A laugh erupted in my chest and flowed up through the taut muscles of my outstretched throat. I lifted my arms and began to spin, stopping only when someone caught me to keep me from falling, or perhaps from floating away.

When the last of the girls had visited the shrine, we took our lanterns and headed back to the main clearing. Phylo brought up the rear, urging the line of initiates forward. In front of me, one of them stopped to stare open-mouthed at a tree, moving her head as if she were following some unseen force traveling through it. I noted this with complete detachment, as if the girls I had just stood with at the shrine were apparitions no more substantial than the spiderwebs that appeared overnight in the eaves of the palace.

I turned to walk again and entered a tunnel of trees that shimmered in oily shades of green and blue, giving way to red and gold as I came nearer the clearing. I stepped into the light, and the aroma of roasting meat found my nostrils. I stopped to examine the smell in a way I never had before, unable to decide whether it was pleasant or foul, and not caring either way. The odor of the meat was a force, drifting outward, just as I was, to mingle with everything else in the universe.

Dark shapes in the firelight changed form and became the women we left behind. They cheered as we came into the clearing, and I felt such great love for them, and for the spirits of fire and trees, and for the circle of torches that enclosed us in the night, that I wanted to cry and laugh at the same time.

The women began to sing, and somehow I just knew the song, knew it in my bones, felt it surge from my scalp to my fingertips. I sent each note out as if I were a wellspring, sending out only what was good and perfect into the world around me.

When I opened my eyes, Helen was seated on her throne. She must have taken another path through the woods, but at the time I was convinced she had the power of a goddess to materialize from nowhere.

She had changed back into the purple robes she had worn for the procession to the grove. She held a tall, thick staff gleaming with gold and topped with stones that glittered in the light of the oil lamps arrayed at her feet. She raised her hand, and one by one we noticed and came to attention.

"Mothers," she said, "your daughters are now women. You have honored the goddess by bringing them to her, but now it is time for you to leave them for the night."

Each woman embraced her daughter. For one painful moment I was left standing alone, until one of the women saw me and took me in her arms without saying a word. Then the mothers left the circle of light, their song drifting up through the black treetops as they disappeared down the path. Other than the initiates, only Helen and her daughter, Phylo and Alcippe, and the musicians were left behind. The musicians' dizzying swirls of sound, which I had found disorienting before my visit to the shrine, made perfect sense to me now as they wafted through the clearing and floated to the heavens. Perhaps the music was the same as before, and only my way of hearing it had changed, but now it sounded like rainfall, a hissing stream, the crackle of new wood on a fire, and waves breaking onto sand, all merging into one as if the world itself were taking a breath.

And then we began to dance. At first we held hands and moved in a circle around a woman playing a lyre, but eventually some of the initiates spun out on their own, and some turned to each other, forming tents with their outstretched fingertips as they swayed.

Phylo took my hand. "Shut your eyes," she whispered. When I did, playing on my eyelids was a vision of Orthia. She had sprouted wings, and I felt the caress of her feathers from my shoulders to my calves.

Perhaps the sensation of the goddess had been the cloth slipping from my body, for when I opened my eyes, I was naked. In the firelight I stared down at my body as if I were seeing it for the first time. Those breasts were mine, part of me. The protruding stomach of my childhood was gone, flattened and contracted into a slender waist that gave way to round hips centered with a triangle of lush dark hair. Before tonight I had seen my naked body as something to wash, reclothe, and ignore, but now I saw the magic in it, saw how Hera and Orthia had been moving secretly inside me to shape me into a woman.

Phylo turned toward me, her eyes like dark pools. She moved her face nearer to mine, tipping it to one side and kissing me on the lips. For a moment I wanted to pull back, but something inside me said to let it happen.

She bent at the waist and brushed each of my nipples with her mouth. A strange feeling came over me in the spot Helen had touched earlier that day. I couldn't resist the urge to put my own hand there, and when I did, Phylo smiled. Placing her fingers over mine, she guided them until I needed to reach out and hang on to her shoulders to keep my knees from buckling.

For a moment I wanted her to stop, mistaking the feeling for that of an urgent need to pass water. And then I could not have stopped if I wanted to. I felt my own wetness cover my fingers as what seemed on the verge of excruciating pain gave way to ripples of such intense delight I moaned aloud. My whole body shuddered, and when it was finally over I realized I was slick with sweat.

"What was that?" I whispered.

"This is a night of mysteries," Phylo said. "The goddess visits us in many ways."

She looked up and I followed her gaze to Helen, who was smiling at me.

"Come," Phylo said. "I need to tend to the queen."

As I approached Helen, I suddenly felt very tired.

"Sit at my feet," she said. "Rest your head on my lap."

She threw a blanket over me and began stroking my hair. "Were you afraid?" she asked.

"Afraid of what?"

"Of meeting Orthia in the shrine."

I had forgotten all about it, so much had happened since.

"No," I said, stifling a yawn.

"I didn't think so." She paused for a moment. "Did you know it was me?"

"Yes."

With my head resting on her lap, I couldn't see her face, but I knew she was smiling. "Only a few girls understand that the power of the goddess is something to rejoice in, not fear," she said. "I saw that you were one of those few."

I wouldn't have called my experience in the hut joyful, but I thought I understood a little of what she was saying. I had briefly inhabited another realm, and it had felt like a home I vaguely re-membered and wanted to visit again. I rubbed my fingers together, feeling the tiny crack in my flesh where Helen had cut me. Though it was a little sore, and I was glad my initiation was over, I put that finger to my lips and kissed it.

I slept at Helen's feet for a little while, but she nudged me awake so I wouldn't miss any more of the festival. She wet a finger and touched it to a powder in a small vial of hollow bone dangling from a gold cord around her neck. "Open your mouth," she said. When I complied, she put her finger on my tongue and gave me a sip of watered wine to rid my mouth of the bitter taste.

"It's a little more of what was in your goblet inside the shrine," she said. "It helps you know the mysteries." I saw Phylo and Alcippe passing among the naked initiates with their own vials of powder, touching the tongues of anyone who came to them with open mouth.

A sudden urge to be with the other women came over me, and I pulled myself away from the refuge of Helen's body and stood up. The blanket fell away, and I felt the tingle of the midsummer night on my skin. I took a few steps toward the fire, but my attention was drawn away somehow to the shadows just outside the glow of lamps around Helen's throne.

For a moment I thought it was the statue of Orthia, grown large as life, as feral and menacing as when I had first laid eyes on her in the shrine. And then the figure moved toward me.

Hermione. I had forgotten she was there. Her eyes glinted as she came out of the shadows. The corners of her lips curled up as she held out her hand.

"Sister," she said, leading me into the firelight and the dance.

* * *

Just before first light, at the moment when the shapes of the world first start to reveal themselves, we put on our chitons and doused the torches. Helen poured a final libation and said the last words of the rite, after which we went down the path out of the grove.

Our clothes were filthy from having been on the ground most of the night, our hair was wild and tangled, and our eyes were red. My thirst was so ferocious I think I would have dropped to the ground and lapped like a dog if I had seen a puddle.

I stayed so close to the queen's chair that if I had crowded in any more I would have tangled with Phylo and Alcippe's feet. I did not drift off to find Hermione as I had the night before, and in fact I did everything I could to keep a safe distance.

I can't say she had done anything out of the ordinary when we danced—strange as the ordinary was that night—but as the new dose of the drug had its effect on me, her body filled out and her face changed form until a wolf looked out at me with yellow, predatory eyes. As we danced she kept her gaze locked on me, and suddenly I found myself running away through the dark woods, just to escape her stare.

Within what seemed like only a few steps, I found myself on the banks of the river. I felt the cool, damp soil under my feet as I gulped air to calm the pounding in my chest. I heard the crack of twigs behind me, and for a moment I thought about jumping into the water to get away from the creature I was sure was bearing down to rip out my throat.

Phylo and Alcippe had come after me, their faces pale and their breath coming hard.

"We saw you run away," Alcippe said in a voice so high it almost didn't come out at all.

"Never do that," Phylo said. "Never leave the clearing alone.

The queen forbids it." She immediately started back, and I followed behind her in the moonlight.

"I was afraid," I said to Phylo's back as we trod along a path of broken reeds. "That's why I ran."

"The drug can do that," she replied. After a moment she added, "Did Hermione say something to you?"

Alcippe was behind me. "We saw her dancing with you and then—"

My frightened run and the clear air by the river had cleared my mind of the effects of the drug, and I felt foolish. Hermione was a person, not a wolf, and earlier that evening she had talked about being friends. I didn't want to jeopardize that over something that existed only in my imagination.

"She called me *sister*," I said. We were by now standing side by side at the edge of the clearing, and I could see them exchange looks.

"I know she isn't," I said, annoyed that they might think I was that stupid. "I was hoping maybe she wished she was. That maybe that might make things—" I thought for a moment. "That it might make things better in the palace."

"It won't," Phylo said, and then realizing how abrupt she had sounded, she went on. "I mean, it's not my place to speak ill of the queen's daughter, but—" Her brow furrowed as she exhaled. "I've said more than I should already." Her voice trailed off as she took a step forward.

I grabbed her arm. "But what?" I demanded.

Phylo looked at Alcippe and then back at me before pulling her arm free to make clear that the conversation was over.

We slept most of the day when we returned to the palace, and when we woke up, it seemed as if nothing at all was different. Phylo made no comment about what had gone on between us when we danced. Hermione disappeared into her quarters again, and for a long time I saw little of her. Menelaus returned from his hunt, the men collected their wives and daughters and left for home, and the palace settled back into its routine.

My daily life was full enough without a thought about the unhappy woman at the other end of the building. In the first few months of my stay in Sparta, my life revolved around the two megarons, one in my quarters and one in the queen's, where I spent much of my time. On a typical day, I rose and ate my breakfast with Adreste, and then sat with my handwork until Helen called for me. Adreste was usually the only one in our quarters by the time I woke up, because Alcippe and Phylo were responsible for getting the queen prepared for her day.

Roughly one morning out of three, Helen was required to go down to sit beside Menelaus to receive guests, but the rest of the time she remained in her chambers. On those days she almost always called for me. I usually wove with her until the midday meal, after which she took a nap, and I went to my quarters to lie down as well. When I awoke I returned to Helen's chambers with Phylo and Alcippe to see what the queen's wishes were for the remainder of the day. In good summer weather, and on days the queen had no banquet to attend in the evening, she might go out with one or more of us to visit a palace workshop or perhaps take a chariot ride into the countryside to look at the progress of the crops in the vineyards and orchards.

On the days Menelaus entertained guests, Helen stayed in all afternoon. Preparing to go down to the grand megaron took much of that time. After we tended to the queen, all of us except Adreste, who rarely went downstairs at all, oiled our skin and brushed our hair until it shone, before pinning it up in graceful waves. Our chitons had to be well oiled and perfectly draped, for she wanted not just her own entrance but also ours to suggest that the guests were experiencing the closest thing to a visit by the gods that mortals were likely to have.

Though we all knew my true identity, and I was not obliged to serve Helen in the ways Phylo and Alcippe were, the distinction became more blurred as time passed. I loved playing with the queen's hair and helping paint her cheeks. Helen, for her part, treated us all more like cherished companions than servants. The only time I ever felt odd about my role was when we went downstairs to greet Menelaus' guests after they had finished their meal and the bard had begun to play. It was strange to stand behind the queen as her maidservant when, if circumstances were different, I would be treated more like a daughter.

The only royal child ever to sit at the table was Menelaus' son, Megapenthes. He was a brute, at least in my estimation, rather like I imagined Antinous had been at my brother's age. He had been born to Menelaus by an Aetolian slave named Getis, when Helen had been unable to conceive again after Hermione's birth. If my wishes were all it took to make something come to pass, Helen would have both me and Hermione by her side. Instead she had neither, and was forced to suffer the indignation of watching a child her husband had sired by someone else grow up as the prince of the realm.

I'd like to think Helen's moments of unhappiness were fleeting. After all, she spent most of her time among people who genuinely cared about her and honored her in the way she deserved. Her quarters were a cocoon against the rest of the world, no more so than when the cold winds of winter drove everyone indoors.

My first winter in Sparta was the harshest in recent memory. I used the time to absorb from Helen everything she could teach me. My mother was an exceptional weaver, but she had little to work with compared to the vast stores of dyes, threads, sequins, and beads Helen used to make clothing for herself, Menelaus, and Megapenthes. To show off the beautiful borders of her cloth, Helen usually wore a short peplos over her chiton, and we worked together to create trims that were each more elaborate and colorful than the one before.

Helen was skilled at many things other than weaving. She learned from women in Egypt how to cast spells, and she had a chest where she kept dried plants and other substances she needed to make potions and cures for ailments. From her stores she supplied the festival of Orthia, and from time to time she drugged the wine at banquets when the guests had grown morose or sullen about the disasters men manage to create for themselves.

The chest itself seemed magical to me, with its neatly lined-up boxes and jars filled with drugs, and its pouches covered with strange embroidered symbols. Inside each was a colorful powder, or a sticky paste, or perhaps a small chunk of something, or a few dried twigs and leaves. These had such power to change the world, or at least one's perception of it, that whenever she opened the chest I held my breath in case some kind of battle between them had taken place inside. After a while, the orderliness of the chest was part of the magic for me, since I was sure only some great power could keep everything looking exactly as it was when she last closed the lid.

Helen seemed relieved to have someone with whom to share her knowledge, as if it were a secret she had despaired of an opportunity to pass down. I was thrilled, of course, to be taken into her confidence. When the anniversary of my arrival in Sparta neared and we all began to think about the next Orthia festival, I nearly toppled at Helen's feet with happiness when she asked if I wanted to begin training as her assistant.

Over the course of the next month, I visited the shrine privately with Helen several times, seeing in daylight the statue of Orthia, which looked quite benign without the smoke and invocations that brought the goddess to inhabit her effigy. We offered her small cakes and poured many libations as we lined up the smaller votive images, cleaned the altar, and made all the other preparations for the ceremony.

Although I wanted to be inside the shrine to share in the mysteries of the initiation, some things Orthia wished only her priestess to know. I would help light the lamps and lay out the items Helen would need, and then I would stay outside helping to coax reluctant girls through the door. Helen wouldn't, and indeed couldn't tell me any of the real secrets of the rite, because she herself didn't know what to say until the fumes possessed her and afterward could not remember most of her words.

Still she had much to tell me about the ceremony. The drugged wine induced each girl not to resist letting her childhood slip away. In its place, her womanhood entered and took up residence. The cut was something Helen flinched at, but compared to the bloody sacrifices of virgins that still happened some places, the price of a nicked finger was a small one.

"And the last thing I say is something I added myself," she told me. "I ask Orthia to be satisfied with a few drops of blood and defend against any woman being further victimized—by god or man."

I thought she was busying herself with something, but when I looked up I saw her staring at me.

"I saw you run away from Hermione at the festival," she said. "It was I who sent Alcippe and Phylo to get you. I nearly ran after you myself."

"I'm sorry I broke your rule," I said. "I didn't know you had one."

"Come outside," she said.

We walked down the path toward the river, and when we were at its bank, Helen stopped. "Things change so much here, and it was night anyway so I'm not sure where it happened."

"Where what happened?"

Her smile was pained and wistful. "What might have happened to you."

"Nothing happened to me." My patience has always been short for those who play around with the answers to my questions, even when the one doing it is the Queen of Sparta. My reply came out sharper than I intended, and I was glad she ignored my tone.

"The night of my own initiation I wandered off, just as you did. An old man—a king used to getting his own way—saw me, and before anyone could rescue me, he threw me down on the reeds and raped me."

She swallowed hard, and her chest filled slowly with a deep in-take of air. "I was eleven years old. My father married me off little more than a year later."

Her eyes followed two waterfowl coming in for a landing on the opposite bank. A frog jumped away from them into the safety of the water.

"You mother sent you here for protection," she said. "I won't let happen to you here what she wanted to avoid there."

She scanned the banks again. "I've never really been comfortable here after that night," she said with a shudder, as she took my arm to head up the path.

We rode back in the chariot that had been waiting for us outside the grove. At first we tried to make conversation, but silence was easier after such a revelation.

When we arrived at the palace we both went to our rooms to lie down. Sleep eluded me, and I got up and went to the outer doors of Helen's quarters, where a servant was always stationed. This time it was a girl of about eight or nine who had fallen asleep in her chair. She woke with a start at the sound of my voice.

"What if the queen was in trouble?" I demanded. "What if someone came here to hurt her while you were asleep?" The girl looked confused. All the posted servants ever had to do was come to our quarters to say that the queen wanted one of us. I wasn't really angry with her—after all, what job could be duller?—but I was still reeling from the story Helen had told me. I shooed the girl away and sat down in her chair.

I had never stood watch outside the queen's chamber before, though Phylo and Alcippe, and even Adreste, often did. It was beneath a princess, I suppose we all assumed.

I don't know why I wanted to sit there. We all know we can't fix the past, but I suppose it was the only way I could think of to say how much I wished I could. I waited outside her room until the afternoon shadows were deep, wanting nothing more than to please her by being there when she awoke.

CHAPTER 13

As False as Brown

Blue and yellow make green. Red and yellow make orange. Red and blue make purple. I twined different colors of thread together in every possible combination and wove them as tightly as I could into a circle at the center of the fabric. Step back across the room, and the eye participates in the falsehood. "That looks like brown," it says, when in fact there is no brown at all.

I bring my face close to the loom and see all the individual colors again. But knowing something isn't true is far different from understanding what is. Perhaps in the future I may be harder to deceive than I was then, when I thought everything was what it appeared to be, and the unpleasant hardness of life could be thrown away by choice, like a pit tossed from a fruit, leaving sweetness to linger on the tongue.

By late summer I was well into my second year in Sparta, and Apollo's rays had once again baked the landscape, ripened the crops in the orchards and robbed the trees of their deepest shades of green.

The Orthia festival was long over. A new group of girls had waited outside the shrine clutching their votive figures and had emerged in much the same condition my group had. Afterward, I helped them back along the path as they pondered for the first time the world Helen's drugs revealed to them.

Orthia's mysteries were not to be taken lightly, and though I shared daily life with Helen and Phylo, neither of them ever touched me again. Some things are meant to be experienced once, and then remembered forever. Since my initiation, I had continued private exploration of my body, but at my second festival I was still not ready to do to another initiate what Phylo had done to me. Only the power of the gods can take over my whole body in the way that particular kind of touch does, and I needed to experience the gods more fully myself before I could be their emissary for others. The whole night of the festival I felt Orthia's presence, and spending the night alongside Alcippe and Phylo, holding my own little pouch of drugs to place on outstretched tongues, was ecstasy enough.

In the summer, the whole palace was driven indoors by the heat, until late-afternoon clouds brought wisps of breeze and, from time to time, the blessing of a thundershower. Usually the women in the queen's wing rested through the hottest part of the day, but no one sat down to take a breath in the days before Helen and Menelaus departed for a wedding in Argos.

Preparing someone as famous as Helen to go out and make an impression on the world bought everyone close to panic. Any imperfection—a snag in a veil, a loose chip of stone in a brooch, a mislaid slipper, a shortage of a particular unguent—sent Phylo and Alcippe into a whirl of glares and recriminations, indignant huffs, and often, at least in Alcippe's case, tearful exits.

Adreste always remained calm and, if anything, bemused by the whole endeavor. She and I spent many mornings trying to stay out of Phylo and Alcippe's way, going through chest after chest of Helen's belongings, unwrapping diadems, necklaces, earrings, and hair combs, and shaking out her collection of robes and veils to hold them up to view.

If it hadn't been so hot I might remember those days I spent parading around in Helen's finery as one of the best times in my years in Sparta. As it was, I spent most mornings naked and slick with perspiration because the queen preferred to remain cool sitting on her throne, while I put on her clothing and jewelry to show her how it looked. For fear of staining a veil or passing out in the heat of a thick robe, I could wear most things only for the time it took to breathe once or twice. As a result, what started out as an amusing game of pretend became a nightmare as I stood on my feet until they ached, trying on each thing in every imaginable combination.

For all my effort, I would not have the reward of going with her. Weddings brought guests from far-off places, and we couldn't risk the possibility that I would be recognized. Only Alcippe and Phylo would attend Helen in Argos, leaving Adreste and me behind.

As the day of Helen's departure neared, Adreste's mouth locked into a little smile at the prospect of time to herself. I suppose I must have looked and sounded much the same, for as much as I would have liked to be part of the grand procession headed for Argos, I wanted calm and quiet more than anything.

I wouldn't have to work myself to a faint over the next ten days, as Alcippe and Phylo would. Even in her thirties, Helen wanted—

no, needed—her beauty to remain unmatched, but I could see the beginnings of fear in her eyes. She knew the day would come when people would not understand why she had been worth a war, and it was up to Alcippe and Phylo to make sure that day did not arrive in Argos.

A little rest from it all sounded better than any excitement I might have as part of Helen's entourage. And besides, plenty of adventures awaited me in Sparta, once the queen was not there to take up so much of my time. We rarely went anywhere without a specific duty to perform, and since my arrival I had never ventured out into the countryside just to be close to the beauty I marveled at from a distance. I was determined to make full use of the time Helen was gone, though I wasn't sure exactly how I would manage to do so.

My answer seemed to come in the form of the shadowy figure I saw observing the king and queen's departure from a watchtower above the palace. When Hermione emerged in the courtyard soon after, she did not go in the direction of her quarters, and once she was out of sight I raced up the same stairs to see where she was going.

The stables were close enough to the palace that I could see how she opened the gate with the efficiency of someone who had done it many times before. Two men came over to speak with her, and after a few moments, they went off in different directions. They came back into my view at the same time, one pulling a small chariot, and the other leading a pair of horses.

Hermione had gone to one side of the stable yard. She shaded her eyes as she looked down the road her parents had taken, but I knew from my vantage point there was already nothing to see.

When the horses had been harnessed to the chariot, she took a whip from the groom, came to the rear, and stepped aboard alone.

I watched as she went out through the stable gates and guided the horses down the path to the main road. Soon she was little more than a speck, but I saw how she turned in the opposite direction to the one Menelaus and Helen had taken, before taking off with such a burst of speed that all I could see was the cloud of dust she left behind.

I made my way down the stairs and back to my quarters. Adreste had already headed off to bed, but I was too perplexed by what I had just seen to be able to lie still, even with the exhaustion of the last few days weighing upon me. I sat with my handwork in our megaron, listening to Adreste snore and waiting for her to wake up and pull back her curtain.

Finally she did. "Quiet!" she said, looking around with a wicked grin. "We should pour a libation."

She was hungry, and I went to find a servant who could bring us something to eat. By the time I got back inside, she was seated in her chair, and though her eyes were closed, her upturned lips said her whole being was smiling.

I sat down near her and picked up my work. "Hermione took off in a chariot," I said, hoping my bluntness might catch the old woman by surprise.

Adreste opened her eyes, but her face was calm. "Where did she go?"

"I don't know. Isn't she supposed to stay inside?

Adreste shrugged. "She isn't a prisoner. The queen doesn't force her to stay in her quarters."

I knew as much. Hermione moved more freely about the palace than I first realized. Many times when Helen didn't need me, I went to the balcony to look out over the grand courtyard, and on a number of occasions I saw Hermione and her maids heading to and from the stairs leading to our wing. In the winter, she spent afternoons in a secluded courtyard at the bottom of a staircase just off her quarters, warming herself in the thin sunlight as she worked on a hand loom.

Still, Hermione did far more that morning than just leave her room. I was annoyed that Adreste was treating a woman riding off by herself as scarcely worth commenting on, while to me it was one of the most unusual things I had witnessed in Sparta.

"Where did she learn to drive a chariot?" I asked.

"It must have been in Mycenae," Adreste said. She thought for a moment, and her face softened. "She's always loved horses. I remember how happy she was when Helen took her riding."

"Helen can ride a horse?"

"She's excellent at it—or used to be. She doesn't ride anymore."

I didn't respond, hoping Adreste would go on. When she did, her voice sounded far away.

"There used to be a child inside Helen—a rather wild one, even after Hermione was born. She was so young when she had her—younger than you, I think—and since her father and mother had given her everything she wanted, Helen thought being queen meant getting her own way and doing whatever she pleased. She wasn't ready to be either a mother or a wife."

I half expected Phylo to burst through the door and tell Adreste to stop telling tales, but the room remained quiet. "Since she came back from Troy, she's been different. Sometimes I think she feels older than I am, with all her burdens."

Adreste picked up her work and said nothing more. I stifled my urge to demand answers, reminding myself I had many days alone with her to find out more.

After I had worked on my own hand weaving for a while, I broke the silence. "If I used the time we're here by ourselves to try to make friends with Hermione, do you think the queen would mind?"

I wish I could say my goal was loftier, but what I most wanted at that moment was a ride in the chariot.

"What makes you think Hermione would want that?" Adreste asked.

The wind, which in my imagination was already whipping my hair as I flew down the road, died with her comment.

"No reason," I admitted. "She probably wouldn't."

Adreste shook her head. "I think she would. I've known both Helen and Hermione since they were babies. They've each had too much to bear to remain the way they were."

Her eyes grew distant. "Hermione was a sweet child," she went on. "So fond of everyone. She'd pick flowers and hold them in her hands while she told stories. 'Here I am kissing my daddy,' she'd say. Or, 'Here's me and Maia coming to a banquet and everyone is clapping because we're so pretty.'"

By now Adreste was wiping her eyes. "Such a shame," she said. "We used to call her our little golden girl. It broke the queen's heart when Hermione came back from Mycenae so bitter."

She thought for a moment. "I don't think the queen would mind at all if you tried to make friends with her daughter. It's more likely to do good than harm. The only thing that would hurt Helen is if you lost any of your loyalty to her because of anything Hermione said."

"I would never do anything to hurt the queen," I said, my voice so choked I could barely get out the words.

"Well then," Adreste said with a quizzical look. "Suppose we see what Hermione has to say."

By the time the afternoon was over, Adreste had arranged for a private dinner with Hermione in her quarters. By making no other preparations than to smooth my hair and adjust the folds of my chiton, I convinced myself I was calm, but my knees felt weak as I went down the corridor.

A young slave girl jumped up when I came into view, and she slipped through a crack in the door without saying a word. Soon she came out, opening it a little wider for me. "The princess is ready," she said, before sitting down again.

Hermione's chambers were like all the others in the palace, arranged around a megaron onto which a sleeping chamber and several other smaller rooms opened. The round hearth in the center of the room was unlit, but several torches hanging from fixtures on the wall provided enough light for a warm summer evening.

Hermione was already seated at the table eating a piece of cheese. "I haven't eaten today, and I was too hungry to wait." She did not get up, but instead motioned me to sit down. "Adreste said you wanted to talk to me."

No greeting, no ritual, no time to adjust. Was I immediately expected to have words flowing, without so much as an offer of wine and food? Not wishing to appear annoyed, but at the same time wanting her to know I thought she was rude, I took a piece of cheese and chewed it slowly. I hoped she understood my meaning—that I was assuming real conversation would not start until the proper time, after we had had our fill and the wine had loosened our tongues. And mine certainly needed loosening, as I was unnerved enough to have forgotten why I had come.

Hermione's hair flowed down her back, and she had taken a bath to remove the dirt of the road. I had formed the impression that she was physically unappealing, with her gangly limbs and long face, but seated and relaxed in her own chambers she seemed, under the golden light of the torches, to have her own kind of radiance. Hermione was not physically beautiful even in the most flattering of settings, but she had inherited from her mother the same powerful sense of her own presence.

"Were you afraid my mother would be angry if you spoke to me?" she asked after I had finished a little more of my meal. "Is that why you waited for her to be gone?" Though I heard the hint of accusation in her voice, her tone was far short of the snarl I had braced for.

I locked my eyes on her in what I hoped was a commanding fashion and deliberately did not answer her question. "I saw you in your chariot today."

She blinked, before shrugging and composing her expression. "And how could you have seen that? Unless of course you were spying on me. Is that what you're doing now too?"

She poured each of us a little more wine. "Tell me, Xanthe, daughter of Odysseus and Penelope, just exactly what you want by coming to share my dinner with me tonight."

Intimidation and anger battled in me for a moment before anger won out. "Look," I said. "If you just want to sit in your room and hate everybody, no one's going to stop you. In case you haven't noticed, you make pretty poor company. And if you just love being alone while you ride around in your chariot, do it."

I was so angry I had already stood up to leave. "I didn't come here tonight for any other reason than to tell you that if you wanted company next time you went out, I'd like to go. But I think I have my answer. And I think now I have other things I'd rather do."

I was already near the door when Hermione called me back. I whirled around, half expecting to see the last traces of a wolf vanishing from her face. Instead I saw the same curious smile she had given me in her sedan chair when she said we should try to be friends.

Perhaps this time she meant it.

"I'll send my servant for you tomorrow," she said. "Be ready after breakfast."

The dirt chewed up by the horses' hooves coated my lips with grit, and my eyes made wet streams across my face from the air ripping across it. Hermione's chariot was smaller and lighter than the one that had brought me from Pylos, and it bounced so violently I had no choice but to hang on with both hands. Hermione kept her balance with only the strength of her legs as she used her whip to urge the horses on.

We hurtled down a road that ran along the Eurotas River, then across a stone bridge and up a hill, where we stopped at a spring to water the animals and let them enjoy the patch of tender grass around a small pool of water.

"Are you all right?" Hermione asked.

I looked down at my chiton, which was now light brown from the dirt, and at the skin of my arms and chest, where the oil from last night's bath had captured dirt in what looked like a mass of black freckles. "I wasn't expecting anything quite so—"

"Fast?" I had never before heard Hermione laugh with what sounded like genuine happiness.

"Exciting," I said, wanting to deny her the pleasure of knowing how scared I had been. "How did you learn to drive like that?"

Hermione tied the reins to a bush and went across the road

to look out over the valley. "From my cousins in Mycenae. All the girls drove—and rode horseback too."

She sat down on a rock and picked a stone from her sandal. "If I go farther I have to take a guard with me, so most of the time I just stay here for a while and go back to the palace."

I pitied the poor soul who would be foolish enough to bother her even far from home, and although I wished I felt comfortable enough to tease her by saying so, I didn't. "Adreste told me you used to ride with your mother," I said.

Hermione's face hardened, and I wished I could take back my words. "I don't want to talk about my mother," she said. "That has to be a rule if you go out with me." With the tip of my sandal, I pushed around a few leaves, but said nothing. "Well, do you agree?" she demanded.

"No," I said. "You don't have to talk to me today, but there are things I want to know, and I'm not saying I won't ask them."

"Like what?" Hermione had been picking up pebbles, and she stood up with a fistful. "Like why I hate her so much?"

I picked up some of my own and stood next to her. "Do they teach girls how to throw rocks in Mycenae?" I threw one, not very well, but better than when I was a child in the olive grove.

"Who needs a teacher for that?" she sneered. "I just find myself wanting to throw things when I start thinking about—" She tossed a stone in a high arc, and her eyes followed it. "—You know."

I cocked back my arm and flung another stone as far up as my strength would let me, losing sight of it for a moment against the looming gray of the Taygetos Mountains on the other side of the valley. How good it felt to throw something away—like banishing an unwanted thought from the mind.

"I think if I stood here long enough, and there were enough

rocks, I could get rid of every one of my problems," I said. "I'd just toss them downhill one at a time."

"They must be simple problems," Hermione sneered.

"Not at all. To start with, I have a brother who *does* need a teacher to learn how to throw a rock. And he's going to be king of Ithaca someday."

"Well, that's something we have in common," Hermione sniffed. "A ridiculous brother."

"This is my last rock," I said. "I'm going to try to hit that bush." My throw broke an outer leaf off my target, and we both cheered my victory.

Our hands were empty now, and we stood facing each other.

"I know we're different in a lot of ways," I said, "but you must remember what it's like to want your mother back." Suddenly I felt tears spring to my eyes. "You have to remember wishing things would be normal again and you could go home. Maybe all that changed for you, but you must have memories of what it felt like then."

Hermione's eyes glittered as the sunlight caught them. She didn't have to say anything. I knew that she recalled perfectly, and that it hurt.

I laced my fingers in my hair, and looked at the sky, a habit I had gotten from my mother to help steady my thoughts. "You're not the only one with a hard story," I said, lowering my gaze to meet her eyes. "Before I left, my mother told me not to give in to hate, because I'd be the one who got hurt by it, and it wouldn't change anything anyway."

"That's what my mother says too," Hermione replied. "I don't know why I can't stop. I just know I can't."

We stood looking out over the valley. Dark shadows of clouds streaked over the fields. Beyond them the Taygetos Mountains were dappled with sunlight. Hawks drifted upward on drafts of air and circled out toward the green meander of the river. Near my feet a lizard pumped its body up and down on skinny legs before scurrying off. Songbirds trilled in the bushes, and the horses nickered softly as they buried their noses in the crystalline water of the spring.

"The horses need feeding," Hermione said. "We should get back."

Adreste was waiting by the meal she had laid for me in our quarters, and when I came to the door, she got up on her bent little body to greet me.

"Zeus, you're filthy," she said, clucking at the coat of grime on my skin and chiton. "I'll call for your bath."

After Adreste had given the orders to a servant passing in the hallway, she came back inside and shut the door. "How was the ride?" she asked conspiratorially.

"We went up to a lookout over the valley," I said, pouring water from a pitcher over my hands and watching the dirt flow off into the basin below. "The horses went so fast they nearly scared me to death."

Hermione had disappeared into her quarters when we returned, without so much as a comment, and though I knew Adreste wanted more, I didn't know what else to say.

And I have to admit I enjoyed toying with her, watching her wrinkled neck crane toward me in anticipation as I chewed silently on a fig. I took the stem out of my mouth with great deliberation and examined it as if there were actually something to see. "And we talked."

The skin from Adreste's eyelids made permanent hoods over

her eyes, and wrinkles carved deep furrows out to her hairline, but when she was happy, her delight was as evident as on the face of a child. "And how was—how did Hermione treat you?"

"Fine," I said in an offhand way, as if I couldn't imagine what she meant. But I was already weary of making her wait. "We threw rocks and talked, but not about much of anything. Mycenae, horses—that's about all."

"About her mother?"

I took a sip of watered wine. "Not except to say she can't stop hating her. But I got the feeling she wishes maybe she could. Stop, I mean, at least a little."

Adreste's pleasure was obvious. "And are you going out again?"

"I don't know. I think she liked having me, but she didn't say so."

"Well," Adreste said, "let her sit and think about it for a while." She gestured to the food. "You've only eaten a fig."

"You have to join me in some wine." Since we had no work to do, I thought I might see if I could get her to relax enough to tell me things she wouldn't otherwise.

"Just a little, then."

I filled her cup to the brim, and she pretended she didn't notice.

I dismissed the servants once they had filled the tub, saying that Adreste could give me all the help I needed. By the time I slipped into the water, she had drunk enough wine to drop onto a stool, having forgotten about assisting me at all.

I leaned back into the water. "I don't think Phylo trusts Hermione," I said, trying to sound casual.

Adreste sniffed. "I was born in this palace, to a handmaiden who served Helen's mother. I've been serving in these quarters since I was younger than you. I think I know a great deal more than Phylo does about who to trust."

I took the scraper and ran it over my arms. "How long have Phylo and Alcippe been here?"

Adreste got up with a grunt and began squeezing water from a sponge over my neck and shoulders. "I thought you knew," she said. "They came from Sidon, in Phoenicia. They were gifts to Helen on her way back from Troy. What would they know about the way things were before?"

I sat up in the bath and turned to her. "Tell me, Adreste. Tell me how it was before. Tell me everything."

CHAPTER 14

A Circle of Gold

When I started weaving Sparta into my story, I knew I would eventually arrive here, where the silver shafts converge. I dreaded every movement of the shuttle as it brought me closer to the point where I would have to decide how Helen could be portrayed. I had no tricks left—no unused color of thread, no texture still to try—and when I could think of nothing, I stopped weaving altogether.

For days I flung myself around my upstairs prison, unable to be comfortable anywhere. Perhaps my mother was right, I thought. I had been wasting my time on something worthless and unbeautiful. I considered taking the weaving off the loom and storing it away deep in a trunk somewhere in a forgotten corner of the palace, but by now it demanded to exist, and I would have felt as if I were burying it alive.

I asked Eurycleia to have servants bring up a chest of my things from the storeroom, and I laid out in my bedchamber all the gifts Helen had sent back with me. I rubbed fragrant oil on my skin and burned frankincense, just as she did in her megaron, hoping somehow I could recall her in a deeper way than simple memory allows. After putting a trace of the drug from the Orthia festival on my tongue, I sat on my bed, draped in a robe and veil Helen had woven and wearing a gold ring that had been passed down to her through her mother, Leda.

The ring was so large it rested on my knuckle and covered part of the adjoining fingers as well. Its face was a thick disk of gold molded with figures of women. On the right side a high priestess sat on her throne, while in the center a bare-breasted woman in a flounced skirt put her hands on her hips and tossed her head. To the left, three smaller figures danced in a circle under the arching branches of trees, while the moon hovered over them.

I've never been sure whether Helen's drugs played tricks with my senses or enabled me to see worlds that were there all along. Whichever it was, as I moved the ring from side to side, admiring its luster in the lamplight, the figures began to stir.

They stood up, moving around on the surface of the ring. Helen the young girl danced on the banks of the river while an old man leered in the shadows. There was Helen flaunting her beauty, and there Helen the high priestess, sitting on her throne.

And she was so much more than that. Daughter of Leda and Tyndareus, although some said of Zeus himself. Horsewoman, prize, bride, queen, young mother. Hostess to many, including the fateful guest from Troy. Abductee or runaway, depending on who told the tale. Penitent returnee. Second mother to me. The closest thing to a goddess I have ever known.

I shut my eyes, picturing the sacred grove in Sparta and imagining the sounds, the smells, the color of the firelight, the feel of the summer night on my body.

When I looked again, the dancers were back in their places. The ring looked just as it had before, but it wasn't the same because the eyes with which I saw it had changed.

I rushed to my loom and began weaving the lower half of the circle, leaving the thread a little loose right at the center so I could tease a hole to *slide the band of the ring through. When it was in place, I secured it from the backside by pushing a twig of kindling through the finger hole. The queen had made her typical grand entrance, taking her place at the center, which in Helen's case was always wherever she was.*

The quiet of our deserted quarters and the effects of the wine cast such a peaceful aura over the room that I thought for a moment Adreste had fallen asleep. I shifted in the tub, and she opened her eyes at the sound of the splashing water.

"Are you finished?" she asked.

I nodded, and Adreste reached out her hand to help me get to my feet. Water pooled on the wood floor as she dried my body. When she had finished, and I had wrapped the dripping ends of my hair in a cloth, we went back out into the megaron.

What happened to Helen? My question hung in the air, filling every corner of the room, but I wasn't sure Adreste was going to answer. I got a clean chiton from my bedchamber and wrapped it around me, pinning up my hair to keep it from soaking the fabric. Then I sat down, wondering if staring at her would be enough, or if I would have to ask a second time.

She took another swallow of the wine she had left behind in her glass. "It's a long story," she said.

"I want to know what happened when Paris came." All other stories could wait.

Adreste shuddered. "Despicable man." Her eyes were as narrow as slits, and her thin upper lip curled to reveal a glimpse of gray teeth.

"He came through the gates of the palace standing in his chariot with his chest puffed out and his chin extended, like he was posing for a fresco of a great warrior," she said, taking another sip of wine. "He was rather exotic, I have to admit. His eyes were dark blue, and his hair was pale and limp as silk thread, all the way down to his shoulders."

She stopped for a moment to think, and then the words began pouring out. "He was more graceful—more refined, I suppose I'd say—than the typical man. Much more so than the king, who's always seemed a little coarse next to Helen, but I suppose that's a thought an old slave should keep to herself. But don't misunderstand—overall, he made a poor impression as a man."

She laughed. "He had no beard, and if he had been wearing more than a little pelt of animal skin around his waist, and a leopard cloak, I would have had to look twice to see that he wasn't a woman. He was wearing more jewelry than I have ever seen on Helen—earrings, hairpins, pendants, bracelets, everything."

I refilled Adreste's cup and took a little more myself. "What did Helen say?"

"I was with her, watching from the balcony. At that time, remember, my back was still straight, and there was no Phylo or Alcippe to help. I thought we'd have a good private joke—something like 'Which goddess is that?'—but when I turned to her, I saw an expression on her face I'd never seen before."

Adreste shook her head. "I hadn't imagined she would find such a man attractive, but she did." Her eyes were locked on a vision only she could see. "Oh yes," she murmured, "she certainly did."

Once Adreste had begun, there was no stopping her, and she told the story until, as night fell, exhaustion stopped her.

Paris was welcomed as a guest, but within a day or two of his arrival, Menelaus left for Crete to attend a funeral. Before he went, he told Helen that because someone as important as a prince of Troy could not be expected to dine alone, she would need to join him. Helen passed two evenings in the megaron with him, coming back upstairs each evening agitated and acting quite unlike herself.

"She told me he was trying to get her into his bed," Adreste said. "It was only the third night of his visit and he already wanted to dishonor the king."

Adreste told me how Helen spent mornings in the great shrine of the palace, stopping first in front of an image of Hera, imploring her protection to keep her marriage safe from harm. Then, because she saw no response, she began prostrating herself in front of an image of Aphrodite, pleading with the goddess to let her go. But Aphrodite never heard, or perhaps she just didn't care. What better sport could there be than to consume a beautiful woman with lust, to watch her grind at herself with her fingers at night, trying to get enough satisfaction so the passion would ebb? And besides, Helen was doomed to lose, for Aphrodite herself had promised Paris that Helen would be his.

"By the fourth day," Adreste went on, "she had Hermione and Megapenthes come to dinner with her. When she came up afterward, she had me lock her in. By the sixth day, even that was not enough."

An inadvertent, husky moan escaped from somewhere deep inside the old woman. She didn't seem to notice how the sound filled the room, as she rocked in her chair, anguish written on her ravaged face. "I came in that morning, as I always did, to stoke the fire and lay out the queen's breakfast. I found her sitting on the platform in front of her throne. Her head was resting on the chair cushion, buried in her arms. She was so still, I would have thought she was asleep, except for the low moaning sounds coming from her. I didn't understand for a moment what had happened. And then the curtain to her bedchamber opened, and there was Paris, naked, with the most horrible grin on his face. 'Well,' he said to me, 'look what I've done.'"

"The queen refused to eat with Paris that evening," Adreste went on, tearing at her ragged cuticles until threads of blood rose at the edges. "And to fight Aphrodite's spell, she asked Hermione to sleep in her bed with her. The next morning when I came in, Hermione was still asleep, but the queen was up, already dressed. I could tell by the red in her cheeks that she had just come in from outside, for the night had been very cold. But something about her had changed. She didn't cry, and she didn't even try to hide what had happened. 'It's too much,' she said to me. 'I want him too badly.'"

Adreste's story had taken long enough for my hair to dry in crisp ropes, but as I combed with my fingers to loosen and rearrange it, I had to put my hands down to control the trembling. My mind was in turmoil, racked by feelings of hopefulness at all of Helen's efforts to resist, even though I knew the story, knew that in the end everything she did would be in vain.

It didn't take long, Adreste told me, for Helen to be overwhelmed with remorse and terrified to face Menelaus. She spent a day filling chests with robes, and jewels, and huge amounts of gold and silver. She was going to smooth over the inhospitality of demanding that a guest leave by showering Paris with far more gifts, and more valuable ones, than he ever could have expected. But that evening in the megaron, she could not make herself send him away.

"The following day, he agreed on his own to go," Adreste said. "I was so relieved I cried. That evening, she sent me to my quarters while she was still dressed, saying she could take care of getting ready for bed herself. I should have realized what might happen, but if I had, what could I have done? The king was gone, and besides, who was likely to listen to the worries of a slave?

"I couldn't sleep, and I got up when the moon was bright overhead. I went out into the hallway outside my quarters and heard the whinny of a horse in the courtyard. I went over to the railing and saw the chariot waiting below. Then I heard a man's voice on the stairs.

"'It's what you said you wanted,' I heard him say.

"And then I heard something that made my hair stand on end. She was crying out like a trapped animal with its killer approaching, pleading to the gods for rescue from her fate."

Adreste fell silent and brushed at the tears on her cheeks.

"And the gods didn't come," I whispered.

"No," Adreste said. "They didn't."

"She went downstairs with Paris, and I saw her standing by his chariot. Her hair was loose and she was in her nightdress. Paris was already aboard, holding the reins firm because the horses wanted to run so badly.

"I called out to her, 'Don't go!' and I saw her turn around and look at me.

"'It's too late,' she cried out to me. The last thing I saw was her gown clinging to her body and her hair blowing back as they went through the gates."

I thought Adreste was finished, but she had one more thing to say.

"Aphrodite was there," she whispered, her gnarled hands clasped in her lap. "I smelled her roses in the air, and the scent of the ocean as she passed. I called out to her to have pity, and I heard her laugh. I swear to this day, I heard her laugh."

* * *

I got up early the following morning. To that point in my life, every terrible story I had heard had taken place elsewhere, and I wanted to visit the rooms where such a tale had actually occurred. Grainy rays of sunlight filtered through the high windows onto the unlit hearth in Helen's quarters. The colors of the frescoed walls were barely visible without torchlight to brighten them. I was not prepared for the odd sensation of seeing Helen's quarters without Helen.

Without Helen. Was this what Hermione had woken up to, coming from her mother's warm bed into a gray room from which the life had flown? And in the days before, had she rushed in to greet her mother in the morning and seen her body draped against her chair as she wept, with a naked man standing in the doorway leading to her bed?

I went across the room to Helen's bedchamber, pulling aside the curtain. The room was darker than the megaron, but I knew what her bed looked like already—soft coverlets heaped inside a frame of dark wood, inlaid with designs in ivory and ebony, and banded with rings of silver and gold. This was the bed to which Paris had come, after Helen unlocked the door to receive him. This was the bed where Hermione, too young to know she was standing guard over her own future, had fallen asleep next to her mother the last few nights Helen was in Sparta.

"What are you doing?"

I whirled around to face Hermione.

"Nothing," I said, instantly regretting how defensive I sounded. "I thought I heard something and I came in to make sure everything was all right."

It was a lie, of course, and I am sure she wasn't fooled by it. "I've never come in before," I added.

Hermione didn't seem to care. "You just surprised me, that's all." She put down the covered basket she was carrying. "It's so dark in here."

"Do you want me to light the torches?" I asked, as if having something to do would make it seem as if I had a reason to be there.

"No!" she said. I heard the alarm in her voice and realized she wasn't supposed to be there either. I had caught her as much as she had caught me.

"On second thought," she said, "go and see if Adreste's up. I'd like her help with something."

Though I was annoyed by her demanding tone, I was glad to get out of the room. When I came back with Adreste, Hermione spoke to her in the same cold voice. "I want to look at my wedding clothes."

Taken by surprise, Adreste rocked back on her hips, lifting her head as much as she could. "Will there be a wedding?"

"No," Hermione said. "I just want to see them. They're in here somewhere." She turned to me. "You can light the torches now."

I was so excited by the prospect of seeing what a Spartan princess would wear to her wedding that I put aside how rude she was to both of us.

"I thought she kept them in the storerooms, but I'll look," Adreste said. She hobbled over to a corner of the room where several chests were stored and pulled open the first one.

Hermione made no move to assist her, so after I finished with the torches, I helped the old woman inch her fingers to the bottom to determine by feel what was inside each one.

"I don't think they're here," she said finally. "I'll go get the housekeeper to see what she knows."

I saw Adreste wincing with pain as she stood up and hurried as fast as she could from the room. Hermione and I were alone again, sitting on two large chests and staring at each other.

"Are you getting married?" I asked.

"Supposedly. My father promised me to Achilles' son Neoptolemus, although he seems to have forgotten about it."

Hermione was twenty-four, very old to remain unmarried. "Well, where is he?" I asked, with the typical lack of tact that now makes me cringe to remember.

"Who knows? He never showed up. Maybe he heard I look more like my father than my mother, and he was sure he could do better."

I wish I could say my thoughts were kinder, but all I could think was that her looks weren't the only thing about her that might deter a man. And I couldn't bring myself to contradict her out of fear she would skewer me for any attempt at flattery.

I had experienced Menelaus' forgetfulness as well. He could never remember I was a princess and the daughter of a friend, and several times already Helen had stepped in to keep him from taking me to bed, as was his right with any slave he fancied.

Menelaus' thoughts seemed locked in time, as if the war had just ended and he had arrived home the day before with fresh stories to tell. He would go on and on, knocking over his wine goblet without noticing as he described a battle for the hundredth time, or weeping uncontrollably as he recounted this or that hero's death. I wasn't surprised that Menelaus didn't seem to comprehend that his daughter's chosen husband had not shown up, and she had already lived almost twice as long as his own wife before he married her.

"Not that I really care," Hermione went on. "The only good thing about it is that I would get out of this horrid place." She sniffed. "Before I shrivel up like old Adreste."

However true her description of the old slave was, speaking of Adreste that way was disrespectful, and I didn't like it. I opened my mouth to defend her, but Hermione had started talking again.

"I'm going to wear the same skirt my sister Iphigenia was wearing the day in Aulis when she thought she was getting married. But I suppose you don't know anything about that."

"You have a sister?"

Hermione's eyes darted. "I think of her that way. Just like I think of Clytemnestra as my mother."

Hermione read the doubt in my expression. "She's a wonderful woman, really. She sent for me just a few days after my father went running off to Troy."

She sniffed. "Funny how things change. Then I was terrified he would kill my mother. Now I wish he had."

"No you don't!" I said. "No one wants that."

"You'd be surprised what people want. Some kill their own children to get what suits them." Hermione's eyes narrowed. "But I suppose you can't imagine that either."

I saw by the cruel smile playing across her lips that she knew she had ensnared me in her story. I would have to hear her out, or look like a fool for closing my ears.

"Do you know what happened to my sister?" she asked. "Two men came to Clytemnestra at Mycenae. They said to bring Iphigenia to the harbor at Aulis, because the Achaeans were getting ready to sail to Troy, and Agamemnon wanted to marry her to Achilles before they left. I'd only been in Mycenae a little while at that point, but I remember how thrilled everybody was."

Hermione's laugh sounded more like a choked growl. "It was all a trick. Her father killed her. Slit her throat, right there in front of her mother's eyes as a sacrifice to the gods. And do you know what happened? All of a sudden the wind came up, and everyone called Agamemnon a great leader for what he'd done."

Hermione's voice grew shrill as her anger mounted, but it dropped again as she continued. "Clytemnestra came home alone, with only Iphigenia's bridal clothes. They're mine now, and I'm using them for my wedding, to remind my parents it's their fault what happened to her."

I wanted to cry out that she was lying, that no father would kill his daughter, no husband would do such a thing to his wife. But I didn't, because no one would say anything that awful unless it was the truth.

Hermione's lip curled with glee at my distress. "And do you want to try to guess what two men came to Mycenae with the story about the wedding? The ones who sat plotting at Aulis with Agamemnon about how to get his wife to bring her daughter to be butchered?"

I was sure I didn't want to know. I shook my head, tears stinging my eyes.

"One of them was my father. And you still can't guess the other?"

"No!" I said. "Stop playing with me!"

"Oh, I think you can. It was Odysseus." She watched me, measuring the effect of her words. "Our fathers. Deceivers of women. Betrayers of daughters. Heroes, wouldn't you say? Brave beyond imagining."

I jumped up, opening my mouth to scream at her that she was mean and hurtful, and that I hated her, but just at that moment Adreste entered the megaron with the housekeeper, both of them empty-handed.

Hermione got up from the chest. "Don't bother," she said. "I don't actually care." She picked up her basket, and without another word to anyone, she swept from the room.

My desire to befriend Hermione vanished that morning. Meanspiritedness was the only explanation for sending an old, crippled woman on an empty errand and using the opportunity to torment me with knowledge I didn't want to have. Hermione wasn't worth knowing, and as far as I was concerned, she could stay at her end of the palace until she turned to dust.

But there wasn't much opportunity to brood, for within a few days Helen and Menelaus returned. With them was a group from Pylos, who would be staying as the king and queen's guests for a few days before finishing their journey home.

All the women were exhausted from the trip. Helen wanted nothing more than to go to bed for days. Alcippe and Phylo kept their backs pointedly turned away from each other and conversed in clipped phrases only when necessary. But Menelaus loved nothing more than company, and that required appearances by the queen. Rest would have to wait.

Helen put off her first royal entrance into the grand megaron for two days, but on the third evening, I went with her to greet the guests after their meal. I was her sole attendant, because by then both Phylo and Alcippe had taken to bed with stuffy heads and coughs.

Most nights, rather than joining the men at the table, Helen would sit near the hearth listening to the bard and making thread with a golden distaff and spindle she had received as a gift in Thebes. That night, however, in acknowledgment of her role as the queen of the palace and host of the guests, she took a seat next to Menelaus. I stood behind her, near enough to reach out and touch her chair if I wanted to. My smile was as glazed as I'm sure hers was, but Helen always managed to be charming, acting as if she were genuinely surprised by having her beauty acclaimed and dazzled by the honeyed words offered in her honor by yet another drunken guest.

But that night, the routine took a sudden turn when Hermione came into the megaron and, with only the most cursory of nods, took her place next to her mother. Signaling a servant, she asked him to pour her some of the concoction Menelaus served all his guests, a wine tasting of resin and honey, cut with the barley beer he drank all day like water. Noticing that her mother's goblet was empty, she motioned the servant to fill it as well.

How thoughtful, I remember thinking. *And how unlike her.*

Menelaus had drunk enough by the time Hermione arrived to throw off his typical world-weary mood in favor of boisterous laughter and exaggerated tales. Still, when he began telling stories, we all knew it was only a matter of time until he would be unable to go on and would signal to the bard to sing so he could retreat into silent melancholy again. Helen always hoped to be gone before he put his head on the table and fell asleep. She wanted to be upstairs already rather than seeing him to bed, since it might require getting in next to him and spending the night.

But tonight, Hermione seemed determined to stretch out the stories at my expense. She prodded her father to give more and more details of Odysseus' trickery and deceit, which of course Menelaus saw as signs of a greatness beyond strength and courage alone. I found myself slowly backing up until I was pressed against a pillar at some distance from the table, too far to see anything but the backs of Menelaus, Helen, and Hermione, and of course Megapenthes, who sat braying on the far side of his father.

I shut my eyes. My temples throbbed. "Please, let's leave," I whispered to myself.

And then, as if a malevolent god had answered my prayer, I heard a commotion around the table. I opened my eyes just in time to see the queen collapse against her husband.

Hermione jumped up and cried out to the heralds to come tend to her mother, but Menelaus had already picked her up. He cradled her under her legs and back as he rushed out of the megaron, across the courtyard and up the stairs to her chambers. Hermione and I were only a few steps behind, and when we reached the top of the stairs, I ran past the queen's door to wake Phylo and the others. Not waiting for them to dress, I rushed back to see that Menelaus had thrown himself on the bed next to his wife.

"Haven't you toyed with her enough?" His wails were loud enough to reach the gods, as he flung his arm over her. "Let us be happy. You have no cause to hate us so."

Looking at Helen's motionless figure on the bed, I saw how small and inconsequential we must appear to the immortals, and how those they have chosen to torment will live forever like birds with broken wings. I had little time for such thoughts because Phylo was now beside me.

"Is she dead?" she asked.

"She's been gasping for breath."

Phylo went over to Menelaus, and, taking him by the shoulder, she turned him toward her. "You need to get up so she can breathe," she said, trying to sound calm, although panic had raised her voice almost as high as Alcippe's. "And so we can take care of her."

In the dim light of the chamber, I could see that his eyes were wild with grief as he allowed Phylo to help him to his feet. *He really loves her,* I thought. What had transpired with another man in this bed, he truly held against the gods and not his wife.

"What happened?" Phylo asked me after she got him seated in the megaron.

I was standing next to the bed, helpless to do anything but hold the queen's hand. "I don't know," I said. "Maybe Hermione saw something. She was sitting next to her."

"Well, where is she?"

We looked around but Hermione was gone.

Coldhearted bitch, I thought, with more gleeful vindication than was seemly, especially when she came back soon after, having apparently left only to change into clothing more suitable for spending the night by her mother's side.

By then we had stripped off Helen's clothing and removed her makeup so it wouldn't stain the bedding. I expected her skin to be paler than usual, but instead it was fading back to normal from a deep flush, as her pulse slowed and she began to breathe more normally. She was still unconscious, but her eyelids fluttered from time to time, and her arms and legs had begun to stir.

"I want to take care of my mother tonight." Hermione's face was wet, but her flat and unwavering voice was at odds with any real emotion.

Phylo's voice was equally stony, but unlike Hermione, she had to clear the tightness in her throat to speak at all. "You may stay," she said, "but it's our job to tend the queen, and we intend to do it."

Hermione took in a breath, as if she were about to rebuke Phylo for daring to cross her, but instead she gave a sigh of annoyance and stared at her as if she were taking her measure.

"Very well," she said. "We'll stay here together."

* * *

When Alcippe, Adreste, and I arrived in her chambers early the following morning, the queen was sitting up, holding her temples in her hands and moaning at the excruciating pain in her head. Phylo was taking a basin of vomit out to the servant in the hall, and she told me to get another clean one before I went in, just in case.

Helen's eyes were unfocused and she didn't seem to know where she was, or who we were at first, but little by little she began to piece together what had happened.

"I shouldn't have tried to go down to the banquet so soon after the journey," she said. "I was still too tired."

"Did the queen have her blood in Argos?" Adreste whispered, and when Alcippe nodded, she added, with a puzzled look, "Then it isn't that."

"Isn't what?" I whispered to Alcippe.

"A baby. It's the first sign. Although she's awfully old." She thought for a moment. "Did she eat something?"

We all knew that was highly unlikely, because the queen rarely ate anything in the presence of guests, and certainly not what Menelaus favored serving—large quantities of meat and very little else.

The queen made hoarse, convulsing sounds deep in her chest, and I ran over with the basin just in time to catch the small amount of vomit that was still inside her. Alcippe took the basin, and I put my arm around Helen's shoulders, resisting the urge to bury my head in her neck and cry at the wretchedness of it all.

"Where's Hermione?" Alcippe asked Phylo.

"She stayed most of the night. When the queen woke up, she said the smell of the vomit was making her sick, so she left."

A servant arrived with hot water infused with herbs, and after Helen drank some, she revived a little. "Was it terrible?" she asked. "Did I embarrass myself?"

No," I said. "You fell over onto Menelaus, and he carried you up here."

"My husband brought me here himself?" Her voice was distant and her face expressionless, but I knew her well enough to tell she was pleased.

And surprised. She put her hand to her forehead and winced at the pain. "I watch him, wondering when his bad thoughts about me will finally come out, but they never do," she murmured.

"I don't think he has any." I could barely hear my own voice, it was so small. "He was crying out to the gods for a chance at happiness with you."

"It's too late to ask for that." She lay down and turned away. I held her hand, listening to her breath grow shallow, as she gave way once again to sleep.

Over the next moon cycle, Helen's illness became more and more mysterious. Some days she was at her loom, seeming to be back to normal, although her arms were noticeably thinner and trembled a little when she held them up. Other mornings her face was red again, and she would talk incoherently as her chest heaved in the struggle to take in air.

And then one morning, I was smoothing the queen's hair as she slept, and my palms came away covered with loose strands. I showed them to Phylo, who went over to the queen and saw for herself how easily the hair came away. Then she bent over the queen's face.

She beckoned to me. "Do you smell anything strange?"

I put my face next to the queen's and held it there for a moment. "She hasn't been eating almonds, but I smell them on her breath."

"That's what I thought," Phylo said. "Come with me."

Adreste and Alcippe were working in our quarters. Phylo walked straight over to Adreste and stood in front of her. "Has Hermione been coming in during your watch?" Phylo demanded.

"Sometimes." Adreste's eyes were defiant as she locked them on Phylo. "She says she doesn't feel comfortable around the rest of you."

"And do you ever leave when she's there?"

"Well, I can't go all night without relieving myself." Adreste adjusted her shoulders with an indignant shrug. "I do take care of that, if you don't mind."

"Does she go with you?"

"Of course not. I don't need help." Adreste's eyes flashed. "And the queen should not be left unattended. You of all people should know that."

Phylo's eyes narrowed. "Of course," she said, staring at Adreste. Adreste stared right back. "I'm sorry to have bothered you," Phylo finally said, turning on her heels and walking out of the megaron. I followed her out, to the sounds of Adreste complaining to Alcippe about people whose hearts were too cold for their own good. When we turned the corner and were well out of earshot, Phylo grabbed my arm, squeezing it so tightly I thought it would leave a bruise. She pulled her head in so close to mine that the fronts of our shoulders brushed.

"Listen," she said. "Can you keep a secret?"

I nodded, wiggling my arm to release her hold.

"I know what's wrong with the queen." She looked around one

more time and lowered her voice even more. "Hermione's poisoning her."

I gasped, not so much from shock but from what was suddenly so obvious. Helen's chest of potions. How stupid I had been not to suspect that Hermione's real reason for coming into the darkened megaron during Helen's absence was inside the basket she was carrying when she left.

When I finished telling Phylo what had happened, she was silent for a long time.

"I'm a slave," she said. "I can't cross the princess. Even the truth would not protect me. Especially the truth, I think, in a situation like this."

And what about me? I was a guest, and I needed to remain welcome. How could I tell my host what I suspected about his daughter? We stared at each other for a moment before Phylo gasped. "We left the queen alone!"

We rushed back to her quarters and heard a faint voice calling for us. She was awake, but more important, she was alive. It would be up to Phylo and me to keep her that way, even if she never knew what we had done.

CHAPTER 15

Madder Red

How better to speak of Hermione's treachery, how better to weave more darkness into the blue and silver than by adding in thin filaments of the queen's hair? I suppose it sounds odd that I saved it, but I didn't know what else to do. I kept all of it, wrapped in a package of silk cloth tied with a gold cord, not because she would ever want it, but because even if she didn't, it felt like stolen property I didn't have the right to throw away.

The poison had indeed stolen something from her. When her hair grew back and her skin looked healthy again, she looked older. And because youth is beauty and beauty is worth, even wealth and power cannot protect a woman from the vulnerability Helen must have felt. During the remaining three and a half years I spent in Sparta, she never traveled again, and she rarely left her quarters to greet guests.

The queen's hair for the darkness, and someone else's, for the light that was also part of my last year there. His locks are interwoven with leftover thread I used for a man's cloak I made in Helen's megaron.

"Weave it even if you don't know who it's for," Helen said. "Weave it, and its magic will help its true owner find you."

Thread dyed in madder red, close enough to the color of his hair to keep the secret that he is there at all. Just the way it was the spring I turned seventeen.

Only the poisoner remained a mystery. When Helen lost all her hair and her skin became lifeless and grainy, everyone knew what had happened. She had come back from Argos weak and unlike herself, and many of the guests there—the women in particular—held grudges against her. Menelaus and his advisers made up a list of wedding guests and settled on more than a dozen people who might have wished her dead. With so many suspects, revenge was impossible, and the subject was dropped. Everyone agreed that it was good the queen was home, away from those who wished her harm.

Phylo and I said nothing to the contrary. We were among those who comforted the queen with reassurances that she was safe. We had done everything we could think of to ensure that she was. Because the more helpless and needy women appear to be, the more men are flattered into giving us what we ask for, we told Menelaus no one in the queen's wing would ever be able to sleep again unless he posted a permanent guard. It wasn't hard to convince him that an enemy could dash across the Spartan countryside, storm the palace gates, and race up the stairs into the queen's room to administer a fatal dose of poisoning before guards could intervene. In his befuddlement, Menelaus eventually came to believe that this had actually happened, and that he had foiled the plot himself just as the enemy held a cup to the cowering queen's lips.

Phylo and I didn't want any men on our wing, so one guard stayed at the bottom and the other at the top of the stairs. Phylo and I, and a few others Phylo trusted, served as sentries outside Helen's quarters, the door to which was now always locked at night.

Hermione would be noticed first by the king's guard and then have to pass the queen's if she wanted to visit her mother. She did so a few times, trying to act as if nothing had changed, but both Phylo and I—for we never breathed a word to Alcippe or Adreste— made it clear through our glares and veiled comments that we knew the truth. And, of course, we never left her alone with her mother for even the time it took to draw a single breath.

No need to break the queen's heart, Phylo and I decided. No need to feel responsible for what Menelaus might be angry enough to do to Hermione if we revealed the truth. We would stay quiet and stand watch, so the king and queen could be at peace.

Whether Helen suspected the truth, I can't say, but unlike be- fore, Hermione was permitted to go visit Clytemnestra for long periods of time. We all were glad when she left, though of course Phylo and I had many anxious moments every time Hermione re- turned with new belongings to unpack. I was no longer curious about her personal life, however, and my interest in her where- abouts extended no farther than an arm's reach from the queen's goblet. Hermione, for all practical purposes, had disappeared.

Several years passed, and I was now seventeen. Mentor came once or twice a year with news so bleak I no longer gave a thought to when I might be going home. On one of his visits he told me Anticleia had died. She had never recovered, he said, from the grief of losing first her son and then her granddaughter. Though I cried long and hard for everything I had been forced to leave behind, every year it was harder to remember details about Ithaca and the people who lived there. By that point, despite frequent thoughts of my mother, Sparta had begun to feel like my true home.

Every month, in acknowledgment of my blood, I wore the traditional saffron-yellow himation Helen and I wove for me. Every few days, I attended Helen in the grand shrine of the palace as she made offerings to the goddesses. Almost every day I ate in her chambers. Every afternoon, I brushed her hair and rubbed oil on her hands, playing games with our fingers to while away the time.

And every year, I assisted at the Orthia festival. Though Helen no longer had the same interest she once had in the physical impression she made, age took away nothing from her role as priestess. In fact, if anything it enhanced it.

But as time passed, the question of my own future became more difficult to ignore. I was thirteen when I arrived, somewhere between childhood and marriage. Now I was seventeen, well beyond the age my mother and Helen had been when they wed, and were it not for the fact that no male guardian had taken charge of me, I would already be a wife.

Even the close friend of a fellow warrior, as Menelaus was to my father, lacked standing to arrange a marriage for me. Presumably Telemachus still thought I was dead, but even if by now he knew I wasn't, my mother was unlikely to bring up the subject of my marriage, for fear of what he might blunder into if he decided to find me a husband himself.

I can't say I minded. I was happy living in the handmaidens' quarters, happy spending my days as a companion to Helen. The swineherd Eumaeus had been right all those years ago. Far worse things could happen than to live as a slave in a great person's house. Unlike him, however, I wasn't really a slave, so I can't say whether the other handmaidens saw life in Sparta differently than I did.

I saw no signs of unhappiness among them. Their petty squabbles and occasional moods were nothing compared to the rage and misery in the hearts of many of the free. On the upper floor of the palace at Sparta we were at greater liberty than most women ever are, and I had more freedom than I am ever likely to experience again.

What has coming back to Ithaca meant to me? The only outlet for my trapped spirit is my loom. I would die without my weaving, for the past is now the only life I have. This palace feels strange to me now, not at all like a home. Here women seem drained of their lifeblood, and men are spilling theirs in a game with only temporary winners.

Downstairs the battle continues, but the megaron is quieting. Here and there, swords clash and men scream like animals, the sounds of defeat and victory surprisingly the same. I no longer recognize any voices, and my senses are so numb, I don't care to try to make out the only voices I want to hear.

Two palaces, two women's wings upstairs. There the similarity between Ithaca and Sparta ends. My room here is cold, and death seeps up through the floor, but when I shut my eyes and remember life in Helen's world, all I recall is warmth and light. But such comparisons go nowhere, and do me no good.

I run my fingers over the places in my weaving where I remember living passionately, touching again the hair of the two people who taught me how. Doing this calms me, gives me hope that a time will come when I will again feel the way I did my last year in Sparta, when the world opened out before me, and I thought my arms could be long enough to wrap around all I had come to love, and hold on forever.

I used to dream of the perfect world, where I could gather around me only the people I wanted and keep out everyone else.

I suppose that's why I so vividly recall hiding from Halia and Eu-rycleia, but most of all from my grandmother. Remembering the surge of power I felt to be momentarily beyond anyone's reach, as I hid in a hollow tree trunk or empty pantry basket, makes me smile even today. Once Helen retreated from public life, a similar feeling of being beyond the control of others pervaded our lives upstairs. The loss we had all felt when Helen's charismatic beauty was not the center of our days began to look in many respects like a gain.

There is a comfort in being among one's own kind, which in this case means being only with women. Once Helen stopped going downstairs, we all did. None of the men in Sparta ever wronged me in any way, but the truth is I just didn't enjoy being around them that much. When Megapenthes' attention wandered after a meal, his favorite entertainment was to clench his fists and watch his arm muscles bulge. Anyone who came to court with a new story found themselves telling it more than once because Megapenthes hadn't understood the first time.

Of all the men in Sparta, only Menelaus seemed moved by any-thing other than the heat of battle. I knew he could cry, knew he could love, but most of the time he was just like everybody else, wiping the grease from his mouth with his arm and belching, be-fore going on with another monotonous tale of blood and glory.

Hiding upstairs in the palace was freedom itself. Sometimes I caught a glimpse of what I had missed as a child by not having other girls to play with. Sometimes all of us, including Helen, told stories until our stomachs ached from laughter. Other times, just for fun, Helen let us use her pots of makeup to draw wild designs on each other's faces.

The mood I remember best is the contentment and relaxation that was never possible when men expected our attention. I loved winter most of all, when Phylo, Alcippe, Adreste, and I would spend the afternoon with Helen around the fire in her megaron. We each had a personal spot, a chair by which we kept a basket with our hand weaving and our spindles. Because the floors were always cold, we took off our shoes and put our feet on the edge of the hearth, soles toward the flames, wiggling our toes while we embroidered ribbon or made woven nets in which to catch our hair.

Five women around a fire. One of them was a queen and the most fabled woman in the world. And though none of us ever forgot that, most days it didn't matter much at all. Helen blossomed again, free of the demand to be perpetually magnificent. Her voice was softer, more dreamlike, without command. She no longer needed to set her shoulders and lengthen her neck every time she entered a room, so as to look a little taller and haughtier.

To me she was more beautiful after her brush with death. She rarely wore any makeup at all, and her face came to life. Her nose crinkled and her lips curled, here with a sly grin, and there with a smile that exploded over her features as she laughed. And when she wanted to cry, she could let the tears flow without causing us all to flutter around her to try to salvage the paint on her face.

Helen's new life had a good effect on her relationship with Menelaus as well. I think his great, unguarded expression of love when he carried her unconscious body up to her room untangled a knot in her heart, and many mornings when I came into her chambers I found her bed empty, or saw signs that he had visited during the night. Her golden spindle and its silver basket had been brought upstairs now that Helen no longer visited the grand megaron, and after each night she spent with Menelaus, she flicked the spindle with a faraway expression, as if she were visiting happy places in her mind.

To go outside, Helen need do no more than put on a thin coating of lotion to protect her skin and cover her head with a thick veil until she was outside the palace grounds. On beautiful days, particularly in the spring and fall, one or the other of us would put down her embroidery or drop her hands from the loom and convince the others it was too nice to be indoors. After sending word to the kitchen to pack us a meal, in no time at all we would be walking to the stables to commandeer a chariot and team of horses to take us wherever we wanted to go.

Helen taught Phylo and me to drive, though we usually did no more than trot down the road to avoid terrifying Alcippe, who never got used to the feeling of traveling faster than she could by foot. We went several more times to the lookout where Hermione and I had stopped. Every time I was glad I had not gone out with her again, so no other beautiful place in Lacedaemon was infected by memories. Helen, of course, had much worse memories of her own, so we avoided the banks of the river, choosing instead to visit the orchards and vineyards, and in the spring, the meadows in flower.

My favorite recollections are of walking down the neat rows of apple, pear, and pomegranate trees, in a cloud of red, pink, and white blossoms in the spring and a blaze of orange and gold in the fall. It was on one such adventure that Helen and I had a conversation that would change my life forever.

Alcippe and Phylo had gone off for a walk, and Helen and I sat on a blanket in the oldest section of a pomegranate orchard, where the trees had grown large enough to provide some shade. The fruits were beginning to set, and falling petals collected on our hair and laps, though there was no hint of a breeze.

Helen got to her feet. "Stand up," she said. "Let me look at you."

I thought I could picture what she was seeing as her eyes ran over me. I had grown a little taller in the last several years, but even after my body had finished reshaping itself, no one would mistake me for a goddess. I was unremarkable in either height or build. My hair had gotten a little darker and was now mostly brown, with glints of gold in bright sunlight. My eyes were too small and shallow to be alluring, and their dark color made what I thought was an unpleasant contrast with fair skin that easily turned pink and freckled when the sun was high.

"You're a very pretty young woman," Helen said.

"No I'm not!" I said, bursting into laughter at the idea of someone like her thinking that of me.

"You shouldn't deny it." Helen's face grew serious. "You should be enjoying this time in your life." She came over and tucked a sprig of red blossoms into my hair. "I wish you could see yourself. See yourself as a man would."

"What man?" My jaw went slack, and I probably looked as dumb as a cow.

She shrugged. "The world is full of men. Take your pick." She put a red sprig in her own hair. "You've never noticed the way the guests in the megaron look at all of you standing behind me?"

Alcippe radiated a golden, fragile beauty. Phylo was all strength, tall and voluptuous. I had seen men eyeing both of them but had never noticed more than the occasional glance my way.

"Of course," Helen went on, "my slaves are my property, off limits unless I give my permission. Phylo and Alcippe have both declined, but I think that's just as well."

Declined what? Permission for what? "Do you mean—" I had no idea how to finish the thought.

Helen hugged me, then stepped back to arm's length with her

hands still on my shoulders. "I mean, dear girl, that it's time you had a lover."

"I can't do that!" The words burst out, and I felt my heart racing in my chest. "I have to be a virgin."

"Why do you think that?"

It seemed like a crazy question, especially coming from someone so worldly, that I could only splutter nonsense in reply. Helen linked her arm in mine and guided me down a path between the trees.

"Why do you think fathers marry girls off so young?" she asked. "They want their daughter's maidenhead to be their prize to give away, and they know if they don't move quickly, she may realize it's hers to give as she pleases."

She turned to face me. "It is, you know. Your virginity doesn't belong to your father, or your brother. It's yours to decide about, but I can tell you one thing with certainty. When the bride is as valuable as the daughter of Odysseus, no one who comes to claim you is going to care if he was there first."

"But what will my mother think?"

Helen took my hand and started down the path again. "No one dreamed you would be here this long. And Penelope was trying to protect you from rape, not womanhood—I'm confident of that."

We walked the length of the orchard in silence. At the end of the trees we looked out over gentle hills and meadows painted with bright splashes of flowers. Two dragonflies buzzed by my head.

"It's an omen," Helen laughed. "It's their time to mate. They've come to have a word with you."

"The gods come as flying bugs now?" I replied, hoping laughter would ease my discomfort. It didn't work, but no matter. Suddenly I was intensely aware of the impossibly blue sky and the red orchard and the purple hills, and a familiar shiver came over me. The world was glowing like a mother holding out her arms to receive her child, and all I had to do to make that happen was know myself better, know who I was and what I wanted.

"Hera," I whispered, confident in my soul that she had come because I needed her, even if I was not aware of having cried out for her help.

Helen murmured something and put her arm around my waist. "Does she give her permission?"

Just then, from nowhere a gust of wind blew through the orchard, sending a storm of red petals fluttering down over us.

"Your face is flushed," Helen said.

Before I could reply, we heard Alcippe and Phylo behind us. Helen put her fingers to her lips. "Just nod for yes," she whispered.

I could never have said out loud the thoughts swarming in my mind. I didn't know what most of them were. But my head was moving. *Yes.*

Helen viewed my introduction to lovemaking much as she viewed the initiation ceremonies at the Orthia festival. If all that was involved was penetrating my body, Megapenthes could have done the job. Unknown to him, he suffered the indignity of never being considered as a potential lover. Helen had endured his presence for years only because she had no choice, and we were all glad not to continue suffering his stupidity once Helen no longer sat near him in the grand megaron.

But who? The answer came at the opening of the next Orthia festival, when Menelaus' friends gathered once again for their annual ritual of shuddering at the temporary dominance of women and fleeing to places of their greatest comfort, which of course inevitably required slaughter of one kind or another.

Though Helen's retreat upstairs was almost complete, she never stopped looking forward to her appearances in the grand megaron at the time of the Orthia festival. This year, during the days of feasting before the men left, we watched them all carefully as I stood behind the queen. My eyes were lined with kohl, and I wore my own brightly colored flounced skirt and a tight jacket too narrow in the front to cover my breasts. My nipples showed through the nearly transparent veil I draped around my neck and tucked in at my waist to create a semblance of modesty. My hair was pulled up with a gold ribbon and fell in loose coils behind my ears, and my braceleted arms and ankles shimmered with fragrant oil.

"I wish you could see yourself," Helen whispered. And if it is true that the best image of oneself is through others, I was a vision. The eyes of every man with a speck of virility left in him never strayed long from me.

At the end of the evening, Helen and I moved through the pools of torchlight on our way out of the megaron. She stepped to one side to ensure that the men had an unobstructed view of the roundness of my body from behind, and to let them follow the easy, seductive sway of hips I had practiced in Helen's quarters.

"Can you feel them looking at you?' Helen asked.

I gave her a sly grin, and we went out into a night exploding with stars.

Menelaus came back from the hunt more befuddled than ever. Men had been sniffing around for information about the pretty handmaiden behind Helen, but all he could remember was that the queen was protecting her for some reason. That was enough to keep the crudest among them from forcing themselves on me if they should ever catch me alone.

I had no doubt men who would do such a thing existed among Menelaus' friends, because many of them reminded me of the suitors back in Ithaca. My only question was whether all men were like that. I was curious about the relationship between a man and a woman, but based on what I had seen, I couldn't understand how the company of any man would be an improvement over being exclusively among women, or in the alternative, being alone.

Aphrodite must be powerful indeed, I thought. Helen had been thrown down on a riverbank and ripped like a neck hole in a tunic, as she described it, yet later she had abandoned her life in Sparta to be with Paris. How could that be? How could something that happened in one small part of my body be enough to affect everything else?

My thoughts danced wild circles in my head, but Helen was all practicality. We had to choose the right man the first time around, because he had to be trusted with my secret. I could not sleep with a man as Eirene, handmaiden to the queen. He had to know whose virginity he was taking. He had to know that the roar of the aggrieved father would come from Odysseus, hero of Troy, if he ever learned of it.

This meant my lover had to be entirely suitable as a husband. Though I probably would end up marrying someone else, at least I would not have dishonored my rank by giving myself to someone unworthy of a princess.

A suitable person proved surprisingly difficult to find. Even one was starting to seem like a gift from the gods. And then, Helen's face began to glow with excitement as a possibility revealed itself. Nestor's youngest son, Peisistratus, had made the trip from Pylos far more often than necessary since the last Orthia festival, always with the same excuse that his father required more horses for his stables. Every time he inquired about me as soon as he arrived, so the queen guessed the real reason he had come.

Peisistratus had been entrusted with the task of getting me unnoticed out of Pylos when I was traveling with Mentor, although he had apparently not recognized me as the slave boy of almost five years ago. And, Helen pointed out, he must have been quite taken with me to make such a journey, because any royal son of Nestor had more young female slaves at home than he could possibly work his way through, if pleasure of the body were his only goal.

In meetings with Peisistratus in the shrine next to the grand megaron, Helen told him who I was and worked out the details of our coming together. He agreed to make chaste visits over the next few months, and if we ended up becoming lovers it would be out of genuine affection and mutual desire.

On each of his visits, Peisistratus rode alongside our chariot in the guise of official escort. Alcippe and Phylo knew about Helen's arrangement, but Peisistratus' attentiveness to us all was so charming, it felt as if he had come along as everyone's friend. Once we were away from the palace and the queen was settled in for a picnic or a tour of a vineyard with Phylo and Alcippe, he and I went off on our own to take in the pleasures of the countryside of Lacedaemon.

He was twenty-five, tall and slender, with a strong chin and a straight nose, and though his eyes were an indistinct color, they were flecked with an appealing touch of green. His hair, the red-brown color of ripe acorns, curled up at the bottom where it touched his shoulders. His hands were veined, with small patches of the same golden hair that covered his arms and legs. From the beginning, so many things made me want to reach out and touch him, even his teeth, which were whiter and less ragged looking than most men's and flashed in the sun when he laughed.

And he laughed a great deal, tilting back his head and crinkling his eyes. Not the brays of men recounting conquests, not the tittering of gossiping slaves, Peisistratus' laughter came from somewhere deep inside. He laughed because things were funny, because he was happy, because he liked being with me. Needless to say, my spirit laughed with his, and before long I was floating around in a hazy glow at just the thought of him.

Since men and women's lives are so different, it surprised me how easy it was for us to talk about almost anything. He told me about hunts, about efforts to save crops from locusts, about horses that refused to be broken, about storms at sea. I told him my most vivid memories of Ithaca—the jellyfish, the day I saved Argos from drowning, my dance with Hera Pais, playing in the olive orchard with Telemachus. Some things seemed as if they had happened yesterday, but sometimes I felt as if I were describing someone else's life, shaping, as a bard does, what is said and what left out.

I skirted the subject of my brother's shortcomings, hoping Peisistratus would not notice. Telemachus used to annoy me, infuriate me, and make me rage with jealousy, but I had changed my view of him. I did not want a weak brother, and the time had passed to smirk at his flaws. Though I loved living in Sparta, especially now that I had Peisistratus for company, I wanted to know what would happen next in my life. Someone needed to take charge of that, because in my world, I couldn't do it myself.

Peisistratus saw through my stories and managed to pry out of me that I wanted a braver and more accomplished brother. When he saw I was ready to acknowledge that, he began telling me more of the news that had been drifting south to Pylos.

Hundreds of suitors were plaguing my house. The sailors who carried stories from port to port were great exaggerators, but half or even a quarter that number was horrifying enough. The people of Ithaca were tired of ill-mannered men infesting their town, and though they admired my mother's loyalty, some were saying she owed it to the people to marry one of the suitors just to get rid of the rest.

The suitors were grumbling loudly and incessantly about how stubborn my mother was, and I took some comfort in that. If anything is a sign that a woman is still in charge, it's a man complaining about not getting what he wants.

I knew Peisistratus well enough to sense that his high spirits seemed a bit forced on his next trip to Sparta. It was summer and we had gone up to watch the sunset from the tower.

My eyes took in the pink glow of the mountains without really seeing. "There's news, isn't there?" I asked.

We were still behaving like acquaintances, but because the attraction between us was strong, that was getting harder to do. I expected him to stay where he was, looking out from the opposite side of the tower from me, but instead he surprised me by coming over and clasping both my hands. His answer sent my world spinning.

"I've heard your mother has agreed to marry one of the suitors."

I blurted out, "Which one?" before realizing that wasn't what really mattered.

"She hasn't said," he told me. "She told them she's going to weave a shroud for Laertes first."

"My grandfather's dead?" How much more bad news was there going to be?

"No," he reassured me. "People say he looks fine. Old, but strong. She says as soon as it's done, she'll choose a new husband."

It made sense that my mother would want to weave Laertes' shroud, since Anticleia was dead and no longer could, but another thought almost immediately came to mind.

"How long ago did she start weaving?" I asked.

Peisistratus had already dropped my hands and gone to look at the clouds, which were now the color of hot coals scattered along the dark outlines of the mountains. "Months," he said. "Maybe a year."

I laughed, and he turned around. "What's so funny?" he asked.

"A shroud would take less than a moon cycle. She's got to be weaving him a story cloth. I don't think my mother has ever tried to make one, and not too many weavers are better than she is. A border all around, scenes from my grandfather's life woven into the middle—"

And then, in a flash, I understood. "Of course, if she makes a mistake, she'll tear it out and start again. She told me once that every flaw screamed at her." I grinned. "And of course, she's in no hurry, is she?"

I was the only one smiling.

"She can't weave forever," Peisistratus said.

"Maybe long enough for my father to come home."

He didn't reply.

"You don't think that's going to happen, do you?" My high spirits vanished as if they had been thrown from the tower to the ground below.

"I'm sorry, Xanthe, but I don't think anyone does." His eyes were sad but so tender that tears sprang into my own. "There hasn't been any real news in several years."

Peisistratus was silent for a moment. Then he pulled his shoulders back and wiggled them with a loud exhalation of breath, the way he always did when he was thinking about what to say.

"Your brother needs to show he's a man, and he needs to do it soon," he said. "You and your mother may not like the choices he makes for your lives, but at least she could stop doing battle, and you could come out in the open again."

I wasn't sure I wanted to be in the open. I liked my life in Sparta, especially now that he was in it. Still, the image of my mother at her loom doing beautiful work and having to pull it out made me want to fly to her side.

"I think my mother would rather die in battle than not choose what she wants for herself," I said.

He laughed. "Men will have much more to fear than sea monsters and giants when all women start thinking like that."

He looked at the fading colors in the clouds. "We should go back down." Then suddenly he took me in his arms. "I'm so sorry for all this," he said.

I forgot everything else for a moment. I wanted to turn my face up, wanted him to lean down and kiss me, wanted it in my lips, my jaw, my spine, my knees, more than I had ever wanted anything in my life. But he didn't.

"I promised," he said, pulling away. "We need to get back."

Helen did not worry about leaving us alone together. She had extracted a pledge from both of us that, if and when the time was right, she would have the pleasure of arranging our first night of love back in the palace. Every day Peisistratus and I spent together frayed the borders of that promise, by a squeeze of the hand, a brush of lips on the cheek, a long embrace. One day that fall, when the leaves were blazing in the sun and the vines were sagging under the weight of grapes yet to be harvested, our pledge almost came unraveled altogether.

We were on our way to one of the orchards so the queen could make an appearance among the workers. The queen's chariot left before he was ready, and we were already well down the main road through the valley when I turned and saw his horse kicking up a cloud of dust. When he pulled up alongside us, his horse snorted and tossed its head, as if it did not want to stop.

"Take me with you and keep going," I teased. "We'll meet the others at the orchard."

I should have realized Helen would call my bluff. "Why not?" she said, pulling the chariot to a stop. With wicked grins on their faces, Phylo and Alcippe jumped off to help me. They laced their fingers together, and over my rather feeble protests that I'd never ridden before, I put my foot into the web they had made and boosted myself onto the horse behind him.

"Put your arms around my waist," he said. As I held him, my head turned toward Helen.

I could never convey all that her eyes told me. *Go*, they said. *Go live.*

Peisistratus gave the horse a nudge with his feet, and we began to trot alongside the chariot, bouncing in a way that was so uncomfortable that if I had gotten off at that point I would concluded that the only good part of horseback riding was the chance to put my arms around him.

"It's actually more comfortable to go faster," he said. "Do you want to try?"

I rubbed my cheek up and down against his back to signal that I did, and after moving far enough ahead of the chariot not to cover it with our dust, Peisistratus told me to hang on tight. He nudged the horse's flanks, and we were off.

The rippling movement underneath me and the speed with which we tore down the road were more frightening than the chariot ride I had taken with Hermione. As I pressed into Peisistratus' back, eventually I began to feel a little safer, and I found my attention focusing more on what it felt like to touch him than on the ride itself.

I sensed the strength of his back and thighs as he kept us firmly in place. I imagined how his shoulders and sun-bronzed arms would feel if I stroked them. Overwhelmed, I buried my face in his tunic and kissed his back, surprising myself because I had done it without forming the intent.

I don't know how far we rode because it felt as if time stopped. It was probably not very long before Peisistratus turned off the main road onto a path leading to the Eurotas River. We came to a spot where the horse could get to the water's edge to drink. Peisistratus held my arm as I slid down from the horse. He got down after me, and as if it were one motion, I found myself in his arms.

I lifted my face as he lowered his, and our lips met, first as soft as a feather, and then harder, as if we were dying of a thirst that could only be quenched by finding some secret well deep inside each other. His hand cupped my breast, and I put my own over it, pressing down as if to say my heart was his to take.

When I think about that afternoon now, it seems as much the end of girlhood as the night in Orthia's grove. The place between my legs felt like the mouth of a cave, and everything inside me was burning. I was ready to fall to the ground and give myself to him, but he pulled away.

"I want you, Xanthe of Ithaca," he said. "I have wanted you from the first moment I saw you. Even before I knew who you were."

I was crying, and he held me closer. "Do you think it's time?" he asked.

I didn't have to ask what he meant. "Yes," I whispered, feeling my breath hot against his chest.

"Then we must go back. Tonight you will talk to Helen."

He made a clicking noise, and the horse looked up from the water and ambled over to him.

"The path's muddy," he said to me. "You should ride."

He boosted me on and held the reins as he walked the horse back to the road, just in time to meet the queen's chariot as it passed.

Saying anything to Helen proved unnecessary. She knew what had occurred just by looking at us.

When we got home, she told Alcippe and Phylo to have servants bring water to her quarters for a bath, clean coverlets for her bed, and a light meal. Once they had done that, she dismissed them for the evening. The bath was for me. For the one and only time in my life, the Queen of Sparta was in service to me, pouring the warm water over my shoulders and massaging me with a sponge.

"Do you know what to expect?" Helen asked.

I wasn't sure how to answer. I had never seen the act except between Melantho and the boy in the woods, but over the course of the years on a few occasions I had seen men's tunics draped over rather monstrous protrusions from their lower body as they leered at servant girls—or, in some cases, boys. I knew what to expect in that sense, but little more.

"Does it hurt?" I asked.

"It might." She twisted the sponge, and the water trickled down my back. "I'm sure he will be gentle. After all, it's not a rape."

I shut my eyes in pain for what Helen must have been thinking. What had happened to each of us at the riverbank could not have been more different. She was giving something to me that she had been robbed of herself.

"Thank you," I whispered.

Helen was using her wet fingers to coax dust out of my hair.

"Thank me for what?" She bent over and kissed the top of my head. "You're like a daughter to me."

She meant it in the softest and sweetest of ways, but I felt another stab of pain at the fact that she wasn't likely ever to have such a moment with Hermione. "I'm sorry," I murmured.

She knew what I meant. "It can't be helped," she said. "Nothing can, unless the gods will it." She squeezed water out of her sponge and put it down. "Are you ready to get out?"

She assisted me to my feet. "Enough sad thoughts. Tonight we'll pour a libation and ask Orthia and Hera to watch over you."

I dressed in an ordinary chiton for dinner with Helen, but before we sat down we made the final preparations to receive Peisistratus. She lent me one of her sheerest oiled linen cloths to drape around my body, adding a weightless green and gold veil she had received as a gift from a Phoenician prince; a pair of gold hoops for my ears; and bracelets with jeweled clasps for my arms.

We removed the coverings from the bed and replaced them with the fresh ones brought by the servants. Though Phylo and the others would know soon enough what had happened, to save me the discomfort of dealing with them that evening, Helen would go quietly to Menelaus and leave her room to me. In this way, the others would go to bed thinking I was still with the queen.

Helen placed small packets of dried rose petals here and there to sweeten the air. The room was quite dark, so she lit two more oil lamps, making the gold tassels and trims of the bedcovers glimmer and the rich colors come to life.

Knowing the bed had been prepared for me, and for such a momentous reason, I began to tremble.

Helen put her arm around my waist. "Come," she said, leading me out of the bedchamber. When we were both standing in front of the grooved channel on the hearth, Helen picked up the crystal rhyton and began to sing, this time not in the wild and unnerving way she did at the Orthia festival, but melodically, like the sound of a flute.

"Golden-throned Hera, daughter of Rhea, hear us as we call in reverence to you, goddess who surpasses all others in honor and beauty. O Royal One, Zeus' blessed queen, bestow your loving care on this virgin, who tonight will know a man for the first time." Helen poured a good portion of wine into the channel, and I heard it trickling into the basin underneath.

"Mighty and serene goddess, may love bless her and do her no harm." Helen's voice broke at these words, and she could barely get out the rest. "And may you keep far from her bed those who bring curses upon mortals."

I was too moved to speak, and I went to the table as if in a trance.

I ate a few bites without tasting anything. When I reached for my wine, Helen stopped my hand. She tapped a small amount of a brownish powder into the cup. "This will taste so bitter you'll want to spit it out, but you must swallow it all," she said.

I didn't ask why. When Helen had a potion, she was not to be resisted or questioned. I swallowed the wine and fought down the immediate urge to vomit.

"What was that?" I spluttered, as if I had just been saved from drowning.

"It's a special root," she said. "It grows by the river. It will keep you from conceiving a child. Tomorrow I'll make you some tea that you will take several times a day for a few days. It's the rest of the remedy."

She patted my hand. "You won't find it any tastier in the morning, but I can't send you back to Ithaca carrying Penelope's grandchild in your arms."

She examined my empty cup. "Good." She gave me a wry smile as she stood up. "I suppose among our prayers we should ask that the lovemaking be worth having to take the tea." I tried to laugh, but the sound never escaped my throat.

I waited by the fire in the megaron after Helen left. At first I tried to calm myself by doing needlework, but after one prick drew blood that left a small mark on my borrowed veil, I put it down and shut my eyes, concentrating on nothing but the warmth of the fire on my skin.

And then I heard the door creak open. Startled, I jumped up, spilling my work to the floor.

Peisistratus came over and picked it up. "You dropped something," he said, putting it on the hearth safely away from the flames before taking me into his arms.

"Xanthe," he said, caressing my name as if I were a goddess who had just revealed herself to him. "You look so beautiful."

Helen and I had settled for only the slightest line of kohl around my eyes and a trace of dark pink on my lips. Makeup was not good for kissing, and it left behind bloodshot eyes in the morning as well as a mess on the bedcovers.

I touched my fingers to his face, feeling how cool and soft his newly shaven skin was. It hadn't occurred to me that he would pay as much attention to being ready for me as I did for him, and knowing that he had was enough to dispel at least some of my nervousness.

"I could hardly wait to see you again," I whispered. "I'm not sure I've been breathing."

He put his hands on the back of my waist and held me tight. His hands wandered over my back, slipping down to cup my buttocks and pulling me to him so forcefully I came up onto my toes. We kissed again and again, as deeply as we had by the river.

But it was not enough. And wonder of wonders, it didn't have to be.

Peisistratus led me toward Helen's bedchamber. I felt as if I were gliding over the ground, disconnected from the ordinary world. When we were inside the curtain, he sat on the edge of the bed.

"Am I going too fast for you?" he asked.

When I shook my head, he stood up and undid the pin on one shoulder of my chiton and then the other, letting the cloth slip down around my waist. I watched his eyes as he took in my breasts. He pulled me to him, kissing my shoulders, my neck, my ears.

I was kissing him too, wherever my lips would reach, taking in a quick, shallow breath and then starting in again. I felt his hand play with the cord at my waist and suddenly my body felt free of all constraints as the robe fell to the floor and cool air flowed over me.

He pulled me with him onto the bed. I lay on my back while he ran his lips over my breasts while his hand moved down between my legs. When I felt for the first time the slip of his fingers along the opening to my body, the experience was almost too intense to bear.

He heard me moan. "Am I hurting you?"

"No," I whispered. "Not at all."

Without another word, he knelt below me on the bed, and lifting my legs by the backs of the knees, he parted them, moving his body closer to mine until I could feel the tip of his phallus touching me. It sent a jolt through my whole body, and I strained against him to feel it again.

Peisistratus moved his hips forward and pressed so hard I cried out. He stopped and then at my insistence he tried again. This time he slipped in and after a moment of searing pain, I felt for the first time the astonishing sensation of being filled up by a man. He moved slowly, watching my reaction, until I began to respond and press my hips against his.

He knelt and lifted my buttocks up with his hands, making small, deliberate movements, building a feeling that spread far beyond where he was touching, down to my toes, out to my fingers and up my spine. It was almost too intense to tolerate, although I didn't want him to stop. Then the feeling Phylo had given me in the sacred grove, the same feeling I sometimes gave myself in the night in my own bed, broke over me more forcefully than ever before, and I gasped with a pleasure so great it bordered on pain.

He was making strange noises too, and then he suddenly pulled away. I felt a warm fluid on my belly, which he dabbed clean with the edge of his robe before lying down beside me and shutting his eyes.

What happened? I wondered, reaching down with my fingers to touch the spot that had throbbed so intensely moments before. I felt another small jolt and moved my fingers away, as if any more might cause me to dissolve altogether.

Peisistratus had rolled onto his side and was looking at me. He brushed back a strand of my hair and kissed my forehead on the spot his fingers had cleared.

"Are you all right?" he asked.

I was too stunned to speak. Finally I whispered, "It wasn't how I imagined."

He laughed. "Is that good or bad?"

I rolled over to face him. "Good."

He drew me close to him. "We'll sleep for a while," he said, "and then I have to leave. I can't be here in the morning without causing a stir. But tomorrow I'll see you and we'll make some plans."

I had a sudden recollection of the cloak on the loom. *Weave it*, Helen had said, *and its magic will help its true owner find you.*

I fell asleep remembering how the wind blew my hair back as Peisistratus' horse flew down the road that morning. I was blazing into my future without fear of anything, through tomorrow, and the next day, and the next, now that the magic had worked, and the two queens, one of Sparta and one of the heavens themselves, had blessed me with such sweet recognition of what I needed, what I craved.

CHAPTER 16

Saffron and Crimson, Swirling

I trace my hand over the chaos of saffron and crimson battling in wild swirls across the next part of my weaving. The colors of womanhood and violence were never far apart in Sparta. Perhaps they never are. Men fight because they want to, and women are their best excuse.

My work tumbles across the loom, struggling to regain its balance, just as I tried to do during my last months in Sparta. I wove without a plan, building up one color here, packing in the other there. I added spatters and patches of other hues at random, sometimes choosing with my eyes shut, much as I imagine the gods do when they toy with our lives.

The result is so disturbing I don't want to look at it. I didn't want to live it either, but I had no choice.

I drifted off in Peisistratus' arms thinking something important had been settled, but when I awoke in the dark and he was gone, my confidence vanished. I felt so strange alone in Helen's bed that I slipped back to my own quarters without waking anyone.

I must have fallen asleep again, because at first light I sat up suddenly, panting in fear. In my dream, Peisistratus and I were hurtling down the road on a chariot. Suddenly the horses lost their footing and we went spinning into the air in a hail of broken bodies, twisted metal, and splintered wood.

I dressed as quietly as I could and slipped downstairs and across the courtyard to the palace shrine. There, where daylight still had not crept in, I stood in front of the statue of Hera, praying that my dream was not an omen, and weeping for the first thing I wanted so badly I was terrified to lose it.

Over the rest of the fall and through the winter, Peisistratus visited me a few more times, as often as he could get away. The women kept my relationship with him secret, treating it with a conspiratorial glee that bordered on giddiness whenever his chariot was spotted near the stables.

Every time I hoped he would come with word that my brother had faced down the suitors and established his manhood, or—equally unlikely—that my father had returned. When the months brought no new developments, he promised to go to Ithaca as soon as the worst sea weather had passed, to talk to my mother and brother about how we might be able to marry.

I was now eighteen, old for a bride, but since Icarius thought I was dead, and my father probably never learned I was alive, it was unlikely I had been promised to someone else. I clung to the probability that another husband had not yet been chosen for me as if it were the equivalent of good news, for there was never any of that.

Peisistratus was not the only one who came and went from the palace. Hermione spent the winter at Mycenae, coming back to Sparta only in time for Hera's spring festival.

Because Peisistratus and I slept in a large and pleasant bedroom next to Hermione's quarters, her return was distressing. We didn't want her to learn our secret, so whenever he visited we had to meet in a tiny, dark room off an interior corridor. Even with Helen's best efforts, it was stifling and oppressive, tolerable only because we were together.

I learned how to toss down Helen's tea without gagging, and I needed a lot of it. She teased me, saying that Peisistratus and I made love so often we were robbing the riverbank of every last protective leaf and root and putting all the other women in Lacedaemon at risk of new babies in their bellies.

Much as I wanted to go off from Sparta as Peisistratus' wife, the novelty of my womanhood was enough to occupy my thoughts and help me see every day through new eyes. Though living with my secrets was frustrating, and every one of his departures left me inconsolable, I could have gone on indefinitely that way, so favorably did it compare to my life before he came into it.

And, as it turned out, compared to the tumult the gods had in store for me now that he had.

I remember in detail the day Orestes arrived in Sparta. The meadows were already green and the fruit trees were blossoming, but the sky had turned heavy and dark, and the sounds of thunder in the mountains rolled through the valley. A late snow was falling, melting as it touched the ground.

Inside Helen's megaron, the fire warmed only the fronts of our bodies as the damp chill seeped through the walls. A messenger came from the king to tell Helen of her nephew's arrival and to ask her to come to a private supper in Menelaus' quarters that evening.

She paced around the room, jumping at sounds as small as a cough or a falling ember on the hearth.

"I'm dressing tonight," she said.

We all heard the nervousness and discomfort in her tone. Orestes was not just any nephew. He was Menelaus' murdered brother Agamemnon's son. We exchanged worried glances as we got up to begin the preparations.

"Why is she going to all this trouble for a little supper upstairs?" I whispered to Adreste as we looked through a chest for the veil Helen wanted.

"She knows what Orestes has come to say."

I gave her a puzzled look as I handed her the veil and shut the lid.

"When men have bloodshed on their minds, women don't exist," Adreste said. "She wants them not to be able to ignore her." She gave me the crafty smile I loved so well. "She'll be wearing so much perfume their eyes will water."

Helen usually took only one attendant to private dinners, and tonight I was going with her. Menelaus and Orestes were well into the wine by the time we arrived. Helen stiffened at the sight of them slouched in their chairs but went with her customary grace to greet Orestes.

"You were hardly more than a baby when I last saw you," she said, touching his cheek and looking into his eyes. "And now, a grown man."

I knew to expect someone my age. When his mother, Clytemnestra, had taken Aegisthus as her lover after Agamemnon left for Troy, Orestes had been about five years old. Fearing that Aegisthus might plan to kill the heir to the throne, his sister Electra spirited him away, and he had been raised in secret far from Mycenae.

No one had seen him all those years, and now he had arrived, exuding such confidence about himself that I could not help comparing him to my brother. Here was someone who wasn't whining for sympathy but doing what was necessary to set things right.

Although he had a pleasant manner about him, when he stood to greet Helen, I saw he was physically unappealing. He was about my height, with legs so thin they looked as if they could break off right under him. His hair was muddy in color and rather thin and lank, and one of his front teeth was badly chipped. His voice was almost as high as Phylo's, rich and deep for a woman, but strange coming from a man.

The king got to his feet as well, revived by seeing his wife looking so radiant. We had taken great pains with her hair, which hung in thick coils over her shoulders and glinted with interwoven threads made of tiny gold beads. Larger gold beads dangled over her temples from her jeweled headband, each one of the strands tipped with an amulet or a disk of glowing amber. Her veil had been perfumed in addition to her skin, and when she entered the room it was as if a goddess had arrived inside a scent and then been embodied in a burst of light.

Even with such a dazzling entrance, the facts of why Orestes had come soon settled in again over the room. The sad history that preceded his nephew had already swallowed Menelaus' joy, and I saw by his red face and cheeks that he had broken down in tears not long before our arrival.

At Helen's request, I was carrying her golden spindle and distaff wound with soft purple roving. When she was settled in with her spinning and the men's cups had been refilled, Menelaus picked up the conversation.

"I told Orestes he must stay for a feast in his honor tomorrow night, but he said no," Menelaus said to Helen. Turning to his guest, he added, "Let's see if you can resist my wife as easily as you do me."

"Oh," Helen said, putting down her work. She exhaled in a manner suggesting that a hidden message meant only for Orestes' ears had just escaped from between her breasts. "You must stay. You can't let us be such bad hosts."

"I'll celebrate when I return," Orestes said, "and we'll pour many libations to the gods."

"Yes," Helen murmured. Something about her voice made me look more closely at her. Her fingers were trembling so noticeably that she spun the top of the spindle too hard and guided the wool through the pads of her fingers with a beginner's lack of dexterity. I knew what would happen, and I watched with my tongue between my teeth as the thread grew thinner and thinner, breaking before it reached the floor.

"You'll leave tomorrow?" Helen asked, picking up the spindle and repairing the break, before starting again to spin a new length of thread.

"At daybreak," Orestes replied.

"And you?" Helen said to Menelaus. Her thread broke again, and with no expression on her face, she handed me the spindle and distaff. Though I took it from her as if nothing were unusual, in all the time I had been with the queen I had never seen her unable to spin. I understood at that moment what had been bothering her all day. It wasn't that Orestes had come for a visit, but that he had probably already asked Menelaus to come with him to Mycenae to kill the murderers of Agamemnon. Menelaus was too broken a man to lift a sword to avenge his brother, but he was sentimental enough to want to try, and not likely to come home alive if he did.

Before Menelaus could reply, we heard voices outside. I recognized in an instant who was demanding that the guard let her by, and almost in the same moment Hermione swept into the room.

She went straight to Orestes without acknowledging anyone else. "It's Hermione," she said. "Do you remember me, or were you too young?"

"Hermione!" Orestes said in a voice so excited I was surprised it didn't squeak.

He turned to Helen. "She was my favorite. I always told her I wished she were my real sister instead of the others. Of course, they were older and not much fun."

Hermione's face glowed in triumph. "You were such a sweet little boy," she said, with a painted-on charm anyone should have seen through.

She turned to her mother. "Don't you remember how sweet he was?" She paused for effect. "No, I suppose you wouldn't."

Hermione had to this point not looked at Menelaus, but now she turned to him. "I know I wasn't invited, but I just needed to say hello."

She took Orestes' hands in her own. "I have to leave now. Please, let's make plans to talk tomorrow." Her voice was strange, not that of a grown woman but of a child who can't sleep on the eve of a big event. Then, without waiting for his reply, she glided out, her eyes straight ahead, acknowledging no one.

The room was silent. We sat for a while in the oppressive air until Helen stood up to go to her quarters. She hung heavily on my arm, forgetting until we were in the courtyard that Menelaus hadn't answered her question.

That night, everyone was roused by a commotion in the palace. As we came to our railing, we could see the stables engulfed in flames. Helen and Phylo stayed behind, but Alcippe and I wrapped cloaks around our bodies, and, not bothering to lace our sandals properly, we tore down the stairs and up the path to the fire.

The stone wall around the stable yard was about as tall as we were, but we found chinks in which to wedge our toes until we climbed high enough to support our weight with our arms on the top of the wall. The flames created their own wind as they swept up into the sky, and the heat even at our distance was like the hottest day of summer. Most of the horses had already gotten out of the stable. Their silhouettes gleamed in the coral-colored light as they ran around the stable yard whinnying in panic.

"Are there any still inside?" I heard one stable hand say to another.

"I don't think so," he replied, "but three are missing."

Just as he spoke, the roof collapsed in a blast of light and heat. Alcippe held her hand to her mouth and cried at the frightening power of the blaze, while I looked as deep as I could into the rubble of the fallen roof, making out what I thought was the outline of the queen's sedan chair.

Early the following morning, a groom came at the queen's request to tell her the damage. They had time only to save horses, and all the chariots and both chairs had been destroyed. Several of the stable hands had been burned, but none seriously. The carcass of one horse was found inside, but no one knew what had happened to the other two.

An idea came to me so suddenly that my feet were moving almost before I finished thinking it. I rushed from the queen's megaron down to Hermione's quarters, throwing open the door without any effort to announce my presence.

I didn't need to. Hermione was gone.

She had taken the two missing horses and Orestes' chariot,

which had been left in the stable yard overnight. No one had to guess where she was going. Menelaus sent a party to borrow a chariot from one of his nearby allies, since he had none left of his own. Now the king would have no choice but to go to Mycenae.

By noon, Helen and I watched from the balcony as Menelaus and Orestes disappeared through the palace gates. We had been so numb all morning that their departure seemed like being woken from a dream. I looked around, surprised to see that, other than the smoldering remains of the stable, everything else was still just the way it always was.

Since there was no longer anything to watch, I turned away, but the queen did not. Her eyes were narrow, and her lips were slightly parted in an expression so troubled I felt a thud of panic in my chest. "Are you worried about the king?" I asked her.

Helen turned to me with a dazed look, as if she had just noticed I was there. "She burned it!" she whispered. Tears pooled in her eyes. Covering her mouth with her fingers, she added, "Poor horse."

Then, as if she had just heard my question, she said, "My husband will be fine. Orestes insists on killing them himself. Menelaus promised me he'll do no more than bring our daughter back." Her brusque formality surprised me more than her tears, but I knew it was meant as a polite sign that prying any further would be unwelcome.

She adjusted the folds of her chiton under her belt as if doing so put everything about the morning into proper order. When she looked up she seemed surprised by the anxiety that must have been apparent on my face.

"I believe him," she said, but her voice was a bit too insistent for comfort. "And I forbid you to worry!" She tried to make her order sound light and playful, but she didn't succeed, and she knew it. "Well then," she said, "let's go make some salve and bring it to the men for their burns."

Half a moon cycle passed with no news. Helen and the handmaidens spent every morning in the shrine, cleaning even the slightest speck of dust from the images of the gods, sprinkling barley and laying flowers and cakes at their feet, and offering gifts of gold, carved ivory, and other treasures, all for Menelaus' safe return with Hermione.

And, because I was sure the queen was not praying for herself, I did so to Hera on her behalf. I trembled with dread in front of her altar at the prospect of Helen's life having even more grief in it. "Most beautiful and radiant queen of the gods," I whispered, "reigning spirit in women's hearts, let her live in peace with her husband."

My next thought was so intense I knew the goddess would hear it even unspoken, so I figured I might as well acknowledge it out loud. "I can't pray for Hermione's safe return because I don't wish it, and you will be angry if I am false," I said in a voice too low to be heard by anyone else. "But please, if you bring her back, don't let her hurt Helen again."

Every time we beseeched the gods in the shrine, we watched their images for signs of acknowledgment. I saw none, and the queen's grim face said the same. Every time we returned, our eyes scanned the altars for signs the gods had honored us with a visit, and we went away more distressed than before that they seemed to have turned their backs on us. Still, what more can mortals do than continue to honor the only ones with power to affect our fates? We prayed and waited, and busied ourselves with our weaving and other duties in a vain attempt to create the illusion that our actions had any influence on destiny at all.

Finally, Menelaus returned. Clytemnestra and Aegisthus were dead. After murdering them both, Orestes stayed in Mycenae to calm the palace and take charge as the heir to the throne.

Menelaus was not alone. Beside him was Hermione, her hair unkempt and her chiton soiled, as if she had not taken care of herself for days. She was rushed straight to her quarters, and a guard was posted outside with directions to admit no one but the servants of Helen's choice, who would bring Hermione her meals and empty her chamber pot.

She never made it to Mycenae. Even though she had taken plenty of gold with her and had managed to bribe someone to take her secretly by boat most of the way—a route that was easier than traveling by road—she and the one slave she had taken with her had been caught near Tiryns, far short of her goal, and she was under guard in the palace there until Menelaus could return to bring her home. Even though I loathed her, when I understood how far she had managed to get on her own, I had to admit I was impressed.

Menelaus sent out his most trusted advisers and servants to go to the surrounding cities and towns for word of Neoptolemus. They were to do everything they could to ensure that he came to Sparta immediately to marry the princess or forfeit his right to do so. Hermione would be married quickly to him, or to someone else, but she was to be out of the palace as soon as possible.

Every day we waited for word from Neoptolemus, if not his actual arrival. In the handmaidens' quarters, friendly wagers were made about what was happening. Had Neoptolemus been warned about Hermione's personality and deliberately stayed away? Would he marry her anyway, to gain access to what was one of the largest dowries ever heard of? If he didn't show up, what would Menelaus do next?

Helen did not involve herself in these wagers. The situation with her daughter had turned out about as badly as it could, and she might as well have put on mourning clothes, so deep was her grief. Still, though she did not participate, she always wanted to know what the rest of us were thinking.

"Phylo and Alcippe go back and forth about whether Neoptolemus will show up," I told her one morning as we passed the shuttle at her loom. "Today they both think he won't."

"And Adreste?" Helen asked as we lifted the heddle rod to change the path of the shuttle across the loom.

"Adreste thinks Menelaus might prefer to marry Hermione to Orestes, and he's hoping Neoptolemus won't show up, so he can get out of his pledge."

Helen smiled as we dropped the heddle and lifted the shed rod. "Clever old woman. He promised our daughter to Orestes while he was still in the cradle, but at Troy he promised her a second time, to Achilles' son."

She held the shuttle in her hand, so lost in thought she forgot to pass it to me. When she spoke her voice was choked with sadness. "He's always been a bit forgetful, even before the war affected his mind. Agamemnon and Achilles both call to him about his promise from the land of the dead." She looked away. "I hear him in his sleep, talking to them."

The conversation had taken an uncomfortably personal turn, so I changed the subject. "I don't suppose Orestes really wants to marry Hermione," I said. "She must hate him now, after what he did."

"No," Helen said, finally noticing the shuttle and passing it to me. "Orestes would marry her. I'm sure of that."

It was my turn to forget to pass the object in my hand. "Hermione is the scariest person I've ever met," I blurted out, unable to understand why anyone would want to bring such horror into his life.

For the first time in as long as I could remember, Helen laughed, really laughed from deep down inside. "You precious girl," she said. "Sad to say about my own child, but I can't imagine Orestes ever sleeping again, not with her in his bed. But he'll want to marry her anyway. And Adreste's right that my husband wants him to."

We took smooth beater sticks and pressed the loose weft threads into the fabric above. "You don't understand, do you?" she said.

"I must not," I sighed, putting down my stick.

"Marriage isn't about what the bride and groom want. I thought you knew that."

My heart sank. All I wanted was Peisistratus, and I tried to calm myself by focusing only on the rhythmic clicks and whooshes the loom and shuttle made as we worked.

Helen went on. "Did you know, for all the stories about how great men competed for my hand, the one who succeeded wasn't there?"

"What?" I asked, glad for the distraction from thoughts of my lover. "Everyone knows Menelaus won."

"He was back in Mycenae, at least at the beginning. Agamemnon came in his place to make a deal with my father. It was never going to matter who actually won the contests."

She stopped weaving and looked at me as if she were assessing how much she could say. "Odysseus was the craftiest of all my suitors," she went on. "When he realized the contest was over before it started, he thought about what else he might be able to get out of coming all that distance. I imagine he already knew what Icarius had in mind for your mother's dowry, so Odysseus made his own deal with my father."

"To make everyone take an oath to defend the man who married you," I said, having been told the story many times before. I had stopped weaving also, and we both stood facing each other in front of the loom.

Helen nodded. "In return for my father making sure that, when the time came, Icarius would declare Odysseus the winner of Penelope's hand."

I was stunned. "My father didn't really win either?"

"No, actually he did. But knowing what Agamemnon had done, he couldn't take the chance that it wouldn't matter in the end."

My head throbbed, and I turned back to the loom to have something to do while I thought about what Helen had told me. If people could not be simple and honest, how could I ever hope to understand anything? Would I have to go through life suspicious of everything and everyone?

Helen reached through her end of the shed and wiggled her fingers to get me to notice that I had the shuttle. "Sometimes I wonder what would have happened if I had married your father," she said. "How many things could have been different."

Her face clouded and she rummaged in a basket as if she were looking for another color of thread to weave in, but since the design did not call for it, I knew she just needed an excuse to be alone with her thoughts. Then her hands went still and she was no longer trying to pretend she was looking for anything. The silence grew so thick it seemed merciful for me to plead a headache and leave us both alone to contemplate what might have been.

* * *

Neoptolemus answered the summons to Sparta only at the last moment, offering no explanation for his delay, nor apparently thinking that the fact he already had a wife had any bearing on his claim to the princess of Sparta. For his efforts at Troy, his share of the spoils had been King Hector's widow, Andromache, who had already borne Neoptolemus a child.

Hermione would be exiled to Scyros, her husband's home, a place that made Ithaca seem rich by comparison, alongside another wife who was reputed still to have considerable charms. Perhaps, I thought, with some satisfaction, having to compete with someone rather like Helen, without one friend or supporter at her side, might finally make Hermione appreciate the mother she had scorned. Or, for that matter, the marriage she might have had, if her parents had not seen her as so much of a threat that she had to be gotten rid of as quickly as possible.

Coincidentally, Megapenthes was set to marry in only a few days, so the simplest plan was to wed Hermione to Neoptolemus at the same time. A few more oxen and pigs would be slaughtered, and extra libations poured, but the bridal feast for Hermione was more a tidy disposal of a problem than a celebration of a momentous event in the life of a princess.

The day of the double wedding arrived, and Helen spent the entire morning getting clothed and painted for the occasion. Everyone's spirits were high. None of us mentioned Hermione or Megapenthes, as if the feast itself were good enough reason to dress up and drink a little wine in Helen's quarters before it began. Even Adreste was persuaded to adorn her hair and wear a colorful veil over her stooped shoulders.

Alcippe, Phylo, and I were wearing our flounced skirts and

tight jackets, with gossamer veils over our breasts. Our hair was pulled up on the back of our heads, decorated with flowers, and left to fall in one fat lock past our shoulders. We finished by painting sunburst designs on our cheeks and lining our eyes with a thick coating of kohl.

In the courtyard a newly painted chariot gleamed. Neoptolemus would use it to take Hermione on the short journey to the port after the ceremony, and she would be gone from Sparta that very day. The chariot would then be returned to the palace, a gift from Neoptolemus to Menelaus, to replace one of those burned in the fire.

We stopped to admire its gold inlay and bright red designs, and Alcippe, made playful by the wine, stepped on board and pretended to drive the horses hard.

"Look at me!" she said, laughing because in real life she would be begging us to stop. He eyes lit on the upper balcony on Hermione's end, and when they stayed there we all turned to look at what she was seeing.

Hermione was coming from her quarters dressed not in Iphigenia's skirt, but in a red-trimmed himation over a shimmering oiled chiton. She was in the middle of a line of attendants, most of them daughters of those who had come for the wedding of Megapenthes.

Helen stepped into her path to greet Hermione as she crossed the courtyard. I held my breath, fearful of a confrontation, and moved closer to the queen to protect her if I needed to.

Hermione's step was heavy, and she stopped without protest in front of her mother. She even permitted Helen to lift her veil. Her face was oddly radiant, and her eyes were glistening but vacant. I saw immediately that she had been drugged. Helen was taking no chances.

"You look lovely," Helen said.

"I'm feeling better already." Hermione's laugh was a loud sniff. She tried to pull back to keep Helen from touching her cheek, but she couldn't move fast enough.

"Go, and may the gods make you happy again," Helen said softly, replacing the veil and motioning her daughter to pass.

We made a quick trip into the shrine to pray for Hermione at Hera's altar, after which we went into the grand megaron, where the feast was already in progress. Additional tables had been brought in, creating three sides and an open end for games and dancing. Palace slaves rattled sistrums and pounded on drums. Boisterous flute melodies had already gotten some guests dancing, while slaves trained as acrobats, dressed in wildly colored tunics and bright hats, flipped backward in full circles in the air and made rings of cartwheels in front of the guests.

Hermione was seated at the head of the table, with Neoptolemus at her side and Megapenthes next to him. Neither man seemed at all interested in his bride, both laughing and banging their hands on the table as they watched the antics in front of them. Megapenthes' bride—I can't now remember her name or anything about her except that she was from somewhere nearby—seemed to be enjoying the entertainment, but Hermione's flaccid stare was straight ahead.

Helen took her seat next to Menelaus, and as usual we all stood behind her. The acrobats stopped to rest for a while, and the bard came into the opening between the tables to sing wedding songs. Megapenthes and most of the other men guffawed with great shakes of their shoulders, since the greatest fun at a wedding seemed to be hearing stories about the gods' violent or sneaky successes at bedding women, who were sometimes willing, sometimes not.

Young men—nobles and princes mostly—got up one pair after another to play games for our entertainment. One young man tossed a ball from under his leg while another caught it and twirled in the air before landing. He cocked his elbow and flicked his wrist as he threw it back, making it spin in the air, while the first man bent forward to bounce it off the back of his neck into his hand. When they ran out of new tricks, they sat down and several other pairs got up and pretended to box.

I grew sadder as the feast continued. The bard's stories weren't funny to me, and all the young men only served as reminders that Peisistratus was not there.

Or so I thought. Phylo nudged me, tilting her head toward the door at the entrance to the megaron.

There he was, coming toward Menelaus' table. In the torchlight, I saw how my lover's freshly bathed skin gleamed with oil, and how strong his shoulders looked under the fleece he had draped over his fresh white tunic. He caught my eye for a moment, and the look that passed between us went straight to that place of greatest pleasure in my body.

So entranced was I that at first I failed to notice the young man next to him. When I did, I gasped at the sight.

Telemachus! My heart pounded. Had Peisistratus already gone to Ithaca, already arranged for our wedding? Were they coming to get me so it could be carried out? What else could it be? Peisistratus and my brother moved in proximity to each other like old friends, and what other bond would suddenly make friends of strangers? I said a silent prayer to Hera that it was so.

I saw Peisistratus turn his chin for a moment in my direction, as if he were indicating to Telemachus where to look for me. My brother searched the faces of the queen's handmaidens until his eyes widened in recognition. I saw his glance go momentarily to my breasts before he looked away. He did not acknowledge me any further, turning instead back to Peisistratus and resuming their conversation.

Getting through the rest of the feast was agony. Peisistratus was seated with my brother at the king's part of the table, so the entire time I could see nothing but his back as he conversed with Telemachus and the others. When Hermione and Neoptolemus went out to their chariot in the courtyard, for the first time I had a chance to work my way toward Peisistratus in the crowd.

He sensed me near him and leaned in my direction. "Say nothing," he said. "Go to our room. I'll come to you later."

I waited in the little cell, my heart soaring at the idea of being with him again, but burdened with the terrible feeling that I wouldn't want to hear any news he was bringing. Finally I heard him opening the door.

He remained fully clothed as he sat on the edge of the bed. "I can't stay," he said. "Telemachus and I are sleeping on the porch, and he'll wonder where I've gone."

I sat up in bed. "What's happening?" I pleaded, unable to keep myself from bursting into tears after the strain of the day.

"Telemachus came to Pylos, looking for news. He told my father Athena sent him. She told him that if he learned Odysseus was dead, he was to come to Sparta, see to your marriage, then go home and marry Penelope to one of the suitors."

My heart slammed against my ribs. "What did he find out?"

In the silence before his reply, my future hovered. A dead father meant Peisistratus would be mine within a day or two, and I could be Xanthe again.

Say he's dead, I thought. *Just say he's dead.*

"My father told him he'd heard he was alive. He came to Sparta to find out what Menelaus had heard."

My stomach felt as if I had swallowed hot rocks. "What did Athena say about that?" I whispered. "What happens if he's not dead?"

Peisistratus took my hand. "Athena told him Odysseus cannot return and the plague on your house cannot be lifted until you come back to Ithaca."

I took in a hoarse gulp of air before bursting into tears again. "Why?" I pleaded.

"The gods don't have to tell us why."

He took me in his arms. "You have to leave Sparta with your brother. I'll go back with you as far as Pylos."

I slumped over on the bed, pulled my knees up, and wrapped my arms around them. I wanted to make myself so small I would disappear, just to get away from all the pain. "I thought when I saw you with Telemachus you were going to tell me we were getting married," I moaned.

"Xanthe, he can't make that happen." He lay down next to me and rocked me in his arms. "Not now. Not yet. But I told him I wanted to."

I felt his shoulders shake, and I knew by the rough sound of his voice that he too was crying. "I made him promise not to give you to anyone else."

"Then we're betrothed? I mean, as good as?" I sat up again, suddenly far less miserable.

"You shouldn't let your hopes get too high. News does travel, and you don't know what your father knows, or what he might already have promised."

Please be dead, I thought again. *Please don't come home and spoil everything.*

Today as I sit at my loom and the silence from downstairs grows around me, I remember something my mother often told me when I was a child. "Be careful what you ask the gods for," she said, "because the one who hears may be in a spiteful mood, and give you what you thought you wanted."

My only salvation, and my mother's, was that I did not invoke any of the gods that night as I wept in Peisistratus' arms. I didn't realize until later that a living Odysseus was the only way everyone's problems could be solved.

"Telemachus spoke with Menelaus and Helen already." Peisistratus stood up. "Tomorrow you pack and attend the feast for your brother. Then, the next day, you're going home."

BOOK III

Ithaca

CHAPTER 17

The Weight of Gray

Gray. I varied the color of the next part of my weaving only by making it darker gray. The color of the boulders in the rain as I left Sparta, the walls at Pylos, the sky, the sea. The gloomy color weighed down the whole life I had woven above it.

Returning to Ithaca, I lay on the bottom of the boat much as I had on my outward journey, wrapping my arms around myself and remembering the secret I had tried to keep five years earlier. The frightened girl who stole into the woods to bury strips of cloth had grown into a confident woman, or so I once thought. Like seawater evaporating after high tide, I left behind only traces of gray as I felt myself disappearing into nothing at all.

The fire in Helen's megaron had not yet been raked and rekindled the next morning, but no one noticed or cared. I suppose we all thought it more appropriate to leave the room cold and dark.

Helen herself packed the red coverlet that lay on my bed to

greet me when I first arrived at the palace. To it she added the most beautiful of her veils, as sheer and golden as Spartan light.

"For your wedding," she said. "In case I can't be there."

Alcippe put her favorite bracelet on top of the neat pile of gifts. "In case none of us can," she said, running from the room with her hand over her mouth in an unsuccessful attempt to hold back tears.

Phylo was wearing a pair of earrings I had always admired. "Please wear these when you leave," she said, brushing the gold hoops with her lips before putting them on me. "The only way I can bear this is to think that at least in some way I'm going with you."

Adreste wasn't in the megaron at all. She had taken to bed, complaining of aches beyond what she could endure on her feet.

"She told me she's too old for any more change," Helen said, brushing my wet cheeks. "You should go to her. She has something for you."

While Helen and the others continued to pack a chest with gifts, I went into Adreste's bedchamber. She looked so frail under the covers as she slept, and more ancient than she had seemed even the day before. I whispered her name, and her eyes opened.

"Xanthe," she said. "I suppose I can call you that now, without making Phylo angry." She managed a weak smile. "Help me sit up, would you?"

When her feet were dangling over the edge of her bed frame, she felt under the covers and pulled out a silk-wrapped package. It was small enough to fit in the palm of my hand, but heavy and solid.

"Open it," she said.

I tugged at the cloth and it fell away to reveal a small figurine. I recognized who it was right away by the owl incised on her shoulder.

"Athena," I whispered.

"The first night you were here, Athena came to see if you were all right. Did you know that?"

The owl in the window. I had forgotten about it. "I didn't know you saw it."

She gave me a wan smile. "Even a goddess makes mistakes. She came to my window first."

She twisted her body toward where I was seated on the bed. "I can't see you very well that way," she said. "Would you mind kneeling in front of an old slave, even though you are a princess?"

I rushed to do what she asked, and she cradled my face in her hands. The tenderness in her eyes made my own burn with tears.

"You're very loyal," she said. "I've always seen that in you. When you came here, you were Hera's alone, but now your heart is more open."

With a fingertip she caught a tear making its way down my cheek. "It isn't disloyal to Hera or Orthia to ask for Athena's help as well," she went on. "She's your father's protector, and your brother's too. Last night I got up when you all were in the megaron, and I saw the owl again from the balcony, perched on the roof. She came because your brother is here."

Adreste took her hands from my face and ran a callused, yellowed finger over the tiny object I was holding.

"It's time you put yourself in Athena's hands," she said. "What happens from now on will be hers to influence more than anyone else's."

Adreste looked at me for a long time with her clouded, watery eyes, as if to fix in memory all the details of my face. Then she asked me to help her get back in bed.

I poured all the love I had into tucking a blanket around her feet and smoothing it across her shoulders. When I bent over to kiss her forehead, a gentle, dreamy smile crossed her face.

"Good-bye," she whispered, shutting her eyes. "And may all the gods be with you."

Adreste died in her sleep that night. Perhaps she breathed her last while we were downstairs at the feast in honor of Telemachus' arrival. We tiptoed into our quarters so as not to disturb her, and nobody thought to check. We didn't find her body until the following morning, when it was already cold.

Though Helen and all the women in the queen's wing would have preferred to stay upstairs and grieve for Adreste, nothing could be done to avoid yet another of Menelaus' feasts, this one in honor of my brother's departure.

Helen disappeared with Menelaus and Megapenthes into a storeroom somewhere in the palace and came out carrying a robe as a gift for Telemachus. She brought it to him at his seat in the place of honor in the grand megaron.

"I made this myself," she said. "I hope you'll honor me by having your bride wear it at your wedding." Her voice was measured and calm. "Until then," Helen went on, "ask your mother to put it in a safe place with her things."

Telemachus took the robe, not recognizing her clear insinuation that in him the marks of adulthood were long overdue.

Helen stood at Menelaus' side while he and Megapenthes presented my brother with a beautiful gold-lipped silver bowl and a two-handled cup. When the king was finished and I took Helen's arm, I felt her knees give way momentarily under her. Phylo and I strained to hold her up as we led her to her chair.

She did not want to sit with the guests, but at a chair near the fire, with me seated next to her. Alcippe had brought Helen's golden distaff and spindle downstairs with us, and Helen handed me her usual ones. We flicked them in silent misery, watching with dull eyes as the filaments spilled out before us.

I hadn't seen Peisistratus all morning. I imagine he deliberately stayed away to give me one less distraction as I spent my last day in Sparta. When he came into the megaron, he ate quickly, perched on the edge of his seat, because the sun was getting high and we needed to be on our way.

Finally Menelaus gave the men leave to get up from the table. He ordered a servant to carry his goblet filled with wine as he accompanied Telemachus and Peisistratus into the courtyard. I got up to follow them, but Helen grabbed my arm.

"Wait a moment," she said. When she pressed her golden distaff and spindle into my hand, I thought she only wanted me to carry it for her, and I turned again to follow the others.

"Xanthe." She said my name in a way that managed to combine a caress with an order. "Look at me."

I didn't want to raise my eyes, didn't want to feel the pain of knowing I was spending my last moments with her. It was almost better to be already on the road than to suffer like that.

"I want you to take these to your mother," she said, touching the objects in my hand. "Tell her it's in thanks for having sent her beautiful daughter to me."

She held me in a long, tight embrace, which I returned as best I could with the precious gifts in my hands. "There's no holding back the sun," Helen finally said. "We can't keep the men waiting."

We walked out of the megaron arm in arm, just as Menelaus was pouring a libation. He was standing in front of one of the two chariots that would be required to transport us, my possessions, and all our gifts back to Ithaca. "Great Zeus, give wings to these horses' feet," he called out in a deep and resonant voice, "and carry the son of Odysseus, beloved of Athena, safely home."

"And his daughter too," I heard Helen whisper. She reached across her body to pat my arm, but neither of us could bear to let our eyes meet.

When Menelaus finished, Telemachus began thanking the king and queen for their gifts and hospitality, but he was interrupted when everyone in the courtyard began shouting and waving their arms.

The biggest eagle I had ever seen had just grabbed a goose from the yard. The goose honked in terror, fluttering its wings to get free of the talons as the eagle swooped low over the courtyard, before disappearing with its prey.

At the commotion, the horses strained as if they wanted to bolt. Peisistratus, who was holding the reins of one team, pulled their heads down toward him to control them. He called out to Menelaus. "Was that an omen for Sparta, or for our journey?"

The king looked bewildered. I thought of Adreste in her dark room. She would have known.

Helen stepped forward and stood next to him. "I'll answer," she said. "The gods put a thought in my mind just as the eagle passed over."

She pulled herself up in the regal way I remembered from my first years in Sparta. "The gods are telling Telemachus that Odysseus is on his way, to seek his vengeance on the fattened suitors in his yard."

All the men cheered, and Telemachus hopped onto one of the chariots. "Let's be gone, then," he said, motioning with his arm that I was to ride with him.

I held back for a moment. My eyes bored into Helen, but she would not look at me. For such a triumphant omen, her face was curiously blank. Was she saying what the omen really meant, or protecting me from the true interpretation? Something or someone healthy and strong would soon be snatched away from the world we knew. The omen had to mean that much. I felt a shudder of misapprehension and had to fight down the contents of my stomach, but I still did not look away from the queen.

Helen turned without meeting my gaze and walked toward the staircase, leaning on Phylo. I could see they were crying by the way their shoulders slumped as they huddled together, crying not just about my leaving, but about the scene they faced upstairs, and the funeral they had to attend to.

Alcippe turned for a moment just as they reached the staircase. Her lips were parted and her eyes pulled down at the corners as if by tiny invisible weights. She looked at me for just a moment before closing her mouth in a tight line and turning to run up the stairs.

Impatiently, the horses tossed their heads. I got aboard, the chariot lurched forward, and I was gone from the palace at Sparta.

My return trip to Pylos was as miserable as my outward journey years before. Helen's interpretation of the omen turned Telemachus into a madman, and he raced over the perilous mountain passes as if demons nipped at the wheels. He acted as if I weren't there, or more accurately, I suppose, as if it didn't matter that I was. He addressed me as *sister* from time to time, but with no more feeling than he might accord a new slave Menelaus had added to the store of gifts. His mind was elsewhere, I suppose, but he made old, taciturn Mentor seem a lively traveling partner by comparison.

I wished I could be with Peisistratus in his chariot, but it was best otherwise. Peisistratus had given Telemachus the impression that he barely knew me and that he could easily wait to marry me until the problems on Ithaca were resolved. He was just a lusty young prince who had seen something he wanted. And besides, I was Telemachus' responsibility, and it was best that he recognize that from the beginning of our journey.

Deep down, I knew being near my lover would be too painful to endure. Our time together was over, at least for now, and we simply had to get through these excruciating last days when nothing could be done and we had to pretend we didn't matter to each other.

When we reached the turnoff to the harbor at Pylos on the second day of our journey, Telemachus entreated Peisistratus to let him be on his way without stopping to say good-bye to Nestor at his court.

I waited in the chariot for his answer to my brother. I hoped he would chastise Telemachus for his rudeness and insist that Nestor be properly honored by affording him the chance to send us off with a feast. The idea of another feast was more than my stomach or my heart could handle, but I yearned for just one night in Pylos, when, knowing the secrets of his own home, my lover could easily come to my bed.

I could see Peisistratus hesitate. And then, without looking at me, he jumped back on his chariot. "To the boat, then," he said.

I felt as if I had been knocked over. The man whose voice made my heart leap when I heard it echoing on the stairs of the palace, the man who by taking my hand could make my knees tremble had just tossed away a night of more value to me than any of the treasures in the chests at my feet. I was shaking too hard to stand in the chariot, and too miserable to care if I was thrown from it altogether as my brother drove the horses toward the bay.

I had not felt more betrayed since the day I was a bedraggled girl in the kitchen at Ithaca listening to Telemachus take credit for saving the dog. How could anyone be so cold? Was I only finding out now that I had been wrong about Peisistratus' heart all along? Had he just been waiting to cast me off and find another lover? Was he really going to send me off with only a quick and indifferent good-bye?

I went off by myself on the beach while the crew loaded everything aboard a rowboat pulled up on the sand. I hoped Peisistratus would come to offer some explanation, but he did not. When Telemachus called to me that it was time to leave, I concentrated on moving shells aside with my toes as I walked back. I looked out the corners of my eyes to be sure my path would not lead me close to Peisistratus, since my feelings had passed quickly from hurt and betrayal to storms of rage.

But the hand helping me into the rowboat was his.

"Xanthe?" he said.

I wanted to pull my hand away, wanted to say a spiteful *What?* and turn my back on him forever, but I couldn't.

"It's better this way," he said in a voice so low no one else could hear.

Almost against my will, I looked at him. His expression was tortured, and because I loved him, I wanted his pain to stop as badly as I wanted mine to.

I knew he was right. There is no good way to tear a bandage from a wound, but getting it done in one quick and unexpected rip is better than teasing it away in small, agonizing steps.

The rowboat was pushing off toward the ship on which I would pretend to be Telemachus' cousin coming for a visit to Ithaca. Peisistratus walked alongside until the water lapped his thighs, looking at the sky as if for a reassuring sign. "I hope Helen was right about the omen," he said.

I looked up too, into a blue that mocked us with its emptiness.

Soon Peisistratus was a speck on the beach. The crew set the mast upright and raised the sail, and with a groan through all its planks, the ship moved toward the open sea.

I spent most of the voyage in a limp heap of self-pity, but as we passed the outer islands of Cephallenia I began to get excited about returning home. I would see my mother again. I would see Eurycleia, Eurynome, and my grandfather as well, since Telemachus told me they were all in good health.

When we reached Ithaca's outer shore, Telemachus ordered the crew to throw out the anchor stones in a cove, so we could eat on the small, rocky beach before sailing up the coast to the harbor. Then, after everyone was full, Telemachus spoke to the crew.

"Go on to the harbor without us," he said. "I want to take my cousin with me to view my lands. I'll meet you in the port tomorrow and pay you for the journey then."

I looked around in shock. Nothing was in sight—no village, no huts, and no sign of a road other than a steep, overgrown path that showed no recent use.

"What are you talking about?" I demanded, pulling him aside so none of the crew could hear.

"Athena came to me last night," he whispered. "The suitors are lying in ambush for me. If I go into the harbor, I'll be killed. And who knows what would happen if they realized who you are."

He looked around as if to make sure no enemy lurked on the lonely beach. "She said to wait here, and someone would come for you."

"For me? What about you?"

"I'm supposed to stay with you until I'm sure you're safe. Then I'm going to the swineherd, to hear what's happened since I left."

He turned and called out to the captain. "Better get going while the wind is still good."

The crew scrambled to their feet, and soon they were back on the ship pulling up the anchor stones and trimming the sail to finish their journey.

As they rounded the edge of the cove and were gone from sight, I turned to Telemachus. "Are they going to be all right?" I asked.

"The crew?" He shrugged his shoulders. "Why not?"

"Did you warn them?"

"About what?" He looked puzzled. "I guess I should have said something to the captain about the ambush, but I didn't think of it."

"And what about all our gifts? All my things?"

"Look, Xanthe," he said, making me glad he rarely called me by name because he put such a sharp edge on it. "Stop being so difficult. Mother's suitors only want me."

"I'm talking about the crew. You're not on board anymore."

I saw a look of fear shoot across his face before it was gone again. What was to keep a crew from sailing off with a huge amount of treasure?

He picked up a piece of driftwood, and, trying to look casual, he tossed it into the water. "Athena wouldn't have told me to stay here if that were going to happen." Something about his tone made me think that if we were still children he might have added, *Would she?*

I can't say Telemachus hadn't changed at all, but he certainly hadn't changed enough. I had nothing more to say, so I found an old, weathered tree trunk to sit on, while Telemachus continued throwing bits of things into the water.

Soon we heard two children giggling as they came down the path. When they reached the beach I saw a girl of about eight and a boy who was a little taller and a few years older.

"Who are you?" asked the girl as she walked toward us on the sand. She was the same age as Melantho when, with the same cocky confidence, she had asked me the same question so many years before.

The boy hadn't come any closer. "I'm Aspasia, and that's my brother," the girl said. "He doesn't talk much."

"Do you come here often?" I asked.

"No, but last night I had a dream there would be something down here, and I wanted to see what it was."

Athena.

Telemachus came over to us, but his eyes showed no recognition of what the children's presence meant.

"Do you know who I am?" he asked.

Aspasia shook her head. Before Telemachus could fill their ears with how he was heir to the throne and their future king, I interrupted him.

"Do you live nearby?" I asked. "Do you think you could take us to your house?"

"It's not very far," she said. "My mother's there now, with the baby."

"We have a baby," the boy said, in a loud but oddly flat voice, like one I had heard before in a man whose mind never grew beyond childhood. Though her brother was older, Aspasia was obviously taking care of him.

"We need to go with her," I told Telemachus.

He shook his head. "We have to wait for Athena."

I looked at him, dumbfounded. "I'm going," I said. "You can wait if you want, but I think she's already sent her messenger."

Telemachus followed us up the path, muttering under his breath. After a while we found ourselves in front of a hut overlooking the same beach where I had been stung by the jellyfish so many years before. Across the bay, the outline of the palace walls smoothed out the top of its rocky perch. I shaded my eyes to get a better look, but the palace was still too far away to see anything.

"Maia!" Aspasia called out. Inside the hut I heard a baby crying.

When there was no reply, she called her mother again, just as a woman with a careworn face and sad eyes came to the doorway, bouncing a wailing infant on her hip. It took me a moment to recognize her.

"Halia?" I asked.

The woman looked bewildered. "How do you know me?"

"It's Xanthe," I said. "Remember?"

She looked even more confused than before. "Xanthe? I saw her buried."

"I'm not dead!" I said, my voice bursting with joy. "It was a lie to keep me safe! And I'm back home now!"

Telemachus grabbed my arm. "You talk too much," he hissed. "What if they run off and tell everyone in the village?."

"Oh, what do you know about anything?" I burst out. "Don't you see Athena brought the girl to us? Don't you know I'm safer here than anywhere on the island?"

Telemachus' eyes burned with anger. "Fine," he said. "Have them take you to the palace tonight. I'll send word to expect you."

He turned his back. "I'm going to see Eumaeus. Figure the rest out yourself."

Halia took me inside the hut. It was as dark and sparsely furnished as her husband's had been, but this one at least did not stink of fish.

"How old is your baby?" I asked, wanting to break the awkwardness of the situation.

"Oh, it's not mine." She was looking for something to offer me to eat and furtively straightening up the meager possessions of the family. "I'm done with that. I'm a widow now."

"What happened to—" I am ashamed to say that *fish man* was the only name I could remember.

"Drowned at sea." Halia gestured with her chin toward Aspasia. "Not too long after she was born."

Aspasia was now holding the baby, and Halia went over to give it a kiss on the top of its head. "This is my first grandchild, by the daughter I was pregnant with when I married Terpias."

I was so relieved to be reminded of his name that I almost missed what Halia said next.

"I thought I was through raising babies by now, but my daughter—" She took in a deep breath and let it out with a sigh. "Her hips were too small. I knew it, but I hoped for the best."

I tried to take it all in. Halia's daughter dead in childbirth before reaching my age. Halia already a widow in her late twenties and a grandmother before I had my own first child.

"I'm sorry," I whispered.

"What for?" Halia asked. "It's not your doing."

"I know. I just wish—"

She held up her hand to stop me. "That it could be different?"

The baby was whimpering, and she put her finger in its mouth to quiet it. "When you live in a fishing village, this is what you expect."

That night I was escorted back to the palace by another of Halia's sons, twelve-year-old Rhexenor. The moon was full, and we went without a torch, to make it harder for anyone to see us. For the first part of our journey we skirted the edge of the bay. The dark water glittered in the moonlight, and soft waves exhaled onto pebbly beaches I had seen only in daylight as a little girl. I gave up trying to recognize any landmark of my native land except the palace that loomed above us on the tallest hill. Its outer walls were dark, but the fire and torches from the megaron sent up a glow into the night sky.

When we turned inland and began climbing toward the palace, the details of my childhood, though transformed by moonlight and the passage of time, began to fall into place. Here was the road that led to the town. Further up to the right, unseen in the darkness, was the scarred field with the jagged thumb. The path to the pig farm went off to the left.

When we got to the top we found a place to hide just outside the palace walls, though no sentries seemed to be posted. When my breathing quieted, I picked up the sounds of boasts and jeers and, whenever the men's voices fell, the faint notes of the bard's lyre.

"What do we do now?" Rhexenor asked.

"Go inside and follow to the left of the courtyard around to the kitchen in the back. Ask for Eurycleia or Eurynome, no one else, and tell them you have me with you." For some reason I couldn't resist adding, "Everyone else thinks I'm dead."

He gave me a quizzical look but didn't ask for an explanation.

"And whatever you do," I went on, "don't go in the megaron.

Try not to let anyone see you, but if someone does, don't talk. Just run away as fast as you can. Those men are too drunk to follow."

I could hear Rhexenor's breath, and I knew he was excited to get started.

"I'll be waiting in the sacred grove," I told him. "The women know where that is."

As he started toward the palace walls, I grabbed him by the arm. "Thank you," I said. "I don't have anything to give you, but I'll send something tomorrow."

"We're fine," he said. "We have enough."

"I'll send something anyway. To your mother. I knew her long before you were born. Ask her when you get back, if you don't believe me."

Rhexenor screwed up his face. "We don't know anyone who lives in the palace."

"You do now," I said. "Go."

He slipped through the open gate of the palace, and I was alone.

I waited for someone to come and fetch me in a stand of trees we always referred to as the sacred grove, just at the beginning of the path to Eumaeus' farm. My mother told me when I was young that Odysseus intended to create a shrine to Athena there, but he had gone to war before he had gotten any further than dragging some large stone blocks into the clearing he'd made. The grove had never been dedicated, but my mother still didn't want Telemachus and me to go inside, because our play was unlikely to be dignified enough to do honor to our father's intentions.

A few times toward the end of my years in Ithaca, when the situation seemed particularly dire, my mother and I went into the grove with flowers and other gifts to ask for Athena's help. Even if some drunken suitor grabbed Rhexenor and squeezed the truth out of him, I knew Athena would not let me be harmed in a place where I had done my best to honor her.

The moonlight filtered through the trees and dappled the ground. The air was still thick with the warmth of the day, but out of nervousness I kept my cloak pulled close around me. My head kept snapping back as I dozed off, and I don't know how much time passed before I heard a familiar voice.

"There she is!" Almost as quickly as I could stand up, Eurynome was hugging me. Eurycleia, with her bad hip, was a few steps behind. We held each other, all three of us rocking and crying, until finally Eurynome pulled away.

"Well, let's have a look at you," she said. Both women clucked as they peered at me in the moonlight.

"All grown," Eurycleia said, and with a cackle she added, "We wouldn't be able to disguise you as a boy now!"

"And so beautiful," Eurynome said, shaking her head in wonder. "From such a scrawny little girl."

My hair was unkempt and my chiton was filthy, but I had learned from Helen not to protest when someone wanted to compliment me. I held out my arms and made a full circle for their inspection.

Eurynome took my arm. "We must get back. Your mother knows you're here, and she's waiting for you."

Soon we were inside the palace gate, hugging the inner wall of the courtyard as we skirted the megaron. The voices had died down enough that we could hear loud snoring on the porch and the sound of two men arguing just inside the hall. Then another roar went up, followed by the sound of wooden benches scraping against the floor.

"Go on ahead, fast as you can," Eurycleia whispered. "They're leaving, and they mustn't see you."

Eurynome and I broke into a run, reaching the safety of the alley leading to the kitchen just as we heard someone berating the snoring man to wake up and go home. When Eurycleia caught up, we went up the back stairway.

I was standing in the corridor leading to the queen's quarters. I heard Eurynome bolting the door behind us, but I was frozen in place, taking in the details of a place that seemed at once as familiar as my own hands, but at the same time as strange as a dream.

"She's in her megaron," Eurycleia said. "Go to her."

The two women held back to let me go in alone. All of a sudden my feet were running. I burst through the door of my mother's quarters, and then I was in her arms, sobbing. I was home at last.

CHAPTER 18

Tatters

*I wove my life, not because I think anyone will care, but because I have
had nothing else to do during the months I've spent barricaded upstairs in
Ithaca. Now, when I unroll my work it falls almost to the floor. Since life
has brought me to my knees, it seems only fitting that, rather than winding
my weaving back over the roller bar to make today's work easier, I take to
the floor as a supplicant to my continuing story.*

*A few threads of gold tell of my joyful homecoming. I doubt anyone else
would notice they were there. I thought about stopping my weaving at that
point and waiting until I knew what would happen next, but life is never
like that. Things happen or they don't, and I am losing my ability to care.
Perhaps that is a blessing.*

*For a few days, I turned the loom to the wall, but it was like turning my
back on myself, when I was all I had. The black patch of soot I had rubbed
into the back mocked me without mercy. Then, when I put the loom back
the right way again, I saw in front of me not just separate colors and textures but the shape of my entire life.*

Yellow for womanhood, and for memories of happiness under Apollo's great sun. Blue for hope, green for youth and foolishness, purple for the privileges I took for granted. Oily, dank shades of brown and oppressive grays for all the forces I could not control. But mostly red, mostly the color of blood. Sometimes the color of warmth and love, sometimes the color of a woman's secret core, but mostly the source of the world's greatest failures and its most profound grief.

But I am not weaving the world, only my piece of it. During this last moon cycle, I have taken every color I had left and made a twisting, swirling pattern of all of them. In the center, I may later embroider a pool of red blood, not in a neat circle, but snaking out everywhere, perhaps through the entire weaving. This day, I now see, has been preordained by the gods, and afterward I will view my whole life as centered around it, colored by inevitability.

From the moment I returned to Ithaca, I had no illusions about escaping from this prison. The only question I have is what man will control me when this day is over. The megaron is silent now, and all I can do is wait to find out what the gods long ago decided.

To calm myself as the battle went on, I continued to weave, thinking of the ragged beggar in the megaron, and how Eumaeus carried my father's bow to him just before Eurycleia and I were ordered upstairs.

I suppose it's a better story if Odysseus threw off his rags to reveal an oiled and glistening body so perfect the suitors thought a god stood before them. I hope it happened that way, hope the fear he struck into the suitors was enough to leave wet patches of mud under them on the floor.

But I don't care much about knowing exactly how the battle started. It's his tatters that speak to me.

I took off the chiton I was wearing this morning and shredded it with a knife. I don't know how long I have been kneeling here alone, naked, powerless, capturing ragged bits of cloth between threads I have smashed into the *weft at the bottom of my weaving. Fall out or stay in, it doesn't matter. My fingers are bloodied, which only fits all the more.*

Tatters. The mess that wild dreams of power make of our lives. The aftermath we must sweep up in order to go on.

The first few days I was back in Ithaca whirled with the excitement of reconnecting with people I loved, but by the time a moon cycle passed, reality closed in.

If the palace had been a prison before I left, it was worse now. Menelaus talked endlessly about the siege of Troy, but this too was a siege, staged by the suitors against the queen and princess upstairs.

When word got out that I was not dead after all but had come back after five years of hiding in Sparta, my mother and brother did their best to protect me by saying I was betrothed. Few of the suitors were deterred.

"Let Peisistratus come to the rescue, after I've used her up," one of them said in the courtyard, in a voice loud enough to be heard upstairs.

"Well, if the little bitch runs off with him to Pylos, don't expect us to go to war for you," another one said, to a roar of approval from the men around them.

"Of course she'll run off," said a third. "Look at the Spartan whore who trained her."

Men such as these were unlikely to cower in fear at the idea of making a new enemy of Peisistratus, and since they had so little respect for anything, it was best not to allow them anywhere near me. That suited me perfectly, even if my mother and brother were unaware that my maidenhead was now far beyond protecting.

I didn't fret as much about being confined as I had when I was younger. I had my memories to absorb me, and I did get out from time to time. The suitors all had rooms in town and spent mornings there, aggravating the shopkeepers and terrifying any women and children who ventured into the streets. Though I could not leave the palace even under guard, I could go downstairs until early afternoon without fear of being harmed, since the suitors would not yet have arrived.

I spent a few mornings with Eurycleia, who struggled to keep up the household. Last night's feast had to be cleaned up after, and that night's feast prepared. The packed dirt floor of the megaron was clotted with grease and covered with bones the men threw at each other. On cold nights, they didn't bother to leave the porch to relieve themselves, and the walls had to be scrubbed to remove the smell of urine, and fresh dirt sprinkled over the spots they left behind. Sometimes in the morning the pillars would be spattered with blood from fistfights or covered with vomit from a punch to the gut or a revolt of the stomach from too much food and drink.

Eurycleia had slaves to help her, and such tasks were not fit for a princess, so eventually I stayed upstairs, out of the way. I had my weaving, and for the first time in years I had my mother.

She was so relieved I was home that a tremor that had developed in her hands was quieting, and a habit of digging at her scalp until she drew blood had disappeared. Her hair was beginning to gray, and the stress of life in the palace made her look far more than five years older. Still, time had softened her eyes and given a smoky tone to her voice that, at least to me, made her more appealing than ever.

I loved to be in her megaron while she worked at her loom, but I couldn't stay long, because the one jagged edge in our relationship was our disagreement about what was on the loom in my own quarters.

"You should be weaving what you need for your marriage," she told me almost every day.

"To whom?" I asked. If I still had any hope it would be to Peisistratus I might have accepted what she said, but no news of him had come from Pylos, and I had begun to doubt whether I had been right about him loving me. Antinous, the likely winner of my hand, could dress in rags, for all he deserved.

"But it's so ugly, Xanthe," she said. "It frightens me. And it will make people afraid of you."

"Let them be," I said. "Perhaps I could learn to shriek like the Harpies too. That should keep the suitors away."

My mother scowled. For all the trouble that being beautiful and feminine had brought her, she still couldn't imagine how a woman could want to be anything else. In the end we simply agreed not to understand each other, but that didn't affect the bond between us. Much as I loved Helen, she was not my mother. She hadn't known me my whole life, hadn't outwitted anyone to protect me, hadn't been miserable for years out of fear for my safety. My mother would do anything for me, and I didn't know the same with certainty about anyone else.

When Telemachus brought me to Ithaca to lift the curse, we all assumed Odysseus would be back quickly. After a month, it was hard to believe Athena had allowed me to come home when such danger still existed. As the reality dawned that the siege might not be lifted anytime soon, I started having nightmares that woke me in such a disturbed frame of mind, I had to bite my hand to keep from screaming at the malevolent gods that keep us all breathing but otherwise dead.

In my mind, the downstairs of the palace became the underworld, a place of gloom and fright no person would choose to visit. One day, after a sleepless night had given way to dozing all morning, I woke up so hungry I decided to put away my fears and slip downstairs to get a piece of cheese and some fruit to take back to my room.

The palace was starting to stir with the preparations for that night's feast, but since at this point only the meats roasting outside required attention, Eurycleia wasn't in the kitchen. I went to a side room where I knew she kept the things she planned to feed the suitors that night.

The door was ajar, but I could hear someone inside. I recognized the kind of sounds they were making and pushed the door open just a little more to see who of the servants would use the storeroom in that way.

I saw a man crouching, and in front of him a woman bent over on all fours. They were at an angle where I could see what was happening, but I could not see either of their faces. He was putting his phallus into her from behind, but not in the usual place. Her chiton was pushed up to her shoulders and I could hear her gasping. The man roared and thrust harder and I heard her yelp like a wounded dog. When he was done, he pulled himself out of her, slapping her behind as if she were a horse he was sending back to the stable.

I recognized her laugh. Melantho scrambled to her feet, pulling her chiton down.

I moved behind the door so they couldn't see me, but I could not retreat any further without being noticed. "Back to work for you," I heard him say. "Your other work, I mean."

Melantho giggled as if she were in on a wonderful private joke.

Eurymachus—the suitor with the best gifts for Icarius, the one my mother was most likely to marry—passed through the doorway where I was hiding. He was too busy scratching his testicles with one hand and blowing his nose into his palm with the other to notice me. Melantho followed, and since she had to close the door behind her, I could not escape being discovered.

"What are you doing out of your cage?" she asked me, curling up her lip in a way I once might have taken for friendliness, but now recognized as mockery.

"I—" I heard the timid voice of the old Xanthe, the one who wanted the approval of the girl in the olive orchard, and I boiled with anger at myself for still feeling so vulnerable.

"I don't owe you an explanation," I said, setting my shoulders and raising my chin. "But I think you owe me one."

"What? For that?"

What did she need to explain? That she was shirking her duties—now only those of a scullery maid since in my absence she had been banished from my mother's chambers for some transgression or another? That she was letting him inside her in that unnatural way? I couldn't say for sure what I wanted an apology for. Perhaps a little of everything that had ever happened between us.

"The queen wouldn't want that happening in the palace." It was the only thing I could think of, and an answer I would immediately regret.

Melantho burst out laughing. "Not happening in the palace? Ask her how she's going to stop it when she marries him? It's the only way he likes to do it. And your brother too. Tell him I'm better at it than those stable boys he fancies."

With a snort and a toss of her head, she walked by me. I could hear her laughter as she passed through the kitchen, and though I didn't move until the sound had faded, the echo in my mind continues today.

A half a moon cycle later—impossible to believe it was just yesterday—a beggar arrived. I was upstairs with my mother when the commotion broke out, and when the taunts grew so loud they disturbed us at the loom, my mother sent down for word about what was happening. A slave girl came back to say that a ragged old man had made the mistake of offending the suitors.

"He said they were beggars too," the girl said, unable to control the play of a smile around her mouth. "He said they eat food they're too lazy to earn—just like he does."

I saw a flicker in my mother's eyes. "What happened then?"

"Antinous threw a stool—the heaviest one—and hit him in the back."

Eurynome and I gasped as loudly as my mother did. Nothing angered the gods more than refusing hospitality to a stranger in need, and Antinous was begrudging food that wasn't even his to begin with.

By habit we all composed ourselves, since it was best that word about what the queen might be thinking not reach the servants' quarters. After the girl was excused, we waited to hear her footsteps on the stairs before snarling in disgust.

"May Apollo repay him with an arrow between his shoulders," my mother said.

"Repay them all that way," Eurynome said, "if our prayers are answered."

"But he's the worst." My mother shuddered. "Black death itself, that's what that man is."

I tried and failed to block from my mind the image of Melantho and Eurymachus in the storeroom and wondered if she would deem Antinous the worst if she had witnessed what I had.

"Repay them all," I affirmed. What did it matter who was worse when they both—when they all—so richly deserved to die?

By midmorning the noise shifted to the courtyard. From a window upstairs we saw a local misfit I knew only by the nickname Irus, squaring off with the man the slave girl had spoken of. The suitors gathered around, having talked the men into entertaining them with a fight.

When the beggar threw off his cloak, I heard my mother's quick intake of breath and saw her hand go to her chest. She curled her fingers into a loose fist and slowly rubbed the area just below her throat, a habit she had when she was thinking hard but did not plan to share her thoughts with anyone.

Under his rags and coating of dirt, the beggar had the shoulders of a boxer and the legs of someone who could run the length of our island and back without stopping to catch his breath. He bounced on his feet and lifted his fists in front of him, while Antinous brayed that if Irus didn't teach the beggar to mind his manners, he knew someone who chopped off the noses and ears of worthless people—and everything else that stuck out too—and fed it to the dogs.

Irus gave out a roar and swung at the beggar, who countered with a single blow to the neck so strong that blood sprayed from Irus' mouth. His knees gave way and he fell headlong into the dirt, where he lay motionless.

"Is he dead?" I asked.

"No," Eurynome said. "I saw his hand move, I think."

Several men dragged Irus to the wall, where they propped his lolling body up. A dog came over and, when Irus lacked the strength to stop him, began licking the blood that trickled from his nose and mouth.

It was disgusting to watch, and Eurynome and I turned away. I assumed my mother would do the same, but I realized she wasn't watching Irus at all. Her eyes were fixed on the beggar, who was wolfing down the sausages he had been given as a prize.

Eurynome clucked. "This isn't suitable for a queen."

My mother startled at her touch. "Come," Eurynome said, escorting her inside.

The day had started out violently, and my sense of unease grew as the sun climbed to the top of its arc in the sky. Although the men feasting at midday in the megaron were their usual loud and crass selves, no birds sang in the trees outside my window, no hoopoes rummaged in the undergrowth, no crows squawked in the sky.

At midday, my room began to darken. I thought nothing of it at first, assuming it was an afternoon cloud temporarily blocking the sun. Almost immediately, I heard the first screams from the courtyard. Forgetting I wasn't supposed to go outside, I ran downstairs, nearly colliding with Eurynome and my mother in the process.

Outside, we clung to each other as we watched the sun being eaten away. Little by little it disappeared until all that remained was a black disk where the sun used to be, with an angry-looking halo around it. I was too frightened to cry. I looked through the dim, murky air at people so pale it looked as if they had been drained of blood.

It was the most terrible omen imaginable, and I had no idea what it meant. Was Apollo so angry with us that he had taken the sun from the world? I looked at my mother's face, and even in the gruesome and poisonous-looking light, I could see in her eyes that she was more calm than I was, trying to figure out what the omen meant.

She turned to me, but before she could speak, Theoclymenus, one of the most respected seers in Ithaca, burst out of the megaron. He turned around and shook his fist at the men inside.

"You mock me?" he roared. "Can't you see how your own funeral shrouds have fallen on your shoulders? Don't you see the rivers of blood running down the walls? The ghosts of the dead are thronging outside, waiting for you. Their mist is creeping over the walls—"

A dozen or so men came out of the megaron, throwing bones at him. Some looked up at the sky, but by then the sun had begun to reappear. Everyone stopped to watch until the world returned to normal, and then the suitors began their barrage again, calling Theoclymenus a crazy old woman and a fraud who had lost his ability to scare them. Finally, after a few punches on his arms and kicks to the backs of his knees, the suitors succeeded in driving the old man outside the palace walls, making a loud show of closing the gates behind him.

All the while, my mother did not take her eyes off the old beggar leaning against a column of the porch, watching the commotion with glittering eyes.

That was yesterday. I woke several times last night with the feeling that spirits were visiting someone in the palace, but they hadn't come for me. In the morning the house seemed different, far too quiet, as if the whole palace were holding its breath.

My mother came into my room clothed to greet guests, though it was still early morning. "Come down with me," she said. "I talked with the beggar last night in the megaron, and the gods put something in my head. I'm going to set up a contest for my hand, and I want you there when I do it."

Somehow the suitors got the message to arrive before the sun was high. Like all travelers passing through, the beggar had spent the night on a bed of skins and blankets on the porch, and I saw him talking with Eumaeus, the swineherd, as we crossed the courtyard. My mother did not go directly to the megaron, but instead took a pair of servants with her into the storerooms.

I had not gone down those stairs since the day of my faked death, but I remembered exactly how the doors to my parents' treasures were laid out along the walls. My mother went straight to the one protecting my father's weapons and armor. Unlocking the double door with a large key made of bronze and ivory, she threw back the bolt. After she motioned to everyone but me to stay back, the two of us went inside.

Her face was pallid in the yellow, dusty light, and her mouth disappeared into a grim line as she looked around. Chests and boxes were stacked to the ceiling two or three thick, crowding halfway into the room. A rack of perhaps twenty double axes of various sizes took up one corner. In the torchlight I saw the glint from rows of bronze helmets lined up on several high shelves along the far wall, under which dangled at least ten shields and an equal number of swords.

"Shine the torch over there," she said, indicating a hook from which a long, thin case was hanging. She had to stand on a chest to remove it, and the weight made her stagger when she stepped back down.

"Put your torch in the standard and help me with this." She sat on a chest and held tight to the top of the case while I slid off the bottom. Inside was a massive bow.

"This is your father's," she said, stroking the wood and fingering the loose bowstring. "No one else can string it. They don't have the strength." She handed it to me and retrieved a quiver of arrows from another hook before calling the servants to pick up a heavy chest and carry it upstairs.

When we arrived in the megaron, we pulled our veils over our faces, and, standing next to one of the pillars in the center of the hall, she called out to the assembled guests.

"You have plagued us long enough," she said. "You say you are only here because of desire for me. Well, here I am. Today will decide whose bride I will become, and tonight I'll be gone with him, and this palace will be only a memory for me."

What was she doing?

She motioned to the servants to open the chest. In it were twelve identical axes unlike any I had ever seen. Their heads were shaped like a crescent moon, leaving a hollow between the shaft and the blade. The metal was too thin to chop wood, and the unwieldy handles were longer than a man's arm, making it obvious their only use was for some kind of game. She called Eumaeus to her side. "You know how this contest is done," she said. "Line up the axes." When she showed him Odysseus' bow, the old swineherd burst into tears at the sight.

"Whoever can string this bow and shoot an arrow clean through these twelve axes will be my husband," she announced to the suitors. They murmured loudly among themselves, some grumbling and some smiling at my mother's decision to have this matter decided by a contest of strength and skill.

Telemachus shuffled his feet, clenching and unclenching his fists. It was obvious he knew no more than I did about our mother's plan. "Let me try the bow first!" he burst out with the impetuousness of someone who thinks about consequences only after it is too late. "If you're leaving, Ithaca's mine, and I need to show I'm man enough to keep it."

My mother's face grew pale as he reached for the bow. I could see the misgivings in her eyes, but nothing could be done. To refuse would be to treat Telemachus as a child in front of the men, and that would be worse than watching him fail.

Fail he did. He tried to bend the bow but put it down unstrung after his third attempt. "I lack only confidence, not strength," he boasted. "Come show me you're my betters, or I won't believe it." Perhaps there was hope for him yet, I thought, since he had managed a show of cockiness when his failure was truly horrifying.

"Well, let's do it then," Antinous cried out, but I noticed he did not take the bow himself. After a few men tried and failed, Antinous did not look so smug. He made some excuse for calling off the contest until the following day, but I knew what he really wanted was not to have to end the day licking his wounds with the other suitors who would not be marrying my mother.

The men were moving to the hearth for the libation and sacrifice, when the beggar spoke. "How about letting me try?" he said in a voice so strong it filled every corner of the hall.

"You?" Antinous sneered. "A beggar courting a queen?"

"Surely you can't think he means that," my mother broke in. "He's just curious." She turned to the beggar. "I'll give you new clothes and a good sword if you can do it. Would that be enough of a prize?"

Antinous drew closer to the queen. "It's not just that." Even though I was standing right there, his voice was so low I could barely make out his words. "Think of the disgrace if a beggar succeeds where the lords of the land have failed!"

Before she could reply, Telemachus broke in. "No need to discuss anything with her," he said. Turning to my mother, he commanded her to go upstairs. "Weaving is for women, not decision making," he said. "I'll be doing all of that from now on."

I could not keep my jaw from dropping. Was this the same

person who had just failed so miserably with the bow? My mother took the insult with the grace of a queen. Only a hint of red flushed her cheeks as she turned and left the room with the other women behind her.

I started to go with her, but Eurycleia grabbed my arm, pulling me behind a pillar. "Stay and watch a little longer," she whispered.

Telemachus had already turned to Eumaeus. "Give the beggar the bow," he said.

Eumaeus walked through the crowd of suitors. He thrust out the bow and put it in the tattered man's outstretched hands.

At that moment, Telemachus saw we were still there. "Eurycleia," he said, coming over to grab her elbow and speak to her in a low voice. "Go upstairs and bolt the doors after you're sure all the women are inside. No matter what you hear, don't open the doors, and don't look out the windows."

He waved us both off. "Tell the women to tend to their weaving. Whatever of this is their business, they'll know soon enough."

As we hurried off, I looked over my shoulder to where the beggar was seated. One hand was clutching the middle of the bow and the other its far end, and I swear it was bending as easily as a green twig in springtime.

Just as Eurycleia threw the bolt on the upstairs doors and locked us all inside, a great crack of lightning split the sky. The women screamed and grabbed on to each other.

Then from below, we heard the beggar's voice. "You dogs!" he cried out. "You thought I'd never come back, didn't you? You thought it would be safe to eat my food? Rape my servants? Marry my wife?"

"Gods in heaven!" I cried out, clutching Eurycleia's hand. "It's my father!"

Eurycleia dissolved into tears as she pulled me aside, out of earshot. "I saw a scar on his leg from a hunting wound when I bathed his feet last night," she whispered. "He told me he'd kill me if I said a word." She fell to her knees in great, heaving sobs of relief. "Oh, great gods, be with us!"

"Does my mother know?" The room was tossing around me like a storm at sea.

"I don't know. She talked with him for a long time last night, and then took herself off to bed without saying anything."

The loud taunting of a man downstairs was cut off suddenly by an agonized scream, full of mortal terror. The serving women began shrieking and sobbing so loudly we could not hear each other speak.

"You wait in your room," Eurycleia told me. "I can deal with them."

I nodded, too dazed to do anything but obey. I shut the door of my room behind me, and, as if by rote, I went to my loom.

The battle raged all day, but my mother knew nothing of it. She fell asleep almost as soon as she got back to her quarters, one of those curious, deep sleeps that come over her. I wove the entire day like someone possessed, trying to hear and not hear, imagine and not imagine, but even awake I knew little more than she did.

The first indication my brother had survived was his voice calling up to Eurycleia from the courtyard, followed a moment later by loud pounding on the door. When Eurycleia opened it, he told her to come downstairs. I followed behind her.

The floor of the megaron was black and wet with blood. Tables and benches were splintered and broken. Sprays of red splashed the pillar and walls, and the cloying smell of fresh slaughter permeated the air. I saw Eumaeus and my father dragging a corpse across the room. The end of an arrow was sticking out just below one of the dead man's nipples, its invisible trajectory downward deep into his gut. They tossed it onto a pile of corpses in the middle of the hall, and in the torchlight, I saw Eurymachus' blank eyes staring upward.

Antinous' body lay nearby, with an arrow through the throat. After flinging his corpse onto the pile, my father stood up. His body was streaked and splattered with blood and gore, and his hair was stiff with it. His tunic was ripped away at the shoulder and held in place around his loins by the rope that had bound it, and he seemed to be unaware that so little of it remained that his private parts hung out below.

"How many women have shamed this house?" he asked Eurycleia.

"Of the fifty, twelve," she said.

"Leave the rest upstairs. Send the guilty ones down to clean this up."

His eyes lit on me. "And who is this?" he asked. "One of the twelve, or the rest?"

I wanted to see a light in his eyes, some recognition of the truth before she could answer, but my hair was unkempt and I had dressed so quickly that one shoulder of my chiton had come unpinned. I looked nothing like a princess as I stood, breathing into my hands, waiting to see what he would do.

"This is your daughter," Eurycleia said. "Born after you left for Troy."

He stood motionless for a moment, looking at me. Was he surprised? I couldn't tell from the cold expression on his face.

Then he spoke. "Is she mine?"

Eurycleia gasped. My body froze. How could he ask such a question? "Of course, my king." Eurycleia's voice trembled as she answered.

"Well, then," he said, without looking at me. "Keep her upstairs with the rest."

He turned to Telemachus and Eumaeus. "Let's finish with the bodies so the little whores can do their work."

I mounted the stairs, stunned as much by my father's indifference as by the scene in the hall. The twelve guilty maids were huddled together just inside the door.

"What did you see?" Melantho asked.

"They'll all dead."

"Every last one?" She let out an unearthly wail and they all began to sob, falling to their knees and clutching one other.

Eurycleia kicked Melantho. "Get up!"

Her lip curled as she pounded everyone her foot could reach, again and again. "Go tend to your lovers."

Looking down at myself, I realized I was still naked from having torn my chiton to shreds at my loom. I clutched a new piece of linen to me and watched from the window as Melantho and some of the other women carried the bodies into the courtyard. The rest of the twelve brought out baskets of blood-caked soil from the floor of the megaron and took inside new dirt to spread a fresh layer.

When they were finished, I saw my brother drive all twelve of them, crying and pleading, into a corner of the yard. There, from a length of ship's cable stretched between two posts, he hung them one by one, until all twelve bodies dangled lifeless at the ends of nooses, like a string of wild birds brought home for supper.

Melantho was last. I heard her begging for her life, but my brother was unmoved. I watched her body fall and her legs and arms twitch, but it gave me no satisfaction, and I could see that it gave Telemachus none either. He stood for a moment in front of his work, then turned and walked away without looking back.

I heard Eurynome's voice as she crossed the room. "Eurycleia says he wants all the rest of the servants downstairs." When she reached the window, she screamed at the sight in the courtyard, grabbing the sill so hard her knuckles whitened.

I put my arm around her as she sobbed into her hands. "There's no joy in it after all," I said, guiding her away from the awful sight.

"No," Eurynome whispered. "There isn't." She looked toward the door. "Your mother slept through the whole thing."

It had been so long since I smiled that my face felt unfamiliar to me. "You go ahead with the others," I said. "I'll wake her."

I heard the women's footsteps and their hushed voices on the stairs, and when I was sure I was alone I left the window and went into my own quarters. Bits of my chiton littered the floor beneath my loom, and as I bent to pick them up, the events of the day hit me and I collapsed on the floor.

When I had enough of crying, I got up and went to my window. The air shimmered with gold and the hills were draped in a robe of purple. Behind me in the palace, life was shifting and incomprehensible, but in front of me birds sang, and the only darkness was a shadow running through a meadow as a cloud passed briefly across the sun.

I was so grateful to be alive in that moment, to see life stretch out in front of me again, that I went to the table and filled a cup with wine.

Standing at my window, I poured a thin stream onto the ground below. I watched it send up wisps of dust as it beaded in the parched dirt, and I raised my voice in praise of the gods who had brought all of us to this day. Then, turning from the window, I pinned my chiton over my naked body and went into my mother's room.

"You did it," I whispered to the sleeping form on the bed. "You defeated them. Just like you said you would."

I touched her shoulder and heard her moan.

"Maia," I said, stroking her hair. "You can wake up now. It's over."

EPILOGUE

I pull the warp knots loose one by one, and my weaving falls into my mother's hands. I can see her relief to see the last of it as she helps me fold it and put it away. I don't want to look at it again either, at least anytime soon. Too much lies ahead to dwell on the past.

The rest of what happened the day of the battle is painful to tell. We all called my mother ungrateful, foolish, stubborn, and things much worse than that, for failing to rush immediately into Odysseus' arms and welcome him back. She was suspicious enough to refuse at first to cross the megaron to where he stood leaning against a pillar in the middle of the room, eyes shut with battle weariness. My mother, Eurycleia, and I had come in so quietly he didn't seem to be aware of our presence, and my mother put her finger to her lips to let us know she wanted to observe him unseen.

The air was hazy with smoke and reeked of the sulfur he

had used to purify the hall, and we pulled our veils over our faces not just from modesty but to ward off the unpleasant, eye-stinging fumes. I pointed without speaking to the long, silver-white scar, still crusted with the dried blood of the suitors, that ran up from the knee into the thigh of the man. My mother shook her head.

"The beggar yesterday had no such scar," she whispered. "I looked."

I was dumbfounded. Had she simply not seen it? That was un-likely. We had been close enough, and I saw how my mother had scrutinized the man. Such trickery could only be the work of the gods, but was the scar, or the lack of it, the disguise?

Odysseus opened his eyes. He saw us but did not move.

"We were talking about your scar," my mother said. Her clear and confident voice echoed around the hall. "It cannot appear and disappear unless a god wills it. But since I don't know whether the god who favors you has good or ill in mind for me, or for my husband, I can go no further now than to thank you for your ser-vice and ask if there is anything you need before you are on your way."

"How dare you?" I heard Telemachus' voice behind us and whirled around. By now he had bathed and changed into a clean tunic and himation. His body seemed filled out and his jaw more resolutely set, as if the gods had showered the appearance of a hero over him as a reward for his valor that day.

Though she kept the veil over her mouth, my mother looked Telemachus firmly in the eyes and did not flinch as he berated her for her unthinkable ingratitude and lack of hospitality to the man who had done such great deeds.

Eurycleia hurried to Odysseus' side. "Perhaps you might see what the rest of us already know," she said to my mother, "after a bath has washed the blood away, and he's dressed like a king." As she led him out of the megaron, my mother turned her back on Telemachus and me, making it clear she didn't want to hear any more.

Telemachus didn't care. "You should stick with your weaving, since your ignorance does such damage." Spittle flew from his mouth as he raged. "I've known my father was back since the day he arrived. He's been living with the swineherd. Who are you to question him if I don't?"

"And what proof did he offer?" my mother asked, turning to face him.

"I know my own father, don't I?"

How could he? I shook my head in wonderment. He was just a baby when our father left.

She arched her brows and asked in a cool voice, "Did Eumaeus recognize him?"

"No," Telemachus said. "Athena disguised him whenever any-one else was around." His face fell, as he realized he had proven my mother's point about the gods and their tricks. "Well," he said, puffing out his chest and shaking his head in annoyance, "I'm sat-isfied. And you should take my word for it."

We all waited in angry silence for Odysseus to return from his bath. My mother went out on to the porch and looked up at clouds growing pink with sunset. Telemachus slouched in a chair, and I stood at the loom, poking the shuttle back and forth with so little attention to the pattern that I had to pull out what little work I managed to do.

After the blood and dirt of battle had been washed away, the man who came into the megaron with his skin glistening with oil and his hair flowing onto his shoulders like clusters of hyacinths looked at least a hand's breadth taller than the beggar of the day before, and far too young to be the battle-scarred hero of Troy. I knew then that my mother was right to doubt him.

She was also the one with the presence of mind to find a way out of the dilemma. When Odysseus ordered Eurycleia to make a pallet on the floor for him, my mother ordered the bed pulled out of her chambers for him.

"What?" His rage filled the megaron. His face turned purple, and my heart pounded with fear, remembering what he had been capable of on that very spot today.

"You'd have to cut that bed down to move it. I built it from an olive tree that grew up from the courtyard. I planed it smooth and inlaid the posts myself." He shook his fists, and I flung my arms around my mother to protect her, though he did not move in our direction. "Did you throw away my—?"

Suddenly his eyes widened and he stepped back so quickly his shoulder hit the pillar. "Or was that the sign you were waiting for?"

My mother knees buckled. "Husband," she said, breaking free of my grip and running into his arms.

I lay awake that night unable to sleep, and feeling more alone than ever. I knew what it meant to lie with a man as my mother finally was, and I missed Peisistratus so desperately that every part of me ached. And my distress was deeper than that. Everything was going to change. My mother would have less time for me, my father would dominate the palace, and Telemachus would somehow manage to be more insufferable than ever.

It was true I was now free from my prison, but would that really mean anything? I was an unmarried woman who needed a husband. Would the stranger in my mother's bed arrange a marriage for me with one of his friends and send me off to a place I had never heard of? If so, it would be soon, since I was already close to twenty years old. I was now free again to go to Hera's shrine, and all the other places on Ithaca that meant so much to me, but only for a little while before I would leave them behind forever.

Dreams had once swirled in my head about how life would be if my father came home, and now that he was here, I wondered whether any of them would come true. I soon learned that my qualms were not misplaced. From the beginning, he threw his arm around Telemachus, and the two of them laughed and joked as if he had been absent about as long as it took to bring home some game for dinner. He had spent twenty years not knowing I existed, and I suppose it wasn't fair to expect him to understand that I was as much his own flesh and blood as the son he had yearned to see. Still, after a month I expected more than the startled, perplexed looks he still gave me when I came down to listen to the bard with my mother.

I had other dreams too, about how he and my mother would rule together. I hoped they would turn out to be much like Helen and Menelaus in Sparta, before going off, as Laertes and Anticleia did, to a contented old age on the farm. And I had matured enough truly to want my brother to grow strong and capable and, in time, rule an untroubled and prosperous land.

After my lover sent me off from Pylos with scarcely a good-bye, the only person I had no dreams for was myself. Strange then, that the dream I didn't dare have appears now to be the only one coming true.

On the seaways word travels fast, and within less than a moon cycle of the battle at the palace, Peisistratus arrived in Ithaca to ask my father for permission to marry me. I tried to greet his arrival with indifference, because I was hurt that there had been no word from him since I left Pylos many moon cycles before. But it was soon clear that our time apart was as painful for him as for me. Born when Nestor was already an advanced age, he was the only unmarried son and the only one available to take care of his father's *oikos*. He actually had sent word to let me know what was happening, but the ship bearing his messenger either sank or fell into the hands of pirates, and it never arrived in Ithaca. To my astonishment, he thought the lack of a reply meant I was betrothed to one of the suitors, and when he heard false rumors to that effect, he thought I would appreciate his discretion in stepping aside and putting our affair behind us. Only when he heard of the slaughter in the palace were his hopes revived.

Peisistratus returned to Pylos a few moon cycles ago to ready a suitable home for us. We will rule an *oikos* rich with olive and fruit trees, the same land I traversed cowering in a chariot headed for Sparta, and again, brokenhearted, on the way back home.

My father will not be at our wedding, which will take place at the new moon in Pylos. He is already gone. Life on an impoverished island, even as its king, does not appeal to him anymore. He gave as an excuse for his departure something about the gods requiring a sacrifice for his safe homecoming in a place where people had never heard of the sea or tasted salt. They hadn't told him where to look, but when he found it, he was to plant an oar, after which the gods would let him come home and die of old age in Ithaca. The story was so ridiculous, even Telemachus had trouble believing it. The old warrior developed a taste for adventure, and nothing else will satisfy him. I doubt we will see him again.

My mother does not seem to care. No one will cause her any more trouble. When she speaks now it is with his voice, his authority, and she will rule as the kind of queen she so richly deserves to be. And though her bed is empty again, she tells me that after all these years she sleeps better alone, and that satisfying the waning urges of her body at night is not worth losing any of her power during the day. She would have chosen a different life for the two of them, but this one happened, and now it is a simple fact that they are both more comfortable apart.

Telemachus, in the end, was the greatest beneficiary of the courage both his parents showed. My mother in her own way, and my father in his, saved the kingdom for him. Telemachus redeemed himself during the battle, showing bravery and skill I'm sure he will never tire of hearing the bards sing about. I can only attribute his day of valor to Athena's intervention. Odysseus needed an accomplice, and no one else was at hand. Since then, Telemachus has been the same half a man, prancing around the palace talking about one day being the king, unthreatened now because all his former tormentors are dead.

My mother is tired of him, though she doesn't say so. I know she mulls over the idea of declaring me the heir, since her dowry will be mine when she's gone. Now that I am to marry a son of the King of Pylos and form a new alliance between the two kingdoms, Cephallenia might be better served with Peisistratus and me sharing a united throne. But that is up to the gods to decide. I have had my fill of violence and greed, and I will not be the cause of anyone's misery or pain. I will be happy in Pylos, with the man I love.

It won't be the two of us for long. Inside me I feel the first tiny kicks from a life that has barely begun to swell my body. Before Peisistratus returned home to prepare a home for us, we found a way to be together, and without Helen's tea, our passion for each other had the predictable consequences.

My last things are packed away. My mother and I are leaving tomorrow for Pylos, accompanied by Telemachus. Helen, Phylo, and Alcippe will meet us there for my wedding.

"Do you have Helen's veil where we can find it?" my mother asks.

"I put it on top." The new girl she is training to be her maidservant is still too shy to look either of us in the eye.

I tousle her hair. "Come on, stop being so afraid. You rescued me on the beach, remember? You talked to me then."

Aspasia rubs the floor with her toe. In time she will be my mother's Alcippe or Phylo, but for now she is just a little girl who will be treated well and whose service will ensure a life of comfort for herself and her family.

We hear the rumble of thunder and the room grows dark.

"Oh no," my mother says. "Today is our last chance."

The pomegranate trees are blooming again. This afternoon we have plans to go to Hera's shrine, taking Aspasia with us for her first, and probably last time. My mother has ordered that a new temple be built, as much like the one of her childhood as can be achieved in a more barren landscape. Athena's temple in the sacred grove is finally being constructed as well. After all, what Adreste said was true. The one who protected my father protected us all.

The room grows bright again, and my mother goes to the window.

"Just a little shower," she says. "The sky is mostly blue."

I join her to look out over the fields and hills of Ithaca. "Look!" I say, pointing to the end of a double rainbow planting itself in the location of Hera's little shrine. Just then a crow flies between the two ribbons of color, as if an invisible heddle rod had moved them out of its path.

"It's an omen," my mother says, and we both smile.

Sometimes the gods call out to us with crows and rainbows, but other times they whisper so softly we only realize much later they were speaking at all. Months ago now, before I started to weave my life, I bunched the loose ends of the warp threads into clusters of four, pulling each group through a hole in a stone weight and knotting it together just above the floor. Between the top and the bottom of my loom, dozens of vertical white lines lay waiting to be filled with my story. From the beginning, the four of us—my father, mother, brother, and I—were gathered together by the bonds of family and weighted down by our collective destiny.

I look at my now-empty loom and think of how the warp determines the pattern to be woven before the first weft thread is laid. Changing the shed pulls the warp apart in predetermined ways and lets the shuttle pass without resistance. Textures emerge in cloth, as in life, by permitting one thing and preventing another. The weft may cover up the warp, but it is there, just as our bodies have bones we cannot see. The gods warp the loom as they please, and all we can do is honor them and hope for their favor.

I go to a chest in the corner of the room and take out Hera's golden pomegranate and crown, now wrapped in two embroidered cloths. I whisper a prayer in her honor before tucking her ornaments into a basket. I hand it to Aspasia to carry and, arm in arm, my mother and I walk out the door.

Reimagining The Odyssey

"You can't mess with Homer," my partner, Jim, said one night as I mulled aloud about the story that would become *Penelope's Daughter*. "Why not?" I asked. "How do we know Odysseus didn't have a daughter? Most of the time Homer doesn't bring in women at all unless they're making trouble for men." I thought about how Anita Diamant used the single biblical mention of the name of Jacob's daughter Dina as the foundation for *The Red Tent*. "Maybe he just didn't think she was important enough to bother with. That happens a lot in ancient epics, you know."

Looking back, I mark this conversation in early 2007 as the point at which I knew I would have to write this novel. From that moment forward, I genuinely believed that Penelope *did* give birth to a daughter after Odysseus left for Troy, and that Homer had left her out only because she was of no interest to him. This actually makes quite a bit of sense. Whether mortal or goddess, relevant women are those who cause disasters of one sort or another to befall the heroes. Only a few, like Penelope, are the opposite, representing the positive impact on a great man's life that a chaste and loyal woman can have. Either way, it's pretty much all about the men.

As I went through the Odyssey over and over again, I pictured Xanthe actually there in the palaces of Ithaca and Sparta when important events were happening. Women *were* there behind the scenes, as the wives, sisters, daughters, and servants of the men. I was as stunned as Xanthe is to discover that Odysseus had a sister, and that Penelope did too. Granted, they aren't essential to the plot—or are they? If *The Odyssey* contains real people and alludes to real events, perhaps these sisters and other women did play an important role, but one that was later brushed aside.

When I added a daughter to the plot, the whole story of *The Odyssey* burst open. The suitors wouldn't want Penelope. This actually doesn't make much sense in Homer's telling of the story anyway, since kingship on Ithaca was Odysseus' right, not his bride's. They would want a son by Odysseus' daughter, so their own flesh and blood would inherit the kingdom once Telemachus was out of the picture.

Penelope was a spoiled princess and a teen bride. I made her sixteen at the time of her wedding, older than she probably would have been, because it was essential to another aspect of the plot. She and her cousin Helen needed to be friends, and that wouldn't be possible if Penelope was a toddler when Helen went off to Troy. Abandoned in a desolate, foreign kingdom, Penelope had to grow up fast to protect herself and others from the increasing lawlessness on Ithaca. If she didn't take the situation in hand through her own cunning, she would see everything collapse, probably violently, around her. Now there, I thought, was the making of a real hero for the story! But even the secondary characters, people like

Eurycleia, Eurynome, and Eumaeus, have to rise to the occasion to protect Penelope and her children. Everyone has a chance to grow in Odysseus' absence.

The word *odyssey* has come down from Homer as a synonym for a long and complicated journey, and of course it goes without saying that the journey at the heart of *The Odyssey* is that of its namesake. However, in *Penelope's Daughter*, Xanthe's narrative allows us to see Penelope as on a journey also, to become a strong and effective queen. Obviously Homer thinks Penelope's and Telemachus' problems with the suitors are important enough to take us away from Odysseus' adventures for long stretches of the poem, but Homer's attitude toward mother and son could not contrast more clearly. Telemachus needs to make a literal and figurative journey—to travel in search of news of his father and somehow transform himself into enough of a man to face up to the situation at home. And Penelope? She needs to be steadfast, an icon of the strength that comes from unwavering virtue. She is supposed to stay in place, right there in the palace, and never change at all.

Homer's view of Penelope is, to put it bluntly, unrealistic. I know it must sound a bit odd to talk about realism in a story replete with monsters and gods, as well as human characters who may never have existed, in places that can't be concretely located. But the Odyssey has its own internal reality, whether anything in it is literally true or not, and within Homer's story the characterization of Penelope makes little sense. Just as I felt I had to rescue a real daughter from oblivion, I needed to rescue the real Penelope from what seemed to me to be Homer's misrepresentation of her story.

Weave and weep? I was tired of hearing Homer imply that was all Penelope did for the nineteen years her husband was gone (Homer has Odysseus come home "in the twentieth year"). And I didn't believe it for a minute. She might have cried buckets at the outset, and I imagine the depression she sinks into at points in the book is probably all too real in her situation, but it's far more interesting to watch a young queen gain the confidence to take charge than to read scene after scene of moaning and groaning about those awful suitors, and how much she misses a husband she hardly had time to get to know. Penelope was, for me, one of the best surprises in my novel. (Yes, it's true—authors too have to wait and see how things turn out!)

Helen was a great surprise as well. Just as Xanthe isn't sure what she'll do when she weaves to the center and has to find a way to represent Helen, I fretted a great deal about the same thing. To begin with, it isn't easy to know what to think of Helen going off to Troy. Was she a victim or a full participant? When Adreste tells Xanthe the story, I'm trying to leave it open to either interpretation. But as I researched Helen, I found she was so much more than a ravishing beauty who left home under questionable circumstances and created havoc in her wake. In fact, not all the Homeric-era sources say she went to Troy at all . . . but that's another story. . . .

Just as it's important to remember that Penelope was painfully young at the beginning of the Trojan War, it's equally important to bear in mind that Helen was fairly old by its end, at least in the reckoning of her time. If Helen was twelve when she was married, as one source says, she would have been at least twenty-one at the time of Paris' fateful arrival in Sparta, since her daughter Hermione was eight. Add the ten years for the Trojan War, and a few more before Penelope sends Xanthe to her, and it's clear that Helen, though still "radiant" in Homer's description, is somewhere in her midthirties by the time we meet her in the novel. (With his typical disinclination to do the math on his female characters,

Homer also describes Hermione as "radiant" on her wedding day, when a woman marrying in her midtwenties, as Hermione did, would be perceived as one step ahead of the grave, rather than a fresh and dewy maiden.)

The Odyssey hints at complexities in Helen, particularly her guilt about having caused the Trojan War, but does little more with her character. Homer speaks of how she drugged guests' wine when the conversations became glum, fulfilling one of the main roles of a wife— good hostess. "Poor old warriors," she seems to be saying. "I just can't stand to see anyone in pain." That's nice, of course, but it's a lot more interesting to think the drugs say something much deeper about who Helen is and her life outside the confines of the poem. And what a life it is!

Most readers are probably no more aware than I was of the numerous other ancient versions of the story told in *The Iliad* and *The Odyssey*. *The Cypria*, *The Little Iliad*, *The Homecoming*, and *The Telegony* do not survive except in fragments and summaries, but they provide a much fuller picture of the range of ideas people had about Helen. It is from *The Cypria*, not *The Odyssey*, that we learn about the rape on the riverbank that Helen describes to Xanthe. Other sources say that Helen was sequestered in Egypt for her own safety throughout the entire Trojan War, which was fought more for plunder and supremacy in the area than to retrieve an errant queen.

What seems clear is that Helen developed quasi-supernatural abilities along the way, which she puts to use back in Sparta through mind-altering drugs and cultic rituals. That she would be the high priestess of Orthia (who would later be subsumed into the goddess Artemis) is only logical, since Helen was not only the Queen of Sparta but a daughter of Zeus, and a woman of such extraordinary charisma that she could destabilize a whole society just by leaving town. She would unquestionably have been the most revered woman in all Lacedaemon, viewed with trepidation and awe by men and women alike.

It has been widely noted that in the Mycenaean era, shortly before the real Helen would have lived (if indeed there was a real Helen), goddesses had the greater power. Zeus, for example, was better known as the husband of Hera than in his own right. As their prophets and priestesses, women had special connections to gods and goddesses. Even those without such powers were respected for the deep, vital force inherent in being female. However, for reasons that are not clear, by the time Homer wrote the story down, leadership was shifting away from the goddesses toward newly powerful gods. Hera became primarily the jealous wife who follows her husband's infidelities with avid interest, and the cult of Orthia would have seemed quaint and devoid of resonance.

Perhaps this role reversal is why Homer had trouble understanding Helen. But oddly enough, Homer has problems understanding Odysseus as well. I was astonished to learn that other versions of the story paint Odysseus in a decidedly different light, viewing him as a dishonorable trickster and cunning manipulator. Homer leaves out altogether what to me is one of the most compelling chapters in Odysseus' story, perhaps because it didn't seem heroic enough. To read about how Odysseus feigned madness and then was forced to turn away the plow to save his infant son, one must go to *The Cypria*, not *The Odyssey*. Homer doesn't include stories of Odysseus' coldblooded murder of a rival, Palamedes, nor the children he sired, according to some sources, while held captive by the goddess Circe. Slick and devious, or creative and resourceful? Self-serving plunderer, or homesick family man? It depends on who's telling the story.

Homer also ends *The Odyssey* a bit prematurely, avoiding plot complications that would show Odysseus as far less faithful to Penelope than she was to him. In *The Telegony*, Odysseus has scarcely left Penelope after his return to Ithaca when he arrives in the land of the Thesprotians; promptly marries Callidice, their queen; and has a son by her. When Callidice dies, Odysseus leaves the kingdom to their son and goes home only to discover—surprise, surprise!—that Penelope had in the interim borne him another son. (You can imagine how I felt when I discovered that a baby born during the father's absence was already part of the story!) Years later, Telegonus, one of his sons by Circe, fails to recognize the father who had abandoned him and his mother as a child and kills him in battle. When he discovers his error, Telegonus takes Telemachus and Penelope, along with Odysseus' corpse, back home to Circe's island. Once there, Telegonus marries Penelope, and Telemachus marries Circe. Perhaps it's best that Homer stopped where he did!

Homer, like everyone else, was a product of his times. I doubt very much that he deliberately shut out existing female characters. By the time he and other writers decided to record what to that point had been transmitted orally, my guess is the women had already been pared down to those essential to a male-dominated plot. Several millennia later, people like me would ask, "Where were the women?" but I think in Homer's era, poets thought they knew the answer. Women were spinning, weaving, birthing, cooking, helping at harvest time—all things of no mythic importance. Those wine-infused evenings listening to the bard tell the story of Odysseus' adventures wouldn't last past dawn, so it was important to stick with the important things—monsters, vengeful gods, mighty battles, testosterone-laden disputes between heroes.

And then there's Xanthe, living in the hidden world of those left behind. I poured all my love for plucky little girls, and my tenderness toward the emotional world of young women, into her character. I must thank my sister, Lynn, once again for her help with this. Our collective memories of our own childhood, plus her experiences raising daughters, were of immense help in getting this right. It may sound oddly anachronistic to say, but I think Xanthe is totally cool—and I absolutely believe there were girls and young women like her.

It's important to remember that Xanthe is not a Greek of the classical era, and in her world there was no Athens serving as a cultural benchmark. If the Homeric legend is true, the people of *The Odyssey* lived in what is often called the Greek "Dark Ages," between the fall of the Mycenaean world in roughly 1200 B.C.E. and the time of Homer about six centuries later. During these years, literacy was lost in the region, so written documents that might help us understand the huge cultural transition taking place simply don't exist. What the world was like for girls and women living then can only be inferred, often weakly, through the mute testimony of archaeological artifacts such as ceremonial objects and jewelry, some of which I describe in the book.

One thing we know for certain is that after the "Dark Ages," during the era of the Peloponnesian and Persian Wars, Spartan women lived quite differently from their Athenian counterparts. Though set apart from the world of men and war, Spartan women were encouraged to be daring, outgoing, strong, athletic, and brave. It's a reasonable assumption, therefore, that a girl in Xanthe's situation would experience both the latitude and the limitations I describe.

What's to be done now with the lost stories of the real Xanthes, other than imagine them? Is it more truthful to leave them out of stories, since we don't (and won't) have the facts? I don't think so. To me, historical fiction about forgotten women is not "made up." After careful research into the facts that do exist, the author imagines and recaptures what is missing—the way stories might have been told all along if the historians and bards had been women. Sure, Odysseus went off to war and had ten years of adventures coming home, but we don't have all night, so we'll have to stick with the important stuff. You see, there was this young bride who was pregnant with a daughter. . . .

ACKNOWLEDGMENTS

First, as always, to my wonderful partner, Jim, who managed to be flexible about his beloved Homer; and to my sister, Lynn, who offered her unique vision to draft after draft.

To my son, Ivan, who is following his star and making his mother very proud.

To Verena Borton, weaver extraordinaire, who helped me look as if I know a lot more about heddles and warps than I actually do, and to my good friend Grace Salvagno, who introduced us.

To Kate Reilly, who saved a piglet once and let me use the story.

To Yanna Faraklou, proprietor of the Hotel Summery in Lixouri, Kefalonia; Tassos Spyratos Athera, Costas and Riki Drosos, and their son Jerry for their hospitality and help in finding the locations relevant to Xanthe's story.

To Maria Kotsaftis (and to the serendipity of making her acquaintance), who paved the way for my extraordinary experiences in Kefalonia, and for her help editing a late draft.

To Adele Lewis Wrench, who had the forbearance to make her parents, Dean and Becca, wait for her to enter this world, so that the day I finished the first draft of *Penelope's Daughter* would be blessed with the best possible omen.

To Meg Ruley of the Jane Rotrosen Literary Agency, who believed in this book, and to Wendy McCurdy, my editor at Berkley Books, who believed in it too. Their validation of me as a writer meant more than I can say.

To the one who started it all. To borrow a phrase, if Homer hadn't existed, we would have to invent him. According to scholars, perhaps we did. In whatever way the story of Penelope, Helen, Eurycleia, and the other women of *The Odyssey* came into being, I am grateful it did.

To all the authors whose work helped shape this story. A more complete bibliography is found here, but I want to single out four people for special accolades. This book simply could not have been written without Bettany Hughes, whose book and documentary *Helen of Troy* helped me understand women of the Bronze Age Aegean, and whose willingness to answer my e-mail kept me going in a plausible direction. Likewise, the pioneering work of Robert Bittlestone (*Odysseus Unbound*) gave me a concrete place, Kefalonia, to envision my story. Third, Raymond Westbrook's article "Penelope's Dowry and Odysseus' Kingship" gave me fresh insight into the nature of the conflict between Penelope and the suitors. And last, Robert Fagels, whose masterful translation of *The Odyssey* is worn to tatters on my bookshelf.

Finally, to all the Greeks I talked to—on ferries, in tavernas, in bookshops, and everywhere I went to research this book— who reacted to the addition of a daughter to their great epic with a shrug of the shoulders. If it makes a good story, why not? That they are Homer's heirs seems undeniable.

GLOSSARY AND PRONUNCIATION GUIDE

Note: The most common English pronunciation and spelling of each word is used here, although in many cases this may differ from the Greek. Names with asterisks (*) are characters taken from The Odyssey. *The others characters are my own creations.*

Achaeans* (*ah-KEE-anz*) the general name Homer used for all the Greeks

Adreste* (*ah-DRES-tee*) one of Helen's handmaidens

Aegisthus* (*ay-JISS-thus*) enemy of Agamemnon; lover of Clytemnestra

Alcippe* (*ahl-SIP-ee*) one of Helen's handmaidens

Anticleia* (*an-tee-CLAY-ah*) mother of Odysseus

Antinous* (*an-TIN-oh-us*) one of the main suitors of Penelope

Aphrodite* (*af-row-DY-tee*) goddess of love; associated with the sea and roses

Argos (*AHR-gos*) Greek kingdom and fortified palace; also the name of Odysseus' favorite hunting dog

Aspasia (*as-PAY-zee-ah*) daughter of Halia; servant to Penelope

Athena* (*ah-THEE-nah*) daughter of Zeus, powerful goddess protecting Odysseus; her symbol is the owl

Cephallenia* (*kef-ah-LEEN-ee-ah*) kingdom comprising Ithaca and the surrounding islands, given as part of Penelope's dowry by her father, Icarius

chiton (*KY-tohn*) women's garment made from one piece of cloth, belted, and pinned at the shoulders

Clytemnestra* (*kly-tem-NES-trah*) wife (and murderer) of Agamemnon; sister of Helen; mother of Orestes, Electra, and Iphigenia; lover of Aegisthus

Ctimene* (*TIM-un-nee*) sister of Odysseus

Dolius* (*DOHL-ee-us*) keeper of the olive groves; father of Melantho and Melanthius

Eirene (*eye-REE-nah*) goddess of peace; Xanthe's alias while in Sparta

Eumaeus* (*you-MAY-us*) swineherd loyal to Odysseus

Eurotas (*you-ROW-tas*) one of the rivers running through Lacedaemon

Eurycleia* (*you-ree-CLAY-ah*) nurse to Odysseus; head housekeeper in the palace

Eurymachus* (*you-RIM-ah-kus*) one of the main suitors of Penelope

Eurynome* (*you-RIN-oh-me*) personal servant to Penelope; head upstairs maid

Halia (*HAY-lee-ah*) wet nurse and first companion to Xanthe

Halitherses* (*hal-uh-THIR-seez*) a seer on Ithaca

Helen* Queen of Sparta; cousin of Penelope

Hera* (*HEH-rah*) wife of Zeus, queen of the gods, patron of women; her symbols are the crow and cuckoo

Hermione* (*her-MY-oh-nee*) daughter of Helen and Menelaus

himation (*hy-MAY-shun*) large piece of cloth thrown over one shoulder as a shawl or cape

Icarius* (*eye-CAIR-ee-us*) father of Penelope

Iphigenia* (*if-uh-jen-EE-ah*) daughter of Agamemnon and Clytemnestra, murdered by her father

Irus* (*EYE-rus*) nickname of the beggar who fights Odysseus to entertain the suitors

Ithaca (*ITH-ah-kah*) island over which Odysseus serves as lord

Lacedaemon (*lass-uh-DEE-mun*) kingdom in the central Peloponnese that includes Sparta

Laertes* (*lay-AIR-teez*) father of Odysseus

libation (*lie-BAY-shun*) ceremonial offering of wine to the gods

madder a rich red dye

Maia (*MY-ah*) Achaean nickname for one's mother

Megapenthes* (*meh-gah-PEN-theez*) illegitimate son of Menelaus by a slave

Melanthius* (*mel-AN-thee-us*) son of Dolius; goatherd on Ithaca

Melantho* (*mel-AN-tho*) daughter of Dolius; house servant to Penelope

Menelaus* (*men-uh-LAY-us*) King of Sparta; husband of Helen

Mentor* (*MEN-tohr*) friend Odysseus entrusted to watch over his family and estate

Mycenae (*my-SEE-nay*) kingdom of Agamemnon

Neoptolemus* (*nee-up-TOLL-uh-mus*) son of Achilles; betrothed of Hermione

Nestor* (*NESS-tohr*) old King of Pylos; father of Peisistratus

Odysseus* (*oh-DIS-ee-us*) King of the Cephallenians; Lord of Ithaca; father of Telemachus and Xanthe; husband of Penelope; son of Laertes and Anticleia

oikos (*oh-EE-kohs*) land, houses, and all goods and property belonging to a man

Orestes* (*oh-RES-teez*) son of Agamemnon; avenger of his murder

Orthia (*OHR-thee-ah*) ancient goddess of women, hunting, and dance; predecessor to Artemis

Paris* prince of Troy; lover of Helen

Peisistratus* (*pye-SIS-trah-tus*) son of Nestor; lover of Xanthe

Penelope* (*Peh-NEL-oh-pee*) mother of Xanthe and Telemachus; wife of Odysseus; daughter of Icarius; cousin of Helen

peplos (*PEEP-lohs*) short women's garment covering the top of the body, worn over a chiton

Phylo* (*FY-loh*) one of Helen's handmaidens

Poseidon* (*poh-SY-don*) "the earth shaker" and god of the sea

Pylos (*PEE-lohs*) kingdom of Nestor, in southwestern coastal Greece

Rhexenor (*rex-EE-nor*) son of Halia; older brother of Aspasia

rhyton (*RY-tohn*) ceremonial pitcher used to pour libations

sistrum (*SIS-trum*) rattle made from balls attached to a paddle with cords

Sparta center of the kingdom of Lacedaemon, site of Menelaus' and Helen's palace

Taygetos (*ty-GET-ohs*) rugged mountain range between Pylos and Lacedaemon

Telemachus* (*tel-LEH-mah-kus*) son of Odysseus and Penelope; brother of Xanthe

Terpias (*TER-pee-as*) husband of Halia

Theoclymenus* (*thee-oh-KLY-men-us*) a seer on Ithaca

Thrasymedes* (*thrah-SIM-uh-deez*) brother of Peisistratus; son of Nestor

Tiryns (*TEER-inz*) fortified city near Mycenae

Xanthe (*ZAN-thee*) daughter of Odysseus and Penelope; sister of Telemachus

BIBLIOGRAPHY

Barber, Elizabeth Wayland. *Women's Work: The First 20,000 Years: Women, Cloth, and Society in Early Times.* New York: Norton, 1994.

Blundell, Sue. *Women in Ancient Greece.* Cambridge, MA: Harvard UP, 1995.

Brule, Pierre. *Women of Ancient Greece.* Edinburgh, UK: Edinburgh UP, 2003.

Cantarella, Eva. *Pandora's Daughters: The Role and Status of Women in Greek and Roman Antiquity.* Baltimore: Johns Hopkins UP, 1987.

Casselman, Karen Leigh. *Craft of the Dyer.* New York: Dover, 1980, 1993.

Castleden, Rodney. *Myceneans.* London: Routledge, 2005.

Chadwick, John. *The Mycenaean World.* Cambridge, UK: Cambridge UP, 1976.

Clayton, Barbara. *A Penelopean Poetics: Reweaving the Feminine in Homer's* Odyssey. Lanham, MD: Lexington Books, 2004.

Cohen, Beth. *The Distaff Side: Representing the Female in Homer's* Odyssey. Oxford, UK: Oxford UP, 1995.

Davies, Malcolm. *The Greek Epic Cycle.* London: Bristol Classical Press, 1989, 2003.

Felson-Rubin, Nancy. *Regarding Penelope: From Character to Poetics.* Princeton, NJ: Princeton UP, 1994.

Forrest, W. G. *A History of Sparta.* New York: Norton, 1968.

Harvey, Nancy. *The Guide to Successful Tapestry Weaving.* Seattle, WA: Pacific Search Press, 1981.

Heitman, Richard. *Taking Her Seriously: Penelope and the Plot of Homer's* Odyssey. Ann Arbor: U of Michigan P, 2005.

BIBLIOGRAPHY

Hughes, Bettany. *Helen of Troy: Goddess, Princess, Whore*. New York: Knopf, 2005.

Karydas, Helen Pournaka. *Eurykleia and Her Successors: Female Figures of Authority in Greek Politics*. Lanham, MD: Rowman and Littlefield, 1998.

Katz, Marylin. *Penelope's Renown: Meaning and Indeterminacy in* The Odyssey. Princeton, NJ: Princeton UP, 1991.

Kruger, Kathryn Sullivan. *Weaving the Word: The Metaphorics of Weaving and Female Textual Production*. Susquehanna, PA: Susquehanna UP, 2001.

Lefkowitz, Mary R. *Heroines and Hysterics*. London: Duckworth, 1981.

Lefkowitz, Mary R., and Maureen B. Fant. *Women's Life in Greece and Rome: A Source Book in Translation*. Baltimore: Johns Hopkins UP, 1982, 1992, 2005.

Pomeroy, Sarah B. *Goddesses, Whores, Wives and Slaves: Women in Classical Antiquity*. New York: Schocken Books, 1975, 1995.

Pomeroy, Sarah B. *Spartan Women*. Oxford, UK: Oxford UP, 2002.

Taylour, Lord William. *The Myceneans*. London: Thames and Hudson, 1964, 1984.

Thalmann, William G. *The Swineherd and the Bow: Representations of Class in* The Odyssey. Ithaca, NY: Cornell UP, 1998.

Literary Sources:

Aeschylus, *The Oresteia*
Euripides, *Orestes* and *Iphigenia in Aulis*
Hesiod, *Works and Days*
Pausanias, *Guide to Greece*
Pliny the Elder, *Natural History*
And of course: Homer, *The Iliad* and *The Odyssey*

READERS GUIDE FOR
Penelope's Daughter

DISCUSSION QUESTIONS

1. Eumaeus the swineherd once tells Xanthe that it is "better to be a worker on the *oikos* of a great man . . . than to be in his own country with no crown, no land, no possessions." What do you think of this view?

2. Helen feels strongly that a girl of Xanthe's age needs a lover, even if she is not yet married. What do you think of Helen's attitude and her actions to ensure that Xanthe does indeed find a man with whom to experience passion?

3. Helen tells Xanthe "it is better to act, even badly and in ways you regret, than to be afraid of life." Do you agree?

4. Do gods and goddesses really visit the mortals in this book, or is it just their imaginations?

5. Do you ever find yourself viewing something as an omen? If so, how does it affect your thoughts or actions?

6. What do you think would have happened if Odysseus' ruse was successful and he had never gone off to the Trojan War? If he had never come home? If he had lost the battle with the suitors?

7. Based on Adreste's story, to what degree should Helen be held responsible for her actions in running off with Paris to Troy?

8. Xanthe uses her weaving as a jumping-off point for the telling of her story. If you were going to tell the story of one period in your own life, how would you represent it as a weaving (or another art form of your preference)?